James Elliot Cabot

A memoir of Ralph Waldo Emerson

Vol. II

James Elliot Cabot

A memoir of Ralph Waldo Emerson
Vol. II

ISBN/EAN: 9783337085759

Printed in Europe, USA, Canada, Australia, Japan

Cover: Foto ©Raphael Reischuk / pixelio.de

More available books at **www.hansebooks.com**

A MEMOIR

OF

RALPH WALDO EMERSON

VOL. II.

A MEMOIR

OF

RALPH WALDO EMERSON

BY

JAMES ELLIOT CABOT

IN TWO VOLUMES

VOL. II.

London

MACMILLAN AND CO.

AND NEW YORK

1887

CONTENTS OF VOLUME II.

RALPH WALDO EMERSON.

CHAPTER XI.

AT the time of the Divinity Hall address, Emerson, as I said, was intending to lecture, the next
winter, in Boston; and he persevered, though he
expected that his audience would be small. When
the lectures began, however, in December, there
was no appearance of any deterrent effect from the
address.

"The lecturing [he writes to his brother William]
thrives. The good city is more placable than it
was represented, and forgives, like Burke, much to
the spirit of liberty."

The attendance was large, and of the same
class of persons as before, most of them, no doubt,
Liberal Christians, but of a liberality that was not
disturbed by his departure from the Cambridge
platform. They came, as Mr. Lowell says, to hear
Emerson, not to hear his opinions. They would
have admitted, most of them, that his opinions

were rather visionary; that his eyes were fixed so
steadily on " the fine horizon line of truth " as to
overlook ordinary mortals and dwell on angelic
forms, too airy and indistinct to be identified with
any of the solid inhabitants of earth. But they
liked to put themselves under the influence of one
who obviously had lived the heavenly life from his
youth up, and who made them feel for the time
as if that were the normal mode of existence.

The subject was " Human Life ; " the soul, the
universal principle in man, unfolding itself in the
individual. The course might have been called
Lectures on Transcendentalism ; a summing-up of
what was to be said for and against the new views.
The indications of development, he says, are not
always agreeable facts. It begins with protest
and rejection, with turbulence and revolution, and
thoughtful persons are apt to overlook, in the rude
and partial expressions, the truth they prefigure.
It is like the rubbish and confusion that go before
the building of a new city ; they are not agreeable,
but they may be welcomed for the sake of what
they announce, — at least for the symptoms of life
and progress.

 " Undoubtedly the movement has its foolish and
canting side. New thoughts will always introduce
a new crop of words, and these are all that the
foolish will get. And yet always there is in man

somewhat incalculable and unexhausted. Men are not made like boxes, a hundred, a thousand, to order, and all alike. Out of the darkness and the awful Cause they come, to be caught up into this vision of a seeing, partaking, acting and suffering life; not foreknown or foremeasurable. Therefore we welcome the unexact extravagant spirits who set routine at defiance, and, drawing their impulse from some profound thought, appear in society as its accusers and its prophets. What if they be, as often such are, monotones, men of one idea? How noble in secret are the men who have never stooped nor betrayed their faith! The two or three rusty, perchance wearisome souls who could never bring themselves to the smallest composition with society, rise with grandeur in the background, like the statues of the gods, whilst we listen to those who stoop a little."

We rest in what we have done, in what we have said, or in what others have done or said, and if we attempt to move, society is against us. "This *deliquium*, this ossification of the soul, is the Fall of Man. The redemption is lodged in the heart of youth. To every young man and young woman the world puts the same question, Wilt thou become one of us? And to this question the soul in each of them says heartily, No. The world has no interest so deep as to cherish that resistance. No matter though the young heart do not yet understand itself, do not know well what it wants, and so contents itself with saying No, No, to unamiable tediousness, or breaks out into sallies of extravagance. There is hope in extravagance; there is none in routine.

" The hostile attitude of young persons toward society makes them very undesirable companions to their friends, querulous, opinionative, impracticable; and it makes them unhappy in their own solitude. If it continue too long it makes shiftless and morose men. Yet, on the whole, this crisis which comes in so forbidding and painful shape in the life of each earnest man has nothing in it that need alarm or confound us. In some form the question comes to each: Will you fulfil the demands of the soul, or will you yield yourself to the conventions of the world? None can escape the challenge. But why need you sit there, pale and pouting, or why with such a mock-tragic air affect discontent and superiority? The bugbear of society is such only until you have accepted your own law. Then all omens are good, all stars auspicious, all men your allies, all parts of life take order and beauty."

In vain shall we expect to redeem society in any way but through the integrity of the individuals who compose it : —

" I am afraid that in the formal arrangements of the socialists the spontaneous sentiment of any thoughtful man will find that poetry and sublimity still cleave to the solitary house. The members will be the same men we know. To put them in a phalanx will not much mend matters, for as long as all people want the things we now have, and not better things, it is very certain that they will, under whatever change of forms, keep the old system."

Two of the lectures ("Tragedy" and "Comedy") were printed a year or two afterwards in the *Dial;* " Demonology," which was the last of the course, nearly forty years later, in the *North American Review.*[1] The others were used in the first series of Essays ; one of them ("Love") is given there almost entire.

In closing the course, Emerson said that it was with regret that he found himself compelled, by the state of his health, to bring it to a somewhat abrupt termination. He had intended to give some completeness to the series by two additional discourses, one on the limitations of human activity by the laws of the world, and one on the intrinsic powers and resources of our nature ; but the execution of these plans he was constrained to postpone.

"My lungs [he writes to Carlyle] played me false with unseasonable inflammation ; " and in letters to his brother William after this time he speaks of troubled health, not amounting to positive illness, but to an indisposition for work : —

[1] *Collected Writings*, viii. 149. "Comedy," x. 7. "Demonology."

" I have not been very strong this summer, contrariwise, very puny, and hoped I should gain vigor
by a journey to the mountains. But I gained little. I am, as usual, neither sick nor well, but, for
aught I see, as capable of work as ever, let once
my subject stand, like a good ghost, palpable before me. But since I came home I do not write
much, and writing is always my meter of health, —
writing, which a sane philosopher would probably
say was the surest symptom of a diseased mind."

" This ill-health of yours and mine and everybody's [he writes to Miss Fuller] is a sore blemish
on the prospects, because on the powers of society.
If you wish to protest (as most ingenious persons
do for some years) against foibles, traditions, and
conventions, — the thing has one face if you live
only long or strong enough to rail, and quite another if you can serenely and in due time broach
your new law, and show the upholsterers the granite
under their whitewash and gingerbread. When it
gets no farther than superciliousness and indignation, the Beckendorfs [Metternich, in " Vivian
Grey "] have every right to ask us what time we
go to bed. Therefore I hate sickness, in common
with all men this side of forty, and am sour and
savage when I anticipate the triumphs of the Philis-
tines. For really, in my best health and hope, it's
always mean to scold, and when I am lean I am
ten times sorry."

Up to the age of forty or thereabouts Emerson was subject from time to time to a tenderness of the lungs and to fits of languor which sometimes alarmed his wife, though he always treated them lightly, as only a symptom of the want of sufficient preoccupation of mind, which he looked upon as the disease of the times.

" Power and aim, the two halves of felicity [he says in one of his letters to Miss Fuller] seldomest meet. A strong mind with a great object finds good times, good friends, good weather, and fair lodging ; but wit without object, and not quite sufficient to make its own, turns all nature upside down, and Rousseau-, Carlyle-, or Byronizes ever. The middle name does not belong in such ill company ; but my friend, I think, wants nothing but work commensurate with his faculty. It must be more the malady, one sometimes thinks, of our day than of others ; for you cannot talk with any intelligent company without presently hearing expressions of regret and impatience whose scope affects the whole order of *good* institutions. Certainly we expect that time will yield some adequate revolution, regeneration, and, under better hours, will fetch us somewhat to do ; but whilst the grass grows, the noble steed starves, — forgive the proverb, — we shall die of the numb-palsy. Ethics, however, remain, when experience and prudence have nothing to show."

The want of definiteness in his subject, where he
wished to protest against the foibles of society, was
due in part to a characteristic slowness to take
sides.   We have a vicious way, he says in one of
these lectures, of esteeming the defects of men
organic. We identify the man with his faults,
judging them from our point of view. We should
rather ask how they appear from his point of view.
Pride, for example, may be an impure form of self-
reliance; the willingness to accept obligations
would only show that he has suffered a fatal slackness in his springs. The love of fighting, beastly
as it may look to us, is the first appearance of the
manly spirit, the willingness to venture all for a
principle. At a certain stage of progress the man
fights, if he be of a sound body and mind. So
again we accuse the people of incapacity for self-
direction; they can only follow their leaders, who
flatter them. But the flattery consists in telling
them that they are capable of governing themselves, and would lose its attraction were they entirely devoid of this capacity. It is possible to be
below these vices as well as to be above them.

In principle, Emerson stood, of course, with the
idealists, the reformers, the party of progress, or
at least of aspiration and hope. But he could not
help seeing that the existing order, since it is here,
has the right to be here, and the right to all the
force it can exert. It is not disposed of (he says)

because we see or think we see something better : still less by merely rejecting it ; but only by its developing in us the force that is needed for putting the better in its place. Nothing is gained by insisting on the omnipotence of limitations, but neither is anything gained by ignoring them ; they are like the iron walls of the gun, that concentrate the force and make it irresistible.

This was very well for a " chimney-corner philosophy," but it did not lend itself readily to the exigencies of the lecturer's desk. The audience must have a definite statement ; but Emerson did not see his way to a comprehensive theory. The reconcilement of fate and freedom — the might of established facts and the rights of the soul — must be made by each man for himself, as the occasion arises for deciding between conformity and following his own bent : it must be realized in a life ; it cannot be stated in propositions.

" We wish [he says in his journal] to sum the conflicting impressions by saying that all point at last to a unity which inspires all, but disdains words and passes understanding. Our poetry, our religions, are its skirts and penumbræ. Yet the charm of life is the hints we derive from this. They overcome us like perfumes from a far-off shore of sweetness, and their meaning is that no tongue shall syllable it without leave ; that only itself can name it ; that by casting ourselves on it and being its voice, it rushes each moment to positive commands, creating men and methods. If we attempt to define it we say nothing.

" We must affirm the endless possibilities in every man that is born, but if we affirm nothing else, we are checked in our speech by the need of recognizing that every fact contains the same, — until speech presently becomes rambling, general, indefinite, and mere tautology. The only speech will at last be action."

He would have preferred, he says in a letter to Carlyle,[1] to retire to his study, hoping to give some form to his " formless scripture." But he had no choice ; money must be had, among other things for advances on Carlyle's account. He had reprinted the " French Revolution," and was now reprinting the " Miscellanies ; " there were bills to be paid, — one bill of five hundred dollars for paper ; and he had already exhausted his credit in borrowing for his friend. Of all which, of course, Carlyle remained blissfully ignorant.

He writes to his brother William : —

CONCORD, *September* 26, 1839.

I have just decided, somewhat unwillingly, to read one more course of lectures in Boston next winter, but their tenor and topics float yet far off and undefined before me.

[1] *Carlyle-Emerson Correspondence,* i. 259.

The topic he fixed upon was the "Present Age." The characteristic trait of the period, he says. is the growing consciousness in the individual man of his access to the Universal Mind. This tends to degrade and weaken all other relations. Superficially it shows itself in a spirit of analysis and detachment. Ours is the age of the first person singular, of freedom and the casting-off of all ties. In the infancy of society, Reason has a kind of passive presence in Dread; a salutary dread defends man in his nonage from crime and degradation. Analysis destroys this check; the world is stripped of love and terror, and is looked upon merely for its economic uses. At bottom, analysis takes place in obedience to the higher instincts: we do not wish to be mastered by things; we wish things to obey us. But it first runs to excess, separates utilities from the labor they should represent, appropriates and monopolizes them. The end to be rich infects the whole world, and shoves by the State and the Church. Government and Education are only for the protection of property, and Religion even is a lever out of the spiritual world to work for this. The decay of piety begets the decay of learning; the fine geniuses of the day decry books, and ostentatiously disdain the knowledge of languages, antiquity. and art. The "self-made" men, of whom we have so large a crop. like to explain how little they owe to colleges and

schools. Of course this is most evident and most
deplorable in the highest sentiment, that is, the
religious : —

" Who can read the fiery ejaculations of St.
Augustine, a man of as clear a sight as almost any
other, of Thomas à Kempis, of Milton, of Jeremy
Taylor, without feeling how rich and expansive a
culture — not so much a culture as a higher life —
they owed to the ceaseless and grand promptings
of this sentiment ; or without contrasting their immortal heat with the cold complexion of our recent
wits ? Side by side with this analysis remains
the surviving tradition, the old state of things in
Church, State, College, and social forms ; number-
ing in its train a multitude composed of those in
whom affection predominates over intellect, and
talent over character : of those who are indisposed
to the exertion which novelty of position demands ;
and, lastly, of those who have found good eating
under the shadow of the old institutions, and therefore hate any change."

Having lost touch of the sentiment which inspired the tradition, this party has nothing to attract the young mind eager for truth, and nothing
to oppose to the disintegrating activity of the understanding. On the other hand, the Movement
Party, though resting on ideas, are infected with
the vice of the age, — the propensity to exaggerate
the importance of visible and tangible facts. They

magnify particular acts and avoidances; they endeavor to vamp and abut principles, and to give a
mechanical strength to the laws of the soul. They
rely on new circumstances; on votes, statutes, associations. They promise the establishment of the
kingdom of heaven, and end with champing un-
leavened bread or dedicating themselves to the
nourishment of a beard. But let us not distrust
our age. Man once for all is an exaggerator; but
let us look at the tendencies. Analysis is the road
to power, and the understanding, with its busy experimenting, steadily tends to place power in the
right hands. The ray of light passes invisible
through space; only when it falls on an object is
it seen. So is spiritual activity barren until it
is directed to something outward. It was Commerce as well as Religion that settled this country,
and it is constantly at work to correct its own
abuses. It matters not with what counters the
game is played, so it be played well. Men rely
upon contrivances and institutions, yet the heat of
the reformers and the resistance to reform make
the discipline and education of the public conscience. On neither side is the cause defended
on its merits. Yet, on the whole, the Movement
Party gains steadily, and as by the movement of
the world itself. The great idea that gave hope to
men's hearts creeps on the world like the advance
of morning twilight, and they have no more part

in it than the watchman who announced the day-
break.

Our part in relation to the projects of reform is
to accept and use them, but not be used by them.
Keep yourself sacred and aloof from the vices of
the partisan, but do not hold yourself excused from
any sacrifice when you find a clear case on which
you are called to stand trial. And be in no haste
to decide. Patience and truth, patience with our
frosts and negations, and few words, must serve.
We find ourselves not expressed in the literature,
the science, the religion of our fathers, and cannot
be trained on their catechism. What has the ge-
neric life of Paris or New York to do with Judæa,
with Moses, or with Paul? The real religion of
the day is reverence for character. This may seem
an abstraction, but there is no thought so delicate
and interior but it can and will get a realization.
One would have said the same of the lowliness of
the blessed soul that walked in Judæa and hal-
lowed that land forever. So will this new perception — which came by no man, but into which all
souls at this era are born — endue its own body
and form, and shine in institutions. See the fruitful crop of social reforms, — Peace, Liberty, Labor, Wealth, Love, Churches of the Poor, Rights
of Women. The reformers, it may be, see not
what they point at. They go forward to ends
whereof they yet dream not, and which the zealots

who work in these reforms would defy. But the heart and the hand go forward to a better heaven than they know.

Not always shall this hope be disappointed. The life of man shall yet be clean and honest, his aims unperplexed. Faith shall be possible and society possible when once there shall be shown to him the infinitude of himself.

Emerson had left the pulpit for the lecturer's desk, because he wished to be entirely free to declare the faith that was in him, without being expected to make it square with any presuppositions. But this freedom had its drawback, since it was no longer sufficient for him to suggest the truth he wished to enforce, trusting that his suggestions would be filled out from the common stock of belief ; they were subversive of the common beliefs ; and yet, since Emerson could never take the polemical tone, and was not ready with a scheme for reconstruction, he found himself condemned to a way of speaking that seemed vague and ineffective, and he felt for a time a disgust at lecturing. He writes in his diary : —

" *October* 18, 1839. Lectures. For the last five years I have read, each winter, a new course of lectures in Boston, and each was my creed and confession of faith. Each told all I thought of the past, the present, and the future. Once more I must renew my work, and, I think, only once in the same form : though I see that he who thinks he does something for the last time ought not to do it at all. Yet my objection is not to the thing, but to the form; and the concatenation of errors called Society, to which I still consent until my plumes be grown, makes even a duty of this concession also. So I submit to sell tickets again. But the form is neither here nor there. What shall be the substance of my shrift? Adam in the garden, I am to new-name all the beasts in the field and all the gods in the sky; I am to invite men drenched in Time to recover themselves and come out of Time and taste their native immortal air. I am to fire, with what skill I can, the artillery of sympathy and emotion. I am to indicate constantly, though all unworthy, the ideal and holy life, the life within life, the forgotten Good, the unknown Cause in which we sprawl and sin. I am to try the magic of sincerity, that luxury permitted only to kings and poets. I am to celebrate the spiritual powers, in their infinite contrast to the mechanical powers and the mechanical philosophy of this time. I am to console the brave sufferers under evils whose end they cannot see, by appeals to the great Optimism self-affirmed in all bosoms."

When the lectures were over he felt that he had come short of his mark.

TO WILLIAM EMERSON.

CONCORD, *February* 25, 1840.

. . . I closed my lectures duly a week ago last Wednesday. I cannot say much for them in any respect. I pleased myself, before I began, with saying I will try this thing once more, because I have not yet done what I would with it. I will agitate men, being agitated myself. I, who rail at the decorum and the harness of society, why should I not speak very truth, unlimited, overpowering? But now unhappily the lectures are ended. Ten decorous speeches and not one ecstasy, not one rapture, not one thunderbolt. Eloquence, therefore, there was none. As the audience, however. were not parties to my intention and hope, they did not complain at my failure. Still, my company was less than the last two years.

(Journal.) " I seem to lack constitutional vigor to attempt each topic as I ought. I ought to seek to lay myself out utterly, large, enormous, prodigal, upon the subject of the week. But a hateful experience has taught me that I can only expend, say twenty-one hours, on each lecture, if I would also be ready and able for the next. Of course I spend myself prudently; I economize: I cheapen; whereof nothing grand ever grew. Could I spend sixty hours on each, or, what is better, had I such

energy that I could rally the lights and mights of
sixty hours into twenty, I should hate myself less;
I should help my friend."

But if the lectures seemed to Emerson tame and
decorous, literary essays rather than effective lay-
sermons, the following letter from Theodore Parker
to Dr. Convers Francis (obligingly communicated
to me by Mr. F. B. Sanborn) shows that such
was not the impression they produced on his audience : —

WEST ROXBURY, *December 6, 1839.*

. . . Are you not to attend Emerson's lectures
this winter? The first was splendid, — better
meditated and more coherent than anything I have
ever heard from him. Your eyes were not dazzled
by a stream of golden atoms of thought, such as he
sometimes shoots forth, — though there was no lack
of these sparklers. It was *Democratic - locofoco*
throughout, and very much in the spirit of Brownson's article on Democracy and Reform in the last
Quarterly [Brownson's Review]. . . . Bancroft
was in cestasies, — he was rapt beyond vision at the
locofocoism of the lecture, and said to me the next
evening, "It is a great thing to say such things
before any audience, however small, much more to
plant these doctrines in such minds: but let him
come with *us*, before the ' Bay State,' and we will
give him three thousand listeners." . . . One grave,

Whig-looking gentleman heard Emerson the other night, and said he could only account for his delivering such a lecture on the supposition that he wished to get a place in the Custom-House under George Bancroft.[1] . . .

Ever yours,   THEODORE PARKER.

"I take it [adds Mr. Sanborn] that the ' Bay State' was a Democratic club. This was the year (1839), when Marcus Morton was elected governor over Edward Everett by one vote."

The next winter (1840–41) he seems to have given no lectures except that on " Man the Reformer." [2] He was busy with his book (the first series of Essays), and the project of a periodical as the organ of the new views was taking definite shape. He writes to his brother William : —

CONCORD. *September* 26, 1839.

. . . George Ripley and others revive at this time the old project of a new journal for the exposition of absolute truth ; but I doubt a little if it reach the day. I will never be editor, though I am counted on as a contributor. My Henry Thoreau will be a great poet for such a company ; and one of these days, for all companies.

[1] Mr. Bancroft was then Collector of the port of Boston.
[2] *Collected Writings*, i. 215.

TO MARGARET FULLER.

CONCORD, *December* 12, 1839.

. . . I believe we all feel much alike in regard to this journal. We all wish it to be, but do not wish to be in any way personally responsible for it. For the sake of the brilliant possibility I would promise honest labor of some sort to each number for a year, but I should wish to leave myself the latitude of supreme indifference, nay abhorrence of such modes of working forever after. But if your labors shall introduce a new age, they will also mould our opinions, and we shall think what you think. But to-day is no writing day with me, so farewell.   R. W. EMERSON.

The plan of the journal had somewhat changed its shape since 1836. It was to have the character of a magazine as well as of a review, and, first of all, it was to furnish means of utterance to the boundless aspirations of the time. Emerson's chief interest in it perhaps lay in the prospect of introducing to the public his friends, Mr. Alcott, Mr. Thoreau, Mr. William Ellery Channing, the unnamed author of " Dolon," and one or two others. " Were I responsible [he writes to Miss Fuller March 30, 1840], I would rather trust for its wit and its verses to the eight or nine persons in whose affections I have a sure place than to eighty or ninety celebrated contributors."

After many conferences and much correspondence, the first number of the *Dial* appeared in
July. Mr. George Ripley and Miss Margaret Fuller were the most active promoters ; Mr. Ripley
undertaking the business management, and Miss
Fuller the literary editorship. It was a rash and
generous enterprise, for the subscribers were few
and the promised contributors for the most part
unpractised writers; and it was sure to have the
dead weight of the reading community against it.
Miss Fuller herself was under no illusions as to
their prospects. " We cannot show high culture
[she writes], and I doubt about vigorous thought."
Her object, however, was not to make a successful
journal, but " to afford an avenue for what of liberal and calm thought might be originated among
us by the wants of individual minds." [1]

It was an experiment worth trying, and even
if it succeeded only in bringing these wants into
clearer consciousness, this of itself ought to give to
the *Dial* a place of honor in our literary annals.
It is much to have uniformly taken the highest tone upon all subjects ; and whatever may be
said of the *Dial*, this praise abundantly belongs
to it.

Success, in the ordinary sense of the word, was
out of the question, — if from no other reason, from

[1] In a letter quoted by Mr. Cooke, in his Life of Emerson,
p. 78.

the lack of complete unity of purpose in the projectors. No two of them precisely agreed as to
what they would have. Some of its oldest friends
had been alienated by the want, or rather the avoid-
ance, of any definite aim. Others soon began to
complain that it still savored of the old order of
things. The practical reformers sniffed at the
superfine idealism of many of its pages. Emerson, for his part, was in favor of the largest liberty
and the most extravagant aspirations, but he winced
in spite of himself at the violations of literary
form, and he confessed, in strict confidence, that he
found some of the numbers unreadable. Miss Fuller, writing to him two years afterwards, when he
relieved her of her charge, says that the change of
editors cannot but change the aim as well as the
character of the journal : —

" You will sometimes reject pieces that I should
not. For you have always had in view to make a
good periodical and represent your own tastes ;
while I have had in view to let all kinds of people
have freedom to say their say, for better, for
worse."

Emerson cared only for the poetry, or for the
poetical point of view; that everything should be
looked upon, as he said, " at large angles ; " and
to this he was extremely tolerant. His criticism
on the first number (in a letter to Miss Fuller)
was that the verse was not sufficiently conspicuous ;

were he the compositor, he would set it in larger
type than the prose. But he did not find that the
public shared his tastes.

"Nowhere [he complains in a letter to Miss
Fuller, July 8, 1840] do I find readers of the *Dial*
poetry, which is my one thing needful in the enterprise. I ask in vain after Z., or H. T., or 'new
contributor,' — of many a one. They wait till I
have done, and then inquire concerning Mr. Parker.
I think Alcott's paper of great importance to the
journal, inasmuch as otherwise, as far as I have
read, there is little that might not appear in any
other journal."

Afterwards, he writes to Miss Fuller, August 4,
1840, he began " to wish to see a different *Dial*
from that which I first imagined. I would not have
it too purely literary. I wish we might make a journal so broad and great in the survey that it should
lead the opinion of this generation on every great
interest, and read the law on property, government,
education, as well as on art, letters, and religion.
. . . It does not seem worth our while to work
with any other than sovereign aims. So I wish we
might court some of the good fanatics, and publish
chapters on every head in the whole art of living.
I am just now turning my pen to scribble and copy
on the subjects of Labor, Farm, Reform, Domestic life, etc., and I asked myself, Why should
not the *Dial* present this homely and grave sub-

ject to the men and women of the land? . . . I
know the dangers of such latitude of plan in any
but the best conducted journal. It becomes friendly
to special modes of reform ; partisan, bigoted, perhaps whimsical ; not universal and poetic. But
our round-table is not, I fancy, in imminent peril
of party and bigotry, and we shall not bruise each
the others' whims by the collision."

And in his diary of the same date : —

" I think our *Dial* ought not to be a mere literary journal, but that the times demand of us all
a more earnest aim. It ought to contain the best
advice on the topics of Government, Temperance,
Abolition, Trade, and Domestic Life. It might
well add such poetry and sentiment as will now
constitute its best merit. Yet it ought to go
straight into life, with the devoted wisdom of the
best men and women in the land. It should —
should it not? — be a degree nearer to the hodi-
ernal facts than my writings are. I wish to write
pure mathematics, and not a culinary almanac or
application of science to the arts."

But he was not easy to suit with any applications that offered themselves, — for instance, Theodore Parker's, though he acknowledged Parker's
earnestness and his power of reaching the ear of
the public with his vigorous rhetoric. Afterwards,
when Emerson had assumed the editorship and the
Dial was in pecuniary straits, Mr. Parker sent a

long article concerning the Reverend John Pierpont's differences with his parish on the subject of
Temperance ; which Emerson wished to reject, but
admitted at last, as he said, *pro honoris causa.*
When that number of the journal appeared, Miss
Elizabeth Peabody, who was then the publisher,
wrote to Emerson that Parker's article had sold
the whole of the issue, and that more copies were
wanted.

Miss Fuller struggled bravely on, with much
labor and no pay, for about two years, and then
Emerson felt obliged to take it up, though very
unwilling.

" The *Dial* [he writes in his diary] is to be sustained or ended; and I must settle the question, it
seems, of its life or death. I wish it to live, but I
do not wish to be its life. Neither do I like to put
it into the hands of the Humanity and Reform men,
because they trample on letters and poetry ; nor in
the hands of the scholars, for they are dead and
dry. I do not like the *Plain Speaker* so well as
the *Edinburgh Review*. The spirit of the last
may be conventional and artificial, but that of the
first is coarse, sour, indigent ; dwells in a cellar-
kitchen and goes to make suicides."

" Poor *Dial!* [he writes Dr. Hedge] — it has not
pleased any mortal. No man cried, God save it !
And yet, though it contains a deal of matter I
could gladly spare, I yet value it as a portfolio

which preserves and conveys to distant persons precisely what I should borrow and transcribe to send them if I could. It wants mainly and only some devotion on the part of its conductor to it, that it may not be the herbarium that it is of dried flowers, but the vehicle of some living and advancing mind. But nobody has yet conceived himself born for this end only."

The *Dial* "enjoyed its obscurity," as Emerson says, two years longer under his charge, and then expired, in April, 1844,[1] to his great relief; having cost him, I conjecture, some money as well as perpetual worry.

Emerson had done what he could to forward the birth of a new spirit in our literature, and Miss Fuller had done her part; but the child refused to be born. The genius of the new era had not as yet got on speaking terms with its day and generation.

About the same time with the *Dial*, another scheme, foreshadowing the later Concord School of Philosophy, appears in a letter from Emerson to Miss Fuller : —

---

[1] Rev. George William Cooke has given, in the *Journal of Speculative Philosophy* (July, 1885), a careful account of the *Dial* and its writers. For a list of Emerson's contributions see Appendix C.

Concord, *August* 16, 1840.

. . . Alcott and I projected the other day a whole university out of our straws. Do you not wish that I should advertise it in the *Dial?* Mr. Ripley, Mr. Hedge, Mr. Parker, Mr. Alcott and I shall, in some country town, — say Concord or Hyannis, — announce that we will hold a semester for the instruction of young men, say from October to April. Each shall announce his own subject and topics, with what detail he pleases, and shall hold, say two lectures or conversations thereon each week ; the hours being so arranged that any pupil may attend all, if he please. We may, on certain evenings, combine our total force for conversations, and on Sunday we may meet for worship, and make the Sabbath beautiful to ourselves. The terms shall be left to the settlement of the scholar himself. He shall understand that the teachers will accept a fee, and he shall proportion it to his sense of benefit received and his means. Suppose, then, that Mr. Ripley should teach the History of Opinion, Theology, Modern Literature, or what else ; Hedge, Poetry, Metaphysics, Philosophy of History ; Parker, History of Paganism, of the Catholic Church, the Modern Crisis, — in short, Ecclesiastical History ; Alcott, Psychology, Ethics, the Ideal life ; and I, Beaumont and Fletcher, Percy's Reliques, Rhetoric, Belles-Lettres. Do you not see that

by addition of one or two chosen persons we might
make a puissant faculty, and front the world without charter, diploma, corporation, or steward? Do
you not see that if such a thing were well and happily done for twenty or thirty students only at first,
it would anticipate by years the education of New
England? Now do you not wish to come here and
join in such a work? What society shall we not
have! What Sundays shall we not have! We
shall sleep no more, and we shall concert better
houses, economics, and social modes than any we
have seen.

What the New England leaders of opinion, even
such as were the least averse to thinking for themselves, thought of their would-be teachers was expressed, though in rather shrill tones, by John
Quincy Adams in his diary at this time: —

"The sentiment of religion is at this time, perhaps, more potent and prevailing in New England
than in any other portion of the Christian world.
For many years since the establishment of the the-
ological school at Andover, the Calvinists and Unitarians have been battling with each other upon the
Atonement, the Divinity of Jesus Christ, and the
Trinity. This has very much subsided, but this
wandering of minds takes the place of that, and
equally lets the wolf into the fold. A young man
named Ralph Waldo Emerson, a son of my once-

loved friend William Emerson, and a classmate of
my lamented George, after failing in the every-day
avocations of a Unitarian preacher and schoolmaster, starts a new doctrine of Transcendentalism,
declares all the old revelations superannuated and
worn out, and announces the approach of new revelations and prophecies. Garrison and the non-
resistant abolitionists, Brownson and the Marat
democrats, phrenology and animal magnetism, —
all come in, furnishing each some plausible rascal-
ity as an ingredient for the bubbling caldron of
religion and politics. Pearse Cranch, *ex ephebis*,
preached here last week, and gave out quite a
stream of Transcendentalism, most unexpectedly." [1]

Emerson for his part did not feel that there had
been any essential change in his position of mind
towards religion since the days when he was a Unitarian preacher. In an address to his old friends
of the Second Church (Sunday, March 10, 1844),
when they were rebuilding their meeting-house in
Hanover Street, he says : —

" I do not think that violent changes of opinion
very often occur in men. As far as I know they
do not see new lights and turn sharp corners, but
commonly, after twenty or after fifty years you
shall find the individual true to his early tendencies. The change is commonly in this, that each

[1] *Memoirs of John Quincy Adams*, x. 345.

becomes a more pronounced character ; that he has thrown off those timidities and excessive regard to the minds of others which masked his own.   I have not the least disposition to prove any consistency in myself ; a great enlargement, a discovery of gross errors corrected, would please me much more ; but as a matter of fact I do not find in the years that have elapsed since I stood here to teach any new varieties of thought, but rather an accumulation of particular experiences to establish, or, I should rather say, illustrate, the leading belief of my youth."

He was looked upon, by John Quincy Adams and by everybody, as the representative Transcendentalist ; yet, in a lecture in 1841, when he was at his farthest in this direction, he defines Transcendentalism as " the Saturnalia or excess of faith."[1] Not as if faith, the vision of the absolute, the look to the ideal as our reinforcement against the tyranny of mere use and wont tending to shut us up in petty cares and enjoyments, — not as if this could ever too much abound ; but that it may want " the restraining grace of common sense, . . . which does not meddle with the absolute, but takes things at their word, things as they appear."[2] This restraint was never wanting to Emerson ; he felt safe against the dangers of " divine discontent," and this feeling made him the more charitable towards

[1] *Collected Writings*, i. 320.   [2] *Ibid.*, viii. 9.

its extreme manifestations. He was as much alive
to the extravagances as anybody, having frequent
occasion to observe them; but our danger he
thought did not lie on that side.

"Buddhism, Transcendentalism [he writes in
his journal], life delights in reducing *ad absurdum*.
The child, the infant, is a transcendentalist, and
charms us all; we try to be, and instantly run
in debt, lie, steal, commit adultery, go mad, and
die."

"The trick of every man's conversation we soon
learn. In one this remorseless Buddhism lies all
around, threatening with death and night. We
make a little fire in our cabin, but we dare not go
abroad one furlong into the murderous cold. Every
thought, every enterprise, every sentiment, has its
ruin in this horrid Infinite which encircles us and
awaits our dropping into it. If killing all Bud-
dhists would do the least good, we would have a
slaughter of the innocents directly."

"It must be admitted that civilization is onerous
and expensive,—hideous expense to keep it up: let
it go, and be Indians again. But why Indians?
That is costly, too. The mudturtle-and-trout life is
easier and cheaper, and oyster cheaper still. 'Play
out the game; act well your part; if the gods have
blundered, we will not.'"

"'T is necessary that you honor the people's
facts. If you have no place for them, the people

absolutely have no place for you. A person, whatever he may have to say or do, to whom politics is nothing, navigation nothing, railroads nothing, money nothing, books nothing, men and women nothing, may have his seat or sphere in another planet, but once for all has nothing to do here. The earth and sea and air, the constitution of things, and all that we call Fate, is on the people's side; and that is a reasoner not liable to a fallacy."

" —— does not do justice to the merits of labor. The whole human race spend their lives in hard work, for simple and necessary motives, and feel the approbation of their conscience; and they meet this talker at the gate, who, as far as they see, does not labor himself, and takes up this grating tone of authority and accusation against them. His unpopularity is not all wonderful. There must be, not a few fine words, but very many hard strokes, every day, to get what even an ascetic wants."

" Let a man hate eddies, hate the sides of the river, and keep the middle of the stream. The hero did nothing apart and odd, but travelled on the highway and went to the same tavern with the whole people, and was very heartily and naturally there; no dainty, protected person."

" I speak [he says] as an idealist," — but his idealism never made him blind to facts, nor did it make him wish to ignore them. Money, for instance, might be, as was then much urged, a very rude certificate of a man's worth and of his claims upon his fellow-men; in a better state of society the "cash-nexus" would be superseded by the bonds of justice and love. Meantime let us not pretend to be better than we are : —

"The cant about money and the railing at mean-souled people who have a little yellow dirt only to recommend them, accuses the railer. Money is a truly admirable invention, and the delicacy and perfection with which this mercury measures our good sense in every transaction in a shop or in a farm ; the Egyptian verdict which it gives : thou hast done well : thou hast overdone : thou hast undone, — I cannot have a better voice of nature.

"Do not gloze and prate and mystify. Here is our dear, grand —— says, You shall dig in my field for a day, and I will give you a dollar when it is done, and it shall not be a business transaction. It makes me sick. Whilst money is the measure really adopted by us all as the most convenient measure of all material values, let us not affectedly disuse the name and mystify ourselves and others ; let us not ' say no and take it.' We may very well and honestly have theoretical and practical objections to it ; if they are fatal to the use of money and barter, let us disuse them ; if they are less grave than the inconvenience of abolishing traffic, let us not pretend to have done with it whilst we eat and drink and wear and breathe it.

"However, I incline to think that among angels the money or certificate system might have some important convenience, — not for thy satisfaction of whom I borrow, but for my satisfaction that I have not exceeded carelessly my proper wants, have not overdrawn."

A sound, sincere, and catholic man, he says, is one who is able to honor at the same time the ideal, or laws of the mind, and Fate, or the order of Nature. "For wisdom does not seek a literal rectitude, but a useful, that is a conditional one, — such a one as the faculties of man and the constitution of things will warrant." [1] With all his idealism Emerson is free from the pedantry of ignoring the actual conditions, or the existing motives by which the ideal must be realized. It is one thing to do what we can to elevate these motives; it is quite another to call upon men to act as if they were different from what they really are. Thus, for instance, in speaking of Education as it ought to be, he describes the prevailing system of emulation and display as " the calomel of culture ; " easy to use and prompt in its effect, but a " quack practice." [2] But once when he found this view too rashly acted on by one of the smaller New England colleges, he calls it an " old granny system.

[1] *Collected Writings,* iv. 47; i. 286. [2] *Ibid.,* x. 151.

President —— has an aversion to emulation, as injurious to the character of the pupils. He therefore forbids the election of members into the two literary societies by merit, but arranges that the first scholar alphabetically on the list shall be assigned to the X and the second to the Y, the third to the X and the fourth to the Y, and so on. ' Well, but there is a first scholar in the class, is there not, and he has the first oration at Commencement?' ' Oh no, the parts are assigned by lot.' The amiable student who explained it added that it tended to remove disagreeable excitement from the societies. I answered, Certainly, and it would remove more if there were no colleges at all. I recommended morphine in liberal doses at the college Commons. I learn, since my return, that the President has resigned; the first good trait I have heard of in the man."

And when a youthful admirer of his, having in mind the description [1] of the spiritual life as that of a man who eats angels' food ; " who, trusting to his sentiments, found life made of miracles; who, working for universal aims, found himself fed, he knew not how; clothed, sheltered, and weaponed, he knew not how," etc., — sent him the autobiography of George Muller, an Englishman, who found himself and a large number of persons under his charge supported entirely by miraculous meth-

[1] *Collected Writings*, i. 319.

ods, Emerson expressed surprise that the book
should be sent to him, and, when he returned it,
says : —

"I send back the book with thanks, and, as I
said, with some wonder at your interest in it. I
sometimes think that you and your coevals missed
much that I and mine found; for Calvinism was
still robust and effective on life and character in
all the people who surrounded my childhood, and
gave a deep religious tinge to manners and conversation. I doubt the race is now extinct, and
certainly no sentiment has taken its place on the
new generation, — none as pervasive and control-
ling. But they were a high tragic school, and found
much of their own belief in the grander traits of
the Greek mythology, Nemesis, the Fates, and the
Eumenides ; and, I am sure, would have raised an
eyebrow at this pistareen Providence of Robert
Huntington and now of George Muller. There is
piety here, but 't is pulled down steadily into the
pantry and the shoe-closet, till we are distressed for
a breath of fresh air. Who would dare to be shut
up with such as these from year to year? Certainly there is a philosophic interest and question
here that well deserves attention, — the success,
namely, to which he challenges scrutiny, through
all these years ; God coming precisely in the mode
he is called for, and to the hour and minute. But
this narrative would not quite stand cross-exam-
ination."

" There is illusion that shall deceive even the
elect ; " and idealism may be one form of it.
Yet the desire for perfection, the discontent with
present attainment, is the spring of all human progress ; there cannot be too much of it, there may
easily be too little. Indeed, what seems excess is
rather defect : an infirm faith that cannot recognize its ideals in the masquerade of every-day life.
Care will be taken that the trees do not grow up
into the sky ; if only sap and vigor be not wanting,
the checks will supply themselves when they are
needed.

" It is a sort of maxim with me never to harp
on the omnipotence of limitations. Least of all do
we need any suggestion of checks and measures ;
as if New England were anything else."

The one thing he feared was an insufficient supply : —

" Of so many fine people it is true that, being so
much, they ought to be a little more, and, missing
that, are naught. It is a sort of King René period ;
there is no doing, but rare thrilling prophecy from
bands of competing minstrels.

" We are wasted with our versatility ; with the
eagerness to grasp on every possible side. The
American genius runs to leaves, to suckers, to ten-
drils, to miscellany. The air is loaded with poppy,
with imbecility, with dispersion, with sloth.

" Allston's pictures are Elysian, fair, serene, but

unreal. I extend the remark to all the American
geniuses: Irving, Bryant, Greenough, Everett,
Channing, — even Webster, in his recorded eloquence, — all lack nerve and dagger.

"Our virtue runs in a narrow rill; we have never
a freshet. One would like to see Boston and
Massachusetts agitated like a wave with some generosity; mad for learning, for music, for philan-
thropy, for association, for freedom, for art. We
have sensibility and insight enough, if only we
had constitution enough. But, as the doctor said
in my boyhood, 'You have no stamina.' What
a company of brilliant young persons I have seen,
with so much expectation! The sort is very good,
but none is good enough of his sort.

"Yet the poorness or recentness of our experience must not deter us from affirming the law of
the soul. Nay, although there never was any life
which in any just manner represented it, yet we are
bound to say what would be if man kept the divine
law, — nay, what already is, and is explained and
demonstrated by every right and wrong of ours;
though we are far enough from that inward health
which would make this true order appear to be the
order of our lives." (Journal, 1839–43.)

CHAPTER XII.

WHEN Emerson said in his letter to Margaret
Fuller that he wished the *Dial* might lead the opinion of the day and declare the law on every great
interest, he was unconsciously borrowing a tone
that did not belong to him. He had no disposition
to play the oracle, or to declare the law upon any
subject. Transcendentalism was to him not a particular set of doctrines, but a state of mind; the
healthy and normal state, in which we resist the
sleep of routine, and think and act for ourselves instead of allowing circumstances to decide for us.

" I told Mr. —— [Emerson writes in his jour-
nal] that he need not consult the Germans, but, if
he wished at any time to know what the Transcendentalists believe, he might simply omit what in

his own mind he added from the tradition, and the
rest would be Transcendentalism."

Emerson's sympathies, in that age of renovation,
of confident outlook to the speedy removal of the
ills that beset man's condition, were of course with
the renovators, the temperance men, the abolitionists, the seekers after improved forms of society.
But "abolition, or abstinence from rum, or any
other far-off external virtue should not divert attention from the all-containing virtue which we
vainly dodge and postpone, but which must be met
and obeyed at last, if we wish to be substance, and
not accidents." The stress that was laid on the
importance of improved conditions, of associations
to help men to escape from bodily or mental bon-
dage, made him think the more strongly of the
prime necessity that the man himself should be renewed, before any alterations of his condition can
be of much help to him.

"If [he writes to a friend] the man were de-
mocratized and made kind and faithful in his heart,
the whole sequel would flow easily out and instruct
us in what should be the new world; nor should
we need to be always laying the axe at the root of
this or that vicious institution."

In Emerson's philosophy "all that we call Fate,"
or external condition, has to be reckoned with, since
it is the counterpart of our internal condition, and
holds its own so long as that remains unchanged.
Here are some extracts from his journal in 1840 : —

" I told —— that I thought he must be a very young man, or his time hang very heavy on his hands, who can afford to think much and talk much about the foibles of his neighbor, or 'denounce,' and play the 'son of thunder,' as he called it. I am one who believe all times pretty much alike, and yet I sympathize so keenly with this. We want to be expressed; yet you take from us War, that great opportunity which allowed the accumulations of electricity to stream off from both poles, the positive and the negative. Well, now you take from us our cup of alcohol, as before you took our cup of wrath. We had become canting moths of peace, our helmet was a skillet, and now we must become temperance milksops. You take away, but what do you give? Mr. Jefts has been preached into tipping up his barrel of rum into the brook; but day after to-morrow, when he wakes up cold and poor, will he feel that he has somewhat for somewhat? If I could lift him up by happy violence into a religious beatitude, or imparadise him in ideas, then should I have greatly more than indemnified him for what I have taken. I should not take away; he would put away, — or rather, ascend out of this litter and sty in which he had rotted, to go up clothed and in his right mind into the assembly and conversation of men.

" We frigidly talk of Reform until the walls mock us. It is that of which a man should never speak, but, if he have cherished it in his bosom, he should steal to it in darkness, as an Indian to his bride, or as a monk should go privily to another monk and say, Lo, we two are of one opinion; a new light has shined in our hearts; let us dare to obey it.

" I have not yet conquered my own house; it irks and repents me. Shall I raise the siege of this hen-coop, and march baffled away to a pretended siege of Babylon? It seems to me that so to do were to dodge the problem I am set to solve, and to hide my impotency in the thick of a crowd.

" Does he not do more to abolish slavery who works all day steadily in his own garden than he who goes to the abolition-meeting and makes a speech? He who does his own work frees a slave. He who does not his own work is a slave-holder. Whilst we sit here talking and smiling, some person is out there in field and shop and kitchen, doing what we need, without talk or smiles. The world asks, Do the abolitionists eat sugar? Do they wear cotton? Do they smoke tobacco? Are they their own servants? Have they managed to put that dubious institution of servile labor on an agreeable and thoroughly intelligible and transparent foundation? Two tables in every house! Abolitionists at one and servants at the other! It is a calumny you utter. There never was, I am persuaded, an asceticism so austere as theirs, from

the peculiar emphasis of their testimony. The
planter does not want slaves; no, he wants his luxury, and he will pay even this price for it. It is
not possible, then, that the abolitionist will begin
the assault on his luxury by any other means than
the abating of his own."

In November, 1837, Emerson was requested to
deliver an address at Concord on the subject of
Slavery. There was some difficulty in getting a
room for the purpose, all agitation of the question
of Slavery being at that time generally deprecated:
at length the Second Church agreed to allow the
use of their vestry. In his speech he dwelt especially on the duty of resisting all attempts to stifle
discussion. It is, he says, the eminent prerogative
of New England, and her sacred duty, to open her
churches and halls to the free discussion of every
question involving the rights of man.

"If the motto on all palace-gates is ' Hush,' the
honorable ensign to our town-halls should be ' Pro-
claim.' I account this a matter of grave importance, because symptoms of an overprudence are
showing themselves around us. I regret to hear
that all the churches but one, and almost all the
public halls in Boston, are closed against the discussion of this question. Even the platform of the
lyceum, hitherto the freest of all organs, is so ban-
daged and muffled that it threatens to be silent.

But, when we have distinctly settled for ourselves the right and wrong of this question, and have covenanted with ourselves to keep the channels of opinion open, each man for himself, I think we have done all that is incumbent on most of us to do. Sorely as we may feel the wrongs of the poor slave in Carolina or in Cuba, we have each of us our hands full of much nearer duties. . . . Let him not exaggerate by his pity and his blame the outrage of the Georgian or Virginian, forgetful of the vices of his own town and neighborhood, of himself. Let our own evils check the bitterness of our condemnation of our brother, and, whilst we insist on calling things by their right names, let us not reproach the planter, but own that his misfortune is at least as great as his sin."

To the abolitionists this tone appeared rather cool and philosophical, and some of his friends tried to rouse him to a fuller sense of the occasion. He was insufficiently alive, they told him, to the interests of humanity, and apt to allow his disgust at the methods or the manners of the philanthropists to blind him to the substantial importance of their work. He was ready to admit that there might be some foundation for the charge : —

"I had occasion to say the other day to Elizabeth Hoar that I like best the strong and worthy persons, like her father, who support the social order without hesitation or misgiving. I like these;

they never incommode us by exciting grief, pity,
or perturbation of any sort. But the professed
philanthropists, it is strange and horrible to say,
are an altogether odious set of people, whom one
would shun as the worst of bores and canters. I
have the same objection to dogmatism in Reform
as to dogmatism in Conservatism. The impatience
of discipline, the haste to rule before we have
served, to prescribe laws for nations and humanity
before we have said our own prayers or yet heard
the benediction which love and peace sing in our
own bosom, — these all dwarf and degrade; the
great names are profaned; our virtue is a fuss and
sometimes a fit. But my conscience, my unhappy
conscience, respects that hapless class who see the
faults and stains of our social order, and who pray
and strive incessantly to right the wrong; this
annoying class of men and women, though they
commonly find the work altogether beyond their
faculty, and their results are, for the present, dis-
tressing. They are partial, and apt to magnify
their own. Yes, and the prostrate penitent also, —
he is not comprehensive, he is not philosophical in
those tears and groans. Yet I feel that under him
and his partiality and exclusiveness is the earth
and the sea and all that in them is, and the axis
around which the universe revolves passes through
his body there where he stands."

It was not fastidiousness nor inertia that made

Emerson averse to active participation in the philanthropic schemes, so much as a necessity of his nature, which inclined him always to look for a relative justification of the offending party or institution ; at any rate, disinclined him, as he said, from coveting the office of constable. In judging ourselves we rightly apply an absolute standard ; but in judging others we ought to consider the circumstances, and take care not to attribute to the individual what belongs to his position : —

" Hostility, bitterness to persons or to the age, indicate infirm sense, unacquaintance with men ; who are really at top selfish, and really at bottom fraternal, alike, identical."

For us to keep slaves would be the sum of wickedness, but in the planter it may indicate only a degree of self-indulgence which we may parallel readily enough nearer home ; in attacking him we are demanding of him a superiority to his conditions which we do not demand of ourselves. He is to blame, of course, but in the same sense the slave is to blame for allowing himself to be held as a slave : —

" The degradation of that black race, though now lost in the starless spaces of the past, did not come without sin. The condition is inevitable to the men they are, and nobody can redeem them but themselves. The exertions of all the abolitionists are nugatory except for themselves. As far as they can emancipate the North from slavery, well.

" The secret, the esoteric of abolition — a secret too from the abolitionists — is that the negro and the negro-holders are really of one party, and that when the apostle of freedom has gained his first point, of repealing the negro laws, he will find the free negro is the type and exponent of that very animal law ; standing as he does in nature below the series of thought, and in the plane of vegetable and animal existence, whose law is to prey on one another, and the strongest has it.

" The abolitionist (theoretical) wishes to abolish slavery, but because he wishes to abolish the black man. He considers that it is violence, brute force, which, counter to intellectual rule, holds property in man; but he thinks the negro himself the very representative and exponent of that brute, base force ; that it is the negro in the white man which holds slaves. He attacks Legree, Mac Duffie, and slave-holders, North and South, generally, but because they are the foremost negroes of the world, and fight the negro fight. When they are extinguished, and law, intellectual law, prevails, it will then appear quickly enough that the brute instinct rallies and centres in the black man. He is created on a lower plane than the white, and eats men, and kidnaps and tortures if he can. The negro is imitative, secondary ; in short, reactionary merely in his successes; and there is no organization with him in mental and moral spheres.

"It is becoming in the scholar to insist on central soundness rather than on superficial applications. I am to demand the absolute right, affirm that, do that; but not to push Boston into a false, showy, theatrical attitude, endeavoring to persuade her she is more virtuous than she is."

Meantime he was heartily glad that men were found willing and able to throw themselves unhesitatingly into the contest. They might be wrong-headed, he said, but they were wrong-headed in the right direction: —

"The haters of Garrison have lived to rejoice in that grand world-movement which, every age or two, casts out so masterly an agent for good. I cannot speak of that gentleman without respect. I found him the other day in his dingy office." (Journal, 1844.)

He went to Garrison's office, perhaps, to concert for a meeting which the abolitionists held in the Concord Court - House[1] on the 1st of August in this year (1844), to celebrate the anniversary of the liberation of the slaves in the British West Indies. Emerson delivered the address, which is

---

[1] None of the churches would open their doors to the convention. At length Thoreau got leave to use the old court-house, and himself rang the bell.

printed in the last edition of his works;[1] a most satisfactory performance (the *Liberator* says) to the abolitionists who were present. In this speech and in one a year later, Emerson went farther than ever before in maintaining the negro's capability of civilization. He esteemed the occasion of the jubilee, he said, to be "the proud discovery that the black race can contend with the white; that in the great anthem which we call History, — a piece of many parts and vast compass, — after playing a long time a very low and subdued accompaniment, they perceive the time arrived when they can strike in with effect and take a master's part in the music. The civility of the world has reached that pitch that their more moral genius is becoming indispensable, and the quality of this race is to be honored for itself."

And in a speech which I know only from the report in the *New York Tribune*[2] (for he never printed it, and seems not even to have preserved the manuscript), on the same anniversary in the next year, at Waltham, he says the defence of slavery in the popular mind is not a doubt of the equity of the negro's cause, nor a stringent self-interest, but the objection of an inferiority of race; a fate, pronouncing against the abolitionist and the philanthropist; so that the good-will of amiable enthusiasts in the negro's behalf will avail him no

[1] *Collected Writings*, xi. 129.   [2] August 7, 1845.

more than a pair of oars against the falling ocean at Niagara.

" And what is the amount of the conclusion in which the men of New England acquiesce ? It is that the Creator of the negro has given him up to stand as a victim, a caricature of the white man beside him ; to stoop under his pack, to bleed under his whip. If that be the doctrine, then I say, if He has given up his cause, He has also given up mine, who feel his wrong. But it is not so ; the universe is not bankrupt ; still stands the old heart firm in its seat, and knows that, come what will, the right is and shall be : justice is forever and ever. And what is the reply to this fatal allegation ? I believe there is a sound argument derived from facts collected in the United States and in the West Indies in reply to this alleged hopeless inferiority of the colored race. But I shall not touch it. I concern myself now with the morals of the system, which seem to scorn a tedious catalogue of particulars on a question so simple as this. The sentiment of right, which is the principle of civilization and the reason of reason, fights against this damnable atheism. The Persians have a proverb : Beware of the orphan ; for, when the orphan is set a-crying, the throne of the Almighty is shaken from side to side. Whatever may appear at the moment, however contrasted the fortunes of the black and the white, yet is the planter's an unsafe and an unblest condition. Nature fights on the other side, and as power is ever stealing from the idle to the busy hand, it seems inevitable that a revolution is preparing, at no distant day, to set these disjointed matters right."

He liked the sun's way of making civilization cast off its disguises better than the storm's. It was always a painful struggle with him when he felt himself constrained to undertake the office of censor: as when, some years earlier than this, another national crime, the violent removal of the Cherokee Indians by the State of Georgia, backed by the army of the United States, forced from him a cry of indignation in a letter to President Van Buren,[1] which that sleek patriot probably never read.

"*April* 19, 1838. This disaster of the Cherokees, brought to me by a sad friend to blacken my days and nights: I can do nothing; why shriek? Why strike ineffectual blows? I stir in it for the sad reason that no other mortal will move, and if I do not, why it is left undone. The amount of it, to be sure, is merely a scream; but sometimes a scream is better than a thesis."

"Yesterday went the letter to Van Buren, — a letter hated of me; a deliverance that does not deliver the soul. I write my journal, I read my lecture with joy; but this stirring in the philanthropic

[1] Appendix D.

mud gives me no peace. I will let the republic
alone until the republic comes to me. I fully sympathize, be sure, with the sentiment I write; but I
accept it rather from my friends than dictate it. It
is not my impulse to say it, and therefore my genius deserts me; no muse befriends; no music of
thought or word accompanies."

The same feeling, that sympathy with the aims
of the reformers must not tempt him beyond his
proper bounds, made him, after some hesitation,
draw back when he was urged to join in the Brook
Farm experiment in 1840.

"What a brave thing Mr. Ripley has done! [he
writes to Miss Fuller;] he stands now at the head
of the Church Militant, and his step cannot be
without an important sequel. For the 'community,' I have given it some earnest attention and
much talk, and have not quite decided not to go.
But I hate that the least weight should hang on
my decision, — of me, who am so unpromising a
candidate for any society. At the name of a society all my repulsions play, all my quills rise and
sharpen. I shall very shortly go, or send to George
Ripley my thoughts on the subject."

(Journal.) "*October* 17, 1840. Yesterday George
and Sophia Ripley, Margaret Fuller, and Alcott
discussed here the new social plans. I wished to
be convinced, to be thawed, to be made nobly mad

by the kindlings before my eye of a new dawn of
human piety. But this scheme was arithmetic and
comfort; a hint borrowed from the Tremont House
and United States Hotel; a rage in our poverty
and politics to live rich and gentlemanlike; an anchor to leeward against a change of weather. And
not once could I be inflamed, but sat aloof and
thoughtless; my voice faltered and fell. It was
not the cave of persecution, which is the palace
of spiritual power, but only a room in the Astor
House hired for the Transcendentalists. I do not
wish to remove from my present prison to a prison
a little larger. I wish to break all prisons."

He wrote to Mr. Ripley, towards the end of the
year, that he had decided, " yet very slowly and,
I may almost say, with penitence," not to join
them; giving his reasons for thinking himself
unfit, and adding some advice from Mr. Edmund
Hosmer, " a very intelligent farmer and a very
upright man in my neighborhood," concerning the
details of the farming.

" I approve every wild action of the experiment-
ers [he writes in his journal] ; I say what they say,
and my only apology for not doing their work is
preoccupation of mind. I have a work of my own,
which I know I can do with some success. It
would leave that undone if I should undertake with
them, and I do not see in myself any vigor equal

to such an enterprise.   So I stay where I am, even
with the degradation of owning bank-stock and
seeing poor men suffer whilst the universal genius
apprises me of this disgrace, and beckons me to
the martyr's and redeemer's office.   This debility
of practice, this staying by our work, is belief too ;
for obedience to a man's genius is the particular
of faith ; by and by shall come the universal of
faith."

The following passage, endorsed " December 12,
1840," was sent to me by the late Reverend
William Henry Channing, as copied by Miss Fuller
from some letter or journal of Emerson's : —

" I have the habitual feeling that the whole of
our social structure — State, School, Religion, Marriage, Trade, Science — has been cut off from its
root in the soul, and has only a superficial life, a
' name to live.'   It would please me then to restore
for myself these fruits to their stock, or to accept
no church, school, state, or society which did not
found itself in my own nature.   I should like, if I
cannot at once abolish, at least to tend to abolish
for myself all goods which are not a part of this
good ; to stand in the world the fool of ideas ; to
demonstrate all the parts of faith ; to renounce a
property which is an accident to me, has no relation to my character or culture, is holden and expended by no sweet and sublime laws, and my
dependence on which is an infirmity and a hurt to

me. I should like to make my estate a document
of my faith, and not an anomalous fact which was
common to me, a believer, with a thousand unbe-
lievers. I know there must be a possible property
which flows directly from the nature of man, and
which may be earned and expended in perfect consent with the growth of plants, the ebb and flow of
tides, and the orbit of planets. But now, as you
see, instead of being the hero of ideas and exploring by a great act of trust those diviner modes
which the spirit will not fail to show to those who
dare to ask, I allow the old circumstance of mother,
wife, children, and brother to overpower my wish
to right myself with absolute Nature; and I also
consent to hang, a parasite, with all the parasites
on this rotten system of property. This is but one
example. Diet, medicine, traffic, books, social in-
tercourse, and all the rest of our practices and
usages are equally divorced from ideas, are empir-
ical and false. I should like to put all my practices back on their first thoughts, and do nothing
for which I had not the whole world for my reason.
If there are inconveniences and what is called ruin
in the way, because we have so enervated and
maimed ourselves, yet it would be like dying of
perfumes to sink in the effort to reattach the deeds
of every day to the holy and mysterious recesses of
life.

" But how will Mr. R.'s project help me in all

this? It is a pretty circuitous route, is it not, to the few, simple conditions which I require? I want my own labor, instead of that which is hired, — or, at least, that the hired shall be honorable and honored. Mr. R.'s plan offers me this, and with another great good for me, namely, direction of my labor. But so would a farm which I should buy, associating to me two or three friends and a hired farmer, secure the same advantages. To Mr. R.'s proposed school I attach no special interest. I am sure that I should contribute my aid as effectually to the education of the country on my own lonely acres as I can in this formal institution. Where a few conditions suffice, is it wise to enter into a complex system? I only wish to make my house as simple as my vocation. I have not the least faith in the enlargement of influence through an external largeness of your plan. Merely the thought in which you work makes the impression, and never the circumstance. I have the dream that a small family of ascetics, working together on a secluded spot, would keep each other's benevolence and invention awake, so that we should every day fall on good hints and more beautiful methods. Then there is no secluding of influences. It is the nature of light to shine."

Nor did he see his way to joining the little community of Fruitlands, established a year or so later than Brook Farm, by Mr. Alcott and some English friends, Messrs. Lane and Wright, in the town of Harvard, not far from Concord : —

" I begged A. to paint out his project, and he proceeded to say that there should be found a farm of a hundred acres, in excellent condition, with good buildings, a good orchard, and grounds which admitted of being laid out with great beauty ; and this should be purchased and given to them in the first place. I replied, You ask too much. This is not solving the problem ; there are hundreds of innocent young persons who, if you will thus establish and endow and protect them, will find it no hard matter to keep their innocency. And to see their tranquil household after all this has been done for them will in no wise instruct or strengthen me. But he will instruct and strengthen me who, there where he is, unaided, in the midst of poverty, toil, and traffic, extricates himself from the corruptions of the same, and builds on his land a house of peace and benefit, good customs and free thoughts. But, replies A., how is this to be done ? How can I do it, who have wife and family to maintain ? I answered that he was not the person to do it, or he would not ask the question. When he that shall come is born, he will not only see the thing to be done, but invent the life ; invent the ways and means of doing it. The way you would show me does not commend itself to me as the way of greatness. The spirit does not stipulate for land and

exemption from taxes, but in great straits and
want, or even on no land, with nowhere to lay its
head, it manages, without asking for land, to occupy and enjoy all land; for it is the law by which
land exists; it classifies and distributes the whole
creation anew. If you ask for application to particulars of this way of the spirit, I shall say that
the coöperation you look for is such coöperation as
colleges and all secular institutions look for, —
money. True coöperation comes in another manner. A man quite unexpectedly shows me that
which I and all souls looked for; and I cry, 'That
is it. Take me and mine. I count it my chief
good to do in my way that very thing.' That is
real coöperation, unlimited, uncalculating, infinite
coöperation. The spirit is not half so slow, or
mediate, or needful of conditions or organs as you
suppose. A few persons in the course of my life
have at certain moments appeared to me not measured men of five feet five or ten inches, but large,
enormous, indefinite; but these were not great proprietors nor heads of communities, but, on the contrary, nothing could be more private. They were
in some want or affliction or other relation which
called out the emanation of the spirit, which dignified and transfigured them to my eyes. And the
good spirit will burn and blaze in the cinders of
our condition, in the drudgeries of our endeavors,
in the very process of extricating us from the evils

of a bad society. But this fatal fault in the logic
of your friends still appears; their whole doctrine
is spiritual, but they always end with saying, Give
us much land and money. If I should give them
anything, it would be from facility and not from
beneficence. Unless one should say, after the maxims of the world, Let them drink their own error
to saturation, and this will be the best hellebore.

"Not this, but something like this I said; and
then, as the discourse, as so often, touched character, I added that they were both intellectual:
they assumed to be substantial and central, to
be the very thing they said, but were not, but
only intellectual; or the scholars, the learned of
the spirit or central life. If they were that,—
if the centres of their life were coincident with
the centre of life,—I should bow the knee; I
should accept without gainsaying all that they said,
as if I had said it,—just as our saint (though
morbid) Jones Very had affected us with what was
best in him,—but that I felt in them the slight
dislocation of these centres, which allowed them to
stand aside and speak of these facts knowingly.
Therefore I was at liberty to look at them, not as
the commanding fact, but as one of the whole circle
of facts. They did not like pictures, marbles, woodlands, and poetry; I liked all these, and Lane and
Alcott too, as one figure more in the various landscape.

" And now, I said, will you not please to pound me a little before I go, just by way of squaring the account, that I may not remember that I alone was saucy ? Alcott contented himself with quarrelling with the injury done to greater qualities in my company by the tyranny of my taste, which certainly was very soft pounding. And so I parted from the divine lotos-eaters." (Journal, November 19, 1842.)

Yet Emerson had so much at heart the results aimed at by these communistic schemes that he had already proposed to Mr. Alcott to join him in the attempt to secure them in a simpler fashion. The inequalities of condition which he saw about him, even in New England, were painful to him, — as indeed they never ceased to be. Later in life he consoled himself, at the sight of great possessions in the hands of men whom he loved and respected, with the thought that these men stood in a just relation to their wealth, having the faculty to use it for the best advantage. None should be rich, he says, but those who understand it ; but there may be such. For himself, he felt at this time a strong desire to clear himself of superfluities and unnatural relations. In a paper on Labor, afterwards rewritten for the lecture on " Man the Reformer," [1] in 1841, he says : —

[1] *Collected Writings,* i. 27.

" Living has got to be too ponderous than that the poor spirit can drag any longer this baggage-train. Let us cut the traces. The bird and the fox can get their food and house without degradation, without domestic servants, and without ties, and why cannot we? I much prefer going without these things to the annoyance of having them at too great cost. I am very uneasy when one waits on me at table. I had rather stretch my arm or rise from my chair than be served by one who does it not from love. Why should not the philosopher realize in his daily labor his high doctrine of self-trust? Let him till the fruitful earth under the glad sun, and write his thought on the face of the ground with hoe and spade. Let him put himself face to face with the facts of dire need, and know how to triumph by his own warlike hands and head over the grim spectres. Let him thus become the fellow of the poor, and show them by experiment that poverty need not be. Let him show that labor need not enslave a man more than luxury; that labor may dwell with thought. This is the heroic life possible in this age of London, Paris, and New York. It is not easy; if it were it would not be heroic. But he who can solve the problem for himself has solved the problem not of a clique or corporation, but of entire humanity. He has shown every young man for a thousand years to come how life may be led indepen-

dently, gracefully, justly. Religion does not seem
to me to tend now to a *cultus*, as heretofore, but to a
heroic life. We find extreme difficulty in conceiv-
ing any church, any liturgy, any rite, that would be
quite genuine. But all things point at the house
and the hearth. Let us learn to lead a man's life.
I have no hope of any good in this piece of reform
from such as only wish to reform one thing; which
is the misfortune of almost all projectors. A partial reform in diet, or property, or war, or the
praise of the country-life, is always an extravagance. A farm is a poor place to get a living
by, in the common expectation. But he who goes
thither in a generous spirit, with the intent to lead
a man's life, will find the farm a proper place. He
must join with it simple diet and the annihilation
by one stroke of his will of the whole nonsense of
living for show. He must take ideas instead of
customs. He must make the life more than meat,
and see, as has been greatly said, that the intellectual world meets man everywhere; in his dwelling, in his mode of living. What a mountain of
chagrins, inconveniences, diseases, and sins would
sink into the sea with the uprise of this doctrine!
Domestic hired service would go over the dam.
Slavery would fall into the pit. Shoals of maladies
would be exterminated, and the Saturnian Age revive."

He writes to his brother William: —

CONCORD, *December* 2, 1840.

. . . I am quite intent on trying the experiment of manual labor to some considerable extent, and of abolishing or ameliorating the domestic service in my household. Then I am grown a little impatient of seeing the inequalities all around me; am a little of an agrarian at heart, and wish sometimes that I had a smaller house, or else that it sheltered more persons. So I think that next April we shall make an attempt to find house-room for Mr. Alcott and his family under our roof; for the wants of the man are extreme as his merits are extraordinary. But these last very few persons perceive; and it becomes the more imperative on those few, of whom I am in some respects nearest, to relieve them. He is a man who should be maintained at the public cost in the Prytaneum; perhaps one of these days he will be. . . . At all events, Lidian and I have given him an invitation to establish his household with us for one year, and have explained to him and Mrs. Alcott our views or dreams respecting labor and plain living; and they have our proposal under consideration.

Mrs. Emerson loyally consented, though the scheme appeared to her a wild one; fortunately Mrs. Alcott declined to come into it.

Meantime an experiment towards putting the domestic service upon a more ideal footing was tried.

TO WILLIAM EMERSON.

CONCORD, *March* 30, 1841.

. . . You know Lidian and I had dreamed that we would adopt the country practice of having but one table in the house. Well, Lidian went out the other evening and had an explanation on the subject with the two girls. Louisa accepted the plan with great kindness and readiness; but Lydia, the cook, firmly refused. A cook was never fit to come to table, etc. The next morning, Waldo was sent to announce to Louisa that breakfast was ready; but she had eaten already with Lydia, and refused to leave her alone. With our other project we are like to have the same fortune, as Mrs. Alcott is as much decided not to come as her husband is ready to come.

Napoleon's saying, " Respect the burden," was a favorite maxim of Emerson's, and often inculcated upon his children. He was very considerate in his treatment of servants ; winced visibly when they were reproved, and was relieved when they left the room, from fear lest something might chance in conversation to make them feel disparagement. He always respected their holidays, even to the inconvenience of their employers, and scrupulously avoided all occasions of unnecessary increase of their work. At a birthday party at his

house, the little guests in their play tumbled over
the hay-cocks, to the vexation of the hired man,
at whose complaint Emerson came out with long
strides: "Lads and lasses! You mustn't undo
hard work. The man has worked in the heat all
day; now all go to work and put up the cocks:"
and stayed and saw it done, working himself.

Another part of the scheme, manual labor, was
no novelty to Emerson: he had been in the habit
of working in his garden, and speaks in his letters
to Miss Fuller of hoeing his corn and tomatoes;
though he confesses that "this day-labor of mine
has hitherto a certain emblematic air, like the
ploughing of the Emperor of China," and that
his son Waldo begs him not to hoe his leg. But
now he wished that he "might make it an honest
sweat, and that these ornamental austerities might
become natural and dear." Accordingly, in the
spring (1841) he invited Thoreau to come and live
with him a year and teach him. "He is to have
his board, etc., for what labor he chooses to do
[Emerson writes to his brother William], and he
is thus far a great benefactor and physician to me,
for he is an indefatigable and a very skilful laborer, and I work with him as I should not without him, and expect to be suddenly well and
strong; though I have been a skeleton all the
spring, until I am ashamed. Thoreau is a scholar
and a poet, and as full of buds of promise as a
young apple-tree."

CONCORD, *April* 22, 1841.

DEAR MARGARET, — Thanks for your kind solicitude, but though feeble, and of late feebler than ever, I have no dangerous complaints, — nothing but ridiculously narrow limits, which if I overpass I must pay for it. As soon as my old friend the south wind returns, the woods and fields and my garden will heal me. Henry Thoreau is coming to live with me, and work with me in the garden, and teach me to graft apples. Do you know the issue of my earlier plans, — of Mr. Alcott, liberty, equality, and a common table, etc. ? I will not write out that pastoral here, but save it for the bucolical chapter in my Memoirs. . . . I am sorry we come so quickly to the kernel and through the kernel of Cambridge society ; but I think I do not know any part of our American life which is so superficial. The Hoosiers, the speculators, the custom-house officers, — to say nothing of the fanatics, — interest us much more. If I had a pocketful of money, I think I should go down the Ohio and up and down the Mississippi by way of antidote to what small remains of the Orientalism (so endemic in these parts) there may still be in me, — to cast out, I mean, the passion for Europe by the passion for America ; and our reverence for Cambridge, which is only a part of our reverence for London, must be transferred across the Alleghany ridge. Yet I, perverse, take an extreme pleasure in reading Au-

brey's Anecdotes, letters, etc., of English scholars,
Oxonian and other; for, next to the culture of
man, the demonstration of a talent is the most attractive thing, and English literary life has been,
if it is no longer, a most agreeable and complete
circle of means and ends. . . . . We ought to have
good verses in the next number [of the *Dial*], for
we must have *levity* sufficient to compensate the
morgue of Unitarianism and Shelley and Ideal
Life and Reform in the last number. Lidian
sends her love to you. She is not well, but thinks
you shall make her well when you come. We read
Porphyry and Duc de St. Simon and Napier's Pe-
ninsular War and Carlyle's lectures, to pass away
the cold and rainy season, and wish for letters
every day from Margaret Fuller. Do you know
that in August I am to go to Waterville, a Baptist
college, and deliver a literary oration to some
young men? For which of my sins? Why should
we read many books, when the best books do not
now avail us to yield that excitement and solid joy
which fifteen years ago an article in the *Edinburgh*,
or almost a college poem or oration, would give?
. . . And yet — and yet — towards evening and
on rainy days I wish to go to Berlin and to Dres-
den before I quite amputate that nonsense called
Europe.

Yours affectionately,   WALDO E.

As to the garden, it did not take him long to find out that he had another garden where he could labor to more advantage. In his journal, before the end of the year, he says : —

"If I judge from my own experience, I should unsay all my fine things, I fear, concerning the manual labor of literary men. If you would be a scholar you must come into the conditions of the scholar. Tell children what you say about writing and laboring with the hands! Can the glass-worker make glass by minding it at odd times? Or the chemist analyze soils? Or the pilot sail a ship through the Narrows? And the greatest of arts, the subtilest and of most miraculous effect, you fancy is to be practised with a pen in one hand and a crow-bar in the other? The writer shall not dig. To be sure, he may work in the garden, but his stay there must be measured, not by the needs of the garden, but of the study." "When the terrestrial corn, beets, onions, and tomatoes flourish [he writes to Miss Fuller] the celestial archetypes do not."

Another small reform he tried about this time, — partly induced, perhaps, by the example of Mr. Alcott, — namely, vegetarianism ; but soon gave it up, finding it of no particular advantage.

In any effort he might feel called upon to make towards better modes of living, Emerson was with-

out help from the love of innovation. There was, to
be sure, a certain presumption in his mind in favor
of opinions which he had not been accustomed to
hold, but, when it came to practice, he was slow to
quit the accustomed ways and glad to return to
them. Of the tendency to *variation*, which plays
so important a part in civil as in natural history,
he had a very small share. He liked to hear of
new projects, because they showed activity of mind;
adoption of them was another matter; it must come
from a distinct call in the individual, and not from
a persuasion that such and such a course is advi-
sable for people in general. Still less sympathy
had he with chiding, or with the people (though
some of them were his friends) who made a duty
of refusing to vote or to pay taxes.

"Don't run amuck against the world. Have a
good case to try the question on. As long as the
State means you well, do not refuse your pistareen.
You have a tottering cause; ninety parts of the
pistareen it will spend for what you also think
good, ten parts for mischief: you cannot fight
heartily for a fraction. Wait till you have a good
difference to join issue upon."

"The non-resistants go about and persuade good
men not to vote, and so paralyze the virtue that is
in the conservative party, and thus the patriotic
vote in the country is swamped. But, though the
non-voting is right in the non-resistants, it is a

patch and pedantry in their converts; not in their system, not a just expression of their state of mind."

"A—— thought he could find as good a ground for quarrel in the State tax as Socrates did in the edict of the Judges. Then, I say, be consistent, and never more put an apple or a kernel of corn into your mouth. Would you feed the devil? Say boldly, There is a sword sharp enough to cut sheer between flesh and spirit, and I will use it, and not any longer belong to this double-faced, equivocating, mixed Jesuitical universe. The abolitionists should resist, because they are literalists; they know exactly what they object to, and there is a government possible which will content them. Remove a few specified grievances, and this present commonwealth will suit them. They are the new Puritans, and as easily satisfied. But you nothing will content. No government short of a monarchy consisting of one king and one subject will appease you. Your objection, then, to the State of Massachusetts is deceptive. Your true quarrel is with the state of Man."

(Journal.) "Jock could not eat rice, because it came west; nor molasses, because it came north; nor put on leathern shoes, because of the methods by which leather was procured; nor indeed wear a woolen coat. But Dick gave him a gold eagle, that he might buy wheat and rye, maple sugar and

an oaken chest, and said : This gold piece, unhappy
Jock, is molasses, and rice, and horse-hide, and
sheep-skin."

" The philosophers of Fruitlands have such an
image of virtue before their eyes that the poetry of
man and nature they never see ; the poetry that is
in a man's life, the poorest pastoral, clownish life,
the light that shines on a man's hat, in a child's
spoon, the sparkle on every wave and on every
mote of dust, they see not."

His position with regard to reform is summed
up in the following fragment of a letter, without
address or date, but written, I conjecture, about
1840 : —

My dear Friend, — My silence is a very poor
account of the pleasure your letter and your book
gave me, and I feel that it is very likely to be mis-
interpreted. . . . Your letter was very grateful to
me, and spoke the language of a pure region. That
language let us always speak. I would willingly
never hear any other. It blended in my ear with
whatever of best and highest I have heard among
my companions, and fortifies my good hope of what
society may yet realize for us. A few persons with
whom I am acquainted do indeed stand in strong
contrast with the general tone of social life. They
think society faithless and base : society in its turn
reckons them dreamers and fanatics. And they

must pass for such until they can make their fine
words good, by adding to their criticism on the
pretension and sensuality of men a brave demonstration to the senses of their own problems.
Certainly virtue has its arithmetic, as well as vice,
and the pure must not eat the bread of the impure, but must live by the sweat of their own face,
and in all points make their philosophy affirmative.
Otherwise it tends so fast downward to mere railing and a greater falseness than that which it rep-
robates. The first impulse of the newly stricken
mind, stricken by light from heaven, is to lament
the death with which it is surrounded. As far as
the horizon it can scarcely see anything else than
tombs and ghosts and a sort of dead-alive population. War, war without end seems then to be its
lot; how can it testify to the truth, to life, but by
affirming in all places that death is here and death
is there, and all which has a name to live is dead?
Yet God has higher and better methods. Come
out, he saith, from this death, once and forever.
Not by hate of death, but by new and larger life
is death to be vanquished. In thy heart is life.
Obey that; it is inventive, creative, prodigal of
life and beauty. Thence heroism, virtue, redemption, succor, opportunity, come to thee and to all.
. . . If thou wouldst have the sense of poverty,
squalid poverty, bestir thyself in endless proclamation of war against the sins of society, thyself

appearing to thyself the only exception. If thou wouldst inherit boundless joyful wealth, leave the war to such as like it.

His opinion of the later agitation for according political functions to women is indicated in the following letter to a lady who had asked him to take part in calling a convention for that purpose : —

CONCORD, *September* 18, 1850.

DEAR MADAM, — I have waited a very long time since I had your letter, because I had no clear answer to give. . . . The fact of the political and civil wrongs of woman I deny not. If women feel wronged, then they are wronged. But the mode of obtaining a redress, namely, a public convention called by women, is not very agreeable to me, and the things to be agitated for do not seem to me the best. Perhaps I am superstitious and traditional, but, whilst I should vote for every franchise for women, . . . if women asked or if men denied it, I should not wish women to wish political functions, nor, if granted, assume them. I imagine that a woman whom all men would feel to be the best would decline such privileges if offered, and feel them to be rather obstacles to her legitimate influence. Yet I confess I lay no great stress on my opinion ; . . . at all events, that I may not stand in the way of any right, you are at

liberty, if you wish it, to use my name as one of
the inviters of the convention, though I shall not
attend it, and shall regret that it is not rather a
private meeting of thoughtful persons sincerely interested, instead of what a public meeting is pretty
sure to be, — a heartless noise, which we are all
ashamed of when it is over.

Yours respectfully,   R. W. EMERSON.

CHAPTER XIII.

THE period from 1835 to 1845, — the thirty-
second to the forty-second year of Emerson's life,
— the heyday of the Boston Transcendentalism,
was also the period of his greatest productivity.
That it took the shape of lectures was due very
much to circumstances, and not to his will. There
was something questionable, if not repugnant, to
him in thus bringing his thoughts to market. "I
feel [he writes in his journal] that my life is frivolous and public; I am as one turned out-of-doors;
I live in a balcony or on the street;" and he is
constantly resolving to withdraw. But there was
really no help; his family expenses were increasing: other children, two daughters and another son,
were born to him; other persons besides those of
his household were partly dependent on him; he
kept open house; and, with the strictest economy,
his outlay outran his income. He published during this period two books (the first and second
series of Essays), which afterwards sold well, but

they brought him at first very little money. Emerson was always careful about his expenditures, and he had nothing of the contempt for money which many persons at that time thought becoming, but he had no skill to earn it. "It is an essential element to our knowledge of the man [he says in his lecture on Wealth] what, was his opinion, practice, and success in regard to the institution of property;" and in this regard Emerson's position has not always been understood. The pains he gave himself with bargaining and with bookseller's accounts for Carlyle, and the common sense he always showed in practical affairs, have sometimes given the impression that he was a shrewd man of business. But in bargaining for himself he was easily led to undervalue his own claims and to take an exaggerated view of those of the other party, and so usually bought dear and sold cheap. Amusing instances could be given, were it on the whole worth while. He had, it is true, from the first, the help of his friend Mr. Abel Adams in his money matters, and afterwards that of other efficient helpers; but he thought it the duty of every man to attend to these things for himself : —

"The gods deal very strictly with us, make out quarter-bills and exact specie payment, allow no partnerships, no stock companies, no arrangements, but hold us personally liable to the last cent and mill. The youth, charmed with his intellectual

dream, can neither do this nor that : ' My father
lived in the care of land and improvements, valued
his meadow, his mill-dam ; why must I be worried
with hay and grass, my cranberry-field, my burned
wood-lot, my broken mill, the rubbish lumber, my
crop, my trees? Can I not have a partner? Why
not organize our new society of poets and lovers,
and have somebody with talent for business to look
after these things, — some deacons of trees and
grass and buckwheat and cranberries, — and leave
me to letters and philosophy?' But the nettled
gods say, Go to ruin with your arrangements ; you
alone are to answer for your things. Leases and
covenants shall be punctually signed and sealed.
Arithmetic and the practical study of cause and
effect in the laws of Indian corn and rye-meal are
as useful as betting is in second-class society to
teach accuracy of statement, or duelling, in countries where the perceptions are obtuse, to hold men
to courteous behavior. To a certain extent every
individual is holden to the study and management
of his domestic affairs. It is a peremptory point
of virtue that his independence be secured, and
there is no more decisive training for all manly
habits than the household. Take from me the feeling that I must depend on myself, give me the
least hint that I have good friends and backers
there in reserve who will gladly help me, and instantly I relax my diligence. I obey the first im-

pulse of generosity that is to cost me nothing, and
a certain slackness will creep over all my conduct
of my affairs."

Emerson's management, however, did not tend
to the positive increase of his worldly goods. "My
prudence [he says] consists in avoiding and going without; not in the inventing of means and
methods; not in adroit steering; not in gentle repairing." For the filling of his purse the only
means he could invent was lecturing. As his name
grew more widely known to the managers of the
country lyceums in New England and then at the
West, he could, with much travelling, collect fees
enough to fill the ever-yawning gap betwixt income
and outgo, though never much more than fill it.
His fees in those days were small; not so large,
perhaps, as more skilful management might have
made them. He writes to Mr. Alexander Ireland
in 1847 that the most he ever received was $570
for ten lectures; in Boston, fifty dollars; in the
country lyceums, ten dollars and travelling expenses. Then, from the liberal style of his house
and his housekeeping, he passed with his neighbors
for a well-to-do man, and paid, his friends thought,
more than a fair proportion of the town taxes. So
it came about that all these years in the forties
were years of unremitted watchfulness and sometimes anxiety to keep out of debt. This appears
from time to time in his letters to his brother William in New York : —

" *August* 3, 1839. Carlyle's accounts have required what were for me very considerable advances, and so have impoverished me in the current months very much. I shall learn one day, if I live much longer, to keep square with the world, which is essential to my freedom of mind.

" *August* 17. I see plainly I shall have no choice about lecturing again next winter. I must do it. Here in Concord they send me my tax-bill for the current year, $161.73.

" *April* 4, 1840. I got home yesterday morning. I crowed unto myself on the way home on the strength of my three hundred dollars earned in New York and Providence. So should I pay my debts. But pride must have a fall: the Atlas Bank declared no dividend; so I find myself pretty nearly where I was before. At Providence I might have enlarged my receipts by undertaking a course of lectures on my own account, after my six were ended; but I preferred not.

" *April* 20, 1840. I suppose that I am now at the bottom of my wheel of debt and, shall not hastily venture 'lower. But how could I help printing ' Chartism,' 103 pages, sent to me for that express purpose, and with the encouragement of the booksellers? They will give T. C. fifteen cents per copy.

" *May* 11, 1840. J. Munroe & Co., in making out the account of T. C. [find] he was in my debt between six and seven hundred dollars, although some important amounts paid by me were not entered in the account.

"*October* 7, 1841. This winter I must hang out my bush again, and try to sell good wine of Castaly at the Masonic Temple. Failing there, I will try the west end of New York, or of Philadelphia, or, as I have lately been challenged to do, of Baltimore.

"*October* 16, 1843. I think not to lecture by courses this winter; only by scattering guerillas, and see if I can make a new book [the second series of Essays], of which the materials collect themselves day by day. Yet I am poor enough to need to lecture."

And lecture he did, every winter but one, from the time he came to Concord, so long as he was able; gradually extending his field from year to year towards the West.

Some of the lectures of the course on the "Present Age," in 1839–40, were repeated in Providence, R. I., and in New York, as well as near Boston. The next winter, 1840–41, he seems to have turned away from lecturing to the preparation of a volume of essays, which came out in the spring of 1841. In the summer, being asked to deliver an address at Waterville College, Maine, he went down to Nantasket for a breath of sea-air. Emerson, though he was born on the edge of the salt water, was a stranger to the sea, and this visit made a strong impression on him.

WORRICK'S HOTEL,
NANTASKET BEACH, *July* 13, 1841.

DEAR LIDIAN : . . . I find this place very good for me on many accounts, perhaps as good as any public place or house full of strangers could be. I read and write, and have a scheme of my speech in my head. I read Plato, I swim, and be it known unto you I did verily catch with hook and line yesterday morning two haddocks, a cod, a flounder, and a pollock, and a perch. . . . The sea is great, but reminds me all the time of Malta, Sicily, and my Mediterranean experiences, which are the most that I know of the ocean ; for the sea is the same in summer all the world over. Nothing can be so bland and delicious as it is. I had fancied something austere and savage, a touch of iron in it, which it hardly makes good. I love the dear children, and miss their prattle. . . . Take great care of yourself, and send me immediate word that you are well and hope everything good. That hope shall the Infinite Benevolence always justify.

Your affectionate husband,

WALDO E.

TO MISS FULLER.

MY DEAR MARGARET: . . . I am here making
a sort of peace-offering to the god of waters,
against whom, ever since my childhood, imprisoned
in streets and hindered from fields and woods, I
have kept a sort of grudge. Until lately every
landscape that had in it the smallest piece of the
sea seemed to me a little vulgarized (shall I say?)
and not quite festal. Now a surfeit of acorns and
whortleberry-pastures has restored the equilibrium
of my eyes and ears, and this beach and grand sea-
line receive me with a sort of paternal love. . . .
I gaze and listen by day, I gaze and listen by
night, and the sea and I shall be good friends all
the rest of my life. I quite comprehend how
Greece should be Greece, lying in the arms of that
sunny sea. Cut off its backwoods from New England, and it would be more likely to repeat that
history of happy genius. Is it these few foolish
degrees of the thermometer that make England
(Old and New) so tough and mighty instead of so
graceful and keen? Really this summer bay glistens
before my eyes so azure and spiritual that I wonder to think that the only question it suggests to
the tall and tanned denizens along these sounding
shores is, " How's fish?" And inland, the same
question, a little magnified and superficially varied,
makes Wall Street and State Street. But Attica

and Peloponnesus were not so easily pleased. I have come down here with by-ends, else I should not be of the true New England blood I celebrate. I hope to find an oration under some of the boulders, or, more probably, within some of the spouting-horns of this shore.

To another friend : —

" I like the sea. What an ancient, pleasant sound is this of the rubbing of the sea against the land : this satiating expanse, too, — the only thing on earth that compares with the sky in contenting the eye, which it more contents beheld from the shore than on the ocean. And then these pretty gliding columnar sail which so enliven and adorn the field."

July 21.

DEAR LIDIAN: . . . I am very glad you get on so happily and hopefully at home, though I do not like what you say of mother's fasting and languor in the heats. It is time her son should come home. I wish he was a better son; but Elizabeth will come back again soon, whose refreshing influences none of us can quite resist. I have read Henry's verses thrice over, with increasing pleasure ; they are very good. I wish I had any to return, but the beach has not yielded me any. If I did not remember that all my life long I had thought To-day always unprofitable and the muses of the Pres-

ent Hour always unkind, I should think myself on
this present 21st of July under some ban, that
nothing tuneful and nothing wise should visit my
heart or be spoken by my lips. But the saying
of the stream is the motto also of men: " And,
the more falls I get, move faster on." We fat on
our failures and by our dumbness we speak. . . .
Thanks again for the news from the nursery. All
angels dwell with the boy and the girl, and with all
who speak and behave to them worthily! In the
pocket of the coat I will put a pebble from the
beach for Waldo. . . .

To his brother William, after his return home : —
CONCORD, *July* 27, 1841.

At Nantasket I found delicious and bracing airs
and sunniest waters, which reminded me of nothing
but my Mediterranean experiences; for I have
never seen so much of the sea before at home. I
hoped there to write an oration, but only my outline grew larger and larger, until it seemed to defy
all possibility of completion. Desperate of success
abroad, I rushed home again ; having before found
that I could write out of no inkstand but my own.
Perhaps not out of that.

Yet, in the Waterville address, delivered on the
11th of August, we seem to find a touch of the
sea, " inexact and boundless," yet distinct in its tone

of suggestion; and Emerson himself, when Mr. Whipple long afterwards praised it to him, confessed that it was " the heat and happiness of what I thought a real inspiration " that was extinguished by the cold reception which the discourse met, and the warning of the presiding minister in his closing prayer against its heresies and wild notions.[1]

TO MISS FULLER.

CONCORD, *September* 8, 1841.

DEAR MARGARET: . . . At Waltham I promised to consider and ascertain whether I could supply you with some prose pages in a fortnight from Phi Beta Kappa night. After turning over many topics, I fancied that I might possibly furnish you with a short article on Landor, and I am now trying to dissolve that pearl or opal in a crucible that is perhaps too small; the fire may be too low, or the menstruum too weak. But something I will send you on Friday or Saturday at farthest. . . . I have nothing to say; not a mouse stirring in all the horizon. Not a letter comes to me from any

---

[1] *Recollections of Eminent Men*, etc. By Edwin Percy Whipple. Boston, 1887: p. 145. The same story is told of the Middlebury (Vt.) address, four years later. Possibly, in his account to Mr. Whipple, Emerson confounded them together. The minister's prayer was that they might be delivered from ever again hearing such transcendental nonsense from the sacred desk. Emerson, the story goes, asked the name of the clergyman, and said, " He seems a very conscientious, plain-spoken man."

quarter; not a new book; not a vision out of the sky of night or noon. And yet I remember that the autumn has arrived, and already I have felt his infusions in the air, — wisest and preciousest of seasons. Presently it will be — will it not? — the rage to die. After so much precocity, apathy, and spiritual bankruptcy, the age of suicide may be shortly expected. We shall die with all manner of enthusiasm. Nothing at the book-shops but Werther, and Cato by Plutarch. Buddhism cometh in like a flood. Sleep is better than waking, death than life. The serpent of the pyramids has begun to swallow himself. The scorpion-stung scorpion is the only cipher and motto. . . .

November 9. . . . I read little, I write little. I seek, but with only my usual gypsy diligence, to drive my loitering troops metaphysical into phalanx, into line, into section; but the principle of infinite repulsion and every one for himself, and the hatred of society which animates their master, animates them to the most beautiful defiance. These are the asserters of immortality; these are they who by implication prove the length of the day in which such agents as we shall work : for in less than millenniums what towers could be built, what brick could be laid, if every straw was enemy to every straw! Gray clouds, short days, moonless nights, a drowsy sense of being dragged easily somewhere by that locomotive Destiny, which, never

seen, we yet know must be hitched on to the cars
wherein we sit, — that is all that appears in these
November weeks. Let us hope that, as often as
we have defamed days which turned out to be benefactors, and were whispering oracles in the very
droning nurses' lullabies which soothed us to sleep,
so this may prove a profitable time. . . .

This was the time of Emerson's Transcendental
apogee, the extreme of his impulse to withdraw
from lecturing and betake himself to solitary contemplation.   Henceforth he lectured diligently.
In the course on " The Times," in the winter 1841–
42, his impatience of the " universal whiggery,"
that is, of decent, self-complacent routine, is bal-
anced by a more explicit recognition of the claims
of the actual order of things, not merely as inevitable, but as the germ of a better.   Three of these
lectures, " The Times," " The Conservative," and
" The Transcendentalist," were published in the
Dial, and afterwards in the first volume of his
collected writings.   The course was repeated in
Providence, in New York, and elsewhere.   In 1843
he read five lectures on " New England " in New
York, Philadelphia, Baltimore, and other places,
spending the whole winter away from home.

BALTIMORE, *January* 7, 1843.

DEAR MARGARET, — I received in Boston your packet for William Channing, and the next morning I left it with my brother in New York. I spent one night at Staten Island [with William] and two nights in Philadelphia, and am here ready to attend high mass in the Cathedral to-morrow morning. In Philadelphia I had great pleasure in chatting with Furness, for we had ten or a dozen years to go over and compare notes upon. . . . And he is the happiest companion. Those are good companions to whom we have the keys. How true and touching in the romance is the saying, " But you can never be to them Vich Ian Vohr "! and each of us is an unsuppliable Vich Ian Vohr to somebody. Furness is my dear gossip, almost a gossip for the gods, there is such a repose of worth and honor in the man. He is a hero-worshipper, and so collects the finest anecdotes, and told very good stories of Mrs. Butler, Dr. Channing, etc. I meant to add, a few lines above, that the tie of school-fellow and playmate from the nursery onward is the true clanship and key that cannot be given to another. At Mrs. Morrison's, last night, I heard Knoop and the Señora de Goni ; which was very good exercise, — " *me satis exercuisti*," said the honest professor to the young Sam. Clarke when he wrangled, — and we are all glad to be turned into strings and finely and thoroughly played upon.

But the guitar is a mean, small-voiced instrument,
and but for the dignity that attaches to every *national* instrument, and its fine form, would not be
tolerated, would it? Very hard work and very
small cry, Señora.

Sunday, P. M. This morning I went to the
Cathedral to hear mass, with much content. It is
so dignified to come where the priest is nothing
and the people nothing, and an idea for once excludes these impertinences. The chanting priest,
the pictured walls, the lighted altar, the surpliced
boys, the swinging censer, every whiff of which I
inhaled, brought all Rome again to mind. And
Rome can smell so far! It is a dear old church,
— the Roman, I mean, — and to-day I detest the
Unitarians and Martin Luther and all the parliament of Barebones. We understand so well the
joyful adhesion of the Winckelmanns and Tiecks
and Schlegels, — just as we seize with joy the fine
romance and toss the learned Heeren out of the
window; unhappily with the same sigh as belongs
to the romance, — "Ah, that one word of it were
true!" ' One small element of new views has, however, got into the American cathedral, namely,
pews; and after service I detected another, a *railroad* which runs from one angle of the altar down
into the broad aisle, for the occasional transporta-
tion of a pulpit. We are as good for that as the
French, who pared apples at dinner with little guil-

lotines. . . . In Baltimore, though I have enquired
as diligently as Herod the king after holy children, I have not yet heard of any in whom the
spirit of the great gods dwelleth. And yet, without doubt, such are in every street. Travelling I
always find instructive, but its lessons are of no
sudden application. I cannot use them all in less
than seven transmigrations of Indur, hardly one of
them in this present mortal and visible. . . .

Your friend,   W ALDO.

TO HIS WIFE.

January 8, 1843.

To-day I heard high mass in the Cathedral
here, and with great pleasure. It is well for my
Protestantism that we have no cathedral in Concord; E. H. and I should be confirmed in a fortnight. The Unitarian church forgets that men are
poets. Even Mr. —— himself does not bear it in
mind.

(Journal.) " The Catholic religion respects
masses of men and ages. It is in harmony with
nature, which loves the race and ruins the individual. The Protestant has his pew, which, of course,
is the first step to a church for every individual
citizen, a church apiece."

In 1844–45 he lectured in many places, and still

more widely in 1845–46, giving, this winter, the course on " Representative Men." He complains in his journal of " the long, weary absences at New York and Philadelphia. I am a bad traveller ; the hotels are mortifications to all sense of well-being in me. The people who fill them oppress me with their excessive virility, and it would soon become intolerable but for a few friends, who, like women, temper the arid mass. Henry James was true comfort ; wise, gentle, polished, with heroic manners, and a serenity like the sun.

" I was born to stay at home, not to ramble. I was not made for an absentee. I have no thoughts, no aims, and seem never to have had any. I must cower down into my own fens presently, and consult the gods again."

He writes to a friend from one of these lecturing-tours : —

" It is strange how people act on me. I am not a pith-ball nor raw silk, yet to human electricity is no piece of humanity so sensible. I am forced to live in the country, if it were only that the streets make me desolate. Yet if I talk with a man of sense and kindness I am imparadised at once. Pity that the light of the heart should resemble the light of the eyes in being so external, and not to be retained when the shutters are closed. Now that I am in the mood for confession, you must even hear the whole. It is because I am so ill a member of society; because men turn me, by their mere presence, to wood and to stone; because I do not get the lesson of the world where it is set before me, that I need more than others to run out into new places and multiply my chances for observation and communion. Therefore, whenever I get into debt, which usually happens once a year, I must make the plunge into this great odious river of travellers, into these wild eddies of hotels and boarding - houses, — farther, into these dangerous precincts of charlatanism, namely, lectures; that out of all the evil I may draw a little good, in the correction which every journey makes to my exaggeration, in the plain facts I get, and in the rich amends I draw for many listless days in the dear society of here and there a wise and great heart. I hate the details, but the whole foray into a city teaches me much."

PHILADELPHIA, *January* 20, 1843.

DEAR LIDIAN: . . . I find that advantage as before in wandering so far from home, that I become acquainted with " the Indians who have the Spirit." . . . I have seen no winter since I left New York, but the finest October weather prevails. The bland speech and courtly manners of these people, too, is as kindly a contrast to our more selfish manners. If I ask my way in the street, there is sure to be some gracefulness in conveying the information. And the service of the negroes in the hotels is always courteous. It looks as if it would be a long time before I get home, and I am getting tired of my picnic. I learn something all the time, but I write nothing, and, as usual, vow each week that I will not play Signor Blitz again. So you must find out, dear wife, how to starve gracefully, — you and I and all of us, another year. Very refreshing is it to me to know that I have a good home. . . . So peace be with you, and joy!

Yours,   WALDO.

TO WILLIAM EMERSON.

PHILADELPHIA, *January* 8, 1843.

I had a very comfortable ride hither from the cabin of the Jersey ferry-boat, and soon got snugly ensconced in the warm entrails of an argument on the divine decrees with a thoroughbred Presbyterian clergyman. B—— was here, but I had tasted him, and preferred the bear's meat which we can never get at home. I can very well afford to set up this lottery. I can never draw quite a blank; for though I wish money to-day, I wish experience always, and a good failure is always a good experience, which is mother of much poetry and prose for me.

TO MISS FULLER.

PORTLAND, *December* 21, 1842.

. . . Many and many a mile, nothing but snow
and pine-trees ; and in travelling it is possible
sometimes to have a superfluity of these fine objects ; the villages few and cold as the Tobolsk and
Irkutsk of Siberia, and I bethought myself, as I
stared into the white night, whether I had not committed some misdemeanor against some Czar, and,
while I dreamed of Maine, was bound a thousand
versts into Arctic Asia. . . . Here have I seen,
besides others, Judge ——, who was lately a com-
missioner on the part of Maine on the Ashburton
negotiations ; a very sensible person, but, what is
remarkable, called a good Democrat here, whilst
his discourse is full of despondency on the entire
failure of republican institutions in this country :
they have neither cherished talent nor virtue ; they
have never had large nor even prudent aims, — none
but low personal ones, and the lowest ; and the officers of government are taken every year from a lower
and lower class. And the root of the whole evil
is universal suffrage. . . . Every man deserves an
answer, but few get one. Words are a pretty game,
but Experience is the only mathematician who can
solve problems ; and yet I amused the man with
my thrum that anarchy is the form and theocracy
the fact to which we and all people are tending.

which seemed to him a pretty soap-bubble. I never see people without observing that strength or weakness is a kind of atmospheric fact: if a man is so related to the topic and the by-standers that he happily expresses himself, well; if not, he is a fool,—quite independently of the relations of both to reason and truth. Plainly we are cackling geese when we do not feel relations, let the Absolute be as grand as he will. Therefore let time and space stand, and man and meeting-house, and Washington and Paris, and phrenology and mesmerism, and the old Beelzebub himself; for relations shall rule, and realities shall strike sail.

It was not merely the incidental annoyances or the disturbance to his habits that made it repugnant to Emerson "to go peddling with my literary pack of notions;" but there was also a recoil from what seemed like a profanation of things dear and sacred. "Are not lectures a kind of Peter Parley's story of Uncle Plato, and a puppet show of the Elcusinian mysteries?"

He felt this sometimes even in the select conversations:—

TO MISS FULLER.

CONCORD, *March* 14, 1841.

The young people wished to know what possessed me to tease you with so much prose, and becloud the fine conversation. I could only answer that it

was not an acute fit of Monday evening, but was
chronic and constitutional with me. I asked them
in my turn when they had heard me talk anything
else. So I silenced them. But how to reply to
your fine Eastern pearls with chuckstones of granite and slate? There is nothing for it but to pay
you the grand compliment, which you deserve if we
can pay it, of speaking the truth. Even prose I
honor in myself and others very often as an awkward worship of truth; it is the plashing and struggling in the water of one who would learn to swim.
I know but one solution to my nature and relations,
which I find in remembering the joy with which in
my boyhood I caught the first hint of the Berke-
leyan philosophy, and which I certainly never lost
sight of afterwards. There is a foolish man who
goes up and down the country giving lectures on
electricity: this one secret he has, to draw a spark
out of every object, from desk and lamp and wooden
log and the farmer's blue frock; and by this he
gets his living. Well, I was not an electrician, but
an idealist. I could see that there was a Cause behind every stump and clod, and, by the help of some
fine words, could make every old wagon and wood-
pile and stone-wall oscillate a little and threaten
to dance; nay, give me fair field, and the select-
men of Concord and the Reverend Pound-me-down
himself began to look unstable and vaporous. You
saw me do my feat, it fell in with your own studies,

and you would give me gold and pearls. Now
there is this difference between the electrician —
Mr. Quimby is his name? I never saw him — and
the idealist, namely, that the spark is to that philosopher a toy, but the dance is to the idealist terror
and beauty, life and light. It is and it ought to
be, and yet sometimes there is a sinful empiric who
loves exhibition too much. This insight is so precious to society that where the least glimmer of it
appears, all men should befriend and protect it for
its own sake. You, instead of wondering at my
cloistered and unfriendly manners, should defend
me. You and those others who are dear to me
should be so rightly my friends as never to suffer
me for a moment to attempt the game of wits and
fashionists, — no, nor even that of those you call
friends; but, by expecting of me a song of laws
and causes only, should make me noble and the
encourager of your nobility. . . .

To lecturing he could reconcile himself, and even
find in it a good side; but it was after all a *pis
aller*, an expedient, not the mode of utterance to
which he aspired. *That* was verse; not so much,
I think, from a direct impulse towards rhythmical
expression as for the sake of freer speech; because,
he says, we may speak ideal truth in verse, but we
may not in prose. It was "the harmony of laws
and causes," not the music of words and images,

that primarily attracted him ; the purely poetical
impulse was so heavily weighted with thought
that it seemed to him feeble, and he lamented his
hard fate in being only "half a bard," or, as
he wrote to Carlyle,[1] "not a poet, but a lover of
poetry and poets, and merely serving as writer, etc.,
in this empty America, before the arrival of the
poets."

Nevertheless, poems of his had been handed
about amongst intimate friends, and there were
already those who found in them a supreme attraction. James Freeman Clarke had got leave to
publish three of them in the *Western Messenger*
(Louisville, Kentucky), of which he was then
the editor, and now applications came from the
Boston publishers.

"Yesterday [Emerson writes to his brother William, December 3, 1843], for the second time, I
had an application from the bookseller to print a
volume of poems ; on which proposition — which
it seems he makes at the instance of others — I
might sit a little, — I, uncertain always whether I
have one true spark of that fire which burns in
verse. When such a request comes to me I am inclined to cut my customary cords, and run to woods
and deserts, into Berkshire, into Maine, and dwell
alone, to know whether I might not yield myself
up to some higher, better influences than any I am

[1] *Carlyle-Emerson Correspondence*, Supplementary Letters, 64.

wont to share in this pewter world. But months and years pass, and the aspirant is found in his old place, unchanged." And two years afterwards he writes to his brother : —

" As for the poems about which you ask once more, a critical friend of mine has discovered so many corrigible and reparable places in them, requiring too the freest leisure and the most favorable poetic mood, that I have laid them aside for two months." It was yet nearly two years before they were published.

One of the last pieces in the volume was the " Threnody " on his eldest child, a beautiful boy, little more than five years old, who died at the beginning of this period (January 27, 1842), after four days' illness of scarlet fever. " A domesticated sunbeam," says a friend of the house, " with his father's voice, but softened, and beautiful dark blue eyes with long lashes. He was his father's constant companion, and would stay for hours together in the study, never interrupting him."

After the first outburst of passionate grief, Emerson was as if stunned, and incapable of expression until long afterwards.

" The innocent and beautiful [he writes to a friend] should not be sourly and gloomily lamented, but with music and fragrant thoughts and sportive recollections. Alas! I chiefly grieve that I cannot grieve. Dear boy, too precious and unique

a creation to be huddled aside into the waste and
prodigality of things; yet his image, so gentle, so
rich in hopes, blends easily with every happy moment, every fair remembrance, every cherished
friendship, of my life. Calm and wise, calmly and
wisely happy, the beautiful Creative Power looked
out from him, and spoke of anything but chaos and
interruption. What was the moral of sun and
moon, of roses and acorns, that was the moral of
the sweet boy's life; softened only and humanized
by blue eyes and infant eloquence."

Some months later, in his answer to the letter of
a lady who had been Waldo's teacher, he says:—

"Meantime life wears on, and ministers to
you, no doubt, as to me its undelaying and grand
lessons, its uncontainable endless poetry, its short
dry prose of scepticism,—like veins of cold air in
the evening woods, quickly swallowed by the wide
warmth of June,—its steady correction of the rash-
ness and short sight of youthful judgments, and its
pure repairs of all the rents and seeming ruin it
operates in what it gave; although we love the
first gift so well that we cling long to the ruin, and
think we will be cold to the new if new shall come.
But the new steals on us like a star which rises behind our back as we walk, and we are borrowing
gladly its light before we know the benefactor. So
be it with you, with me, and with all."

To Miss Fuller two years later:—

Concord, *January* 30, 1844.

When, last Saturday night, Lidian said, "It is two years to-day," I only heard the bell-stroke again. I have had no experience, no progress, to put me into better intelligence with my calamity than when it was new. I read lately, in Drummond of Hawthornden, Ben Jonson's narrative to him of the death of his son, who died of the plague in London. Ben Jonson was at the time in the country, and saw the boy in a vision; " of a manly shape, and of that growth, he thinks, he shall be at the resurrection." That same preternatural maturity did my beautiful statue assume the day after death; and so it often comes to me, to tax the world with frivolity. But the inarticulateness of the Supreme Power how can we insatiate hearers, perceivers, and thinkers ever reconcile ourselves unto? It deals all too lightly with us low-levelled and weaponed men. Does the Power labor as men do with the impossibility of perfect application, that always the hurt is of one kind and the compensation of another? My divine temple, which all angels seemed to love to build, and which was shattered in a night, I can never rebuild: and is the facility of entertainment from thought, or friendship, or affairs an amends? Rather it seems like a cup of Somnus or of Momus. Yet the nature of things, against all appearances and specialities whatever, assures us of eternal benefit. But

these affirmations are tacit and secular; if spoken,
they have a hollow and canting sound. And thus
all our being, dear friend, is evermore adjourned.
Patience, and patience, and patience! I will try,
since you ask it, to copy my rude dirges to my dar-
ling, and send them to you.

Emerson gave much more of his time and
thought to his children, from their infancy, than
was usual with busy fathers in New England forty
years ago, or is, perhaps, now. "There is nothing
[he writes in his journal] that is not of the greatest interest in the nursery. Every tear and every
smile deserves a history, to say nothing of the
stamping and screaming;" and he kept a record
of their childish doings and sayings, in which these
"pretty oracles" are chronicled like the anecdotes
of Plutarch. Their play and their work, their
companions and their lessons, their out-of-door
rambles and their home occupations, were objects
of his constant care. The home discipline was
never neglected, though it was enforced by the
gentlest methods. The beginning of a childish
quarrel, outbursts of petulance and silliness, were
averted by requests to run into the study and see
if the stove-door was shut, or to go to the front
gate and look at the clouds for a minute. "His
interest and sympathy about every detail of school
affairs, school politics and school pleasures [says

one of his children] were unbounded. We told him
every word as we should have told our mates, and
I think he had as much enjoyment out of it as we.
He considered it as our duty to look after all the
strangers that came to the school; at his desire
we had large tea-parties every year, to be sure to
have all the out-of-town boys and girls come to the
house. He used to ask me, when I told him of a
new scholar, 'Did you speak to her?' 'No, I
had n't anything to say.' 'Speak, speak, if you
have n't anything to say. Ask her, Don't you
admire my shoe-strings?' And he was always
kind and friendly to them when they came to tea;
made them talk and entered into what they said.
On Sunday afternoons he came into the front
entry at four o'clock, and whistled or said, 'Four
o'clock,' and we all walked with him, from four
to eight miles, according to the walking and the
flowers we went to see; as, when a rare flower was
in bloom, we went to find it, in Becky Stow's Hole,
or Ledum Swamp, or Copan, Columbine Rock or
Conantum. Mr. Channing often gave the names
to the spots, and showed them to father in their
glory; then he would conduct us to see the show,
or take us to places he had found beautiful in the
course of the week; full of pretty speeches about
what we were to see, making it a great mystery.
Once I expressed my fear that he would cut down
his Walden grove or sell it: he answered, 'No, it

is my camel's hump. When the camel is starving in the desert and can find nothing else, he eats his own hump. I shall keep these woods till every-thing else is gone.' One day when he saw smoke in the direction of the grove, he cried out with such love and fear in his voice, ' My woods, my beauti-ful woods ! ' and hurried off to the rescue. A baby could not be too young or small for him to hold out his hands instantly to take it into his arms. As long as he was strong enough to bear it, the [grand]children were constantly in his study."

The following extract from a letter to his wife shows that even at the time when he most jealously guarded the retirement of his study the babies were not excluded : —

" *February* 19, 1838. . . . Here sits Waldo be-side me on the cricket, with mamma's best crimson decanter-stand in his hand, experimenting on the powers of a cracked pitcher-handle to scratch and remove crimson pigment. News comes from the nursery that Hillman has taught him A and E on his cards, and that once he has called T. All roasted with the hot fire, he at present gives little sign of so much literature, but seems to be in good health, and has just now been singing, much in the admired style of his papa, as heard by you only on several occasions."

At New Year's time he planned with them about their little presents to the cousins in New York. He writes to his brother William : —

Concord, *February* 3, 1845.

The precious gifts of the cousins to the cousins arrived as safely as such auspicious parcels should; which doubtless have all angels that love children to convoy them to their destination. A happy childhood have these babes of yours and mine; no cruel interferences, and what store of happy days! We cannot look forward far, but these little felicities, so natural and suitable to them, should be introductory to better, and not leading into any dark penumbra. We must arm them with as much good sense as we can, and throw them habitually on themselves for a moral verdict.

I do not wonder that you and Susan should delight in the boys. I spend a great deal of time on my own little trinity, — for my own pleasure, too, — if we could divide it from theirs. But these interests are luckily inseparable, and all our cordial study of the bewitching manners and character of the children is a more agreeable kind of self-knowledge, and a repairing of the defects of our memory of those earliest experiences.

On the birth of his first grandchild he writes: —

My DEAR ——: Happy wife and mother that you are, and not the less, surely, that the birth of your babe touches this old house and its people and neighbors with unusual joy. I hope the best gifts and graces of his father and mother will combine for this blossom, and highest influences hallow and ripen the firm and perfect fruit. There is nothing in this world so serious as the advent of a child, with all his possibilities, to parents with good minds and hearts. Fair fall the little boy! he has come among good people. I do not grudge to —— and you the overflow of fondness and wonder; and to the boy it is the soft pillow prepared for him. It is long before he will come to himself, but I please myself already that his fortunes will be worthy of these great days of his country; that he will not be frivolous; that he will be noble and true, and will know what is sacred.

Emerson was playful and winning in his ways with his children, but he did not often romp with them, and he discouraged their devoting the early hours, even of a holiday, to amusement. " He taught us that at breakfast all must be calm and sweet, nothing must jar; we must not begin the day with light reading or games; our first and best hours should be occupied in a way to match the sweet and serious morning."

From the age of thirteen or fourteen he thought they should be encouraged as much as possible to regulate their own conduct. He would put the case, and leave them to think and act for themselves; and he did not fear to inculcate, even at this

age, the whole of his own doctrine of self-reliance.
To one of his daughters who was away from home,
at school, he writes : —

"Finish every day and be done with it. For
manners and for wise living it is a vice to remember. You have done what you could; some blunders and absurdities no doubt crept in; forget
them as soon as you can. To-morrow is a new day;
you shall begin it well and serenely, and with too
high a spirit to be cumbered with your old nonsense. This day for all that is good and fair. It is
too dear, with its hopes and invitations, to waste a
moment on the rotten yesterdays."

Soon after his son's death Emerson went upon a
lecturing-tour to Providence and New York, and
paid a visit to his brother William.

STATEN ISLAND, *March* 1, 1842.

DEAR LIDIAN: . . . Yesterday I dined with Mr.
Horace Greeley and Mr. Brisbane, the socialist, at
a Graham boarding-house. Mr. Brisbane promised
me a full exposition of the principles of Fourierism and Association as soon as I am once lodged at
the Globe Hotel. One must submit, yet I foresaw,
in the moment when I encountered these two new
friends here, that I cannot content them. They
are bent on popular actions. I am, in all my theory, ethics, and politics, a poet; and of no more

use in their New York than a rainbow or a firefly. Meantime they fasten me in their thought to "Transcendentalism," whereof you know I am wholly guiltless, and which is spoken of as a known and fixed element, like salt or meal. So that I have to begin by endless disclaimers and explanations: "I am not the man you take me for." One of these days shall we not have new laws forbidding solitude, and severe penalties on all separatists and unsocial thinkers? . . . Those poor little girls whose crown of glory is taken from them interest me still, if it were only for pity, and I would gladly know how they fare. Tell mother that Susan and William had greatly hoped to see her in the winter, but now that they learn how formidable the journey looked to her they are content that she did not come. They say she shall come when you and I make a summer visit here. They are the same faultless, affectionate people here that they ever were. In their temple of love and veneration Elizabeth [Hoar] holds undisputed possession of the highest niche. William is not the isolated man I used to find or fancy him, but, under the name of "the judge," seems to be an important part of the web of life here in his island. . . . Write to me all the particulars of home, including Elizabeth, you can; that you are yourself very peaceful and still beneficent to me and to all. Give my love to Henry and a kiss to each of the babes.

Yours affectionately, W.

Thanks, dear Lidian, for this morning's welcome letter, which informed me of what I most wished to know. . . . We had a pretty good company in the lecture-room, although the hall is small, and I see not how it will hold people enough to answer any of my profane and worldly purposes, which you and I at this moment have so much at heart. And for the sacred purposes of influence and provocation, — why, we know that a room which will hold two persons holds audience enough; is not that thy doctrine, O unambitious wife? . . . This p. m. Mr. Brisbane indoctrinated me in the high mysteries of Attractive Industry, in a conversation which I wish you all might have heard. He wishes me, "with all my party," to come in directly and join him. What palaces! what concerts! what pictures, lectures, poetry, and flowers! Constantinople, it seems, Fourier showed was the natural capital of the world, and when the earth is planted, and gardened, and templed all over with " groups" and " communities," each of 2000 men and 6000 acres, Constantinople is to be the metropolis; and we poets and miscellaneous transcendental persons who are too great for your Concords and New Yorks will gravitate to that point for music and architecture and society such as wit cannot paint nowadays. Well, to-morrow p. m. I am to hear the rest of the story, so you shall have

no more of it.   I doubt, I doubt if I find anything
here in New York of gain, outward or inward,
that it is at all worth while to break up my dull routine for.   I should have invented a better expedient at home, and stayed there, and come hither later,
in another or a following year.   However, my Ides
of March are not quite gone yet.   Thanks for all
the tidings, of Elizabeth too.   Perhaps she will
yet want to write to me, though I really might not
care, in this empty, listless, homeless mood, to write
her in reply!   Chat away, little Ellen; might all
her words countervail one the Boy should speak.
. . . William and Susan are the best of husband
and wife, brother and sister, host and friend, that
can be to sad, estranged, misadventured, estrayed

WALDO EMERSON.

These years, as I have said, were years of strait-
ened circumstances to the Concord family; strait-
ened in part by extraordinary expenses, some
unavoidable, others such as, on the whole, Emerson did not choose to avoid: for instance, in the
purchase of land to preserve a bit of his favorite
woodlands from the otherwise inevitable axe.

TO WILLIAM EMERSON.

CONCORD, *October* 4, 1844.

I have lately added an absurdity or two to my

usual ones, which I am impatient to tell you of. In one of my solitary wood-walks by Walden Pond I met two or three men who told me they had come thither to sell and to buy a field, on which they wished me to bid as purchaser. As it was on the shore of the pond, and now for years I had a sort of daily occupancy in it, I bid on it and bought it, eleven acres, for $8.10 per acre. The next day I carried some of my well-beloved gossips to the place, and they deciding that the field was not good for anything if Heartwell Bigelow should cut down his pine-grove, I bought, for $125 more, his pretty wood-lot of three or four acres, and am now landlord and water-lord of fourteen acres, more or less, on the shore of Walden, and can raise my own blackberries.

Emerson found great satisfaction in his woodlot. " My spirits," he says, " rise whenever I enter it. I can spend the entire day there with hatchet and pruning-shears, making paths, without the remorse of wasting time. I fancy the birds know me, and even the trees make little speeches, or hint them."

He had more misgivings over the purchase of a piece of land adjoining his homestead on the east. It was needful in order to prevent a threatened interruption of his only free outlook; but it was arable land, and had to be " improved " with orchard and kitchen-garden. The orchard was a pure delight to him, but the addition to his agriculture involved additional responsibilities and worries, and it involved expenses which had to be met by lecturing. The passage in " Wealth " [1] about the scholar who pulls down his wall and adds a field to his homestead was a reflection on this piece of his own experience.

Perhaps the need of replenishing his stock of materials for lectures may have weighed with him in deciding upon an offer which came to him at this time from England.

" I had lately an irregular application from different quarters in England [he writes to his brother William, December 29, 1846], proposing to me to come thither to lecture, and promising me engagements to that end in the great towns if I would. And I understand the Queenie (not Victoria, but Lidian) to say that I must go."

The invitation came at a good time, for he was in need of recreation, and this he could find only in some fresh task. Emerson's method of work left him without the momentum which in general serves the man of letters to carry him over the dead-points of life. Wanting the fly-wheel of a regular, continuous occupation, the impulse had to be supplied wholly from within.

---

[1] *Collected Writings*, vi. 113.

Now he had come to one of those dead-points, those " solstices when the stars stand still in our inward firmament, and when there is required some foreign force, some diversion or alterative, to prevent stagnation." [1]   " As I manage it now [he writes to Miss Fuller], I who have never done anything never shall do anything." And to another friend who was in Europe : —

" No news or word from abroad, no lion roars, no mouse cheeps ; we have discovered no new book ; but the old atrophy, inanition, and drying-up proceeds at an accelerated rate, and you must hasten hither before any high wind shall sweep us into past and pluperfect tenses."

" Here am I [he writes in his journal] with so much all ready to be revealed to me as to others, if only I could be set aglow. I have wished for a professorship : much as I hate the Church I have wished the pulpit, that I might have the stimulus of a stated task. R. spoke more truly than he knew, perchance, when he recommended an abolition-campaign to me. I doubt not a course of mobs would do me much good."

An English audience, he fancied, might furnish "that stimulation which my capricious, languid, and languescent study needs. The Americans are too easily pleased. We get our education ended a little too quick in this country. As soon as we

---

[1] *Collected Writings*, vi. 142.

have learned to read and write and cipher we are
dismissed from school and set up for ourselves ; we
are writers and leaders of opinion, and we write
away without check of any kind, play what prank,
indulge what spleen or oddity or obstinacy, comes
into our dear head, and even feel our complacency
therein ; and thus fine wits come to nothing. We
are wits of the provinces, Cæsars in Arden, who
easily fill all measures, and lie on our oars with the
fame of the villages. We see none who calls us to
account, and so consult our ease ; no Douglas cast
of the bar, no pale Cassius, reminds us of inferiority. In the acceptance that my papers find among
my thoughtful countrymen in these days, I cannot
help seeing how limited is their reading. If they
read only the books that I do, they would not exaggerate so wildly."

He wished to find those powerful workers, those
well-equipped scholars, whom he admired from a
distance ; to see them close at hand and feel himself among them. He did not mean to thrust himself upon them : he might accept a challenge, but
he would offer none. He said nothing to Carlyle.
not wishing that the smallest pains should be taken
to collect an audience for him. But in the course
of the winter he received, through the friendly offices of Mr. Alexander Ireland, regular invitations
to lecture before various Mechanics' Institutes in
Lancashire and Yorkshire, which he accepted for

the following autumn (1847). Carlyle, too, hearing of his intentions, wrote to promise him " an audience of British aristocracy " in London.

In the spring before he sailed there were meetings at his house looking to a new quarterly review which should be more alive than was the *North American* to the questions of the day. Theodore Parker and Dr. Samuel Gridley Howe, I think, were the persons most forward in the matter. Mr. Sumner came up and spoke approvingly of the undertaking, but doubted whether the time was quite ripe for it. Thoreau was there, but contented himself with asking whether any one present found difficulty in publishing in the existing journals anything that he might have occasion to say. On the whole, but little zeal was manifested, nor would anybody promise definite contributions. But it was taken for granted that the new review was to be; the main discussion was about the editor. Mr. Parker wished to put Emerson forward, but Emerson declined; other persons were talked of, but nothing was distinctly agreed upon, that I remember, except a committee, consisting of Emerson, Parker, and Howe, for the drafting of a manifesto to the public. This Emerson wrote, and he seems to have supposed his office thereby discharged. But when the first number of the *Massachusetts Quarterly Review* reached him in England, he found himself set down, with Mr. Parker and me,

" assisted by several other gentlemen," as the editors. He did not like this, but suffered his name to stand upon the covers until, after his return home, the fourth number appeared with the announcement that he would now "of course" contribute regularly. Then he insisted upon withdrawing, and Mr. Parker became, what in fact he had always been, sole editor. Emerson had no part in it beyond writing the Editor's Address.

This spring, also, he went to Nantucket to lecture, and while there, at the request of the minister of the place, he read (I suppose for the last time) a Sunday discourse from the pulpit. The subject was Worship. He said he was not a clergyman; he had long ceased to take any active part in churches, and perhaps also had private objection that withheld him from the pulpit. But he was unwilling to refuse to speak on a topic which concerns not only every churchman, but every man, — the cardinal topic of the moral nature.

Somewhat earlier in the year he had lectured in New Bedford, and no doubt met there some of his Quaker friends, one of whom (probably Miss Mary Rotch) wrote him a letter, to which he made the following reply : —

CONCORD, *March* 28, 1847.

MY DEAR FRIEND, — It was a great pleasure to hear from you, if only by a question in philosophy.

And the terrors of treading that difficult and quaking ground shall not hinder me from writing to you. I am quite sure, however, that I never said any of those fine things which you seem to have learned about me from Mr. Griswold, and I think it would be but fair, as he deduces them, that he should explain them, and, if he can, show that they hold. No, I never say any of these scholastic things, and when I hear them I can never tell on which side I belong. I never willingly say anything concerning " God " in cold blood, though I think we all have very just insights when we are " in the mount," as our fathers used to say. In conversation sometimes, or to humility and temperance, the cloud will break away to show at least the direction of the rays of Absolute Being, and we see the truth that lies in every affirmation men have made concerning it, and, at the same time, the cramping partiality of their speech. For the science of God our language is unexpressive and merely prattle : we need simpler and universal signs, as algebra compared with arithmetic. Thus I should affirm easily *both* those propositions, which our Mr. Griswold balances against one another ; that, I mean, of Pantheism and the other *ism*.

Personality, too, and impersonality, might each be affirmed of Absolute Being ; and what may not be affirmed of it, in our own mind ? And when we have heaped a mountain of speeches, we have still

to begin again, having nowise expressed the simple
unalterable fact.

So I will not turn schoolman to-day, but prefer
to wait a thousand years before I undertake that
definition which literature has waited for so long
already. Do not imagine that the old venerable
thought has lost any of its awful attraction for me.

I should very heartily — shall I say, *tremulously,*
— think and speak with you on our experiences or
gleams of what is so grand and absorbing; and I
never forget the statements, so interesting to me,
you gave me many years ago of your faith and that
of your friends. Are we not wonderful creatures
to whom such entertainments and passions and
hopes are afforded?

Yours with respect and affection,

R. W. EMERSON.

CHAPTER XIV.

1847–1848.

EMERSON sailed from Boston in the packet-ship *Washington Irving*, on the 5th of October, reached Liverpool on the 22d, and soon afterwards proceeded to London.

CHELSEA, LONDON, *October 27, 1847.*

DEAR LIDIAN : . . . I found at Liverpool after a couple of days a letter which had been once there seeking me (and once returned to Manchester before it reached my hands) from Carlyle, addressed to " R. W. E., on the instant he lands in England," conveying so hearty a welcome and so urgent an invitation to house and hearth that I could no more resist than I could gravitation ; and finding that I should not be wanted for a week in the lecture-rooms, I came hither on Monday, and, at ten at night, the door was opened to me by Jane Carlyle, and the man himself was behind her with a lamp in the entry. They were very little changed from their old selves of fourteen years ago (in August), when I left them at Craigenputtock.

" Well," said Carlyle, " here we are, shovelled together again." The floodgates of his talk are quickly opened, and the river is a great and constant stream. We had large communication that night until nearly one o'clock, and at breakfast next morning it began again. At noon or later we went together, Carlyle and I, to Hyde Park and the palaces (about two miles from here), to the National Gallery, and to the Strand, — Carlyle melting all Westminster and London down into his talk and laughter as he walked. We came back to dinner at five or later; then Dr. Carlyle came in and spent the evening, which again was long by the clock, but had no other measures. Here in this house we breakfast about nine ; Carlyle is very apt, his wife says, to sleep till ten or eleven, if he has no company. An immense talker he is, and altogether as extraordinary in his conversation as in his writing, — I think even more so. You will never discover his real vigor and range, or how much more he might do than he has ever done, without seeing him. I find my few hours' discourse with him in Scotland, long since, gave me not enough knowledge of him, and I have now at last been taken by surprise. . . . Carlyle and his wife live on beautiful terms. Nothing can be more engaging than their ways, and in her bookcase all his books are inscribed to her, as they came, from year to year. each with some significant lines.

But you will wish to hear more of my adventures, which I must hasten to record. On Wednesday, at the National Gallery, Mrs. Bancroft greeted me with the greatest kindness, and insisted on presenting me to Mr. Rogers, who chanced to come into the gallery with ladies. Mr. Rogers invited me to breakfast, with Mrs. B., at his house on Friday. . . . The smoke of London, through which the sun rarely penetrates, gives a dusky magnificence to these immense piles of building in the west part of the city, which makes my walking rather dream-like. Martin's pictures of Babylon, etc., are faithful copies of the west part of London ; light, darkness, architecture, and all. Friday morning at half past nine I presented myself at Mr. Bancroft's door, 90 Eaton Square, which was opened by Mr. Bancroft himself! in the midst of servants whom that man of eager manners thrust aside, saying that he would open his own door for me. He was full of goodness and of talk. . . . Mrs. Bancroft appeared, and we rode in her carriage to Mr. Rogers' house. . . . Mr. Rogers received us with cold, quiet, indiscriminate politeness, and entertained us with abundance of anecdote, which Mrs. Bancroft very skilfully drew out of him, about people more or less interesting to me. Scott, Wordsworth, Byron, Wellington, Talleyrand, Mme. de Staël, Lafayette, Fox, Burke, and crowds of high men and women had talked and feasted in these

rooms in which we sat, and which are decorated
with every precious work. . . . I think it must be
the chief private show of London, this man's collection. But I will not bore you with any more particulars. From this house Mrs. Bancroft carried me to
the cloister of Westminster Abbey and to the Abbey itself, and then insisted on completing her boun-
ties by carrying me in her coach to Carlyle's door
at Chelsea, a very long way. . . . At five P. M. yesterday, after spending four complete days with my
friends, I took the fast train for Liverpool, and
came hither, 212 miles, in six hours; which is
nearly twice our railway speed. In Liverpool I
drank tea last Saturday night with James Martineau, and heard him preach on Sunday night last.
He is a sincere, sensible, good man, and though
greatly valued as a preacher, yet I thought him superior to his books and his preaching. I have seen
Mr. Ireland, also, at Manchester on my way to
London, and his friends. It seems I am to read
six lectures in this town in three weeks, and at the
same time three lectures in each week in Manchester, on other evenings. When this service is ended
I may have as many new engagements as I like,
they tell me. I am to begin at Manchester next
Tuesday evening.

November 1, *Tuesday evening.* I am heartily
tired of Liverpool. I am oppressed by the seeing
of such multitudes : there is a fierce strength here

in all the streets; the men are bigger and solider far than our people, more stocky, both men and women, and with a certain fixedness and determination in each person's air, that discriminates them from the sauntering gait and roving eyes of Americans. In America you catch the eye of every one you meet; here you catch no eye, almost. The axes of an Englishman's eyes are united to his backbone. . . . Yesterday morning I got your welcome letter (by Mr. Ireland). I am greatly contented to know that all is so well with you. . . .

Ever affectionately yours, WALDO E.

In a fragment, apparently a rough draft of some letter at this time, he says : —

" I had good talk with Carlyle last night. He says over and over for months, for years, the same thing. Yet his guiding genius is his moral sense, his perception of the sole importance of truth and justice, and he too says that there is properly no religion in England. He is quite contemptuous about *Kunst* also, in Germans, or English, or Americans. . . . His sneers and scoffs are thrown in every direction. He breaks every sentence with a scoffing laugh, — 'windbag,' 'monkey,' 'donkey,' 'bladder;' and let him describe whom he will, it is always 'poor fellow.' I said : ' What a fine fellow are you, to bespatter the whole world with this oil of vitriol!' 'No man,' he replied, 'speaks truth to

me.' I said: 'See what a crowd of friends listen
to and admire you.' 'Yes, they come to hear me,
and they read what I write; but not one of them
has the smallest intention of doing these things."

MANCHESTER, December 1, 1847.

DEAR LIDIAN, — What can be the reason that I
have no letter by this Caledonia which has arrived?
It is just possible that letters have gone to London
and back to Liverpool, and will reach me to-night.
Care of Alexander Ireland, Esq., Examiner Office,
Manchester, is still for the present the best address. You cannot write too often or too largely.
After January 1, I believe there is a steamer once
a week, and if you will enclose anything to Abel
Adams, he will find the right mail-bag. I trust
you and the children are well, — that you are well,
and the children are well, — two facts, and not one;
two facts highly important to an exile, you will believe. Ah! perhaps you should see the tragic spectacles which these streets show, — these Manchester
and those Liverpool streets, by day and by night,
— to know how much of happiest circumstance,
how much of safety, of dignity, and of opportunity,
belongs to us so easily, that is ravished from this
population. Woman is cheap and vile in England,
it is tragical to see; childhood, too, I see oftenest
in the state of absolute beggary. My dearest little
Edie, to tell you the truth, costs me many a penny.

day by day. I cannot go up the street but I shall see some woman in rags, with a little creature just of Edie's size and age, but in coarsest ragged clothes and barefooted, stepping beside her; and I look curiously into *her* Edie's face, with some terror lest it should resemble *mine*, and the far-off Edie wins from me the halfpence for this near one. Bid Ellen and Edie thank God they were born in New England, and bid them speak the truth, and do the right forever and ever, and I hope they and theirs will not stand barefooted in the mud on a bridge in the rain all day to beg of passengers. But beggary is only the beginning and the sign of sorrow and evil here.

You are to know in general that I am doing well enough in health and in my work. I have, which is a principal thing, read two new lectures in the last two weeks: one on Books, or a course of reading: and the other on the Superlative, which was my lecture on Hafiz and my Persian readings. The next new one I get out will be the Natural Aristocracy, or some such thing.

I have had the finest visit to Mrs. Paulet, at Seaforth House, near Liverpool, where I was lodged in Canning's chamber in a grand *château :* also a visit to be thankful for to Mr. Rathbone at Green-bank.

BIRMINGHAM, *December* 16. 1847.

DEAR LIDIAN: . . . I find very kind friends

here, and many such. I have even given up my caprice of not going to private houses, and now scarcely go to any other. At Nottingham I was the guest on four nights of four different friends. At Derby I spent two nights with Mr. Birch, Mr. Alcott's friend. Here also I am hospitably received; and at towns which I have promised to visit I have accepted invitations from unknown hosts. . . . The newspapers here report my lectures (and London papers reprint) so fully that they are no longer repeatable, and I must dive deeper into the bag and bring up older ones, or write new ones, or cease to read. Yet there is great advantage to me in this journeying about in this fashion. I see houses, manufactories, halls, churches, landscape, and men. There is also great vexation. At any moment I may turn my back on it and go to London; and, if it were not winter, might embark and come home. So give my love to mother, — to whom you must send all my letters, for I do not write to her, — and say I much doubt whether I go to France. Love to all the darlings at home, whom I daily and nightly behold. I am much disappointed that no steamer yet arrives from you; it is overdue by a day, or two, or three. I dare not begin to name the friends near and nearest in these lines, they are so many and so loved, but I have yet no letter from Elizabeth II., and none from George Bradford. Tell George that I respect the

English always the more, the sensible, handsome, powerful race ; they are a population of lords, and if one king should die, there are a thousand in the street quite fit to succeed him. But I shall have letters from you, I trust, to-morrow, so good-night.

W.

Alexander Ireland approves himself the king of all friends and helpful agents ; the most active, un-weariable, imperturbable. . . . A wonderful place is England ; the mechanical might and organizations it is oppressive to behold. I ride everywhere as on a cannon-ball (though cushioned and comforted in every manner), high and low, over rivers and towns, through mountains in tunnels of three miles and more, at twice the speed and with half the motion of our cars, and read quietly the *Times* newspaper, which seems to have mechanized the world for my occasions.

MANCHESTER, *December* 25, 1847.

DEAR LIDIAN, — I did not receive your letters by the last steamer until the moment when my own must be forwarded, so that I could not write the shortest note to Mrs. Ripley, nor to you. I shall write to her a letter to accompany this.[1] Sudden and premature and shattering so many happy plans

---

[1] Reverend Samuel Ripley died very suddenly soon after his removal to Concord.

as his death does, yet there was so much health and
sunshine and will and power to come at good ends
in him that nothing painful or mournful will attach to his name. He will be sure to be remembered as living and serving, and not as suffering.
I am very sorry that I should not have been at
home, for he, who was so faithful to all the claims
of kindred, should have had troops of blood-rela-
tions to honor him around his grave. I think
often how serious is his loss to mother. I remember him almost as long as I can remember her, and,
from my father's death in my early boyhood, he
has always been an important friend to her and her
children. You know how generous he was to me
and to my brothers in our youth, at college and
afterwards. He never ceased to be so, and he was
the same friend to many others that he was to us.
I am afraid we hardly thanked him ; it was so
natural to him to interest himself for other people
that he could not help it. And whenever or wherever we shall now think of him, we shall see him
engaged in that way. . . . You must see Mrs. Ripley as much as you can. We cannot afford to live
as far from her (in habits, I mean) as we have
done. . . . I am a wanderer on the face of this
island, and am so harried by this necessity of reading lectures — which, if accepted, must be accepted
in manner and quantity not desirable — that I shall
not now for a fortnight or three weeks have time

to write any good gossip, you may be sure. What reconciles me to the clatter and routine is the very excellent opportunity it gives me to see England. I see men and things in each town in a close and domestic way. I see the best of the people (hitherto never the proper aristocracy, which is a stratum of society quite out of sight and out of mind here on all ordinary occasions) — the merchants, the manufacturers, the scholars, the thinkers, men and women — in a very sincere and satisfactory conversation. I am everywhere a guest. Never call me solitary or Ishmaelite again. I began here by refusing invitations to *stay* at private houses, but now I find an invitation in every town, and accept it, to be at home. I have now visited Preston, Leicester, Chesterfield, Birmingham, since I returned from Nottingham and Derby, of which I wrote you, and have found the same profuse kindness in all. My admiration and my love of the English rise day by day. I receive, too, a great many private letters, offering me house and home in places yet unvisited. You must not think that any change has come over me, and that my awkward and porcupine manners are ameliorated by English air ; but these civilities are all offered to that deceiving Writer who, it seems, has really beguiled many young people here, as he did at home, into some better hope than he could realize for them. . . . To-day is Christmas, and being

just returned yesterday P. M. from a long circuit, I
am bent on spending it quite domestically, and
Mr. Ireland and Mr. Cameron are coming presently to dine with me. On Wednesday I go spinning again to Worcester, and then presently to
those Yorkshire engagements which at home were
first heard of. Parliament is now in holidays
again until February, and of course London empty.
But it looks as if I should not arrive there for any
residence until March. I am often tempted to slip
out of my trade here, by some shortest method,
and go to London for peace. . . . At Leicester I
just missed seeing Gardiner, author of the "Music
of Nature." At Chesterfield I dined in company
with Stephenson, the old engineer who built the
first locomotive, and who is, in every way, one of
the most remarkable men I have seen in England.
I do not know but I shall accept some day his reit-
erated invitations " to go to his house and stay a
few days, and see Chatsworth and other things."
. . . Every word you send me from the dear children is excellent. Our Spartan-Buddhist Henry is
père or *bonhomme malgré lui*, and it is a great
comfort daily to think of him there with you. . . .
You ask for newspapers, but you do not want reports of my lectures, which they give too abundantly; nor the attacks of the clergymen upon them;
nor the pale though brave defences of my friends:
there are such things, but I do not read them.

When there is, if there should be, anything really
good, I will send it. But first there must be something really good of mine to build it upon. Ah
me! Elizabeth has written the best and fullest of
letters, and I dare not say that I shall write to her
by the going steamer. Tell Ellen that I fear I
shall not see Tennyson, for, though Dr. John Carlyle writes me yesterday that he has just met him at
his brother's, he is going to Rome, and I hardly
think I shall follow him there. He has not three
children who say all these things which my wife
records. . . . Elizabeth says that aunt Mary thinks
to come to Concord; by all means, seduce her into
the house, and make her forget, if it be possible,
her absurd resolutions and jealousies. . . . Here
is no winter thus far, but such days as we have at
the beginning of November. I am as well in body
as ever, and not worse in spirit than when I am
spinning to winter lectures at home. But mortal
man must always spin somewhere, and I bow to my
destiny.

TO MISS ELIZABETH HOAR.

MANCHESTER, *December* 28, 1847.

DEAR ELIZABETH, — You are the best of sisters, and good by yourself and without provocation.
. . . How generously you give me trust for indefinite periods! You must believe, too, that I appreciate this magnanimity, though too dull and heavy

to make a sign. The hour will come and the world,
wherein we shall quite easily render that account
of ourselves which now we never render, and shall
be very real brothers and sisters. . . . When I
see my muscular neighbors day by day I say, Had
I been born in England, with but one chip of English oak in my willowy constitution! . . . I have
seen many good, some bright, and some powerful
people here, but none yet to fall in love with, neither man nor woman. I have, however, some
youthful correspondence — you know my failing —
with some friendly young gentlemen in different
parts of Britain. I keep all their letters, and you
shall see. At Edinburgh I have affectionate invitations from Dr. Samuel Brown, of whom I believe
you know something. He saw Margaret F. At
Newcastle, from Mr. Crawshay, who refused the
tests at Cambridge after reading my essays! as he
writes me. And so with small wisdom the world
is moved, as of old. In the press of my trifles I
have ceased to write to Carlyle, and I hear nothing
from him. You have read his paper in *Fraser?* [1]
He told me the same story at his house, but it
reads incredible, and everybody suspects some
mystification, — some people fancying that Carlyle
himself is trying his hand that way! But Carlyle
takes Cromwell sadly to heart. When I told him

---

[1] December, 1847. *Thirty-five Unpublished Letters of Oliver
Cromwell.* Communicated by Thomas Carlyle.

that he must not expect that people as old as I could look at Cromwell as he did, he turned quite fiercely upon me. . . . If I do not find time for another note, am I the less your constant brother?

WALDO.

MANCHESTER, *January* 8, 1848.

DEAR LIDIAN : . . . There is opportunity enough to read over again a hundred times yet these musty old lectures, and when I go to a new audience I say, It is a grossness to read these things which you have, fully reported, in so many newspapers. Let me read a new manuscript never yet published in England. But no, the directors invariably refuse. " We have heard of these, advertised these; there can be no other." It really seems like China and Japan. But the great profession and mystery of Bards and Trouveurs does hereby suffer damage in my person, and I fear no decent man in London will speak to me when I come thither ; to say nothing of the absolute suspension and eclipse which all my faculties suffer in this routine, so that, at whatever perils, I must end it. I have had a letter from George Bradford, very good to read ; never one from Parker or any of the *Massachusetts Quarterly* men. Their journal is of a good spirit, and has much good of Agassiz, but no intellectual tone such as is imperatively wanted ; no literary skill, even, and, without a loftier note than any in this number, it will sink into a *North American* at once. In a day or two I shall have good news again from you, and news from the nursery and school, ever heartily welcome. . . . I hope you keep — you must keep — a guest-chamber *with a fire* this winter and every winter, as last winter we had none. I may send you a young Mr. Stansfield, a Leeds merchant, who offers to carry letters for me, and the nephew of Mr. Stansfield, of Halifax, who showed me great hospitality; and it would chill my bones to believe that he passed a New England winter night without fire, so unprepared by the habits of English at home. I shall perhaps say to Mr. S., if he wishes to go into the country and look, you will gladly give him a night's lodging. And if he comes, — or any Englishman, — give him bread and wine before he goes to bed, for these people universally eat supper at nine or ten P. M., and therefore must be hungry in Concord; which would make me hungry all my life, they have been so careful of me. Farewell. Yours,   W.

MANCHESTER, January 26, 1848.

DEAR LIDIAN: . . . I have been at York and at Flamborough Head since I wrote you last. I have no special notes to write of these places — and persons; persons are like stars, which always keep afar. No angel alights on my orb, — such presences being always reserved for angels. But I was proceeding to tell you that I am now spending a few peaceful days at Manchester, after racketing about Yorkshire in the last weeks. I was disgusted with reading lectures, and wrote to all parties that I would read no more; but in vain. Secretaries had misunderstood, had promised and pledged me. I myself had not forbidden it. Did not Mr. E. remember? etc., etc. And at last I have consented to drudge on a little longer after this peaceful fortnight is ended, and shall go to Edinburgh on the 7th February, and end all my northern journeys on the 25th. Then I return hither and proceed to London to spend March and April, and (unless I go to Paris) May also. I am writing in these very days a lecture which I will try at Edinburgh, on Aristocracy. The other night at Sheffield I made shift, with some old papers and some pages suggested lately by the Agassiz reports, to muster a discourse on Science. Last night I heard a lecture from Mr. Cameron, whom I have heretofore mentioned, on some poetic and literary matters. He talked, without note or card or compass, for his hour, on Readers and Reading; very manly, very gaily; not quite deeply enough, — it did not cost him enough, — yet what would I not do or suffer to buy that ability? "To each his own." A manly ability, a general sufficiency, is the genius of the English. They have not, I think,

the special and acute fitness to their employment
that Americans have, but a man is a man here; a
quite costly and respectable production, in his own
and in all other eyes. To-morrow evening I am
to attend what is called the " Free-Trade Banquet,"
when Cobden, Bright, Fox, and the free-traders
are to speak. . . . Peace be with all your household; with the little and with the larger members!
Many kisses, many blessings, to the little and the
least. I am glad the children had their good visit
to Boston and Roxbury; but I would keep them
at home in winter. You speak of Ellen's letter;
surely I wrote one to Edith also, and if Eddie will
wait, or will only learn to read his own name, he
shall have one too, at least a picture. So with
love to all,   Yours,   W.

GATESHEAD IRON WORKS, *February* 10, 1848.

. . . I have written a lecture on Natural Aristocracy, which I am to read in Edinburgh to-morrow, and interpolated besides some old webs with
patches of new tapestry, contrary to old law. The
day before leaving Manchester we had a company
of friends assembled at Dr. Hodgson's house and
mine: two from Nottingham, Neuberg and Sutton;
Mr. Gill from Birmingham; one from Hudders-
field; and Ireland, Cameron, Espinasse, and Bal-
lantyne from Manchester. I gave them all a dinner on Sunday. These are all men of merit, and

of various virtues and ingenuities. I have been
once more at Mr. Stansfield's in Halifax ; and yesterday, at Barnard Castle, I found myself in the
scene of Scott's Rokeby. . . . I find here at Newcastle a most accomplished gentleman in Mr. Crawshay, at whose counting-room in his iron works I
am now sitting, after much conference on many
fine and useful arts. . . . My reception here is
really a premium often on authorship; and if
Henry [Thoreau] means one day to come to England, let him not delay another day to print his
book. Or if he do not, let him print it.

PERTH, *February* 21, 1848.

DEAR LIDIAN : . . . All these touching anecdotes and now drawings and letters of my darlings
duly come, and to my great joy, and ought to draw
answers to every letter and almost to every piece
of information. I cannot answer but with most
ungrateful brevity, but you shall have a short
chronicle of my late journeys. Well, then, I came
from Newcastle to Edinburgh [and after some
mischance, delaying him on the way, reached the
lecture-room a quarter of an hour late]. It was
really a brilliant assembly, and contained many remarkable men and women, as I afterwards found.
After lecture I went home with my friend, Dr.
[Samuel] Brown, to his lodgings, and have been
his guest all the time I was in Edinburgh. There

I found David Scott, the painter, a sort of Bronson
Alcott with easel and brushes, a sincere great man,
grave, silent, contemplative, and plain. . . . The
next day I was presented to Wilson (Christopher
North), to Mrs. Jeffrey, and especially to Mrs.
Crowe, a very distinguished good person here.
. . . I looked all around this most picturesque of
cities, and in the evening met Mr. Robert Chambers (author of the " Vestiges of Creation ") by
appointment at Mr. Ireland's (father of Alexander), at supper. The next day at twelve, I visited
by appointment Lord Jeffrey, . . . and then to
Mrs. Crowe's at 5.30 to dine with De Quincey and
David Scott and Dr. Brown. De Quincey is a small
old man of seventy years, with a very handsome
face, and a face, too, expressing the highest refinement ; a very gentle old man, speaking with the
greatest deliberation and softness, and so refined in
speech and manners as to make quite indifferent
his extremely plain and poor dress. For the old
man, summoned by message on Saturday by Mrs.
Crowe to this dinner, had walked on this stormy,
muddy Sunday ten miles, from Lass Wade, where
his cottage is, and was not yet dry ; and though
Mrs. Crowe's hospitality is comprehensive and minute, yet she had no pantaloons in her house.
Here De Quincey is very serene and happy among
just these friends where I found him ; for he has
suffered in all ways, and lived the life of a wretch

for many years, but Samuel Brown and Mrs. C. and one or two more have saved him from himself, and defended him from bailiffs and a certain Fury of a Mrs. Macbold (I think it is), whom he yet shudders to remember, and from opium ; and he is now clean, clothed, and in his right mind. . . . He talked of many matters, all easily and well, but chiefly social and literary; and did not venture into any voluminous music. When they first agreed, at my request, to invite him to dine, I fancied some figure like the organ of York Minster would appear. In *tête-à-tête*, I am told, he sometimes soars and indulges himself, but not often in company. He invited me to dine with him on the following Saturday at Lass Wade, where he lives with his three daughters, and I accepted. The next day I breakfasted with David Scott, who insists on sittings for a portrait; and sat to him for an hour or two. . . . This man is a noble stoic, sitting apart here among his rainbow allegories, very much respected by all superior persons. Of him I shall have much more to say. At one o'clock I went to Glasgow, and read my story there to an assembly of two or three thousand people, in a vast lighted cavern called the City Hall. . . . Next day I dined at Edinburgh with Robert Chambers, and found also his brother William. . . . This day I went to the University to see Professor Wilson, and hear him lecture (on Moral Philosophy) to his

class. We, that is always Dr. B. and I, went first
into his private retiring-room and had a pretty long
talk with him.   He is a big man, gross almost as
S——, and tall, with long hair and much beard,
dressed large and slouching.   His lecture had
really no merit.   It was on the association of ideas,
and was a very dull sermon, without a text, but
pronounced with great bodily energy, sometimes
his mouth all foam ; he reading, the class writing,
and I at last waiting a little impatiently for it to be
over.   No trait was there of Christopher North ; not
a ray.   Afterwards we went to Sir William Ham-
ilton's lecture on Logic.   He is the great man of
the college, master of his science, and in every way
truly respected here. . . . In the evening, at Mr.
Stoddart's, I saw George Combe, who had called
on me and had invited me to breakfast. . . . Next
morning I breakfasted with Mr. Combe.   Mrs.
Combe is the daughter of Mrs. Siddons, whom she
more and more resembles, they all say, in these
days.   Combe talked well and sensibly about
America.   But, for the most part, there is no elas-
ticity about Scotch sense ; it is calculating and
precise, but has no future.   Then to Glasgow, and
spent the night at Professor Nichol's observatory,
well appointed and rarely placed, but a cloudy
night and no moon or star.   I saw, next day, the
Saut Market and oh ! plenty of women (fishwives
and others) and children, barefooted, barelegged,

on this cold 18th of February, in the streets. . . .
At Edinburgh again I dined with Mr. Nichol,
brother of the Professor, and in the evening, by
invitation, visited Lord Jeffrey, with Mrs. Crowe.
. . . Jeffrey, as always, very talkative, very dis-
putatious, very French ; every sentence interlarded
with French phrases ; speaking a dialect of his
own, neither English nor Scotch, marked with a
certain *petitesse*, as one might well say, and an affected elegance. I should like to see him put on
his merits by being taxed by some of his old peers,
as Wilson, or Hallam, or Macaulay ; but here he
is the chief man, and has it all his own way. . . .
The next day I dined with De Quincey and his
pleasing daughters. A good deal of talk, which I
see there is no time to relate. We carried our
host back with us to Edinburgh, to Mrs. Crowe's,
and to my lecture ! De Quincey at lecture ! And
thereat I was presented to Helen Faucit, the actress, who is a beauty ; and to Sir William Allan,
the painter, Walter Scott's friend ; and to Professor Simpson, a great physician here ; and to others.
Next day I sat to Scott again, and dined again with
Mrs. Crowe, and De Quincey and Helen Faucit
came to tea, and we could see Antigone at our ease.
One thing I was obliged to lose at Edinburgh, with
much regret. Robert Chambers is the local anti-
quary, knows more of the " Old Town," etc., than
any other man, and he had fixed an hour to go and

show me some of the historical points and crypts
of the town ; but I was obliged to write and excuse
myself for want of time. . . . What I chiefly regret is that I cannot begin on the long chronicle
of our new Paracelsus here, Dr. Samuel Brown,
who is a head and heart of chiefest interest to me
and to others, and a person from whom everything
is yet to be expected.[1] . . . On Saturday I leave
Scotland, and shall stop a day, I think, at Amble-
side, with Harriet Martineau, and visit Wordsworth, if it is practicable, on my way to Manchester. There I shall pack up my trunk again (for it
is always there) and go to London. . . . Excuse
me to everybody for not writing ; I simply cannot.
Ah! and excuse me to my dear little correspondents. . . . Papa never forgets them, never ceases
to wish to see them, and is often tempted to run
ignominiously away from Britain and France for
that purpose. . . . Love to all who love — the
truth! and continue you to be merciful and good
to me.   Your affectionate   W.

On his way to London he stayed, he writes to
Miss Fuller, "two days with Harriet Martineau,
and spent an hour and a half with Wordsworth,
who was full of talk on French news, bitter old

[1] Dr. Brown was expecting to reduce several chemical elements (perhaps all matter) to one substance, a line of speculation always fascinating to Emerson.

Englishman he is; on Scotchmen, whom he contemns; on Gibbon, who cannot write English; on Carlyle, who is a pest to the English tongue; on Tennyson, whom he thinks a right poetic genius, though with some affectation; on Thomas Taylor, an English national character; and on poetry and so forth. But, though he often says something, I think I could easily undertake to write table-talk for him to any extent, for the newspapers; and it should cost me nothing and be quite as good as any one is likely to hear from his own lips. But he is a fine, healthy old man, with a weather-beaten face, and I think it is a high compliment we pay to the cultivation of the English generally that we find him not distinguished. . . . To-morrow, through all these wondrous French news which all tongues and telegraphs discuss, I go to London."

At London and on the way he received many invitations to lecture there, but apparently of a kind that seemed to pledge him to subjects which did not suit him; at all events, none that he wished to accept, though his home-letters told him of claims that made it desirable for him to earn money if he could. Six weeks after he reached London he was still undecided about lecturing. Meantime he was making good use of his social opportunities. A day or two after his arrival he writes:—

DEAR LIDIAN : . . . Ah, you still ask me for
that unwritten letter, always due, it seems, always
unwritten from year to year by me to you, dear
Lidian; I fear, too, more widely true than you
mean, — always due and unwritten by me to every
sister and brother of the human race. I have only
to say that I also bemoan myself daily for the same
cause; that I cannot write this letter, that I have
not stamina and constitution enough to mind the
two functions of seraph and cherub, — oh, no! let
me not use such great words; rather say that a
photometer cannot be a stove. . . . Well, I will
come home again shortly, and behave the best I
can. Only I foresee plainly that the trick of soli-
tariness never, never can leave me. My own pursuits and calling often appear to me like those of
an Astronomer Royal, whose whole duty is to make
faithful minutes which have only value when kept
for ages, and in one life are insignificant.

I have dined once with Carlyle, and have found
the Bancrofts again very kind and thoughtful for
me. Mr. B. has supplied me with means of access
to both Houses of Parliament, and Mrs. Bancroft
sends me a card to Lady Morgan's *soirées*, where
she assures me I shall see good people. Bancroft
shares, of course, to the highest point, in the enthusiasm for the French. So does Carlyle in his way,
and now for the first time in his life takes in the

Times newspaper daily. . . . I also read the *Times* every day. I have been to the House of Lords one evening, and attended during the whole sitting; saw Wellington. Once also to the Commons; to the British Museum, long an object of great desire to me. . . . Last night, by Carlyle's advice, I attended a meeting of Chartists, assembled to receive the report of the deputation they had sent to congratulate the French Republic. It was crowded, and the people very much in earnest. The Marseillaise was sung as songs are in our abolition meetings. London is disturbed in these days by a mob which meets every day this week, and creates great anxiety among shopkeepers in the districts where it wanders, breaking windows and stealing. London has too many glass doors to afford riots. . . . Yet, though there is a vast population of hungry operatives all over the kingdom, the peace will probably not be disturbed by them; they will only, in the coming months, give body and terror to the demands made by the Cobdens and Brights who agitate for the middle class. When these are satisfied, universal suffrage and the republic will come in. But it is not this which you will wish to hear now. The most wonderful thing I see is this London, at once seen to be the centre of the world: the immense masses of life, of power, of wealth, and the effect upon the men of running in and out amidst the play of this vast machinery; the effect

to keep them tense and silent, and to mind every
man his own. It is all very entertaining, I assure
you. I think sometimes that it would well become
me to sit here a good while and study London
mainly, and the wide variety of classes that, like
so many nations, are dwelling here together. . . .

March 23. . . . I have seen a great many peo-
ple, some very good ones. Mr. and Mrs. Bancroft,
and Carlyle, and Milnes have taken kind care to
introduce me. At Mr. Bancroft's I dined with
Macaulay, Bunsen, Lord Morpeth, Milman, Milnes,
and others. Carlyle, Mr. and Mrs. Lyell, Mrs.
Butler, and others came in the evening. At Mr.
Milman's I breakfasted with Macaulay, Hallam,
Lord Morpeth, and a certain brilliant Mr. Charles
Austin. . . . At Mr. Procter's (Barry Cornwall)
I dined with Forster of the *Examiner*, Kinglake
(Eothen), and others. . . . Carlyle carried me to
Lady Harriet Baring, who is a very distinguished
person, and the next day to Lady Ashburton, her
mother, and I am to dine with them both. . . .
Mrs. Jameson I have seen a good deal. Then
there is a scientific circle of great importance. Mr.
Owen, who is in England what Agassiz is in
America, has given me a card to his lectures at
the College of Surgeons, and shown me the Hun-
terian Museum. His lecture gratified me the more,
or entirely, I may say, because, like Agassiz, he is
an idealist in physiology. Then Mr. Hutton, to

whom Harriet Martineau introduced me, carried me to the Geological Society, where I heard the best debate I have heard in England, the House of Commons and the Manchester banquet not excepted; Buckland (of the Bridgewater treatise), a man of great wit and sense and science, and Carpenter, and Forbes, and Lyell, and Daubeny being among the speakers. I was then presented to the Marquis of Northampton, who invited me to his *soirée*. These people were all discoverers in their new science, and loaded to the lips, so that what might easily seem in a newspaper report a dull affair was full of character and eloquence. Some of these above-named good friends exerted themselves for me to the best effect in another way, so that I was honored with an election into the Athenæum Club during my temporary residence in England, a privilege one must prize. . . . Milnes and other good men are always to be found there. Milnes is the most good-natured man in England, made of sugar; he is everywhere and knows everything. He told of Landor that one day, in a towering passion, he threw his cook out of the window, and then presently exclaimed. " Good God, I never thought of those poor violets ! " The last time he saw Landor he found him expatiating on our custom of eating in company, which he esteems very barbarous. He eats alone, with half-closed windows, because the light interferes with the taste.

He has lately heard of some tribe in Crim Tartary
who have the practice of eating alone, and these
he extols as much superior to the English. . . .
Macaulay is the king of diners-out. I do not know
when I have seen such wonderful vivacity. He
has the strength of ten men, immense memory, fun,
fire, learning, politics, manners, and pride, and
talks all the time in a steady torrent. You would
say he was the best type of England. . . .

March 24. Yesterday, or rather last night, I
dined at Mr. Baring's (at eight o'clock). The
company was, Lord and Lady Ashburton, Lord
Auckland, Carlyle, Milnes, Thackeray, Lord and
Lady Castlereagh, the Bishop of Oxford (Wilber-
force), and in the evening came Charles Buller :
who, they say in introducing me to him, " was the
cleverest man in England until he attempted also
to be a man of business." . . . French politics are
incessantly discussed in all companies, and so here.
Besides the intrinsic interest of the spectacle, and
the intimate acquaintance which all these people
have with all the eminent persons in France, there
is evidently a certain anxiety to know whether our
days also are not numbered. . . . Carlyle de-
claimed a little in the style of that raven prophet
who cried, " Woe to Jerusalem," just before its fall.
But Carlyle finds little reception even in this company, where some were his warm friends. All his
methods included a good deal of killing, and he

does not see his way very clearly or far. The
aristocrats say, " Put that man in the House of
Commons, and you will hear no more of him." It
is a favorite tactics here, and silences the most
turbulent. There he will be permitted to declaim
once, only once ; then, if he have a measure to propose, it will be tested ; if not, he must sit still.
One thing is certain : that if the peace of England
should be broken up, the aristocracy here — or, I
should say, the rich — are stout-hearted, and as
ready to fight for their own as the poor ; are not
very likely to run away. . . . You will wish to
know my plans. Alas, I have none. As long as
I have these fine opportunities opening to me here,
I prefer to use them and stay where I am. France
may presently shut its doors to me and to all peaceful men ; so that I may not go there at all. But I
shall soon spend all my money if I sit here, and I
have not yet taken any step in London towards
filling my pocket. How can I ? I must soon decide on something. I have declined such lecturing
as was offered me ; you do not wish me to read
lectures to the Early-closing Institution ? I saw
Macready the other night as Lear, and Mrs. Butler as Cordelia. Mrs. Bancroft is very happy and
a universal favorite. She sees the best people of
all the best circles, and she has virtues and graces
which I see to greater advantage in London than
in Boston ; for her true love of her old friends and

her home is very obvious. Her friend Miss Murray
and Mrs. Jameson were concocting a plot for introducing me to Lady Byron, who lives retired and
reads ——! . . . . But I shall, no doubt, remember
many traits and hues of this Babylonish dream
when I come home to the woods.

April 2. Yesterday night I went to the *soirée*
of the Marquis of Northampton, where may be
found all the *savants* who are in London. There
I saw Prince Albert, to whom Dr. Buckland was
showing some microscopic phenomena. The prince
is handsome and courteous, and I watched him for
some minutes across the table, as a personage of
much historical interest. Here I saw Mantell,
Captain Sabine, Brown the great botanist, Crabbe
Robinson (who knew all men, Lamb, Southey,
Wordsworth, Madame de Staël, and Goethe), Sir
Charles Fellowes, who brought home the Lycian
marbles; and many more. Then I went, by an invitation sent me through Milnes, to Lady Palmerston's, and saw quite an illustrious collection, such
as only London and Lord Palmerston could collect:
princes and high foreigners; Bunsen; Rothschild
(that London proverb) in flesh and blood; Disraeli, to whom I was presented, and had with him
a little talk; Macaulay; Mr. Cowper, a very courteous gentleman, son of Lady Palmerston, with
whom I talked much; and many distinguished
dames, some very handsome. . . . Lord Palmer-

ston is frank and affable, of a strong but cheerful
and ringing speech. But I ought to have told you
that on the morning of this day when I saw all these
fine figures I had come from Oxford, where I spent
something more than two days, very happily. I
had an old invitation from Mr. Clough, a Fellow of
Oriel, and last week I had a new one from Dr.
Daubeny, the botanical professor. I went on
Thursday. I was housed close upon Oriel, though
not within it, but I lived altogether on college hospitalities, dining at Exeter College with Palgrave,
Froude, and other Fellows, and breakfasting next
morning at Oriel with Clough, Dr. Daubeny, etc.
They all showed me the kindest attentions, . . .
but, much more, they showed me themselves; who
are many of them very earnest, faithful, affectionate, some of them highly gifted men ; some of
them, too, prepared and decided to make great sacrifices for conscience' sake. Froude is a noble
youth, to whom my heart warms; I shall soon see
him again. Truly I became fond of these monks of
Oxford. Last Sunday I dined at Mr. Bancroft's
with Lady Morgan and Mrs. Jameson, and accepted Lady Morgan's invitation for the next evening to tea. At her house I found, beside herself
(who is a sort of fashionable or London edition of
aunt Mary; the vivacity, the wit, the admirable
preservation of social powers, being retained, but
the high moral genius being left out), Mrs. Gore,

of the fashionable novels, a handsome Lady Moles-
worth, a handsome, sensible Lady Louisa Tennyson, Mr. Kinglake, Mr. Conyngham, a friend of
John Sterling's, and others.

Pray, after this ostentation of my fashionable acquaintance, do you believe that my rusticities are
smoothed down, and my bad manners mended?
Not in the smallest degree. I have not acquired
the least facility, nor can hope to. But I do not
decline these opportunities, as they are all valuable
to me, who would, at least, know how that "other
half of the world" lives, though I cannot and
would not live with them. I find the greatest simplicity of speech and manners among these people;
great directness, but, I think, the same (or even
greater) want of high thought as you would notice
in a fashionable circle in Boston. Yes, greater.
But then I know these people very superficially.
I have not yet told you, I believe, of my dinner at
Lord Ashburton's, where I sat between Mr. Hallam
and Lord Northampton, and saw Lockhart, Buckland, Croker, Lady Davy (of Sir Humphrey D.),
Lord Monteagle, and more. Another day I went
to the house, and Lord Ashburton showed me all
his pictures, which are most precious and renowned. Hallam was very courteous and com-
municative, and has since called on me. To-morrow I am to dine with Mr. Lyell, and the next
day with the Geological Club at the invitation

of — oh, tell not Dr. C. T. J. [Dr. Charles T. Jackson, his brother-in-law, geologist and man of science] — Sir Henry Delabeche, the president. . . . I spend the first hours of the day usually in my chamber, and have got a new chapter quite forward, if it have rather a musty title. Whether to go to France or not, I have not quite determined : I suppose I must, in all prudence; though I have no money, nor any plain way of obtaining any.

LONDON, *April* 20, 1848.

DEAR LIDIAN, — The steamer is in : everybody has letters, and I have none, none from you or the dear little Ellen who writes me short, pert, good notes, — all blessings fall on the child ! It must be that you too have decided that boats run a little too often for mere human pens moved by hands that have many more things to drive. . . . I have been busy during the last fortnight, but have added no very noticeable persons to my list of acquaintances. A good deal of time is lost here in their politics, as I read the newspaper daily, and the revolution, fixed for the 10th instant, occupied all men's thought until the Chartist petition was actually carried to the Commons. And the rain, too, which falls at any time almost every day, — these things, and the many miles of street you must afoot or by 'bus or cab achieve to make any visit, put me, who am, as you know, always faint-hearted

at the name of visiting, much out of the humor of
prosecuting my social advantages. I have dined with
Mr. and Mrs. Lyell one day, and one with a good
Dr. Forbes, who carried me to the Royal Institution to hear Faraday, who is reckoned the best lecturer in London. It seems very doubtful whether
I shall read lectures here even now. Chapman
makes himself very busy about it, and a few people,
and I shall, no doubt, have a good opportunity, but
I am not ready, and it is a lottery business, and I
do much incline to decline it, — on grounds that I
can only tell you of at home, — and go to Paris for
a few weeks, get my long-promised French lesson,
and come home to be poor and pay for my learning.
I have really been at work every day here with my
old tools of book and pen, and shall at last have
something to show for it all.

The best sights I have seen lately are, the British
Museum, whose chambers of antiquities I visited
with the Bancrofts on a private day, under the guidance of Sir Charles Fellowes, who brought home
the Xanthian marbles, and really gave us the most
instructive chapter on the subject of Greek remains
that I have ever heard or read of. . . . Then the
King's Library, which I saw under the guidance of
Panizzi, the librarian, and afterwards of Coventry
Patmore, a poet, who is a sub-librarian. Then I
heard Grisi the other night sing at Covent Garden,
— Grisi and Alboni, the rivals of the opera. Being

admitted an honorary member of the Reform Club, I went over all that magnificent house with Mr. Field, through its kitchen, reckoned the best in Europe, which was shown to me by Soyer, renowned in the literature of saucepan and soup. Another day through, over, and under the new Houses of Parliament, . . . among the chiefest samples of the delight which Englishmen find in spending a great deal of money. Carlyle has been quite ill lately with inflamed sore throat, and as he is a very intractable patient, his wife and brother have no small trouble to keep him in bed or even in the house. I certainly obtained a fairer share of the conversation when I visited him. He is very grim lately on these ominous times, which have been and are deeply alarming to all England.

I find Chapman very anxious to establish a journal common to Old and New England, as was long ago proposed. Froude and Clough and other Oxonians and others would gladly conspire. Let the *Massachusetts Quarterly* give place to this, and we should have two legs and bestride the sea. But what do I, or what does any friend of mine in America, care for a journal? Not enough, I fear, to secure any energetic work on that side. . . . 'T is certain the *Mass. Q. R.* will fail unless Henry Thoreau and Alcott and Channing and Charles Newcomb — the fourfold-visaged four — fly to the rescue. I am sorry that Alcott's editor, the Du-

mont of our Bentham, Baruch of our Jeremiah, is so
slow to be born. . . . Young Palgrave at Oxford
gave me a letter to Sir William Hooker, who pre-
sides over Kew Gardens, and Mr. and Mrs. Bancroft
having a good will to go there, and being already
acquainted with him, we went thither yesterday in
their carriage, and had the benefit of this eminent
guide through these eminent gardens. The day was
the finest of the year, and the garden is the richest
on the face of the earth. Adam would find all his
old acquaintances of Eden here. Since I have been
in London I have not earned a single pound. The
universal anxiety of people on political and social
dangers makes no favorable theatre for letters and
lectures. The poor booksellers sell no book for the
last month. Neither have I yet had any new chapters quite ripe to offer for reading to a private class.
But all this question must very shortly decide itself. Either I shall undertake something in London, or go to Liverpool or to Bristol, as has been
proposed, or renounce all such thought, and determine to pay for my pleasures by publishing my
new papers when I get home. My newest writing
(except always an English journal which grows a
little day by day) is a kind of " Natural History of
Intellect;" very unpromising title, is it not? and,
you will say, the better it is, the worse. I dined with
the Geological Club yesterday, and in the evening
attended the meeting of the Society, and had a very

good opportunity of hearing Sedgwick, who is their best man, Ramsay, Jukes, Forbes, Buckland, and others. To-day I have heard Dr. Carpenter lecture at the Royal Institution. . . . Dear love to all the children three, and to dear friends whom I do not begin to name for fear to choose. I never name any without a sense of crying injustice, so multitudinous are my debts, happy, unhappy man that I am! Fare you well.   WALDO.

May 4. I am going on Saturday to Paris. I mean to read six lectures in London, which will be forthwith advertised, to begin three weeks from next Tuesday. And I shall spend the interim in France. I had all but decided not to read in London, but was much pressed, and came at last to have a feeling that not to do it was a kind of skulking. I cannot suit myself yet with a name for the course. I am leading the same miscellaneous London life as when I have written before ; dining out in a great variety of companies, seeing shilling shows, attending scientific and other societies, seeing picture-galleries, operas, and theatres. One day I met Dickens at Mr. Forster's, and liked him very well. Carlyle dined there also, and it seemed the habit of the set to pet Carlyle a good deal, and draw out the mountainous mirth. The pictures which such people together give one of what is really going forward in private and in public life are inesti-

mable. Day before yesterday I dined with the
Society of Antiquaries, sat beside the veritable
Collier (of Shakspeare criticism) and discussed the
Sonnets. Among the toasts my health was actually
proposed to the company by the president, Lord
Mahon, and I made a speech in reply ; all which
was surprising enough. To-morrow I am to dine
with Tennyson, whom I have not yet seen, at Coventry Patmore's. . . . Miss Martineau is here, not,
as I supposed, for a frolic after so much labor,
but to begin, with Knight, hard work for a twelve-
month in writing a penny journal called *Voice of
the People;* which the government have procured
these two to emit in these wild times, and which
seems to foolish me like a sugar-plum thrown to a
mad bull. . . .

(Journal.) " I saw Tennyson first at the house
of Coventry Patmore, where we dined together.
I was contented with him at once. He is tall and
scholastic-looking, no dandy, but a great deal of
plain strength about him, and, though cultivated,
quite unaffected. Quiet, sluggish sense and thought;
refined, as all English are, and good-humored.
There is in him an air of general superiority that
is very satisfactory. He lives with his college set,
. . . and has the air of one who is accustomed to
be petted and indulged by those he lives with.
Take away Hawthorne's bashfulness, and let him

talk easily and fast, and you would have a pretty good Tennyson. I told him that his friends and I were persuaded that it was important to his health an instant visit to Paris, and that I was to go on Monday if he was ready. He was very good-humored, and affected to think that I should never come back alive from France; it was death to go. But he had been looking for two years for some-body to go to Italy with, and was ready to set out at once, if I would go there. . . . He gave me a cordial invitation to his lodgings (in Buckingham Place), where I promised to visit him before I went away. . . . I found him at home in his lodgings, but with him was a clergyman whose name I did not know, and there was no conversation. He was sure again that he was taking a final farewell of me, as I was going among the French bullets, but promised to be in the same lodgings if I should escape alive. . . . Carlyle thinks him the best man in England to smoke a pipe with, and used to see him much; had a place in his little garden, on the wall, where Tennyson's pipe was laid up.

PARIS, *May* 17, 1848.

DEAR LIDIAN, — I came to Paris by Boulogne Saturday night, May 6. I have been at lodgings ever since, in the Rue des Petits Augustins, where I manage to live very comfortably. On Monday (day before yesterday), as you will read in the

papers, there was a revolution defeated which came
within an ace of succeeding.   We were all assured
for an hour or two that the new government was
proclaimed and the old routed, and Paris, in terror,
seemed to acquiesce ; but the National Guards, who
are all but the entire male population of Paris, at
last found somebody to rally and lead them, and
they swept away the conspirators in a moment.
Blanqui and Barbès, the two principal ringleaders,
I knew well, as I had attended Blanqui's club on
the evenings of Saturday and Sunday, and heard
his instructions to his Montagnards, and Barbès'
club I had visited last week, and I am heartily
glad of the shopkeepers' victory.   I saw the sudden
and immense display of arms when the *rappel* was
beaten, on Monday afternoon ; the streets full of
bayonets, and the furious driving of the horses
dragging cannon towards the National Assembly ;
the rapid succession of proclamations proceeding
from the government and pasted on the walls at
the corners of all streets, eagerly read by crowds
of people ; and, not waiting for this, the rapid passage of messengers with proclamations in their
hands, which they read to knots of people and then
ran on to another knot, and so on down a street.
The moon shone as the sun went down ; the river
rolled under the crowded bridges, along the swarming quays ; the tricolor waved on the great mass of
the Tuileries, which seemed too noble a palace to

doubt of the owner; but before night all was safe,
and our new government, who had held the seats for
a quarter of an hour, were fast in jail. . . . I have
seen Rachel in Phèdre, and heard her chant the
Marseillaise. She deserves all her fame, and is
the only good actress I have ever seen. I went to
the Sorbonne, and heard a lecture from Leverrier
on mathematics. It consisted chiefly of algebraic
formulas which he worked out on the blackboard;
but I saw the man. I heard Michelet on Indian
philosophy. But, though I have been to many
places, I find the clubs the most interesting; the
men are in terrible earnest. The fire and fury of
the people, when they are interrupted and thwarted,
are inconceivable to New England. The costumes
are formidable. All France is bearded like goats
and lions; then most of Paris is in some kind
of uniform, — red cap, red sash, blouse perhaps
bound by red sash, brass helmet, and sword, and
everybody supposed to have a pistol in his pocket.
But the deep sincerity of the speakers, who are
agitating social, not political questions, and who are
studying how to secure a fair share of bread to
every man, and to get God's justice done through
the land, is very good to hear. . . . Clough, my
Oxford friend, is here, and we usually dine together.
. . . I have just sent my programme of lectures
to London, but am not to begin until the 6th of
June; thence count three long weeks for the

course to fill, and I do not set out for Boston until
almost the 1st of July. By that time you must
make up your minds to let me come home. And
I am losing all these weeks and months of my
children : which I daily regret. I shall bring
home, with a good many experiences that are well
enough, a contentedness with home, I think, for
the rest of my days. Indeed, I did not come
here to get that, for I had no great good-will to
come away, but it is confirmed after seeing so many
of the " contemporaries."

I think we are fallen on shallow agencies. Is
there not one of your doctors who treats all disease
as diseases of the skin? All these orators in blouse
or broadcloth seem to me to treat the matter quite
literarily, and with the ends of the fingers. They
are earnest and furious, but about patent methods
and ingenious machines.

May 24. I find Paris a place of the largest liberty
that is, I suppose, in the civilized world ; and I am
thankful for it, just as I am for etherization, as a
resource when the accident of any hideous surgery
threatens me ; so Paris in the contingency of my ever
needing a place of diversion and independence : this
shall be my best-bower anchor. All winter I have
been admiring the English and disparaging the
French. Now in these weeks I have been correcting my prejudice, and the French rise many entire
degrees. Their universal good-breeding is a great

convenience; and the English and American
superstition in regard to broadcloth seems really
diminished, if not abolished, here. Knots of people
converse everywhere in the street, and the blouse,
or shirt-sleeves without blouse, becomes as readily
the centre of discourse as any other; and Superfine and Shirt, who never saw each other before,
converse in the most earnest yet deferential way.
Nothing like it could happen in England. They
are the most joyous race, and put the best face on
everything. Paris, to be sure, is their main performance; but one can excuse their vanity and pride,
it is so admirable a city. The Seine adorns Paris;
the Thames is out of sight in London. The Seine
is quayed all the way, so that broad streets on both
sides the river, as well as gay bridges, have all the
good of it, and the sun and moon and stars look
into it and are reflected. At London I cannot remember seeing the river. Here are magnificent
gardens, neither too large nor too small for the
convenience of the whole people, who spend every
evening in them. Here are palaces truly royal. If
they have cost a great deal of treasure at some
time, they have at least got a palace to show for it,
and a church too, in Notre Dame; whilst in England there is no palace, with all their floods of millions of guineas that have been spent. I witnessed
the great national *fête* on Sunday last, when over
120,000 people stood in the Champ de Mars, and

it was like an immense family; the perfect good-humor and fellowship is so habitual to them all. . . . You will like to know that I heard Lamartine speak to-day in the Chamber ; his *great* speech, the journals say, on Poland. Mr. Rush lent me his own ticket for the day. He did not speak, however, with much energy, but is a manly, handsome, gray-haired gentleman, with nothing of the rust of the man of letters, and delivers himself with great ease and superiority. . . . Clough is still here, and is my chief dependence at the dining hour and after-wards. I am to go to a *soirée* at De Tocqueville's to-night. My French is far from being as good as Madame de Staël's.

LONDON, *June* 8, 1848.

I came from Paris last Saturday hither, after spending twenty-five days there, and seeing little of the inside of the houses. I had one very pleasant hour with Madame d'Agout. . . . An artist of the name of Lehmann offered me also good introduc-tions, and I was to see Quinet, Lamennais, and others, but I turned my back and came to London. Still, Paris is much the more attractive to me of the two; in great part, no doubt, because it yields itself up entirely to serve us. I wholly forget what I have already written you concerning Paris, and must not venture on repeating my opinions, which are stereo-typed as usual, and will surely come in the same words. Besides, I have no right to be writing you

at all, dear wife, as I have been writing all day,
have read my second lecture to-day, and must
write all to-morrow on my third for Saturday. We
have a very moderate audience, and I was right, of
course, in not wishing to undertake it; for I spoil
my work by giving it this too rapid casting. . . .
It is a regret to me to lose this summer; for in
London all days and all seasons are alike, and I
have not realized one natural day. . . . Carlyle
talks of editing a newspaper, he has so much to
say about the evil times. You have probably already seen his articles. I send you two of them
in the *Spectator*. . . . It grieves me that I cannot
write to the children: to Edie for her printed letter, which is a treasure; to Ellen, who must be my
own secretary directly. I cannot hear that the
railroad bridge is built, and you would not have
me come home till I can go clean from Boston to
Concord? Will this idle scrawling tell you the
sad secret that I cannot with heavy head make the
smallest way in my inevitable morrow's work?

June 16. My last lecture is to-morrow, and is
far from ready. Then do not expect me to leave
England for a fortnight yet, for I must make
amends for my aristocratic lecturing in Edwards
Street, at prices which exclude all *my* public, by
reading three of my old chapters in Exeter Hall
to a city association. Our little company at
Marylebone has grown larger on each day, and is

truly a dignified company, in which several notable
men and women are patiently found. . . . Carlyle
takes a lively interest in our lectures, especially in
the third of the course [on the "Tendencies and
Duties of Men of Thought"], and he is a very
observed auditor, 't is very plain. The Duchess of
Sutherland, a magnificent lady, comes, and Lady
Ashburton, and Lord Lovelace, who is the husband
of "Ada, sole daughter of my house and heart,"
and Mrs. Jameson, and Spence (of Kirby and
Spence), and Barry Cornwall, and Lyell, and a
great many more curiosities ; but none better than
Jane Carlyle and Mrs. Bancroft, who honestly
come. Love to the little saints of the nursery. . . .

LONDON, *June* 21.

We finished the Marylebone course last Saturday
afternoon, to the great joy, doubt not, of all parties. It was a curious company that came to hear
the Massachusetts Indian, and partly new, Carlyle
says, at every lecture. Some of the company probably came to see others ; for, besides our high
Duchess of Sutherland and her sister, Lord Morpeth and the Duke of Argyle came, and other
aristocratic people ; and as there could be no pre-
diction what might be said, and therefore what
must be heard by them, and in the presence of
Carlyle and Monckton Milnes, etc., there might be
fun ; who knew? Carlyle, too, makes loud Scot-

tish-Covenanter gruntings of laudation, or at least
of consideration, when anything strikes him, to
the edifying of the attentive vicinity. As it befell,
no harm was done; no knives were concealed in
the words, more's the pity! Many things — supposed by some to be important, but on which the
better part suspended their judgment — were propounded, and the assembly at last escaped without
a revolution. Lord Morpeth sent me a compliment
in a note, and I am to dine with him on the 28th.
The Duchess of Sutherland sent for me to come to
lunch on Monday, and she would show me her
house. Lord Lovelace called on me on Saturday,
and I am to dine with him to-morrow, and see Byron's daughter. I met Lady Byron at Mrs. Jameson's, last week, one evening. She is a quiet, sensible woman, with this merit among others, that
she never mentions Lord Byron or her connection
with him, and lets the world discuss her supposed
griefs or joys in silence. Last night I visited
Leigh Hunt, who is a very agreeable talker, and
lays himself out to please; gentle, and full of anecdote. And there is no end of the Londoners.
Did I tell you that Carlyle talks seriously about
writing a newspaper, or at least short off-hand
tracts, to follow each other rapidly, on the political
questions of the day? I had a long talk with him
on Sunday evening, to much more purpose than we
commonly attain. He is solitary and impatient of

people ; he has no weakness of respect, poor man,
such as is granted to other scholars I wot of, and I
see no help for him. . . . I have been taxed with
neglecting the middle class by these West-End lectures, and now am to read expiatory ones in Exeter
Hall ; only three, — three dull old songs.

TO MISS HOAR.

LONDON, *June* 21, 1848.

DEAR ELIZABETH, — I have been sorry to let
two, or it may be three, steamers go without a word
to you since your last letter. But there was no
choice. Now my literary duties in London and
England are for this present ended, and one has
leisure not only to be glad that one's sister is alive,
but to say so. I believe you are very impatient of
my impatience to come home, but my pleasure, like
everybody's, is in my work, and I get many more
good hours in a Concord week than in a London
one. Then my *atelier* in all these years has gradually gathered a little sufficiency of tools and con-
veniences for me, and I have missed its apparatus
continually in England. The rich Athenæum
(Club) library, yes, and the dismaying library of the
British Museum could not vie with mine in convenience. And if my journeying has furnished
me new materials, I only wanted my *atelier* the
more. To be sure, it is our vice — mine, I mean
— never to be well ; and to make all our gains by

this indisposition. So you will not take my wish-
ings for any more serious calamity than the common lot. And yet you must be willing that I
should desire to come home and see you and the
rest. Dear thanks for all the true kindness your
letter brings. How gladly I would bring you such
pictures of my experiences here as you would bring
me, if you had them! Sometimes I have the
strongest wish for your daguerreotyping eyes and
narrative eloquence, but I think never, more than
the day before yesterday. The Duchess of Sutherland sent for me to come to lunch with her at
two o'clock, and she would show me Stafford House.
Now you must know this eminent lady lives in the
best house in the kingdom, the Queen's not excepted.
I went, and was received with great courtesy by
the Duchess, who is a fair, large woman, of good
figure, with much dignity and sweetness, and the
kindest manners. She was surrounded by company,
and she presented me to the Duke of Argyle, her
son-in-law, and to her sisters, the Ladies Howard.
After we left the table we went through this magnificent palace, this young and friendly Duke of Argyle
being my guide. He told me he had never seen so
fine a banquet hall as the one we were entering;
and galleries, saloons, and anterooms were all in
the same regal proportions and richness, full everywhere with sculpture and painting. We found the
Duchess in the gallery, and she showed me her

most valued pictures. . . . I asked her if she did
not come on fine mornings to walk alone amidst
these beautiful forms; which she professed she
liked well to do. She took care to have every best
thing pointed out to me, and invited me to come
and see the gallery alone whenever I liked. I assure you in this little visit the two parts of Duchess
and of palace were well and truly played. . . . I
have seen nothing so sumptuous as was all this.
One would so gladly forget that there was anything
else in England than these golden chambers and
the high and gentle people who walk in them!
May the grim Revolution with his iron hand — if
come he must — come slowly and late to Stafford
House, and deal softly with its inmates! . . .

Your affectionate brother,   WALDO.

TO HIS WIFE.

LONDON, *June* 28.

. . . All my duties will be quite at an end on Friday
night at Exeter Hall, and I have then to determine
which to choose of all the unseen spectacles of England. I have not seen Stonehenge, nor Chatsworth,
nor Canterbury, nor Cambridge, — nor even Eton
and Windsor, which lie so near London. I have
good friends who send for me, but I do not mean
to engage myself to new people or places. As Mr.
Burke said, " I have had my day; I can shut the
book." I am really very willing to see no new face

for a year to come, — unless only it were a face
that made all things new. There is very much to
be learned by coming to England and France.
The nations are so concentrated and so contrasted
that one learns to tabulate races and their manners
and traits as we do animals or chemical substances,
and look at them as through the old Swedish eye-
glass, each as one proper man. Also, it must be
owned, one meets now and then here with wonder-
fully witty men, all-knowing, who have tried everything and have everything, and are quite superior
to letters and science. What could they not, if
they only would? I saw such a one yesterday, with
the odd name, too, of Arthur Helps. On Sunday
I dined at Mr. Field's at Hampstead, and found the
Egyptian *savant* Mr. Sharpe, Rowland Hill (of
the Penny Post), Stanfield the painter, and other
good men. I breakfasted next morning with Stanfield, and went with him to see a famous gallery of
Turner's pictures at Tottenham. That day I dined
with Spence, and found Richard Owen, who is the
anatomist. To-morrow he is to show me his museum. I esteem him one of the best heads in England. Last evening I went to dine with Lord
Morpeth, and found my magnificent Duchess of
Sutherland, and the Duke and Duchess of Argyle,
and the Ladies Howard, and Lady Graham, and Mr.
Helps, so omniscient, as I said. . . . This morning
I breakfasted with him and Lady Lovelace, as Lord

L. wished to read me a certain paper he had been
writing on a book of Quetelet. We had quite a
scientific time, and I learned some good things. I
am to go there again to-morrow evening, to see Mrs.
Somerville. . . .

And so on, day after day while he is in London.
I have detailed at such length (though still far
from the whole) the breakfast, dinners, and recep-
tions, in order to show how much Emerson had at
heart to learn his London lesson. There was much
to learn, and he would not neglect his opportunities,
but the process was not altogether enjoyable to
him. "I find [he writes to Miss Fuller] that all
the old deoxygenation and asphyxia that have, in
town or in village, existed for me in that word 'a
party' exist unchanged in London palaces." But
he liked to see everything at its best. "To see the
country of success [he writes in his journal] I, who
delighted in success, departed." He writes to a
friend : —

LONDON, *March* 20, 1848.

. . . What shall I say to you of Babylon ? I see
and hear with the utmost diligence, and the lesson
lengthens as I go ; so that at some hours I incline
to take some drops or grains of lotus, forget my
home and selfish solitude, and step by step establish my acquaintance with English society. There
is nowhere so much wealth of talent and character

and social accomplishment; every star outshone
by one more dazzling, and you cannot move without coming into the light and fame of new ones.
I have seen, I suppose, some good specimens,
chiefly of the literary-fashionable and not of the
fashionable sort. . . . They have all carried the
art of agreeable sensations to a wonderful pitch;
they know everything, have everything; they are
rich, plain, polite, proud, and admirable. But,
though good for them, it ends in the using. I shall
or should soon have enough of this play for my
occasion. The seed-corn is oftener found in quite
other districts. . . . Perhaps it is no fault of Britain, — no doubt 't is because I grow old and cold,
— but no persons here appeal in any manner to
the imagination. I think even that there is no person in England from whom I expect more than
talent and information. But I am wont to ask
very much more of my benefactors, — expansions,
that amount to new horizons.

"I leave England [he writes to Miss Fuller]
with an increased respect for the Englishman. His
stuff or substance seems to be the best of the world.
I forgive him all his pride. My respect is the
more generous that I have no sympathy with him,
only an admiration."

The Englishman, Emerson says in a lecture
after his return, stands in awe of a fact as some-

thing final and irreversible, and confines his
thoughts and his aspirations to the means of dealing with it to advantage ; he does not seek to comprehend it, but only to utilize it for enjoyment or
display, at any rate to adapt himself to it ; and he
values only the faculties that enable him to do this.
He admires talent and is careless of ideas. " The
English have no higher heaven than Fate. Even
their ablest living writer, a man who has earned
his position by the sharpest insights, is politically
a fatalist. In his youth he announced himself as 'a
theoretical *sans-culotte*, fast threatening to become
a practical one.' Now he is practically in the English system, a Venetian aristocracy, with only a private stipulation in favor of men of genius. The
Norse heaven made the stern terms of admission
that a man could do something excellent with his
hands, his feet, or with his voice, eyes, ears, or with
his whole body ; and it was the heaven of the English ever since. Every Englishman is a House of
Commons, and expects you will not end your speech
without proposing a measure ; the scholars no less ;
a stanza of the ' Song of Nature ' they have no ear
for, and they do not value the expansive and medicinal influence of intellectual activity, studious of
truth, without a rash generalization."

It was this feeling, perhaps, that made him hesitate so long about lecturing in London, and made
his lecturing, when it was done, seem to him rather

ineffectual. The Marylebone course does not appear to have attracted much notice ; it was hardly mentioned in the London literary newspapers. He was careful in his letters to guard against the inference that his friends were slack, or that they had been too confident in their assurances, but it comes out incidentally in a letter to his brother William that instead of £200, which he had been led to expect, he received but £80 for the six lectures, when all expenses were paid.

The lack of response, at which he hints in the letter at the close of the course, would be the more felt by him because on this occasion he had made a new departure, in pursuance of a scheme he had long cherished of reading a series of connected discourses on the first principles of philosophy. In a letter to Miss Fuller, he says : —

" I am working away in these mornings at some papers which, if I do not, as I suppose I shall not, get ready for lectures here, will serve me in a better capacity as a kind of book of metaphysics, to print at home. Does not James Walker [Professor of Moral Philosophy at Harvard College] want relief, and to let me be his lieutenant for one semester to his class in Locke ? "

For the ordinary metaphysics he felt something as near contempt as was possible for so undogmatic a nature as his. " Who [he asks in his introduc-

tory lecture] has not looked into a metaphysical
book? And what sensible man ever looked twice?"
Yet the repulsiveness lay, he thought, not in the
subject, but in the way in which it is treated.
"Why should it not be brought into connection
with life and nature? Why cannot the laws and
powers of the mind be stated as simply and as at-
tractively as the physical laws are stated by Owen
and Faraday? Those too are facts, and suffer
themselves to be recorded, like stamens and verte-
bræ. But they have a higher interest as being
nearer to the mysterious seat of creation. The
highest value of physical science is felt when it
goes beyond its special objects and translates their
rules into a universal cipher, in which we read the
rules of the intellect and the rules of moral practice. It is this exceeding and universal part that
interests us, because it opens the true history of
that kingdom where a thousand years is as one day.
The Natural History of the Intellect would be an
enumeration of the laws of the world, — laws common to chemistry, anatomy, geometry, moral and
social life. In the human brain the universe is
reproduced with all its opulence of relations; it is
high time that it should be humanly and popularly
unfolded, that the Decalogue of the Intellect
should be written." He was not so hardy, he said,
as to think any single observer could accomplish
this, still less that he could; but he would attempt
some studies or sketches for such a picture.

" If any man had something sure and certain to tell on this matter, the entire population would come out to him. Ask any grave man of wide experience what is best in his experience, he will say: A few passages of plain dealing with wise people. The question I would ask of my friend is: Do you know what you worship? What is the religion of 1848? What is the mythology of 1848? Yet these questions which really interest men, how few can answer! Here are clergymen and presbyteries, but would questions like these come into mind when I see them? Here are Academies, yet they have not propounded these for any prize. Seek the literary circles, the class of fame, the men of splendor, of *bon-mots*, — will they yield me satisfaction? Bring the best wits together, and they are so impatient of each other, so vulgar, there is so much more than their wit, a plain man finds them so heavy, dull, and oppressive with bad jokes and conceit and stupefying individualism, that he comes to write in his tablets, ' Avoid the great man who is privileged to be an unprofitable companion.' The course of things makes the scholars either egotists, or worldly and jocose. O excellent Thersites! when you come to see me, if you would but leave your dog at the door. And then, was there ever prophet burdened with a message to his people who did not cloud our gratitude by a strange confusion of private folly with his public wisdom?

Others, though free of this besetting sin of sedentary men, escape from it by adopting the manners and estimate of the world, and play the game of conversation as they play billiards, for pastime and credit. Who can resist the charm of talent? The lover of truth loves power also. Among the men of wit and learning he could not withhold his homage from the gaiety, the power of memory, luck and splendor; such exploits of discourse, such feats of society! These were new powers, new mines of wealth. But when he came home his sequins were dry leaves. What with egotism on one side and levity on the other, we shall have no Olympus. And then you English have hard eyes. The English mind, in its proud practicalness, excludes contemplation. Yet the impression the stars and heavenly bodies make on us is surely more valuable than our exact perception of a tub or a table on the ground."

The English aristocracy, Emerson remarks in " English Traits," have never been addicted to contemplation; and Emerson's idealism, thus abruptly presented, was not calculated to win them to it. In his " Natural History of the Intellect," metaphysical notions are treated as if they were poetical images, which it would be useless and impertinent to explain. I shall return to this point on occasion of his resumption of the same topic in later years;

meantime it is obvious that, so conceived, there is little to be said about them to those who do not see things as we do. We can only lament that they are blind of their spiritual faculties, and use only their senses and their understanding; and they on their side will think that we are dreaming. Emerson's London audience, to be sure, would probably in any case have given themselves but little concern with his ideas; it was not the ideas, but the man, that attracted them, so far as they were attracted. Crabbe Robinson writes : [1] —

" It was with a feeling of pre-determined dislike that I had the curiosity to look at Emerson at Lord Northampton's a fortnight ago; when in an instant all my dislike vanished. He has one of the most interesting countenances I ever beheld, — a combination of intelligence and sweetness that quite disarmed me. I can do no better than tell you what Harriet Martineau says about him, which I think admirably describes the character of his mind: 'He is a man so *sui generis* that I don't wonder at his not being apprehended till he is seen. His influence is of an evasive sort. There is a vague nobleness and thorough sweetness about him which move people to their very depths without their being able to explain why. The logicians have an incessant triumph over him, but their triumph is of no avail. He conquers minds as well as hearts wherever he goes, and, without convincing any-

[1] *Diary of Henry Crabbe Robinson.* Boston, 1869 : p. 371.

body's reason of any one thing, exalts their reason
and makes their minds of more worth than they
ever were before.' "

Emerson seems to have felt no encouragement
to continue his "Song of Nature." Of the six lectures, but three were concerned with the Natural
History of the Intellect; the rest were miscellaneous papers which he had read in the North of England. At Exeter Hall he repeated three more of
these, and he seems afterwards to have read another
at Marylebone.

"At Exeter Hall [he writes to his wife] Carlyle
came on Tuesday evening, and was seated, by the
joyful committee, directly behind me as I spoke ; a
thing odious to me. Perhaps he will go with me
to Stonehenge next week. We have talked of it."

Carlyle at this time was in a mood in which Emerson's optimism was apt to call forth " showers
of vitriol "upon all men and things. They did not
meet often nor with much pleasure on either side ;
but their regard and affection for each other were
unabated, and when the time of Emerson's departure drew near, it was agreed between them that
they should make an excursion together to some
place of interest which Emerson had not seen.
Stonehenge was selected, and they made the visit
which Emerson records in " English Traits."

He sailed from Liverpool on the 15th of July,
and reached home before the end of the month.

CHAPTER XV.

LECTURING AT THE WEST. — DEATH OF MARGARET
FULLER. — DEATH OF EMERSON'S MOTHER. —
THE ANTI-SLAVERY CONFLICT.

1848-1865.

AFTER his return, Emerson lectured on "England," — keeping his notes by him, however, until they were published, seven years later, as "English Traits," — also on "France," and on various topics, in many places, extending his range gradually westward, until, in 1850, he went as far as St. Louis and Galena. Thenceforth, for nearly twenty years, a Western lecturing-tour was a regular employment of his winter; sometimes taking up the greater part of it. From one of these winter rounds he writes : —

"This climate and people are a new test for the wares of a man of letters. All his thin, watery matter freezes; 't is only the smallest portion of alcohol that remains good. At the lyceum the stout Illinoisian, after a short trial, walks out of the hall. The committees tell you that the people want a hearty laugh; and Saxe and Park Benjamin, who give this, are heard with joy. Well, I think, with Governor Reynolds, the people are always right (in a sense), and that the man of letters is to say, These are the new conditions to which I must conform. The architect who is asked to build a house to go upon the sea must not build a Parthenon, but a ship; and Shakspeare, or Franklin, or Esop, coming to Illinois, would say, I must give my wisdom a comic form, and I well know how to do it. And he is no master who cannot vary his form and carry his own end triumphantly through the most difficult conditions."

For his own part, he made no attempt to give his wisdom a comic form, though he took some pains with anecdotes and illustrations to make it more acceptable to a chance audience. But in the lectures of this time, for instance, those on the " Conduct of Life," if we compare them with " Nature " and the early lectures, we may observe a less absolute tone ; the idealism of ten years before remains as true as ever, but there is more explicit recognition of the actual conditions. In a lecture on the " Spirit of the Age," in 1850, he says of the idealists, " I regard them as themselves the effects of the age in which we live, and, in common with many other good facts, the efflorescence of the period, and predicting a good fruit that ripens, but not the creators they believe themselves. Compacts of brotherly love are an absurdity, inasmuch as they imply a sentimental resistance to the gravities and

tendencies which will steadily, by little and little,
pull down your air-castle. I believe in a future of
great equalities, but our inexperience is of inequalities. The hope is great, the day distant; but as
island and continents are built up by corallines, so
this juster state will come from culture on culture,
and we must work in the assurance that no ray of
light, no pulse of good, is ever lost."

He found in the West, on the whole, abundant
acceptance and sometimes a fellowship of thought
and feeling that made bright places in the dull expanse. The country and the people were interesting, could he have seen them at leisure and on his
own terms. Here was the heroic age come again :
" Here is America in the making, America in the
raw. But it does not want much to go to lecture,
and 't is pity to drive it. Everywhere the young
committees are the most friendly people." He was
much invited, and he was glad to go ; at any rate
for the sake of the money, which was needful to
him, his books still bringing him little in that kind.
Like his friend Agassiz, he could not afford the
time to make money ; but he would not be ham-
pered by the want of it, if the want were removable
by any reasonable amount of exertion. Upon his
return from one of these winter excursions he writes
in his journal : —

" 'T was tedious, the obstructions and squalor of

travel. The advantage of these offers made it
needful to go. It was, in short, — this dragging a
decorous old gentleman out of home and out of
position, to this juvenile career, — tantamount to
this : ' I 'll bet you fifty dollars a day for three
weeks that you will not leave your library, and
wade, and freeze, and ride, and run, and suffer all
manner of indignities, and stand up for an hour
each night reading in a hall ; ' and I answer, ' I 'll
bet I will.' I do it and win the nine hundred dollars."

PITTSBURGH, *March* 21, 1851.

DEAR LIDIAN, — I arrived here last night after
a very tedious and disagreeable journey from Philadelphia, by railway and canal, with little food and
less sleep ; two nights being spent in the rail-cars
and the third on the floor of a canal-boat, where the
cushion allowed me for a bed was crossed at the
knees by another tier of sleepers as long-limbed as
I, so that in the air was a wreath of legs ; and the
night, which was bad enough, would have been far
worse but that we were so thoroughly tired we
could have slept standing. The committee wished
me to lecture in the evening, if possible, and I, who
wanted to go to bed, answered that I had prelim-
inary statements to make in my first lecture, which
required a little time and faculty to make ready,
which now could not be had ; but if they would

let me read an old lecture I would omit the bed
and set out for the hall. So it was settled that I
should read poor old " England " once more, which
was done; for the committee wished nothing better, and, like all committees, think me an erratic
gentleman. only safe with a safe subject. . . .

SPRINGFIELD, ILLINOIS. *January* 11, 1853.

Here am I in the deep mud of the prairies, mis-
led, I fear, into this bog, not by a will-o -the-wisp,
such as shine in bogs, but by a young New Hampshire editor, who overestimated the strength of both
of us, and fancied I should glitter in the prairie
and draw the prairie birds and waders. It rains
and thaws incessantly, and if we step off the short
street we go up to the shoulders, perhaps, in mud.
My chamber is a cabin ; my fellow-boarders are
legislators. . . . Two or three governors or ex-
governors live in the house. But in the prairie we
are all new men just come, and must not stand for
trifles. 'T is of no use, then, for me to magnify
mine. But I cannot command daylight and solitude for study or for more than a scrawl, nor, I
fear, will my time here be paid for at any such
rate as was promised me. . . .

January 3, 1856. A cold, raw country this, and
plenty of night-travelling and arriving at four in
the morning to take the last and worst bed in the
tavern. Advancing day brings mercy and favor to

me, but not the sleep. . . . Mercury 15° below
zero. But I pick up some materials, as I go, for
my chapter of the Anglo-American, if I should
wish to finish that. I hope you are not so cold
and not so hard riders at home. I find well-dis-
posed, kindly people among these sinewy farmers
of the North, but in all that is called cultivation
they are only ten years old; so that there is plenty
of non-adaptation and yawning gulfs never bridged
in this ambitious lyceum system they are trying to
import. Their real interest is in prices, in sections
and quarter-sections of swamp-land.

As late as 1860 he writes : " *February* 13. . . .
I had travelled all the day before through Wis-
consin, with horses, and we could not for long
distances find water for them ; the wells were dry,
and people said they had no water, but snow, for
the house. The cattle were driven a mile or more
to the lake.

" *Marshall*, 17. At Kalamazoo a good visit, and
made intimate acquaintance with a college, wherein
I found many personal friends, though unknown to
me, and one Emerson was an established authority.
Even a professor or two came along with me to
Marshall to hear another lecture. My chief ad-
venture was the necessity of riding in a buggy
forty-eight miles to Grand Rapids; then, after lecture, twenty more on the return ; and the next

morning getting back to Kalamazoo in time for
the train hither at twelve. So I saw Michigan and
its forests and the Wolverines pretty thoroughly."

And in 1867 : " Yesterday morning in bitter cold
weather I had the pleasure of crossing the Mississippi in a skiff with Mr. ——, we the sole passengers, and a man and a boy for oarsmen. I have
no doubt they did their work better than the Harvard six could have done it, as much of the rowing
was on the surface of fixed ice, in fault of running
water. But we arrived without other accident than
becoming almost fixed ice ourselves ; but the long
run to the Tepfer House, the volunteered rubbing
of our hands by the landlord and clerks, and good
fire restored us."

Among the new lectures of the early part of this
period were those on the " Conduct of Life," afterwards elaborated in the first six essays of the volume of that title which appeared in 1860. The
elaboration consisted in striking out whatever could
be spared, especially anecdotes and quotations.
What was kept remained mostly as it was first
spoken ; but, in repeating his lectures, Emerson
was in the habit of using different papers together,
in a way that makes the particular title often an
uncertain indication of what was actually read upon
a given occasion. What was nominally the same
lecture was varied by the substitution of parts of

others, as one or another aspect of a group of subjects was prominent to his mind.   This practice,
together with his objection to reports in the newspapers and his carelessness to preserve his manuscripts after they were printed, makes it difficult
to assign precise dates to his writings after his return home in 1848.

He begins already to complain of failing productivity. " I scribble always a little, — much less than
formerly," he writes to Carlyle.[1]   Yet he was then
writing the "chapter on Fate," and the other essays
of the " Conduct of Life " which Carlyle reckoned
the best of all his books. And he was at the height
of his fame as a lecturer.   Even N. P. Willis, who
hitherto, he says, "had never taken the trouble to
go and behold him as a prophet, with the idea that
he was but an addition to the prevailing Boston
beverage of Channing-and-water," was attracted
to hear the lecture on " England," and gave a description [2] of Emerson's voice and appearance which
is worth reading, — with due allowance : —

" Emerson's voice is up to his reputation.   It
has a curious contradiction in it which we tried in
vain to analyze satisfactorily. But it is noble, altogether.   And what seems strange is to hear such a
voice proceeding from such a body. It is a voice

---

[1] *Carlyle-Emerson Correspondence*, ii. 217.

[2] Reproduced in *Hurrygraphs*, New York. 1851.

with shoulders in it, which he has not; with lungs
in it far larger than his; with a walk which the
public never see; with a fist in it which his own
hand never gave him the model for; and with a
gentleman in it which his parochial and 'bare-
necessaries-of-life' sort of exterior gives no other
betrayal of. We can imagine nothing in nature
(which seems too to have a type for everything)
like the want of correspondence between the Emerson that goes in at the eye and the Emerson that
goes in at the ear. . . . A heavy and vase-like blossom of a magnolia, with fragrance enough to per-
fume a whole wilderness, which should be lifted by
a whirlwind and dropped into a branch of an aspen,
would not seem more as if it could never have grown
there than Emerson's voice seems inspired and
foreign to his visible and natural body.   Indeed
(to use one of his own similitudes), his body seems
'never to have broken the umbilical cord' which
held it to Boston; while his soul has sprung to the
adult stature of a child of the universe, and his
voice is the utterance of the soul only."

In 1849 Emerson collected his separate addresses
and "Nature" in one volume. In July, 1850,
"Representative Men" was published.   In the
same month, Margaret Fuller, returning home from
Italy, was shipwrecked and drowned, with her husband and child, on Fire Island beach.

Whatever "fences" there may have been between them, she was perhaps the person most
closely associated with the boundless hope and the
happy activity of the Transcendental time, and he
readily joined her friends, William Henry Channing and James Freeman Clarke, in the Memoirs
that were published in 1852. As to his own contribution he writes in his journal : —

"All that can be said is that she represents an
interesting hour and group in American cultivation ; then that she was herself a fine, generous,
inspiring, vinous talker, who did not outlive her
influence ; and a kind of justice requires of us a
monument, because crowds of vulgar people taunt
her with want of position."

But he was glad that her nearer friends were
able to say much more.

In 1853 Emerson's mother died at his house,
where she had lived since his marriage. He writes
to his brother William : —

CONCORD, *November* 19, 1853.

. . . It was an end so graduated and tranquil,
all pain so deadened, and the months and days of
it so adorned by her own happy temper and by so
many attentions of so many friends whom it drew
to her, that even in these last days almost all gloom
was removed from death. Only as we find there is

one less room to go to for sure society in the house, one less sure home in the house. I would gladly have asked, had it been anywise practicable, that the English liturgy should be read at her burial : for she was born a subject of King George, and had been in her childhood so versed in that service that, though she had lived through the whole existence of this nation, and was tied all round to later things, it seemed still most natural to her, and the Book of Common Prayer was on her bureau.

After the " Conduct of Life," Emerson's chief occupation was " English Traits," which was published in 1856. The essays that make up " Society and Solitude " were all written before 1860 ; most of them long before, though the book was not published until 1870.

Emerson showed little appearance of old age during the period of which I am writing, yet he had long since begun to think and speak of himself as an old man, because, he says, he did not so readily find a thought waiting for him when he went to his study in the morning. In 1847 (when he was forty-four) he writes to Carlyle : " In my old age I am coming to see you." And, ten years before, he writes in his diary : " After thirty a man is too sensible of the strait limitations which his physical constitution sets to his activity. The stream feels its banks, which it had forgotten in the run and overflow of the first meadows." In 1850 he writes: "Unless I task myself I have no thoughts." Whether it would have been better for him had he tasked himself by some regular occupation may be a question. He seems at times to have thought so. I suppose the visit to England was undertaken partly with this feeling, and the compiling of his notes served him to some extent as a regular task during the next six or seven years.

Meanwhile his tranquil meditations on his own topics were more and more broken in upon by the noise of external affairs. A matter which had always been of grave moment, but hitherto had not seemed to touch him specially, became of pressing instance, — the encroachments of slavery. The thunder-clouds which had long been muttering on the Southern horizon, certain to come up some day, began to rise higher and to growl menace to the peace and the honor of New England. The imminence of the crisis did not force itself upon him all at once. In January, 1845, Emerson, as one of the curators of the Concord Lyceum, had urged upon his colleagues the acceptance of a lecture on slavery, by Wendell Phillips, on two grounds: —

" *First*, because the Lyceum was poor, and should add to the length and variety of the entertainment by all innocent means, especially when a discourse from one of the best speakers in the common-wealth was volunteered. *Second*, because I thought, in the present state of the country, the particular subject of slavery had a commanding right to be heard in all places in New England, in season and out of season. The people must be content to be plagued with it from time to time until something was done and we had appeased the negro blood so."

In the same month a public meeting was held in the Concord Court-House (January 26, 1845), to take counsel about the case of Mr. Samuel Hoar, of Concord, who had been sent to South Carolina as the agent of Massachusetts to protect the rights of her colored citizens, and was expelled by the mob : also upon the question of the annexation of Texas. Emerson was one of the business committee (Dr. John Gorham Palfrey being the chairman), who reported, says a writer in the *Liberator* (January 31), resolutions rather mild in character, declining to countenance anything that looked to the dissolution of the Union. On the 22d of September there was a convention at Concord of persons opposed to the annexation. Emerson was present, and, I suppose, made a speech; at least I find among his papers what seems to be the partial draft of a speech of that time, though it is not mentioned in the *Liberator*, being regarded, perhaps, as of too mild a type for the occasion. It was but lately that he had decided — moved, per-

haps by the eloquence of his friend William Henry
Channing — against annexation. In 1844 he writes
in his journal : —

"The question of the annexation of Texas is
one of those which look very differently to the centuries and to the years. It is very certain that
the strong British race, which have now overrun
so much of this continent, must also overrun that
tract, and Mexico and Oregon also ; and it will, in
the course of ages, be of small import by what
particular occasions and methods it was done."

In the paper of 1845 he says: "The great majority
of Massachusetts people are essentially opposed to
the annexation, but they have allowed their voice to
be muffled by the persuasion that it would be of no
use. This makes the mischief of the present con-
juncture, — our timorous and imbecile behavior,
and not the circumstance of the public vote. The
event is of no importance ; the part taken by Massachusetts is of the last importance. The addition
of Texas to the Union is not material; the same
population will possess her in either event, and
similar laws ; but the fact that an upright community have held fast their integrity, — that is a great
and commanding event. I wish that the private
position of the men of this neighborhood, of this
county, of this State, should be erect in this matter. If the State of Massachusetts values the
treaties with Mexico, let it not violate them. If it

approves of annexation, but does not like the authority by which it is made, let it say so. If it
approves the act and the authority, but does not
wish to join hands with a barbarous country in
which some men propose to eat men, or to steal
men, let it say that well. If on any or all of these
grounds it disapproves the annexation, let it utter a
cheerful and peremptory No, and not a confused,
timid, and despairing one."

In 1851 the mischief had come nearer; it was
in the streets, it was at the door. The Fugitive
Slave Law of 1850 made every man in Massachusetts liable to official summons in aid of the return
of escaped slaves. And it had been passed with
the aid of Massachusetts votes, and with the outspoken advocacy of the foremost Massachusetts
man. Mr. Webster had gone about upholding the
righteousness of the law, and declaring that he
found no serious opposition to it in the North.
And, in fact, instead of being execrated and resisted, it appeared to be received with acquiescence,
if not with approval, by most men of standing and
influence in the State. Here, Emerson felt, was
an issue which he had not made and could not
avoid. On Sunday evening, May 3, 1851, he delivered an address to the citizens of Concord, " on
the great question of these days," in a tone which
must have been more satisfactory to his abolitionist friends. He accepted the invitation to speak,
he said, because there seemed to be no option : —

"The last year has forced us all into politics. There is an infamy in the air. I wake in the morning with a painful sensation which I carry about all day, and which, when traced home, is the odious remembrance of that ignominy which has fallen on Massachusetts. I have lived all my life in this State, and never had any experience of personal inconvenience from the laws until now. They never came near me, to my discomfort, before. But the Act of Congress of September 18, 1850, is a law which every one of you will break on the earliest occasion, — a law which no man can obey or abet the obeying without loss of self-respect and forfeiture of the name of a gentleman."

Such was his indignation against "this filthy law" that it moved him for once in his life to personal denunciation, and this of a man who had hitherto been to him an object of admiration and pride. From his boyhood he had been an eager listener to Mr. Webster; he exulted in the magnificent presence of the man, and in the very tones of his voice. In 1843 Webster came to Concord to argue an important case, and was a guest at Emerson's house, where there was a gathering of neighbors to meet him.

"Webster [he writes in his journal] appeared among these best lawyers of the Suffolk bar like a schoolmaster among his boys. Understanding language and the use of the positive degree, all his

words tell. What is small he shows as small; and
makes the great, great. His splendid wrath, when
his eyes become fires, is good to see, so intellectual
it is, — the wrath of the fact and cause he espouses,
and not all personal to himself. One feels every
moment that he goes for the actual world, and
never for the ideal. Perhaps it was this, perhaps
it was a mark of having outlived some of my once
finest pleasures, that I found no appetite to return
to the court in the afternoon. He behaves admirably well in society. These village parties must be
dish-water to him, yet he shows himself just good-
natured, just nonchalant enough; and he has his
own way, without offending any one or losing any
ground. He quite fills our little town, and I doubt
if I shall get settled down to writing until he is
well gone from the county. He is a natural emperor of men; they remark in him the kingly talent
of remembering persons accurately, and knowing
at once to whom he has been introduced, and to
whom not. It seems to me the quixotism of criticism to quarrel with Webster because he has not
this or that fine evangelical property. He is no
saint, but the wild olive-wood, ungrafted yet by
grace, but, according to his lights, a very true and
admirable man. His expensiveness seems necessary to him; were he too prudent a Yankee it
would be a sad deduction from his magnificence.
I only wish he would not truckle; I do not care
how much he spends."

In 1851 the truckling had gone too far, and Mr. Webster's example seemed to have debauched the public conscience of Emerson's native town. His beloved Boston, "spoiled by prosperity, must bow its ancient honor in the dust. The tameness is indeed complete; all are involved in one hot haste of terror, — presidents of colleges and professors, saints and brokers, lawyers and manufacturers; not a liberal recollection, not so much as a snatch of an old song for freedom, dares intrude on their passive obedience. I met the smoothest of Episcopal clergymen the other day, and, allusion being made to Mr. Webster's treachery, he blandly replied, 'Why, do you know, I think that the great action of his life.' I have as much charity for Mr. Webster, I think, as any one has. Who has not helped to praise him? Simply he was the one eminent American of our time whom we could produce as a finished work of nature. We delighted in his form and face, in his voice, in his eloquence, in his daylight statement. But now he, our best and proudest, the first man of the North, in the very moment of mounting the throne, has harnessed himself to the chariot of the planters. Mr. Webster tells the President that he has been in the North, and has found no man whose opinion is of any weight who is opposed to the law. Ah! Mr. President, trust not to the information. This 'final settlement,' this 'measure of pacification and union,'

has turned every dinner-table into a debating-club
and made one sole subject for conversation and
painful thought throughout the continent, namely,
slavery. Mr. Webster must learn that those to
whom his name was once dear and honored disown him ; that he who was their pride in the woods
and mountains of New England is now their mortification. Mr. Webster, perhaps, is only following
the laws of his blood and constitution. I suppose
his pledges were not quite natural to him. He is
a man who lives by his memory; a man of the
past, not a man of faith and of hope. All the
drops of his blood have eyes that look downward,
and his finely developed understanding only works
truly and with all its force when it stands for animal good; that is, for property. He looks at the
Union as an estate, a large farm, and is excellent
in the completeness of his defence of it so far.
What he finds already written he will defend.
Lucky that so much had got well written when he
came, for he has no faith in the power of self-gov-
ernment. Not the smallest municipal provision, if
it were new, would receive his sanction. In Massachusetts in 1776, he would, beyond all question,
have been a refugee. He praises Adams and Jefferson, but it is a past Adams and Jefferson. A
present Adams or Jefferson he would denounce.
The destiny of this country is great and liberal,
and is to be greatly administered; according to

what is and is to be, and not according to what is
dead and gone. In Mr. Webster's imagination the
American Union was a huge Prince Rupert's drop,
which, if so much as the smallest end be shivered
off, the whole will snap into atoms. Now the fact is
quite different from this. The people are loyal, law-
abiding. The union of this people is a real thing;
an alliance of men of one stock, one language, one
religion, one system of manners and ideas. It
can be left to take care of itself. As much union
as there is the statutes will be sure to express. As
much disunion as there is, no statutes can long conceal. The North and the South, — I am willing to
leave them to the facts. If they continue to have
a binding interest, they will be pretty sure to find
it out; if not, they will consult their peace in parting. But one thing appears certain to me, that the
Union is at an end as soon as an immoral law is
enacted. He who writes a crime into the statute-
book digs under the foundations of the Capitol.
One intellectual benefit we owe to the late disgraces.
The crisis had the illuminating power of a sheet of
lightning at midnight. It showed truth. It ended
a good deal of nonsense we had been wont to hear
and to repeat, on the 19th April, the 17th June,
and the 4th July. It showed the slightness and
unreliableness of our social fabric. . . . What is
the use of admirable law forms and political forms
if a hurricane of party feeling and a combination

of moneyed interests can beat them to the ground?
. . . The poor black boy, whom the fame of Boston had reached in the recesses of a rice-swamp or
in the alleys of Savannah, on arriving here finds all
this force employed to catch him. The famous
town of Boston is his master's hound. . . . The
words of John Randolph, wiser than he knew, have
been ringing ominously in all echoes for thirty
years : ' We do not govern the people of the North
by our black slaves, but by their own white slaves.'
. . . They come down now like the cry of fate, in
the moment when they are fulfilled.

  " What shall we do? First, abrogate this law;
then proceed to confine slavery to slave States, and
help them effectually to make an end of it. Since
it is agreed by all sane men of both parties (or
was yesterday) that slavery is mischievous, why
does the South itself never offer the smallest counsel of her own? I have never heard in twenty
years any project except Mr. Clay's. Let us hear
any project with candor and respect. It is really
the project for this country to entertain and accomplish. It is said it will cost a thousand millions of
dollars to buy the slaves, which sounds like a fab-
ulous price. But if a price were named in good
faith, I do not think any amount that figures could
tell would be quite unmanageable. Nothing is impracticable to this nation which it shall set itself
to do. Were ever men so endowed, so placed, so

weaponed? their power of territory seconded by a
genius equal to every work. By new arts the earth
is subdued, and we are on the brink of new wonders. The sun paints; presently we shall organize
the echo, as now we do the shadow. These thirty
nations are equal to any work, and are every moment stronger. In twenty-five years they will be
fifty millions; is it not time to do something besides ditching and draining? Let them confront
this mountain of poison, and shovel it once for all
down into the bottomless pit. A thousand millions
were cheap.

"But grant that the heart of financiers shrinks
within them at these colossal amounts and the em-
barrassments which complicate the problem, and
that these evils are to be relieved only by the wisdom of God working in ages, and by what instru-
ments none can tell; — one thing is plain. We
cannot answer for the Union, but we must keep
Massachusetts true. Let the attitude of the State
be firm. Massachusetts is a little State. Countries have been great by ideas. Europe is little,
compared with Asia and Africa. Greece was the
least part of Europe; Attica a little part of that,
one tenth of the size of Massachusetts, yet that
district still rules the intellect of men. Judæa
was a petty country. Yet these two, Greece and
Judæa, furnish the mind and the heart by which
the rest of the world is sustained. And Massa-

chusetts is little, but we must make it great by
making every man in it true. Let us respect the
Union to all honest ends, but let us also respect an
older and wider union; the laws of nature and rectitude. Massachusetts is as strong as the universe
when it does that. We will never intermeddle
with your slavery, but you can in no wise be suffered to bring it to Cape Cod or Berkshire. This
law must be made inoperative. It must be abro-
gated and wiped out of the statute-book; but,
whilst it stands there, it must be disobeyed. Let
us not lie nor steal, nor help to steal, and let us not
call stealing by any fine names, such as union or
patriotism."

Dr. Palfrey was then candidate for Congress
from Emerson's district, and Emerson repeated his
speech at several places in Middlesex County, hoping, he said, to gain some votes for his friend;
among other places, Cambridge, where he was interrupted by clamors from some of "the young
gentlemen from the college," Southern gentlemen,
the newspaper said; but this was denied by a Southern student, who wrote to say that Southern gentlemen had too much respect for themselves and regard for the rights of others to condescend to any
such petty demonstrations of dissent, and that the
disturbers were Northern men who were eager to
keep up a show of fidelity to the interests of the
South. Mr. Whipple, in his reminiscences of Em-

erson,[1] says that Emerson was not disturbed by the
hissing, but seemed absolutely to enjoy it. This
would argue a temperament more alive than Emerson's to the joys of conflict. He would not be disturbed, but he must have been profoundly grieved
to see men of his own order — young men, too,
whom above all others he would have wished to
influence — so utterly wrong - headed. Professor
James B. Thayer, who was present, says in a note
to me : —

" The hisses, shouts, and cat-calls made it impossible for Mr. Emerson to go on. Through all this
there never was a finer spectacle of dignity and com-
posure than he presented. He stood with perfect
quietness until the hubbub was over, and then went
on with the next word. It was as if nothing had
happened : there was no repetition, no allusion to
what had been going on, no sign that he was
moved, and I cannot describe with what added
weight the next words fell."

The college authorities were supposed to be on
the side of the South, and upon another occasion
Mr. Horace Mann, speaking in Cambridge, was interrupted by shouts of applause for " Professor
—— and Mr. Potter, of Georgia," a collocation
not distinctly understood, but felt to convey a general Southern sentiment. In fact, all the " author-

---

[1] *Recollections of Eminent Men.* By Edwin Percy Whipple.
Boston, 1887: p. 140.

ities," nearly all the leading men among the scholars and the clergy, as well as the merchants, were
upon that side or but feebly against it. This, to
Emerson, was a most depressing experience; it
seemed, he said, to show that our civilization was
rotten before it was ripe. He could not take a very
active share in the agitation of the question, but
he made no secret of his opinion, and the *Boston
Daily Advertiser* remarked, more in sorrow than
in anger, that Mr. Emerson attended the anti-
slavery meetings, and might be fairly looked on as
a decided abolitionist.

On the 7th of March, 1854, the anniversary of
Webster's famous speech in 1850, Emerson read
in New York the address on the Fugitive Slave Law
which has been published in his writings.[1] In
January of the following year he delivered one of
the lectures in a course on slavery, at the Tremont
Temple in Boston, in which men of different sentiments, from all parts of the country, were invited
to take part. He writes to his brother William : —

CONCORD, *January* 17, 1855.

. . . I am trying hard in these days to see some
light in the dark slavery question, to which I am
to speak next week in Boston. But to me as to so
many 't is like Hamlet's task imposed on so unfit
an agent as Hamlet. And the mountains of cot-

---

[1] *Collected Writings,* xi. 203.

ton and sugar seem unpersuadable by any words as
Sebastopol to a herald's oration. Howbeit, if we
only drum, we must drum well.

"The subject [he said in his speech] seems exhausted, and it would perhaps have been well to
leave the discussion of slavery entirely to its pa-
trons and natural fathers. But they, with one or
two honorable exceptions, have refused to come;
feeling, perhaps, that there is nothing to be said.
Nor for us is there anything further to say of slavery itself. An honest man is soon weary of crying 'thief;' it is for us to treat it, not as a thing
by itself, but as it stands in our system. A high
state of general health cannot coexist with mortal
disease in any part. Slavery is an evil, as cholera
or typhus is, that will be purged out by the health
of the system. Being unnatural and violent, we
know that it will yield at last, and go with canni-
balism and burking; and as we cannot refuse to
ride in the same planet with the New Zealander, so
we must be content to go with the Southern planter, and say, You are you and I am I, and God
send you an early conversion. But to find it here
in our own sunlight, here in the heart of Puritan
traditions, under the eye of the most ingenious, in-
dustrious, and self-helping men in the world, stag-
gers our faith in progress; for it betrays a stupen-
dous frivolity in the heart and head of a society

without faith, without aims, dying of inanition.
An impoverishing scepticism scatters poverty, disease, and cunning through our opinions, then
through our practice. Young men want object,
want foundation. They would gladly have somewhat to do adequate to the powers they feel, some
love that would make them greater than they are ;
which not finding, they take up some second-best,
some counting-room or railroad or whatever credit-
able employment, — not the least of whose uses is
the covert it affords. Among intellectual men you
will find a waiting for, an impatient quest for, more
satisfying knowledge. It is believed that ordina-
rily the mind grows with the body; that the moment of thought comes with the power of action ;
and that, in nations, it is in the time of great external power that their best minds have appeared.
But, in America, a great imaginative soul, a broad
cosmopolitan mind, has not accompanied the immense industrial energy. Among men of thought,
the readers of books, the unbelief is found as it is
in the laymen. A dreary superficiality; critics
instead of thinkers, punsters instead of poets.
Yes, and serious men are found who think our
Christianity and religion itself effete ; forms and
sentiments that belonged to the infancy of mankind.

"I say intellectual men ; but are there such? Go
into the festooned and tempered brilliancy of the
drawing-rooms, and see the fortunate youth of both

sexes, the flower of our society, for whom every favor, every accomplishment, every facility, has been
secured. Will you find genius and courage expand-
ing those fair and manly forms? Or is their beauty
only a mask for an aged cunning? No illusions for
them. A few cherished their early dreams and resisted to contumacy the soft appliances of fashion.
But they tired of resistance and ridicule, they fell
into file, and great is the congratulation of the refined companions that these self-willed protestants
have settled down into sensible opinions and practices. God instructs men through the imagination.
The ebb of thought drains the law, the religion, the
education of the land. Look at our politics, — the
great parties coeval with the origin of the government, — do they inspire us with any exalted hope?
Does the Democracy stand really for the good of
the many? Of the poor? For the elevation of
entire humanity? The party of property, of education, has resisted every progressive step. They
would nail the stars to the sky. With their eyes
over their shoulders they adore their ancestors, the
framers of the Constitution. What means this
desperate grasp on the past, except that they have
no law in their own mind, no principle, no hope, no
future of their own? Some foundation we must
have, and if we can see nothing, we cling desper-
ately to those who we believe can see.

" There are periods of occultation, when the light

of mind seems partially withdrawn from nations as well as from individuals. In the French Revolution there was a day when the Parisians took a strumpet from the street, seated her in a chariot, and led her in procession, saying, 'This is the Goddess of Reason.' And in 1850 the American Congress passed a statute which ordained that justice and mercy should be subject to fine and imprisonment, and that there existed no higher law in the universe than the Constitution and this paper statute which uprooted the foundations of rectitude and denied the existence of God. This was the hiding of the light. But the light shone, if it was intercepted from us. What is the effect of this evil government? To discredit government. When the public fails in its duty, private men take its place. And we have a great debt to the brave and faithful men who, in the hour and place of the evil act, made their protest for themselves and their countrymen by word and deed. When the American government and courts are false to their trust, men disobey the government and put it in the wrong.

"Yet patriotism, public opinion, have a real meaning, though there is so much counterfeit, rag-money abroad under the name. It is delicious to act with great masses to great aims. The State is a reality; Society has a real function, that of our race being to evolve liberty. It is a noble office;

for liberty is the severest test by which a government can be tried. All history goes to show that it is the measure of all national success. Most unhappily, this universally accepted duty and feeling has been antagonized by the calamity of Southern slavery; and that institution, through the stronger personality, shall I say, of the Southern people, and through their systematic devotion to politics, has had the art so to league itself with the government as to check and pervert the natural sentiment of the people by their respect for law and statute. But we shall one day bring the States shoulder to shoulder and the citizens man to man to exterminate slavery. Why in the name of common sense and the peace of mankind is not this made the subject of instant negotiation and settlement? Why not end this dangerous dispute on some ground of fair compensation on one side, and of satisfaction on the other to the conscience of the Free States? It is really the great task fit for this country to accomplish, to buy that property of the planters, as the British nation bought the West Indian slaves. I say buy, — never conceding the right of the planter to own, but that we may acknowledge the calamity of his position, and bear a countryman's share in relieving him; and because it is the only practicable course, and is innocent. Here is a right social or public function, which one man cannot do, which all men must do. 'T is said it will cost two thousand millions of dollars. Was there ever any contribution that was so enthusiastically paid as this will be? We will have a chimney-tax. We will give up our coaches, and wine, and watches. The churches will melt their plate. The father of his country shall wait, well pleased, a little longer for his monument; Franklin for his; the Pilgrim Fathers for theirs; and the patient Columbus for his. The mechanics will give; the needle-women will give; the children will have cent-societies. Every man in the land will give a week's work to dig away this accursed mountain of sorrow once and forever out of the world."

In all these years from the passage of the Fugitive Slave Bill in 1850 to its natural fruit in 1861, the politics of the day occupy an unusual space in Emerson's journals, and intrude themselves upon all his speculations. A lecture on Art has an exordium on the state of the country; in Morals, his impatience of the lukewarm good-nature of the North gives value even to malignity: —

" I like to hear of any strength; as soon as they speak of the malignity of Swift, we prick up our ears. I fear there is not strength enough in America that anything can be qualified as malignant. I fancy the Americans have no passions; alas! only appetites."

He did not doubt that the right would win; but he did not believe that it would win easily: —

" Our success is sure ; its roots are in our poverty, our Calvinism, our schools, our thrifty habitual
industry ; in our snow and east wind and farm-life.
But it is of no use to tell me, as Brown and others
do, that the Southerner is not a better fighter than
the Northerner, when I see that uniformly a Southern minority prevails and gives the law. Why,
but because the Southerner is a fighting man, and
the Northerner is not ? "

He had been much impressed in his college-days
by the forceful personality of the Southern boys ;
he says he always fell a prey to their easy assurance, and he had seen the same effect on others
ever since. In a lecture on " New England " in
1843, he says : —

" The Southerner lives for the moment ; relies
on himself and conquers by personal address. He
is wholly there in that thing which is now to be
done. The Northerner lives for the year, and does
not rely on himself, but on the whole apparatus of
means he is wont to employ ; he is only half present
when he comes in person ; he has a great reserved
force which is coming up. The result corresponds. The Southerner is haughty, wilful, generous, unscrupulous ; will have his way and has it.
The Northerner must think the thing over, and his
conscience and his common sense throw a thousand
obstacles between himself and his wishes, which
perplex his decision and unsettle his behavior. The

Northerner always has the advantage at the end of
ten years, and the Southerner always has the advantage to-day."

The disadvantage of the reflective temperament
and the habit of thinking what may be said for the
other side, in comparison with the impulsive habit
that needs no self-justification but acts at once, was
illustrated at large in the behavior of the North
twenty years later. Emerson himself was an example of it. He had not the happiness of being
able to look upon slaveholding simply as an outrage, to be resisted and put down without parley; he
could not help feeling some relative justification for
the slaveholder ; and this feeling debarred him from
complete sympathy with the abolitionists. He admired their courage and persistence, but he could
not act with them, — any more than they could
entertain his scheme for buying the slaves, or re-
press their scorn when he spoke of the " calamity "
of the planter's position. He says (in his journal)
of one of the foremost abolitionists : —

" —— is venerable in his place, like the tart
Luther ; but he cannot understand anything you
say, and neighs like a horse when you suggest a
new consideration, as when I told him that the fate
element in the negro question he had never considered."

But, as events thickened towards the crisis, he
was forced to see that the encroachments of slavery

must be resisted by force. In May, 1856, in his speech at Concord, on occasion of the assault upon Mr. Sumner in the Senate-Chamber of the United States, he says: "I think we must get rid of slavery or we must get rid of freedom." And at the Kansas-Relief meeting at Cambridge, in September of that year, he warmly advocated the sending of arms to the settlers in Kansas, for resistance to the pro-slavery raids from Missouri, and thought that aid should be contributed by the legislature of Massachusetts. In 1857 John Brown came to Concord, and gave, Emerson says, "a good account of himself in the Town Hall last night to a meeting of citizens. One of his good points was the folly of the peace party in Kansas, who believed that their strength lay in the greatness of their wrongs, and so discountenanced resistance. He wished to know if their wrong was greater than the negro's, and what kind of strength that gave to the negro."

In a lecture on "Courage," in Boston (November, 1859), Emerson quoted Brown's words about "the unctuous cant of peace parties in Kansas," and called upon the citizens of Massachusetts to say, "We are abolitionists of the most absolute abolition, as every man must be. Only the Hottentots, only the barbarous or semi-barbarous societies, are not. We do not try to alter your laws in Alabama, nor yours in Japan or the Feejee Islands, but we

do not admit them or permit a trace of them here.
Nor shall we suffer you to carry your Thuggism
north, south, east, or west, into a single rod of territory which we control. We intend to set and
keep a *cordon sanitaire* all round the infected
district, and by no means suffer the pestilence to
spread." Speaking of the different kinds of courage corresponding to different levels of civilization,
he says : " With the shooting complexion, like the
cobra capello and scorpion, that abounds mostly in
warm climates, war is the safest terms. That marks
them, and if they cross the line they can be dealt
with as all fanged animals must be."

It does not appear that Emerson was acquainted
in advance with Brown's Virginia project, but in
this lecture, which was delivered while Brown was
lying in prison under sentence of death, he spoke
of him as " that new saint, than whom none purer
or more brave was ever led by love of men into
conflict and death, — the new saint awaiting his
martyrdom, and who, if he shall suffer, will make
the gallows glorious like the cross." In the essay
as published ten years later, these passages were
omitted ; distance of time having brought the case
into a juster perspective.

But the strongest mark of the disturbance of
Emerson's native equilibrium is to be found in his
condemnation of the judges and the state officials
for not taking the law into their own hands. Law,

he said, is the expression of the universal will; an immoral law is void, because it contravenes the will of humanity. And he passed at once to the conclusion, not merely that the Fugitive Slave Law was to be disobeyed by those who felt it to be immoral, but that the official interpreters and the executive were bound to make and enforce righteous laws of their own; than which nothing could well be more opposed to his own principles. " Justice was poisoned at the fountain. In our Northern States no judge appeared of sufficient character and intellect to ask, not whether the slave law was constitutional, but whether it was right. The first duty of a judge was to read the law in accordance with equity, and, if it jarred with equity, to disown the law." (Speech of January 26, 1855.) Yet no one could be more prompt than he to repudiate the claim of any one to decide for other people what is right, or what is the will of humanity. He had been protesting against such assumptions all his life.

The speech about John Brown spoiled his welcome in Philadelphia, and an invitation to lecture there was withdrawn; apparently also to some extent in Boston, though he lectured in other parts of New England and at the West. He made no more anti-slavery speeches at this time, but being invited by Mr. Wendell Phillips to speak at the annual meeting of the Massachusetts Anti-Slavery Society in 1861 (Tremont Temple, January 24), he took a place on the platform, and, when he was called upon, tried to make himself heard, but in vain.[1] " Esteeming such invitation a command [he writes in his journal], though sorely against my inclination and habit, I went, and, though I had nothing to say, showed myself. If I were dumb, yet I would have gone, and mowed and muttered, or made signs. The mob roared whenever I attempted to speak, and after several beginnings I withdrew."

The outbreak of the war relieved Emerson from his worst apprehension, that some show of peace and union would be patched up when no real union existed. For two winters (1859–61) he had given no course of lectures in Boston, though he had frequently addressed Theodore Parker's congregation in the absence and after the death of their pastor. But in April, 1861, he was in the midst of a course on " Life and Literature," when the news came of the attack on Fort Sumter; not unexpected, yet with an effect on the public temper that took Emerson as well as others by surprise. In place of the lecture which had been announced, on the " Doctrine of Leasts," he gave one entitled

[1] There is an account of the meeting in the *Liberator*, February 1, 1861.

" Civilization at a Pinch," in which he confessed
his relief that now, at length, the dragon that had
been coiled round us and from which we could not
escape, had uncoiled himself and was thrust outside the door. " How does Heaven help us when
civilization is at a hard pinch? Why, by a whirlwind of patriotism, not believed to exist, but now
magnetizing all discordant masses under its terrific
unity. It is an affair of instincts; we did not
know we had them; we valued ourselves as cool
calculators; we were very fine with our learning
and culture, with our science that was of no country, and our religion of peace; — and now a sentiment mightier than logic, wide as light, strong as
gravity, reaches into the college, the bank, the
farm-house, and the church. It is the day of the
populace; they are wiser than their teachers.
Every parish-steeple marks a recruiting - station;
every bell is a tocsin. Go into the swarming town-
halls, and let yourself be played upon by the stormy
winds that blow there. The interlocutions from
quiet-looking citizens are of an energy of which I
had no knowledge. How long men can keep a secret! I will never again speak lightly of a crowd.
We are wafted into a revolution which, though at
first sight a calamity of the human race, finds all
men in good heart, in courage, in a generosity of
mutual and patriotic support. We have been very
homeless, some of us, for some years past, — say

since 1850; but now we have a country again. Up
to March 4, 1861, in the very place of law we
found, instead of it, war. Now we have forced
the conspiracy out-of-doors. Law is on this side
and War on that. It was war then, and it is war
now; but declared war is vastly safer than war un-
declared. This affronting of the common sense of
mankind, this defiance and cursing of friends as
well as foes, has hurled us, willing or unwilling,
into opposition; and the nation which the Seces-
sionists hoped to shatter has to thank them for a
more sudden and hearty union than the history of
parties ever showed."

War, upon such an issue, was to be welcomed.
He asked a friend to show him the Charlestown
Navy-Yard, and looking round upon the warlike
preparations he said, " Ah! sometimes gunpowder
smells good." On the 19th of April, the anniversary of Concord Fight, a company of his townsmen
left home to join the army. He writes the next
day : —

DEAR ——: You have heard that our village
was all alive yesterday with the departure of our
braves. Judge Hoar made a speech to them at
the depot; Mr. Reynolds made a prayer in the
ring; the cannon, which was close by us, making
musical beats every minute to his prayer. And
when the whistle of the train was heard, and George

Prescott (the commander) — who was an image of manly beauty — ordered his men to march, his wife stopped him and put down his sword to kiss him, and grief and pride ruled the hour. All the families were there. They left Concord forty-five men, but, on the way, recruits implored to join them, and when they reached Boston they were sixty-four.

He was slow to believe (as indeed who was not?) that the disrupted fragments of the country could, within any assignable time, come together with mutual good-will in a political union. It was " a war of manners," the conflict of two incompatible states of civilization; and, for the present, could only end in a separation in which the incompatibilities should be acknowledged and somehow provided for. "No treaties, no peace, no constitution, can paper over the red lips of that crater. Only when at last the parts of the country can combine on an equal and moral contract to protect each other in humane and honest activities, — only such can combine firmly." For the time it was enough that the United States had become the country of free institutions, of which hitherto we had bragged most falsely. To the Southern States also the war had been of signal benefit: "I think they have never, since their first planting, appeared to such advantage. They have waked to energy, to self-help, to economy, to valor, to self-knowledge and progress. They have put forth for the first time their sleepy, half-palsied limbs, and as soon as the blood begins to tingle and flow, it will creep with new life into the moribund extremes of the system, and the 'white trash' will say, 'We, too, are men.'"

In the first lecture of the course, delivered on the 9th of April, three days before the bombardment of Fort Sumter, he had spoken with equanimity of "the downfall of our character-destroying civilization;" and in the next, a few days later, even speculates on the advantages of its downfall : —

"The facility with which a great political fabric can be broken, the want of tension in all ties which had been supposed adamantine, is instructive, and perhaps opens a new page in civil history. These frivolous persons with their fanaticism perhaps are wiser than they know, or indicate that the hour is struck, so long predicted by philosophy, when the civil machinery that has been the religion of the world decomposes to dust and smoke before the now adult individualism; and the private man feels that he is the State, and that a community in like external conditions of climate, race, sentiment, employment, can drop with impunity much of the machinery of government, as operose and clumsy, and get on cheaper and simpler by leaving to every man all his rights and powers, checked by no law but his love or fear of the rights and powers of his neighbor.

" Property has proved too much for the man; and now the men of science, art, intellect, are pretty sure to degenerate into selfish housekeepers, dependent on wine, coffee, furnace, gaslight, and furniture. We find that civilization crowed too soon, that our triumphs were treacheries; we had opened the wrong door and let the enemy into the castle. Civilization was a mistake, and, in the circumstances, the best wisdom was an auction or a fire; since the foxes and birds have the right of it, with a warm nest or covert to fend the weather, and no more."

The echoes of Sumter put an end to these fancies. The war, as he said afterwards, was "an eye-opener, and showed men of all parties and opinions the values of those primary forces that lie beneath all political action. Every one was taken by surprise, and the more he knew probably the greater was his surprise. We had plotted against slavery, compromised, made state laws, colonization societies, underground railroads; and we had not done much; the counteraction kept pace with the action; the man-way did not succeed. But there was another way. Another element did not prove so favorable to slavery and the great political and social parties that were roused in its de-

fence; namely, friction, an unexpected hitch in the
working of the thing. With everything for it, it
did not get on; California and Kansas would have
nothing of it, even Texas was doubtful; and at last
the slaveholders, blinded with wrath, destroyed
their idol with their own hands. It was God's doing, and is marvellous in our eyes.

"The country is cheerful and jocund in the belief that it has a government at last. What an
amount of power released from doing harm is now
ready to do good! At the darkest moment in the
history of the republic, when it looked as if the
nation would be dismembered, pulverized into its
original elements, the attack on Fort Sumter crys-
tallized the North into a unit, and the hope of mankind was saved. If Mr. Lincoln appear slow and
timid in proclaiming emancipation, and, like a bashful suitor, shows the way to deny him, it is to be
remembered that he is not free as a poet to state
what he thinks ideal or desirable, but must take a
considered step, which he can keep. Otherwise his
proclamation would be a weak bravado, without
value or respect."

Still, Emerson himself was not without his fears.
The hold of slavery upon the national capital
seemed not yet entirely broken. In January, 1862,
being at Washington, he took occasion to bear his
testimony at the seat of government to the sentiment of the North. "A nation [he said in a lec-

ture at the Smithsonian Institution [1] on " American Civilization "] is not a conglomeration of voters, to be represented by hungry politicians empowered to partition the spoils of office, but a people animated by a common impulse and seeking to work out a common destiny. The destiny of America is mutual service; labor is the corner-stone of our nationality,—the labor of each for all. In the measure in which a man becomes civilized he is conscious of this, and finds his well-being in the work to which his faculties call him. He coins himself into his labor; turns his day, his strength, his thought, his affection, into some product which remains as the visible sign of his power; to protect that, to secure his past self to his future self, is the object of all government. But there is on this subject a confusion in the mind of the Southern people, which leads them to pronounce labor disgraceful, and the well-being of a man to consist in sitting idle and eating the fruit of other men's labor. We have endeavored to hold together these two states of civilization under one law, but in vain; one or the other must give way. America now means opportunity, the widest career to human activities. Shall we allow her existence to be menaced through the literal following of precedents? Why cannot

---

[1] In the presence, Mr. Conway says (*Emerson at Home and Abroad.* By Moncure Daniel Conway. Boston, 1882: p. 313), of the President and his Cabinet. But this seems doubtful.

the higher civilization be allowed to extend over the whole country? The Union party has never been strong enough to kill slavery, but the wish that never had legs long enough to cross the Potomac can do so now. Emancipation is the demand of civilization, the inevitable conclusion reached by the logic of events. The war will have its own way; one army will stand for slavery pure and one for freedom pure, and victory will fall at last where it ought to fall. The march of ideas will be found irresistible, and this mountainous nonsense insulting the daylight will be swept away, though ages may pass in the attempt. But ideas must work through the brains and arms of good and brave men, or they are no better than dreams. There can be no safety until this step is taken."

On the 22d of September, Mr. Lincoln, who up to the last moment had been anxiously pondering the matter under pressure of " the most opposite opinions and advice," at length issued his proclamation that slavery would be abolished on the 1st of January, 1863, in those States which should then be in rebellion against the United States. At a meeting in Boston soon afterwards, Emerson expressed his hearty satisfaction with the President's action (which was violently condemned by some of the Boston newspapers and rather pooh-poohed, as ineffectual, by others), his appreciation of the difficulties of the President's decision, and his confidence that the step thus taken was irrevocable.

On the day when the Emancipation went into effect a "Jubilee Concert" was given at the Music Hall, and Emerson read there his "Boston Hymn" by way of prologue.

If the geographical position of Washington and the traditions of Southern rule made the politicians there less alive than they should be to the American idea, the patriotism of New England was affected with a like apathy from a different cause. the colonial spirit that still lingered in the well-to-do class of persons, the mimicking of English aristocratic ideas. In a lecture in Boston in 1863, the darkest period of the struggle, on the "Fortune of the Republic," Emerson said that with all the immense sympathy which at first and again had upheld the war, he feared that we did not yet apprehend the salvation that was offered us, and that we might yet be punished to rouse the egotists, the sceptics, the fashionist, the pursuers of ease and pleasure. These persons take their tone from England, or from certain classes of the English : —

"To say the truth, England is never out of mind. Nobody says it, but all think and feel it. England is the model in which they find their wishes expressed, — not, of course, middle-class England, but rich, powerful, and titled England. Our politics threaten her. Her manners threaten us. A man is coming, here as there, to value himself upon what he can buy."

In this class of Englishmen we had found, instead of sympathy, only an open or ill-concealed satisfaction at the prospect of our downfall. They are worshippers of Fate, of material prosperity and privilege; blind to all interests higher than commercial advantage or class prejudice. Never a lofty sentiment, never a duty to civilization, never a generosity, is suffered to stand in the way of these; and we are infected with this materialism. But, thanks to the war, we were coming, he hoped, to a nationality and an opinion of our own. " Nature says to the American, I give you the land and the sea, the forest and the mine, the elemental forces, nervous energy. Where I add difficulty I add brain. See to it that you hold and administer the continent for mankind. Let the passion for America cast out the passion for Europe. Learn to peril your life and fortune for a principle, and carry out your work to the end."

A year later, in November, 1864, on the second election of Mr. Lincoln, Emerson says in a letter to a friend who was in Europe : —

" I give you joy of the election. Seldom in history was so much staked on a popular vote. I suppose never in history. One hears everywhere anecdotes of late, very late remorse overtaking the hardened sinners, and just saving them from final reprobation."

And in beginning a course of lectures in Boston he congratulated his countrymen " that a great portion of mankind dwelling in the United States have given their decision in unmistakable terms in favor of social and statute order ; that a nation shall be a nation, and refuses to hold its existence on the tenure of a casual gathering of passengers at a railroad station or a picnic, held by no bond, but meeting and parting at pleasure ; that a nation cannot be trifled with, but involves interests so dear and so vast that its unity shall be held by force against the forcible attempt to break it. What gives commanding weight to this decision is that it has been made by the people sobered by the calamity of the war, the sacrifice of life, the waste of property, the burden of taxes, and the uncertainty of the result. They protest in arms against the levity of any small or any numerous minority of citizens or States to proceed by stealth or by violence to dispart a country. They do not decide that if a part of the nation, from geographical necessities or from irreconcilable interests of production and trade, desires a separation, no such separation can be. Doubtless it may, because the permanent interest of one part to separate will come to be the interest and good-will of the other part. But at all events it shall not be done in a corner, not by stealth, not by violence, but as a solemn act, with all the forms, on the declared opinions of the entire population concerned, and with mutual guarantees and compensations."

The Union, whatever its extent, should be the expression of a real unity, and not a contrivance to make up for the want of it.

The subject of the lecture to which this was the exordium was Education. What chapters of instruction, he said, has not the war opened to us! It has cost many valuable lives, but it has made many lives valuable that were not so before, through the start and expansion it has given. It has added a vast enlargement to every house, to every heart. Every one of these millions was a petty shopkeeper, farmer, mechanic, or scholar, driving his separate affair, letting all the rest alone if they would let him alone, abstaining from reading the newspapers because their mean tidings disgraced him or froze him into selfishness. But in every one of these houses now an American map hangs unrolled: the symbol that the whole country is added to his thought. "I often think, when we are reproached with brag by the people of a small home-territory like the English, that ours is only the gait and bearing of a tall boy by the side of small boys. They are jealous and quick-sighted about their inches. Everything this side the water inspires large prospective action. America means freedom, power, and, very naturally, when these instincts are not supported by moral and mental

training they run into the grandiose, into exaggeration and vaporing. This is odious; and yet let
us call bad manners by the right name.

"I think the genius of this country has marked
out her true policy, — hospitality; a fair field and
equal laws to all; a piece of land for every son of
Adam who will sit down upon it; then, on easy
conditions, the right of citizenship, and education
for his children."

In the early part of the war the drying-up of all
sources of income threatened Emerson with pecuniary straits. He writes to his brother William in
1862 : —

"The 1st of January has found me in quite as
poor a plight as the rest of the Americans. Not a
penny from my books since last June, which usually
yield five or six hundred a year ; no dividends
from the banks or from Lidian's Plymouth property. Then almost all income from lectures has
quite ceased ; so that your letter found me in a
study how to pay three or four hundred dollars
with fifty. . . . I have been trying to sell a wood-
lot at or near its appraisal, which would give me
something more than three hundred, but the purchaser does not appear. Meantime we are trying
to be as unconsuming as candles under an extin-
guisher, and 't is frightful to think how many rivals
we have in distress and in economy. But far better
that this grinding should go on bad and worse than

we be driven by any impatience into a hasty peace or any peace restoring the old rottenness."

In 1863 he was lecturing again. This year he was appointed by the President (probably at Charles Sumner's suggestion) one of the visitors to the Military Academy at West Point. Mr. John Burroughs, who saw him there in June, writes to me :

" My attention was attracted to this eager, alert, inquisitive farmer, as I took him to be. Evidently, I thought, this is a new thing to him ; he feels the honor that has been conferred upon him, and he means to do his duty and let no fact or word or thing escape him. When the rest of the Board looked dull or fatigued or perfunctory, he was all eagerness and attention. He certainly showed a kind of rustic curiosity and simplicity. When, on going home at night, I learned that Emerson was on that Board of Visitors at the Academy, I knew at once that I had seen him, and the thought kept me from sleep. The next day I was early on the ground with a friend of mine who had met Emerson, and through him made his acquaintance and had a chat with him. In the afternoon, seeing us two hanging about, he left his associates and came over and talked with us and beamed upon us in that inimitable way. I shall never forget his serene, unflinching look. Just the way his upper lip shut into his lower, imbedded itself there, showed to me the metal of which he was made."

CHAPTER XVI.

In his review of the institutions for public education, the common school and the college, in his
lecture in 1864, Emerson dotted out, with a remarkable prevision, the new departure upon which
his own college soon afterwards entered. The college, he said, is essentially the most radiating and
public of agencies; it deals with a force which it
cannot monopolize or confine, cannot give to those
who come to it and refuse to those outside. "I
have no doubt of the force, and, for me, the only
question is whether the force is inside. If the colleges were better, if they really had it, you would
need to set the police at the gates to keep order in
the in-rushing multitude. Do the boat-builders in
Long Island Sound forget George Steers and his
yacht America, or the naval men omit to visit a

new Monitor of Ericsson? But see in colleges
how we thwart this natural love of learning by
leaving the natural method of teaching what each
wishes to learn, and insisting that you shall learn
what you have no taste or capacity for. It is right
that you should begin at the beginning, to teach the
elements, but you shall not drive to the study of
music the youth who has no ear, or insist on making a painter of him if he have no perception of
form. The college, which should be a place of
delightful labor, is made odious and unhealthy, and
the young men are tempted to frivolous amuse-
ments to rally their jaded spirits. External order,
verbal correctness, the keeping of hours, the absence of any eccentricity or individualism disturb-
ing the routine, is all that is asked. Then, in the
absence of its natural check, the city invades the
college ; the habits and spirit of wealth suppress
enthusiasm. Money and vulgar respectability have
the ascendant. The college and the church, which
should be counterbalancing influences to , the
spirit of trade and material prosperity, do now conform and take their tone from it. I wish the democratic genius of the country might breathe something of new life into these institutions. I would
have it make the college really literary and scientific, and not worldly and political; drive out cox-
combs as with a broom, and leave only scholars.
I would have the studies elective, and I would hand

over the police of the college to the ordinary civil
government. The student shall, by his merits,
make good his claim to scholarships; to access to
still higher instruction in such departments as he
prefers. The class shall have a certain share in
the election of the professor: if only this, of making their attendance voluntary. Then, the imagination must be addressed. Why always coast on
the surface, and never open the interior of Nature?
— not by science, which is surface still, but by
poetry. Shakspeare should be a study in the university, as Boccaccio was appointed in Florence to
lecture on Dante. The students should be educated not only in the intelligence of, but in sympathy with, the thought of great poets. Let us have
these warblings as well as logarithms."

The mistake of confining higher education to a
rigid system of studies prescribed for all, without
regard to individual aptitudes, was illustrated, as
was natural, from his own experience with mathematics. " Great," he said, " is drill. It is better
to teach the child arithmetic and Latin grammar
than rhetoric or moral philosophy, because they
require exactitude of performance, and that power
of performance is worth more than the knowledge.
Then, too, it is indispensable that the elements of
numbers be taught, since they are the base of all
exact science. But there are many students, and
good heads, too, of whom it is infatuation to re-

quire more than a grounding in these. Yet they find this learning, which they do not wish to acquire, absorbing one third of every day in the two first academic years, — often two thirds, — a dead weight on mind and heart, to be utterly cast out the moment the youth is left to the election of his studies. The European universities once gave a like emphasis to logic and to theology. Until recently, natural science was almost excluded; now natural science threatens to take in its turn the same ascendant. A man of genius, with a good deal of general power, will for a long period give a bias in his own direction to a university. That is a public mischief, which the guardians of a college are there to watch and counterpoise. In the election of a president, it is not only the students who are to be controlled, but the professors; each of whom, in proportion to his talent, is a usurper who needs to be resisted."

Some of these utterances reached the watchful ear of Agassiz, whose persuasive eloquence, in spite of the distractions of the time, was drawing grant after grant from the legislature of Massachusetts in behalf of natural history and the Museum, as well as large sums from private contributors. He, not unnaturally, took these remarks to himself, and wrote to Emerson [1] in a tone of good-humored re-

---

[1] See their letters in the *Life and Correspondence of Louis Agassiz.* Edited by E. C. Agassiz. Boston, 1885: ii. 619.

monstrance at being thus wounded, as he thought, in the house of his friend.

Emerson had no difficulty in assuring him that they were not so meant, and that he wished him and the Museum Godspeed. It was true he had no predilection for systematic science, but natural history had a more attractive sound. Above all, he had no intention of making invidious comparisons between the different departments of learning: he only wished to protest against exclusiveness, wherever it was found; and of this no one could accuse Agassiz.

The cordial relation between them, begun, I suppose, some years before, at the Saturday Club, was not for a moment interrupted, and it was an unfailing source of refreshment to Emerson at their monthly meetings. The abundant nature of the other, his overflowing spirits, his equal readiness for any company and any and every subject, and a simplicity of manner which was the outcome of quick and wide sympathies, gave Emerson a sense of social enjoyment such as he rarely found. Never, he said of Agassiz, could his manners be separated from himself; and never was any separation felt to be desirable.

They met, also, together with Judge Hoar, Mr. Lowell, Jeffries Wyman, and other peers of the Saturday table, in the excursions of the Adirondack Club (an offshoot of the Saturday), among the wilds of northern New York, in 1858 and afterwards : of which Emerson has given a poetical sketch.[1] Emerson bought a rifle for the occasion, and learned to use it, but never used it, I believe, upon any living thing. He had himself paddled out one night to see a deer by the light of the jack-lantern, and saw "a square mist," but did not shoot. He liked above all to talk with the guides, and to please his imagination with their marvellous exploits.

Emerson was one of the original members of the Saturday Club, — indeed, Dr. Holmes tells us, the nucleus around which the club formed itself; and we might expect, as Dr. Holmes says, to find in his diaries some interesting references to it. I find only the following sentence : —

"*February* 28, 1862. Cramped for time at the club, by late dinner and early hour of the return train ; a cramp which spoils a club. For you shall not, if you wish good fortune, even take the pains to secure your right-and-left-hand men. The least design instantly makes an obligation to make their time agreeable, — which I can never assume."

He enjoyed the meetings, and went regularly until the time came when loss of power to recall the right word made talking painful to him. I have often heard him extol the conversational powers of some of his distinguished associates, but his own

[1] *Collected Writings.* ix. 150.

attitude there was that of a listener, eager to hear
what the clever men about him were saying, rather
than forward to take part himself. Dr. Holmes
describes him as sitting " generally near the Longfellow end of the table, talking in low tones and
carefully measured utterances to his neighbor, or
listening, and recording any stray word worth remembering on his mental phonograph." And in
the delicately touched portrait at the Massachusetts
Historical Society he says : " Emerson was spar-
ing of words, but used them with great precision
and nicety. If he had been followed about by a
short-hand-writing Boswell, every sentence he ever
uttered might have been preserved. To hear him
talk was like watching one crossing a brook on
stepping-stones. His noun had to wait for its verb
or its adjective until he was ready ; then his speech
would come down upon the word he wanted, and
not Worcester or Webster could better it from all
the wealth of their huge vocabularies. . . . He was
always courteous and bland to a remarkable degree ; his smile was the well-remembered line of
Terence written out in living features. But when
anything said specially interested him, he would
lean towards the speaker with a look never to be
forgotten, his head stretched forward, his shoulders
raised like the wings of an eagle, and his eye
watching the flight of the thought which had attracted his attention, as if it were his prey, to be

seized in mid-air and carried up to his eyry." This
last touch is important. Emerson could join readily enough in the talk about a piece of literary history or a commonplace of criticism, but a striking
thought or expression was apt to send him home
to his own meditations, and prevent reply. He
seemed on such occasions to come, as Carlyle said,[1]
with the rake to gather in, and not with the shovel
to scatter abroad. This reticence was not, I think,
the mere effect of a solitary habit, or a dislike to
discussion, but in part also of that nicety in the use
of language which Dr. Holmes remarks. This
made him hesitate, where the matter interested
him, to commit himself to the first words that came
to mind. In one of his early journals he says : " I
had observed, long since, that, to give the thought
a just and full expression, I must not prematurely
utter it. It is as if you let the spring snap too
soon." The consequence was that the spring, too
constantly bent, lost the power of acting on a sudden. Though he was a public speaker all his life,
he rarely attempted the smallest speech impromptu,
and never, I believe, with success. I remember
his getting up at a dinner of the Saturday Club on
the Shakspeare anniversary in 1864, to which some
guests had been invited, looking about him tran-
quilly for a minute or two, and then sitting down ;
serene and unabashed, but unable to say a word

---

[1] *Carlyle's life in London.* By J. A. Froude. New York,
1884 : i. 355.

upon a subject so familiar to his thoughts from
boyhood. The few instances that may be cited of
his speaking in public without preparation may
usually be explained, I imagine, as Mr. Lowell explains the ready flow of the Burns speech, by a
manuscript in the background. He rarely wrote a
letter of any importance without a rough draft;
and even in conversation, though no one could be
more free from any purpose of display, his pains in
the choice of words helped, I think, to produce the
" paralysis " of which he complains.

The most serious consequence (if I am not fanciful in ascribing it to this cause) was that afterwards, in his old age, as exertion grew more difficult,
this painstaking habit left him more and more at a
loss for the commonest words of every-day life.

He readily found compensations for his want of
fluency. The American genius, he says, is too
demonstrative; most persons are over-expressed,
beaten out thin, all surface without depth or substance.

" The thoughts that wander through our minds
we do not absorb and make flesh of, but we report
them as thoughts; we retail them as stimulating
news to our lovers and to all Athenians. At a
dreadful loss we play this game."

Yet it would be giving a false impression of Emerson to represent him as taciturn or inclined to
hold himself apart, or even as afflicted with the shy-

ness which may coexist, as in Hawthorne, with entire openness towards intimate friends. No one
could be more affable and encouraging in his address, or more ready to take his part in any company; and this not of set purpose, but from a
spontaneous hospitality of mind which no one who
met him could help feeling. No one who knew
him, however slightly, but must have been struck
with the ever-ready welcome that shone in his eyes
upon a casual meeting in the street, and with the
almost reverential way in which he received a
stranger. It is true he sometimes resisted intro-
ductions. " Oh, Elizabeth [he said to Miss Hoar,
when some one applied for an introduction], whom
God hath put asunder why should man join together?" And there was no doubt an inner circle
of thought and feeling in him which it was always
hard to penetrate, hard for him to open. But the
man of his aspirations was not the moralist, sitting
aloof on the heights of philosophy and overlooking
the affairs of men from a distance, but the man of
the world, in the true sense of the phrase ; the man
of both worlds, the public soul, with all his doors
open, with equal facility of reception and of communication, — such as Plato, such as Montaigne.

" With what security and common sense [he
writes to Miss Hoar] this Plato treads the cliffs
and pinnacles of Parnassus, as if he walked in a
street, and comes down again into the street as if

he lived there! My dazzling friends the New Platonists have none of this air of facts and society about them."

In himself he felt a "want of stomach and stoutness," a quasi-physical sensitiveness that made it uncomfortable for him to be in the street. "The advantage of the Napoleon temperament [he writes in one of his early diaries], impassive, unimpressible by others, is a signal convenience over this other tender one, which every aunt and every gossiping girl can daunt and tether. This weakness, be sure, is merely cutaneous, and the sufferer gets his revenge by the sharpened observation that belongs to such sympathetic fibre."

On the whole, he doubtless exaggerated his social defects; and I expect to hear that I have exaggerated them in my account of him.

Another trait, touched upon by Mr. Lowell in his sketch of Emerson at the Saturday symposium, in his poem on Agassiz, was the dislike of being made to laugh : —

> " Listening with eyes averse I see him sit
> Pricked with the cider of the judge's wit,
> (Ripe-hearted homebrew, fresh and fresh again,)
> While the wise nose's firm-built aquiline
>   Curves sharper to restrain
> The merriment whose most unruly moods
> Pass not the dumb laugh learned in listening woods
>   Of silence-shedding pine."

Several of Emerson's friends were good laughers, notably Carlyle and Agassiz, and he never found their mirth intemperate; but, for himself, "the pleasant spasms we call laughter," when he was surprised into them, seemed almost painful.

" The hour will come, and the world [Emerson writes to Miss Hoar from England], wherein we shall quite easily render that account of ourselves which now we never render." But by this time, without effort and in spite of some occasions for unfavorable impressions, he had rendered account of himself, and found acceptance and, we may say, reverence for what he was, even from those who took but little account of his writings and sayings, or perhaps would have counted them folly or worse.

" The main thing about him [says Mr. James [1]] was that he unconsciously brought you face to face with the infinite in humanity;" and this made its own way without help or hindrance. His lectures had not attracted a great variety of persons; it was always the same set, and not a large or an influential set. In certain quarters something of the odium of the Divinity Hall address still lingered, and yet more widely everything connected with Transcendentalism presented itself in rather a ludicrous aspect. One can hardly say that his doctrines had gained many converts; he had never identified himself with his precepts, but was always

[1] *Literary Remains*, 201.

ready to reverse them, however categorical they might be, with equal emphasis and as coolly as if he had never heard of them. He was not compiling a code ; he was only noting single aspects of truth as they struck him, trusting that every one would do the like for himself.

"I have been writing and speaking [he writes in his journal in 1859] what were once called novelties, for twenty-five or thirty years, and have not now one disciple. Why? Not that what I said was not true ; not that it has not found intelligent receivers ; but because it did not go from any wish in me to bring men to me, but to themselves. What could I do if they came to me? They would interrupt and encumber me. This is my boast, that I have no school and no followers. I should account it a measure of the impurity of insight if it did not create independence."

"I would have my book read as I have read my favorite books, — not with explosion and astonishment, a marvel and a rocket, but a friendly and agreeable influence, stealing like the scent of a flower or the sight of a new landscape on a traveller. I neither wish to be hated and defied by such as I startle, nor to be kissed and hugged by the young whose thoughts I stimulate."

He wished to stand aside and leave what he had written or said to rest on its own merits. He writes to a distant correspondent on occasion of some criticism in the newspapers : —

" Sorry I am that it is still doubtful whether books or words of mine are of doubtful health and safety; but, so long as it seems so, so long you must think so, and beware. I too am only a spectator, of your impressions as well as of my own things, and cannot set aside that fact any more than this. So we will not affirm or deny my sanity at present, but leave that hanging between heaven and earth for probation."

The increased sale of his books in this period shows that he was more widely read, but the effect he produced is not entirely accounted for by his writings. What gave Emerson his position among those who influence thought was not so much what he said, or how he said it, as what made him say it, — the open vision of things spiritual across the disfigurements and contradictions of the actual: this shone from him, unmistakable as the sunlight, and now, when his time of production was past, more and more widely, as the glow of the winter sky widens after the sun has set.

After 1866 he wrote but little that was new; indeed, for some time already he had been working up metal brought to the surface long before. He still lectured as much as ever, mostly away from home, at the West, where he often read a lecture nearly every day (sometimes twice a day) for weeks together in the winter; travelling all the time.

In July, 1865, he was asked to speak at the

commemoration by Harvard College of the close
of the war and the return of her contingent. "To
him more than to all other causes together did the
young martyrs of our civil war [says Mr. Lowell,
thinking of the Harvard boys] owe the sustaining
strength of thoughtful heroism that is so touching
in every record of their lives : " it was fitting that
he should be there to welcome the survivors. He
made the short address to them which has been
printed in his collected writings.[1]

The close of the war was marked also by a joyful event in Emerson's family circle, — the marriage of his younger daughter to Colonel William
H. Forbes. He writes to his old friend, Mr. Abel
Adams : —

CONCORD, *October* 1, 1865.

Edith's note will have given you the day and
the hour of the wedding, but I add this line to say
that I rely on the presence of you and your family
as on my own, . . . and I entreat you not to let
any superable obstacle stand in your way hither.
My own family connection has become so small
that I necessarily cling to you, who have stood by
me like a strong elder brother through nearly or
quite forty years. You know all my chances in
that time, and Edward's [2] career has depended on

---

[1] *Collected Writings*, xi. 317.

[2] Emerson's son, the cost of whose college course Mr. Adams
had paid.

you. Tuesday will not be the day I look for unless you are here. . . .

Yours affectionately,   R. W. EMERSON.

In 1867 he was chosen orator on Phi Beta Kappa day at Cambridge, as he had been thirty years before; but not now as a promising young beginner, from whom a fair poetical speech might be expected, but as the foremost man of letters of New England. In 1866 he received the honorary degree of LL. D. from Harvard, and was elected overseer by the Alumni.

He had not grown more orthodox, but opinion had been advancing in his direction. In the matter of religion, although his speech at the meeting for organizing the Free Religious Association (May 30, 1867), the speech at the Horticultural Hall in 1871, and his Sunday discourses to the Parker Fraternity in these years would have been regarded at the time of the Divinity Hall address as being still more outspoken in dissent, yet it was noised about that he had begun to see the error of his ways, and to return from them. When these reports came to Emerson he authorized his son to contradict them; he had not retracted, he said, any views expressed in his writings after his withdrawal from the ministry. What was true, I think, was that when his mind was quiescent, and nothing happened to stir up reflection, his feelings went back with complacency to the sentiments and the observances of his youth. He liked that everybody should go to church but himself, as aunt Mary Emerson liked that other people should be Calvinists; and a special motive — the appeal of some unpopular body like the Free Religious Association — was needed to bring him out on the side of innovation. A good instance of this unconscious drift transpired from the Board of Harvard Overseers, on occasion of a motion to dispense with the compulsory attendance at morning prayers in the college; which, it was understood, would have prevailed but for Emerson's vote. He should be loath, he is reported to have said, that the young men should not have the opportunity afforded them, each day, of assuming the noblest attitude man is capable of, — that of prayer. That he should decide, upon the whole, against the change, would not perhaps have been surprising; but it naturally excited surprise that the objections that were urged did not present themselves with special force to his mind. The truth was, he was simply dwelling in his early associations.

He served two terms as overseer, from 1867 to 1879, though it was with some difficulty that he was withheld from resigning before the close of the second. He felt himself to be unfit and now growing more unfit for the business. He attended the meetings regularly, however, sitting intent and as one astonished at the wisdom of those about him; now and again stooping forward with knit brows and lips slightly parted, as if eager to seize upon some specially important remark, but rarely taking part in the debates. He visited some of the courses in the college, and was chairman, from time to time, of committees, of whose reports I find fragmentary drafts among his papers, mostly of a general character; insisting that the aim of the college being to make scholars, the degrees, honors, and stipends should be awarded for scholarship, and not for deportment; and that scholarship is to be created not by compulsion, but by awakening a pure interest in knowledge. "The wise instructor accomplishes this by opening to his pupils precisely the attractions the study has for himself. He is there to show them what delights and instructs himself in Homer, or Horace, or Dante, and not to weigh the young man's rendering, whether it entitles to four or five or six marks. The marking is a system for schools, not for the college; for boys, not for men; and it is an ungracious work to put on a professor."

I find also the recommendation of greater attention to elocution, which was a favorite matter with him in the Concord schools; and the suggestion in a report on the library that a library counsellor, to guide the gazing youth amidst the multitude of books to the volume he wants, is greatly needed.

It was not Emerson's way to follow up his general
views into their detailed application, nor to insist on
them in debate. So he sat, as I have said, mostly
in silence, but always interested in what was going
on, and pleased at feeling himself within the atmosphere of the college. For, in spite of some un-
pleasant recollections, and of the "whiggery" of
which he had sometimes accused it, Emerson kept
always a feeling of loyalty towards his college,
came regularly to the Phi Beta Kappa festivals
and often to Commencement, and, when the building of a Memorial Hall was proposed, busied himself in collecting contributions from his class ; giving, in his proportion, more largely towards it, I
suppose, than any of them.

I find in his journal this record of the proceedings on the day when the corner-stone was laid : —
" *October* 6, 1870.   To-day at the laying of the
corner-stone of the Memorial Hall, at Cambridge.
All was well and wisely done.   The storm ceased
for us; the company was large; the best men and
the best women were there, or all but a few ; the
arrangements simple and excellent, and every
speaker successful.   Henry Lee, with his uniform
sense and courage, the manager.   The chaplain,
Reverend Phillips Brooks, offered a prayer in which
not a word was superfluous and every right thing
was said.   Henry Rogers, William Gray, and Dr.
Palfrey made each his proper report.   Luther's

hymn in Dr. Hedge's translation was sung by a
great choir, the corner-stone was laid, and then
Rockwood Hoar read a discourse of perfect sense,
taste, and feeling, full of virtue and of tenderness.
After this, an original song by Wendell Holmes
was given by the choir. Every part in all these
performances was in such true feeling that people
praised them with broken voices, and we all proudly
wept. Our Harvard soldiers of the war were in
their uniforms, and heard their own praises and the
tender allusions to their dead comrades. General
Meade was present and 'adopted by the college,'
as Judge Hoar said, and Governor Claflin sat by
President Eliot. Our English guests, Hughes,
Rawlins, Dicey, and Bryce, sat and listened."

He was much gratified when he was invited, in
1870 (in pursuance of a scheme, soon abandoned,
of lectures to advanced students by persons not
members of the Faculties), to give a course of university lectures in Cambridge. Emerson welcomed
the proposal as an opportunity for taking up and
completing his sketches of the "Natural History
of the Intellect," which he appears to have regarded as the chief task of his life. As early as
1837 he had proposed to himself "to write the
natural history of reason," and he had returned to
the project again and again ; in the London lectures in 1848, repeated in the two succeeding years
at Boston and New York ; in 1858, in a course on

the " Natural Method of Mental Philosophy ; " in
1866, in lectures on " Philosophy for the People : "
but had never got beyond the general announcement of his principle. Now he would make a supreme effort and bring together what he wished to
say. He worked hard over his papers for some
months before the course began, and in the intervals between the lectures ; but the result, as his
letter to Carlyle [1] shows, was still far from satisfactory to himself.

No one would expect from Emerson a system
of philosophy ; he had always declared his small
esteem of metaphysical systems, charts of the universe or of the mind, and he could not have intended now to attempt one. But he had long
cherished the thought of a more fruitful method
for the study of the mind, founded on the paral-
lelism of the mental laws with the laws of external
nature, and proceeding by simple observation of
the metaphysical facts and their analogies with the
physical, in place of the method of introspection
and analysis : —

" We have an invincible repugnance to introversion, study of the eyes instead of that which the
eyes see. The attempt is unnatural, and is punished by loss of faculty. 'T is the wrong path. For
fruit, for wisdom, for power, the intellect is to be
used, not spied. I want not the logic, but the power,

---

[1] June 17, 1870. *Carlyle-Emerson Correspondence,* ii. 327.

if any, which it brings into science and literature. The adepts value only the pure geometry, the aerial bridge ascending from earth to heaven, with arches and abutments of pure reason. I am fully contented if you tell me where are the two termini. My metaphysics is purely expectant; it is not even tentative. Much less am I ingenious in instituting *experimenta crucis* to extort the secret and lay bare the reluctant lurking law. No, I confine my ambition to true reporting. My contribution will be simply historical. I write anecdotes of the intellect, a sort of Farmers' Almanac of mental moods."

He tries to speak graciously, as always, of the system-makers, the pretenders to universal knowledge, who draw their circle and define every fact by its relations in a general scheme of experience, but he cannot conceal his disgust at their pretensions. " 'T is the gnat grasping the world. We have not got on far enough for this. We have just begun and are always just beginning to know." Yet the metaphysicians on their side might ask: Does not knowledge consist in the perception of universal relations? Or what is a fact but the instance of a law of nature, a way in which every one will be affected under the given circumstances? This is the paradox of knowledge, that this gnat we call John or Peter can grasp a law of the universe; and it is involved already in the very be-

ginnings of our experience, in every distinction of
facts from vain imaginations and dreams. What
is truth but system, order seen through the chance
medley of events? Emerson says the same thing
himself: —

" If one can say so without arrogance, I might
suggest that he who contents himself with dotting
only a fragmentary curve, recording only what
facts he has observed, without attempting to arrange them within one outline, follows a system
also, a system as grand as any other, though he
does not interfere with its vast curves by prematurely forcing them into a circle or ellipse, but
only draws that arc which he clearly sees, and
waits for new opportunity, well assured that these
observed arcs consist with each other."

What he resists is not metaphysics, nor the idea
of system, but dogmatism; the haste to realize the
idea in a final statement, to call a halt and exclude
all further implications in our facts beyond what
is contained in our definitions. In beginning his
first lecture, he says : —

" My belief in the use of a course on philosophy
is that the student shall learn to appreciate the miracle of the mind; . . . shall see in it the source of
all traditions, and shall see each of them as better
or worse statement of its revelations; shall come to
trust to it entirely, to cleave to God against the
name of God. And, if he finds at first with some

alarm how impossible it is to accept many things which the hot or the mild sectarian will insist on his believing, he will be armed by his insight and brave to meet all inconvenience and all resistance it may cost him."

In particular, perhaps, the recollection how the authorities of the Divinity School and the Liberal Christians, many of them just and acute men and well-equipped reasoners, had concluded that because they were right he must be wrong, and that there could be no reality in his religious perceptions, because, from the nature of the case, no such perceptions could be, made him distrust all attempts to verify our beliefs by systematic reasoning. But this feeling carries him so far that, as the Germans say, he empties out the child with the bath; he throws overboard not merely the claim to prescribe the conclusions to which our data must lead us, but every attempt to distinguish the grounds of belief from the momentary impression : —

" My measure for all the subjects of science, as of events, is the impression on the soul. Every thought ranks itself, on its first emergence from the creative night wears its rank stamped upon it. This endless silent procession of the makers of the world, — wonderful is their way and their sequence! They have a life of their own and their own proper motion, independent of the will. They

are not to be tampered with or spied upon, but
obeyed. Do not force your thoughts into an arrangement, and you shall find they will take their
own order, and that the order is divine.

" The ethics of thought is reverence for the
source, and the source lies in that unknown country which, in the despair of language, we call Instinct; a sheathed omniscience to which implicit
obedience is due. Instinct compares with the
understanding as the loadstone compares with a
guide-post.

" 'T is certain that a man's whole possibility lies
in that habitual first look which he casts on all objects. What impresses me ought to impress me."

On this showing there would seem to be small
place for philosophy ; its first word will be its last,
for if we have only to obey our impressions, no further counsels will be needed. Nor would there,
in Emerson's view, be any place for philosophy,
were our sensibilities always alive to the informa-
tions of experience. Every impression is a fact in
nature, as much as the freezing of water or the fall
of an apple, and carries the law with it. In the
healthy or obedient soul the creative thought real-
izes itself in the image in which it is expressed,
without any interval or any need of reasons for
connecting them. The inspired man, the poet,
the seer, and not the reasoner, is the right philosopher : —

" Philosophy is still rude and elementary. It will one day be taught by poets. The poet sees wholes and avoids analysis; the metaphysician, dealing as it were with the mathematics of the mind, puts himself out of the way of the inspiration, loses that which is the miracle and creates the worship. The poet believes; the philosopher, after some struggle, has only reasons for believing."

But in our colder moods, in default of clear vision, we may assure ourselves of the reality of our thoughts and the justness of their connections by seeing them reflected back to us from the face of nature. Things tally with thoughts because they are at bottom the same; knowledge is the perception of this identity. We first *are* the things we know, and then we come to speak and to write them, — translate them into the new sky-language we call thought. And it is this natural logic, and not syllogisms, that can help us to understand and to verify our experience.

In the second lecture, on the " Transcendency of Physics," he says : —

" The world may be reeled off from any one of its laws like a ball of yarn. The chemist can explain by his analogies the processes of intellect; the zoölogist from his ; the geometer, the mechanician, respectively from theirs. And in the impenetrable mystery which hides (and hides through

absolute transparency) the mental nature, I await
the insight which our advancing knowledge of natural laws shall furnish."

And in one of the London lectures : —

" If we go through the British Museum, or the
Jardin des Plantes, or any cabinet where is some
representation of all the kingdoms of nature, we
are surprised with occult sympathies. Is it not a
little startling with what genius some people take
to hunting, to fishing, — what knowledge they still
have of the creature they hunt? I see the same
fact everywhere. The chemist has a frightful in-
timacy with the secret architecture of bodies. As
the fisherman follows the fish because he was fish,
so the chemist divines the way of alkali because he
was alkali."

Emerson was not constructing a system of philosophy ; he was not even formulating a method ;
he was only indicating after his own fashion the
problem of philosophy, and the direction in which
a solution is to be sought. The problem is the
coming together of thought and thing in our assent
to a fact. A fact is a thought, an impression in
our mind ; yet it is also a part of nature, outside
and independent of us and of our thinking : the
business of philosophy is to explain and to justify
the connection, and thereby distinguish knowledge
from the mere association of ideas. Now if we
were sure that everything impresses us just as it

ought to impress us, there would be no need to look beyond the image in the mind in order to be certain that things are just what they appear to us. Unhappily, as Emerson remarks in the essay " Experience," [1] we have discovered that we do not see directly, but mediately, and that we have no means of correcting these colored and distorting lenses which we are. The real world, we learn, is not the world we think. But if we get rid of the discrepancy, as he seems to propose, by striking out the difference of thought and object, on the ground of their ultimate identity, — this is not solving the problem, but ignoring it. The question how we can know anything is answered to the effect that there is nothing to know ; that knowledge is simply the mind's consciousness of itself and of the unreality of everything outward. Emerson had said such things in his essays, throwing them out as poetical images to illustrate the power of intellect to dissolve nature "in its resistless menstruum ;" but they could not be stated as a doctrine, since the statement falls at once into a tautology. In this view nothing can be said of any impression except that it exists, or is felt ; and in this respect all impressions are the same. In Emerson's psychology, Instinct, Perception, Imagination, Reason, even Memory, all come back to recipiency and " the dissolving of the fact in the laws

[1] *Collected Writings.* iii. 77, 85.

of the mind," or in the one law of identity with itself. The one operation of thought is to set aside
all diversity as merely apparent, — a diversity of
names for one fact. The Natural History of the
Intellect will resolve itself, then, into a progressive
discovery of illusions, a perpetual coming up with
our facts, and finding them to be old acquaintances
masquerading in novel disguises.

The lectures appear to have been well received
by a little audience of some thirty students, one of
whom, in an account of the course in the *Atlantic
Monthly* (June, 1883, p. 818), says they were
" poetry and music." But Emerson, on this occasion, was intending something more. It could not
have been his intention to unfold the poetical paradox of his " Xenophanes" [1] in a series of university lectures, or to inculcate, as a doctrine, that the
mind, like nature,

> . . .   " an infinite paroquet,
> Repeats one note."

What he wished to impress on the young men,
if I understand him, was not the identity but the
infinity of truth ; the residuum of reality in all
our facts, beyond what is formulated in our definitions. So that no definition is to be regarded as
final, as if it described an ultimate essence whereby
the thing is utterly discriminated from all other

1 *Collected Writings*, ix. 121.

things, but only as the recognition of certain of its
relations; to which, of course, no limit can be set.
In this view Nature is the counterpart of the mind
beholding it, and opens new meanings as fast as
the capacity is there to receive them. This, at
any rate, was Emerson's characteristic doctrine, but,
in his exposition, he sets forth the ideal unity, on
which the perception of relation is founded, so
strongly and exclusively that no room is left for the
diversity in which it is to be realized, or for any relation save that of identity.

He must have felt the difficulty, I think, from
the outset. Any way, upon his return home after
the first lecture, he seemed disheartened. "I have
joined [he said, quoting Scott's " Dinas Emlinn "]
the dim choir of the bards who have been." It
was but a momentary feeling; he soon recovered
his spirits, supplemented the lectures by readings
from the Oriental Mystics and the Platonists, contented himself with " anecdotes of the intellect,"
without much attempt to deduce any conclusions,
and finished the course (which he made shorter by
two lectures than he had intended) in good heart,
trusting for better things the next year. At the
close of the last lecture, he thanked the class for their
punctual and sympathetic attention, and said that
although the discourses had been " quite too rapid
and imperfect to be just to questions of such high

and enduring import," yet the act of reading them
had given much assistance to his own views, and
would, he hoped, enable him to give a greater completeness to the leading statements.

He repeated the course (with slight changes) the
next year, but with no greater feeling of success.
It was, he wrote Carlyle,[1] " a doleful ordeal," and
when it was over he was much in need of the
refreshment that was offered him by his friend and
connection, Mr. John Forbes, in a six weeks' trip
to California, of which an account is preserved in
Professor Thayer's little volume.[2]

There was much in the circumstances to make
travelling, for once, enjoyable to Emerson, — a
company of near friends, entire absence of responsibility, a private Pullman car, well stored with all
that was needful ; and he seems to have thoroughly
enjoyed it. He talked more freely than was his
wont, was in excellent spirits, and impressed Mr.
Thayer with the sense he seemed to have of "a
certain great amplitude of time and leisure." He
put all cares behind him and enjoyed the passing hour, astonishing his young companions by
being "so agreeable all the time without getting
tired."

---

[1] *Carlyle-Emerson Correspondence*, Supplementary Letters, 78.
[2] *A Western Journey with Mr. Emerson.*   By James Bradley
Thayer.   Boston, 1884.

DEAR LIDIAN, — We live to-day and every day
in the loveliest climate. Hither to-day from San
Francisco, by water and by rail, to this village of
sulphur springs, with baths to swim in, and heal-
ing waters to drink, for all such as need such medi-
caments ; you may judge how religiously I use such
privilege, — as that word *wont* has two meanings.
Last night I read a lecture in San Francisco, and
day after to-morrow should read a second, and
perhaps still another later; for even in these vales
of Enna and Olympian ranges every creature sticks
to his habit. Our company is, as you know, New
England's best, the climate delightful, and we fare
sumptuously every day. The city opens to us its
Mercantile Library and its City Exchange, one
rich with books, the other with newspapers ; and
the roads and the points of attraction are Nature's chiefest brags. If we were all young — as
some of us are not — we might each of us claim
his quarter-section of the government, and plant
grapes and oranges, and never come back to your
east winds and cold summers : only remembering
to send home a few tickets of the Pacific Railroad
to one or two or three pale natives of the Massachusetts Bay, or half-tickets to as many minors.
. . . Of course, in our climate and condition the
leanest of us grows red and heavier. At the first
Dearborn's balance that we saw, Mr. Thayer and I

were weighed with the rest, and each of us counted the same pounds, 140½. I have not tried my luck again, but shall dare to by and by. . . . I stay mainly by San F. until the whole party shall go to the Yo Semite, which it were a little premature to seek at once, and the mammoth groves are in its neighborhood. . . . But I have not said what was in my mind when I began, that we three went to San Rafael on Tuesday, to Mr. Barber's, and spent the day and night there. It is a charming home, one of the beauties of this beautiful land. All shone with hospitality and health. They showed us every kindness. The house is new and perfectly well built and appointed. His place has seventy-one acres of plain and wood and mountain, and he is a man of taste and knows and uses its values. Three or four wild deer still feed on his land, and now and then come near the house. The trees of his wood were almost all new to us — live-oak, madrona, redwood, and other pines than ours ; and our garden flowers wild in all the fields.

TRUCKEE, *May* 20, 1871.
254 miles east from San Francisco.

We began our homeward journey yesterday morning from San Francisco, and reviewed our landscapes of four weeks before. The forest has lost much of its pretension by our acquaintance with grander woods, but the country is everywhere rich in trees and endless flowers, and New England starved in comparison. Another main advantage is that every day here is fair, if sometimes a wind a little raw or colder blows in the afternoon.

The soil wants nothing but water, which the land calls aloud for. The immense herds of horses, sheep, and cattle are driven to the mountains as the earth dries. Steps begin to be taken to meet this want of the plains and the cities, which the Sierras that keep their snow-tops all summer stand ever ready to supply. 'T is a delightful and a cheap country to live in, for a New Englander, though costly enough to the uproarious, unthrifty population that drift into it. One of my acquaintances, Mr. Pierce, a large owner and very intelligent, much-travelled man, thinks California needs nothing but hard times and punishment to drive it to prudence and prosperity; the careless ways in which money is given and taken being a ruinous education to the young.

Its immense prospective advantages, which only now begin to be opened to men's eyes by the new railroad, are its nearness to Asia and South America; and that with a port such as Constantinople, plainly a new centre like London, with immense advantages over that, is here. There is an awe and terror lying over this new garden, all empty as yet of any adequate people, yet with this assured future in American hands; unequalled in climate

and production. Chicago and St. Louis are toys to
it in its assured felicity. I should think no young
man would come back from it.

Lake Tahoe. We have driven through twelve
miles of forest to this fine lake, twenty or more
miles in diameter, with sulphur hot springs on its
margin and mountains for its guardians; yet silver
trout, I suspect, were the magnet in the mind of
our commanders. . . . It would have an additional
charm for me if it were not a *détour*, instead of an
advance to the blue northeast, which can only be
reached by retracing our way to Truckee. Friday
night I went to Oaklands (the Brooklyn of San
Francisco) to read a lecture, . . . and returned at
eleven o'clock P. M. by rail and boat to San Francisco. Edith had packed my trunk in the mean
time, and we departed for these places at eight in
the morning.

He came home refreshed, stopping on his way at
Niagara Falls, and in the autumn went again to
the West, lecturing. But the effort of the Cambridge course had left a strain from which he never
recovered; or perhaps it only betrayed the decline
which had already begun. At all events, the de-
scent was steady from this time. In 1868 he had
given the course of lectures in Boston of which Mr.
Lowell says that Emerson's older hearers could perceive in it no falling-off in anything that ever was es-

sential to the charm of his peculiar style of thought
or phrase. And in 1869 he gave ten readings in
English Poetry and Prose at Chickering's Hall in
Boston; the second address to the Free Religious
Association, and several lectures : in none of which,
so far as I know, were any signs of failing powers
observed. But the same thing could not often be
said after 1870.

Emerson never grew old ; at heart he was to the
last as young as ever, his feelings as unworn, his
faith as assured as in the days of his youth. Many
visions he had seen pass away, but the import of
them remained, only confirmed and enlarged in
scope. Nor were bodily infirmities swift to come
upon him. His hair remained thick and its brown
color unchanged up to rather a late period, when
suddenly it began to come off in large patches.
His eyesight, which sometimes failed him in his
youth and early manhood, was remarkably strong
in the latter part of his life. He used no glasses
in reading his lectures until he was sixty-four, when
he found the need of them in his Phi Beta Kappa
speech in 1867, and was thrown into some confusion, attributed by the audience to the usual dis-
array of his manuscript.

Dr. Hedge, in his recollections of Emerson in
1828, notes the slowness of his movements; but I
think most persons who saw him first in more advanced years will have been struck with the rapid

step with which he moved through the Boston
streets, his eye fixed on the distance. I count myself a good walker, but I used to find myself kept
at a stretch when I walked with him in the Concord woods, when he was past seventy. Miss Elizabeth Hoar and one or two other persons who remembered him from his youth have told me that he
seemed to them more erect in carriage, better "set
up," in later years. A life so much in the open
air no doubt had gradually strengthened an originally feeble habit of body. Emerson was never
quite willing to acknowledge the fact of sickness
or debility.

"You are bound [he writes to one of his chil-
dren] to be healthy and happy. I expect so much
of you, of course, and neither allow for nor believe
any rumors to the contrary. Please not to give
the least countenance to any hobgoblin of the sick
sort, but live out-of-doors, and in the sea-bath and
the sail-boat and the saddle and the wagon, and,
best of all, in your shoes, so soon as they will
obey you for a mile. For the great mother Nature
will not quite tell her secret to the coach or the
steamboat, but says, One to one, my dear, is my
rule also, and I keep my enchantments and oracles
for the religious soul coming alone, or as good as
alone, in true-love."

Yet there are traces from time to time, growing
less frequent latterly, of precarious health.

He loved warm weather: the Concord summer was never too hot for him; he revelled in the " rivers of heat;" but he seemed also impassive to cold, and would go without an overcoat when another man would have felt the need of one. Though here allowance must be made for his unwillingness to acknowledge bodily inconveniences.

But, from this time, the decay of some of the vital machinery began to make itself felt in ways that would not be denied. He began to find extraordinary difficulty in recalling names, or the right word in conversation. By degrees the obstruction increased, until he was forced at times to paraphrase his meaning, and to indicate common things — a fork or an umbrella — by a pantomimic representation, or by a figure of speech; often unintentionally, as one day, when he had taken refuge from the noontide glare under the shade of a tree, he said, in a casual way to his companion, who was sitting in the sun, " Is n't there too much heaven on you there?" Meeting him one day in the street in Boston, seemingly at a loss for something, I asked him where he was going. " To dine [he said] with an old and very dear friend. I know where she lives, but I hope she won't ask me her name;" and then went on to describe her as " the mother of the wife of the young man — the tall man — who speaks so well;" and so on until I guessed whom he meant. For himself, he took a

humorous view of his case. Once, when he wanted
an umbrella, he said, "I can't tell its name, but I
can tell its history. Strangers take it away." But
the disability led him at last to avoid occasions of
conversation with persons with whom he was not
intimate, thinking it unfair to them. He spoke of
himself as a man who had lost his wits, and was
thereby absolved for anything he might do or omit,
only he must learn to confine himself to his study,
"where I can still read with intelligence." How
clear his intelligence still was in spite of these superficial obstructions is manifest in the introduction which he wrote in the summer of 1870 for
Professor Goodwin's revision of the translation,
"by several hands," of Plutarch's Morals. This
little essay,[1] at which he worked diligently for a
month or more, buying a Greek Plutarch to compare with the old version (always even to its idiom
a prime favorite of his), was, I suppose, his last
effort at composition; old affection for the book
bringing the needed stimulus.

The anthology of English poetry, published in
1874 under the title "Parnassus," received some
additions at this time and afterwards, and some
pieces were admitted which at an earlier time he
would probably have passed over. He had begun
as early as 1855 to have his favorites copied out
for printing, and the selection was mostly complete

[1] *Collected Writings*, x. 275.

before 1865; but in the years after 1870 some
pieces were inserted, rather (in the opinion of those
who stood nearest to him) on the strength of a skilful reading or some other accidental circumstance
than upon a critical consideration of their merits.
The preface belongs substantially to the earlier time.

In the spring of 1872 he gave a course of six
lectures in Boston, and in July had just returned
from reading an address at Amherst College when
a cruel calamity fell upon him in the burning of
his house. About half past five in the morning of
July 24 he was waked by the crackling of fire, and
saw a light in the closet, which was next the chim-
ney. He sprang up, and, not being able to reach
the part that was in flames, ran down partly dressed
to the front gate and called out for help. He was
heard at a considerable distance, and answered instantly. The neighbors came running in from all
sides, and, finding it too late to save the house, applied themselves to removing the books and manuscripts and then the furniture, which was done with
so much promptitude and skill and by such a concourse of persons eager to help that, of the movables, but little of value was destroyed or even injured;
hardly anything except some papers in the garret
where the fire began. One of his kind townsmen
was in the chambers, and barely escaped when the
roof fell. By half past eight the fire was out; the
four walls yet standing, but the roof gone and the

upper parts much injured. It had been raining
in the night and everything was soaked; a circumstance which saved the trees Emerson had planted
close about the house, but also was the cause of
many colds and rheumatisms. Emerson himself
had a feverish attack, from walking about in the
rain, partially clad, in his solicitude about the letters and papers from the garret, which were carried about far and wide by the wind.

Many houses were at once offered for their reception, and Mr. Francis Cabot Lowell, Emerson's
classmate and friend, soon arrived from Waltham
with provision for removing the family to his own
house. They decided, however, to accept Miss
Ripley's invitation to the Manse. A day or two
afterwards, Mr. Lowell came again, and left with
Emerson a letter which was found to contain a
check for five thousand dollars, as the contribution
of a few friends for present needs. He did it,
Emerson said, "like the great gentleman he is,
and let us have his visit without a word of this."
Another of Emerson's old friends, Dr. Le Baron
Russell, had long been thinking it was time he
should be relieved from his lecturing and induced
to take a vacation, and with this additional reason
the suggestion was at once taken up by those within
reach, and between eleven and twelve thousand
dollars sent in, and felicitously conveyed to Mr.
Emerson by Judge Hoar.[1]

[1] See Appendix D.

Emerson at first resisted; he had been allowed, he said, so far in life, to stand on his own feet. He felt the great kindness of his friends, but he could not so far yield to their wishes. But on reflection he saw that there was no reason for declining, and he would not cast about for any.

His books and papers, meanwhile, had been carefully removed to the Court House (then out of use), and a temporary study fitted up for him there.

It was to be expected that such a blow would have serious consequences. Apart from the physical exposure, the shock of finding himself thus violently turned out of his home, his library, and all his accustomed surroundings, the apprehension for the moment that it might be forever, — this, for a man whose life was so much in his study, was most severe. It was natural that the loss of memory and of mental grasp which was afterwards noticed should be dated from this time. But the disability had begun earlier, and already showed itself to watchful eyes in his lectures in the spring and at Amherst in July; and the proof-sheets of a new volume of essays ("Letters and Social Aims"), which he had undertaken to select and arrange for a London publisher, showed that before the fire he had begun to find insuperable difficulty in a continuous effort of attention. I have spoken, in a prefatory note to that volume in the collected edi-

tion, of the circumstances under which it was undertaken and of the small progress he had made at
this time. The thought of it was a serious addition
to the burden that was pressing upon him.

On the whole, he was less disturbed than had been
expected, "though [one of his children writes] he
is so faithfully careful never to mention himself
that it is hard to know; but he looks happy." He
took cold at the time of the fire and had an attack
of low fever, but soon recovered, and went to the
seashore for a change of air and scene. Meantime
another visit to Europe was urged upon him ; this
time to include Greece and the Nile, which had
been a day-dream of his. At first he thought it
impossible, on account of the book which he was
bound to get ready. But it was obvious that the
book could not be proceeded with at present, and
this being represented to the publishers, they acceded to a year's delay. He then consented to
the foreign tour, and sailed, October 28, from
New York for England, accompanied by his eldest
daughter.

CHAPTER XVII.

1872–1882.

THE air of the sea, as in his younger days,
proved a tonic to Emerson. A few days before
sailing, he had found some difficulty in making a
little speech at a dinner of welcome to Mr. Froude
in New York; but, on the day he reached England,
being invited to a meeting of the Archæological
Society at Chester, and his presence noticed with a
request that he would second a motion of thanks
to the speakers of the evening, he did so with such
readiness and force that his son, who had come to
meet him there, was much relieved from anxiety
concerning him.

He greatly enjoyed the enforced rest and freedom from care, and in London gladly yielded him-

self to the attentions of the friends who welcomed him. He saw Carlyle again. He writes to his wife : —

LONDON, *November* 8, 1872.

. . . Yesterday I found my way to Chelsea, and spent two or three hours with Carlyle in his study. He opened his arms and embraced me, after seriously gazing for a time: " I am glad to see you once more in the flesh," — and we sat down and had a steady outpouring for two hours and more, on persons, events, and opinions. . . . As I was curious to know his estimate of my men and authors, of course I got them all again in Scottish speech and wit, with large deduction of size. He is strong in person and manners as ever, — though so aged-looking, — and his memory as good.

He spent ten days in England, quite content to sit still and do nothing. " When I cast about for some amusement or business [his daughter writes], he says, ' Old age loves leisure. I like to lie in the morning. And one gets such good sleep in this country, — good strong sleep.' " Next, to Paris, where Emerson was rejoiced to find Mr. Lowell and Mr. John Holmes. Thence to Marseilles, Nice, Italy, and the Nile before the end of December, stopping for a while in Rome.

He admired the beautiful scenery that came in his way, but would go nowhere to see anything,

and was always happy in the prospect of a halt.
Persons, as always, were the chief objects of interest to him: the dead, as at the tombs of Santa
Croce in Florence; and the living friends at Rome
and Naples.

The entrance of the Nile was not promising:
"Nothing could argue wilder insanity than our
leaving a country like America, and coming all this
way to see bareness of mud, with not even an inhabitant. Yes! there are some inhabitants; they
have come to drown themselves."

At Cairo he was affectionately received by Mr.
George Bancroft, — "a chivalrous angel to Ellen
and me," — who took him to breakfast with the
Khedive and showed him the sights. Early in
January they joined a party in taking a boat up
the river, and went as far as Philæ "and the tem-
ple-tomb of him who sleeps there." But he did
not find the Nile of his imagination. He was often
gay when riding about on shore on his donkey;
rejoiced at seeing the lotus, and the date-palm, and
"a huge banian tree" in the hotel yard at Cairo;
admired the groups of country people, "looking
like the ancient philosophers going to the School of
Athens;" praised the mandarin oranges: "They
even go ahead of pears, I'm afraid. They charm
by their tractability, their lovely anticipation of
your wishes. One may call them Christianity in
apples; an Arabian revenge for the fall of man."

Yet, his daughter writes, " he makes homesick speeches, and, if he should follow his inclination, would doubtless take a bee-line for home. He says he shall cheerfully spend a fortnight in Paris with Mr. Lowell, and in England desires to find Tennyson, Ruskin, and Browning. He never speaks of the beauty of the views here, only of the trees; but he prospers in health."

Here is one of the few entries in his diary : —

" All this journey is a perpetual humiliation, satirizing and whipping our ignorance. The people despise us because we are helpless babies, who cannot speak or understand a word they say; the sphinxes scorn dunces; the obelisks, the temple-walls, defy us with their histories which we cannot spell. The people, whether in the boat or out of it, are a perpetual study for the excellence and grace of their forms and motions."

He was improving in bodily health, his hair growing thick again in places and quite brown, but he was disinclined to mental exertion; " absolutely cannot write."

Away from his library his resource for mental stimulus was enlivening conversation, and for this there were few opportunities on the Nile. One or two lively young Englishmen whom he met were a godsend to him, and at Cairo, upon his return, Professor Richard Owen and General Stone. He writes to his son-in-law from Alexandria : —

DEAR WILL, — I ought to have long since acknowledged your letters, one and two, so kindly
ventured to an old scribe who for the first time in
his life recoils from all writing. Ellen sits daily
by me, vainly trying to electrify my torpid conscience and mend my pen ; but the air of Egypt
is full of lotus, and I resent any breaking of the
dream. But to-day we are actually on board of
the Rubattino Line steamer for Messina and Naples, and though to this moment of writing she refuses to lift her anchor, — the sea being too rough
outside for the pilot to return in his boat, — I can
believe that the dream is passing, and I shall return to honester habits. Egypt has been good and
gentle to us, if a little soporific. Nothing in our
life, habit, company, atmosphere, that did not suffer change. . . .

But I am not so blind or dependent but that I
could wake to the wonders of this strange old land,
alone, or with such friends as we brought with us
or found here. These colossal temples scattered
over hundreds of miles say, like the Greek and like
the Gothic piles, O ye men of the nineteenth century, here is something you cannot do, and must
respect. And 't is all the more wonderful because
no creature is left in the land who gives any hint
of the men who made them. One of the wonders
is the profusion of these giant buildings and sculp-

tures; sphinxes and statues by fifties and hundreds at Thebes. The country, too, so small and limitary, no breadth, nothing but the two banks of the long Nile. Forgive me for teasing you with this old tale. But I believe I have written nothing about it, and 't is all we have had to think of. Continue to be a good angel to me. With dear love to Edith and the children,

Yours, R. W. EMERSON.

In Rome, his friends thought him greatly improved in appearance, and Hermann Grimm, in Florence, said he looked as if he were made of steel. He began at this time to work with some heart upon the selection and revision of his poems for a new edition.

He had his fortnight with Mr. and Mrs. Lowell at Paris in March, "to our great satisfaction. There also I received one evening a long and happy visit from Mr. James Cotter Morison. At the house of M. Laugel I was introduced to Ernest Rénan, to Henri Taine, to Elie de Beaumont, to M. Tourgennef, and to some other noted gentlemen. M. Taine sent me the next day his ' Littérature Anglaise.' "

In England, upon his return, he declined all public speaking, except once at the Workingmen's College, at the request of his friend Mr. Thomas Hughes. Two of the workingmen sent him two

sovereigns towards the rebuilding of his house. He
declined all lecturing and formal speaking, but he
accepted many of the daily invitations to break-
fasts, lunches, and dinners, and was glad to go.
He breakfasted twice with Mr. Gladstone, and he
saw many people whom he had wished to see,
among them Mr. Browning. He saw Carlyle
again, but, from various mischances, they met but
seldom. After about three weeks' stay in London
he went northward on his way to Liverpool.

"At Oxford I was the guest of Professor Max
Müller, and was introduced to Jowett, and to Ruskin, and to Mr. Dodson, author of "Alice in Won-
derland," and to many of the university dignita-
ries. Prince Leopold was a student, and came
home from Max Müller's lecture to lunch with us,
and then invited Ellen and me to go to his house,
and there showed us his pictures and his album,
and there we drank tea. The next day I heard
Ruskin lecture, and then we went home with Ruskin to his chambers ; where he showed us his pictures, and told us his doleful opinions of modern
society. In the evening we dined with Vice-Chan-
cellor Liddell and a large company."

Mr. Ruskin's lecture he thought the model, both
in manner and in matter, of what a lecture should
be. His gloomy view of modern civilization Emerson could not away with. It was as bad, he said,
as Carlyle's, and worse ; for Carlyle always ended

with a laugh which cleared the air again, but with
Ruskin it was steady gloom.

He had a happy visit to Oxford. except that he
did not find Dr. Acland, nor Dr. Pusey, who had
lately sent him a book with a poetical inscription
which pleased him. From Oxford they went to
Mr. Flower at Stratford-on-Avon for three days,
and thence to Durham, which Dean Lake made
very interesting and delightful to him ; thence to
Edinburgh, where he dined with Professor Fraser
and with Dr. William Smith, and saw Dr. Hutch-
ison Stirling and other friends ; from Edinburgh
(where there was a gathering of persons to see him
off, one of whom asked to kiss his hand) by way of
the Lakes to Mr. Alexander Ireland. who hospitably received him for the two days before he sailed,
and brought together to meet him many of his
friends and hearers of 1847–48.

He reached home in May, and was received at
the station in Concord by a general gathering of
his townspeople, who had arranged that the approach of the steamer should be notified by a peal
of the church-bells, which tolled out the hour when
he would come. The whole town assembled, down
to the babies in their wagons, and as the train
emerged from the Walden woods the engine sent
forth a note of triumph, which was echoed by the
cheers of the assemblage. Emerson appeared, sur-

prised and touched, on the platform, and was escorted with music between two rows of smiling school-children to his house, where a triumphal arch of leaves and flowers had been erected. Emerson went out to the gate and spoke his thanks to the crowd, and then returned to make a delighted progress through the house, which had been restored, with some improvements, under the careful supervision of Mr. Keyes and Mr. W. R. Emerson, the architect, — the study unchanged, with its books and manuscripts and his pictures and keepsakes in their wonted array.

He appeared greatly refreshed and restored in spirits by his vacation. " He is very well [Mrs. Emerson writes], and if there is a lighter-hearted man in the world I don't know where he lives." On the 1st of October he read an address at the opening of the public library given to the town by Mr. William Munroe ; and though his notes, after the beginning, were fragmentary, flying leaves from former discourses, he connected them neatly together into a whole in the delivery. On the 16th of December, the anniversary of the emptying of the tea into Boston Harbor, he read at the celebration in Faneuil Hall his poem " Boston," [1] written many years before in the anti-slavery excitement, but now remodelled, with the omission of some of the stanzas, and the addition of those relating to the seizure of the tea.

[1] *Collected Writings,* ix. 182.

During the next year (1874), " Parnassus " was finished, and was published in December.

In the early part of this year, much to his surprise, he was asked by the Independent Club of Glasgow University to be one of the candidates for the Lord Rectorship, and letters came to him from the young men in Glasgow and from graduates in New York, urging him to accept the nomination, which he did, receiving five hundred votes against seven hundred for the successful candidate, Mr. Benjamin Disraeli.

In February, 1875, he was asked to lecture in Philadelphia, and also received an affectionate invitation from his old friend Dr. Furness : to which he replied in the following letter : —

CONCORD, *February* 10, 1875.

MY DEAR FRIEND, — Oldest friend of all, old as Mrs. Whitwell's school, and remembered still with that red-and-white handkerchief which charmed me with its cats and dogs of prehistoric art ; and later, with your own native genius with pencil and pen, up and upwards from Latin school and Mr. Webb's noonday's writing, to Harvard, — you my only Mæcenas, and I your adoring critic ; and so on and onward, but always the same, a small mutual-admiration society of two, which we seem to have founded in Summer Street, and never quite forgotten, despite the three hundred miles — tyran-

nical miles — between Philadelphia and Concord.
Well, what shall I say in defence of my stolid
silence at which you hint? Why, only this: that
while you have, I believe, some months in advance
of me in age, the gods have given you some draught
of their perennial cup, and withheld the same from
me. I have for the last two years, I believe, written nothing in my once-diurnal manuscripts, and
never a letter that I could omit (inclusive too of
some I ought not to omit), and this applies to none
more than yours. Now comes your new letter, with
all your affectionate memories and preference fresh
as roses. . . . I must obey it. My daughter Ellen,
who goes always with my antiquity, insists that we
shall. . . . So you and Mrs. Furness receive our
affectionate thanks for the welcome you have sent
us. My love to Sam Bradford, if you meet him.

    Your affectionate   R. W. EMERSON.

My wife — too much an invalid — sends you her
kindest regards.

He went in March, accordingly, and "the three
of us," including Mr. Samuel Bradford, spent day
after day together, to Emerson's great enjoyment,
celebrating their reunion by going to be photo-
graphed in a group.

On the 19th of April, the centennial anniversary
of Concord Fight was commemorated at the bridge
by an oration from Mr. George William Curtis

and a poem from Mr. Lowell, and there was a
great concourse of persons from far and near. Mr.
Daniel French's spirited statue of the Minute-Man,
which had been put in position on the spot where
the militia stood to defend the North Bridge, was
unveiled.   Ebenezer Hubbard, a Concord farmer
who inherited land in the village on which the
British troops had committed depredation, and who
never neglected to hoist the stars and stripes there
on the 19th of April and the 4th of July, had been
deeply grieved that the monument erected by the
town in 1836 should mark the position occupied
by the enemy instead of that of the defenders in
the skirmish, and he bequeathed a sum of money to
the town on the condition that a monument should
be placed on the very spot where the minute-men
and militia had stood, and another sum to build a
foot-bridge across the river where the old bridge
was in 1775. Mr. Stedman Buttrick, a descendant
of Major Buttrick, who gave the command to return the fire, provided the site; the sculptor was
a Concord youth ; and Emerson made the address.
It was a raw day, with a bitter wind, and the waiting crowd suffered from the cold as the visitors in
1775 had suffered from the heat. Emerson ad-
verted to the contrast in his little speech, which
was the last piece written out with his own hand.

Soon after this, the dead weight of the book he

had undertaken for the London publisher, Mr. Hotten, which had been staved off, Emerson fondly supposed, by Mr. Hotten's death, fell back upon him. He learned that Messrs. Chatto & Windus had taken Mr. Hotten's place, and that they were inquiring when the volume would be ready. The thought of it worried him : he felt that he could not go on to make the selections and see the book through the press without assistance. He needed the help of some one who was familiar with his published writings and could devote the time that was necessary, and he at length allowed his daughter to invite me to undertake it. I went to Concord accordingly in September, and thereafter from time to time until the book ("Letters and Social Aims") was finished and came out in December. I have given in a note to that volume, in the Riverside edition, an account of the way in which it was compiled. Only one or two of the pieces had been fixed upon ; the rest were added with Mr. Emerson's approval, but without much active coöperation on his part, except where it was necessary to supply a word or part of a sentence.

After this, I used to go up at intervals for five or six years, — so long as he continued to read lectures, — for the purpose of getting ready new selections from his manuscripts, excerpting and compounding them as he had been in the habit of doing for himself. There was no danger of dis-

turbing the original order, for this was already
gone beyond recovery. In using separate lectures
together at different times, as he was wont to do,
he had mixed them up so thoroughly, with various
pagings and headings, or without any, and with no
obvious means of connection, that my efforts ever
since to get them back into their first shape have
met with but partial success. The difficulty is increased by his persistent objection to full reports
of his lectures, and even, it was understood, to the
taking of private notes.

He still liked to read a paper occasionally, when
he was asked to do so, and would often read with
much of his old skill and power when he retained
but a slight recollection of what he had written,
and would comment on it as if it were another person's. " A queer occasion it will be [he said, when
he was to read a lecture at the Concord Lyceum
in 1878], — a lecturer who has no idea what he is
lecturing about, and an audience who don't know
what he *can* mean."

It was thus that the essays published for the
first time in the last two volumes of the Riverside
edition received their final arrangement. Everything in them, except a few passages taken directly
from his journals, was in some earlier lecture; but
the title of the essay does not always indicate the
lecture to which the sentences originally belonged.

He was always pleased at my coming upon this

errand, and would often intimate the feeling of an immense and unspeakable service I was doing him, and his uneasiness at trespassing so much upon my time, without its ever occurring to him that I, and not he, was the party obliged. When I was at his house thus employed, he would come in from his study in the early afternoon and take me off for a walk, saying that I had worked long enough; and would go on a stroll in the Walden woods, or over Sleepy Hollow and Peter's field, or sometimes on a drive to the other side of the river. And in the evening he would come again about ten o'clock, and take me to his study for a cigar before bedtime.

To me there was nothing sad in his condition; it was obvious enough that he was but the shadow of himself, but the substance was there, only a little removed. The old alertness and incisiveness were gone, but there was no confusion of ideas, and the objects of interest were what they always had been. He was often at a loss for a word, but no consciousness of this or of any other disability seemed to trouble him. Nor was there any appearance of effort to keep up the conversation. He liked perhaps to listen rather than to talk; he " listened and smiled " as a man might who was recovering from illness, and felt himself removed for a time from his ordinary activities, but he often talked freely. I never could get him to talk about himself, his

early days, or even much of Boston as he first
remembered it; he did not seem averse, but he
glided away to other topics. His usual topics were
the splendors of the age and the miracles it has
wrought in the relation of nations to each other,
— the steamboat, railroad, electric telegraph, the
application of the spectroscope to astronomy, the
photograph; the remarkable and admirable persons he had known, — Dr. Channing, Mr. Everett,
and living friends; then European politics, — Mr.
Gladstone, and how superior in *kind* he was to the
common run of statesmen; the college, and what
a godsend President Eliot was, what an all-accom-
plished man; then the manifold virtues of his
Concord townsmen of all degrees. In general, his
memory of persons was good, even though they
might be recent acquaintances. Sometimes there
was a strange lapse, as once when I asked him
about John Sterling, with whom he had been
in correspondence up to the time of Sterling's
death. He could not remember to have heard the
name.

He did not often touch upon literary matters,
unless to inquire about some new book. His reading seemed to lie mostly in the books of all sorts
which had been sent to him and lay at his hand
upon the table. I found him reading Dr. Stirling's "Secret of Hegel," and he spoke in praise
of Professor Caird's book on Kant, but it was the

tone of the writing rather than the subject that attracted him. He liked to feel himself in the atmosphere of letters, and continued to feel and enjoy literary ability in a passive way after his mind had ceased to occupy itself much with the substance of what he read. But what was chiefly remarkable in his conversation, and always new and striking, although it belonged to the stuff of which his whole life was made, was its uniform and un-forced cheerfulness. He did not need to turn away from gloomy things, from uncomfortable presages in society about him, or from the ever-narrowing line that bound in his own activities on earth; for he saw beyond them, and as clearly now as when, forty years before, he had sounded the notes that told that the lofty soul of Puritanism was not dead in the decay of its body.

To go back a little. In the spring of 1876, be-ing invited by the Washington and Jefferson lit-erary societies of the University of Virginia to deliver the address at their joint celebration on the 28th of June, he readily acceded, thinking it of happy omen that they should send to Massachu-setts for their orator. In his reply he said he had given up speaking, but could not refuse an invita-tion from Virginia. He went, accordingly, with his daughter Ellen. After a fatiguing journey, in which they suffered much from the heat and dust, they were kindly received and lodged in the house of one of the professors. It speedily appeared, however (what perhaps a less confiding disposition might have allowed him to foresee), that no miracle had been wrought in the temper of the community, and that the predominant feeling was still one of bitter indignation at Northern aggression. The visitors were treated with every attention in the society of the place. there was no intentional discourtesy, but the Southern self-respect appeared to demand that they should be constantly reminded that they were in an oppressed and abused country. And the next day, at Emerson's address, the audience in general — mostly young women with their admirers, but also children, as well as older persons — seemed to regard the occasion chiefly as one for social entertainment, and there was so much noise that he could not make himself heard. Some of the students (probably his inviters) came to the front and listened with attention, but most of them, finding that they could not hear, gave up the attempt, and turned to whispering and even talking and laughing aloud; until Emerson, after contending with the din for half an hour, sought out a suitable passage and swiftly came to a close.

It was not in flesh and blood not to feel indignant, but whatever Emerson felt he kept to himself. No one heard of it, and when I afterwards asked him about his reception all he said was, "They are very brave people down there, and say just what they think." What was more remarkable, perhaps, than this free-and-easy treatment of the Boston idealist was his meeting there several persons who had read his books and expressed their pleasure at seeing him. And the next day, in the train going North, he was an object of attention to many of his fellow-travellers, some of whom asked to be introduced to him or introduced themselves, saying they were from Arkansas, Louisiana, Alabama, going to the Philadelphia Exhibition.

All over the country, indeed, there were by this time here and there readers for whom he had a special charm, and letters came to him with tributes of thankfulness from distant States. In his own neighborhood he received silent greetings wherever he went. Here is an incident that might be matched any day in these years : —

A writer (Mrs. Helen Hunt Jackson ?) in the *Atlantic Monthly*, September, 1882, p. 424, says : "Many years ago, I was one day journeying from Brattleboro to Boston, alone. As the train went on from station to station, it gradually filled, until there was no seat left unoccupied in the car excepting the one by my side. At Concord the door of the car opened, and Mr. Emerson entered. He advanced a few steps into the car, looked down the aisle, turned, and was about to go out, believing the car to be entirely full. With one of those sudden impulses which are acted upon almost before they are consciously realized, I sprang up, and said, 'Oh, Mr. Emerson, here is a seat!' As he came towards me, with his serene smile slowly spreading over his face, my courage faltered. I saw that he expected to meet in me an acquaintance; and, as he looked inquiringly and hesitatingly in my face, I made haste to say, 'You do not know me, Mr. Emerson. I never had the pleasure of seeing you before. But I know your face, and I could not resist the temptation of the opportunity to speak with you. You know that so many people who are strangers to you know you very well.' 'Perhaps there should not be the word stranger in any language,' he answered slowly, in a tone and with a kindly look which at once set my timidity at ease. I do not know any good reason for it.' "

Everywhere in his own part of the country he was silently watched over by an unknown bodyguard, some one of whom could usually be reckoned on to provide a seat, a carriage, or to render any needed service.

In the autumn of this year, at the commemoration by the Latin School Association in Boston (November 8, 1876) of the centennial anniversary [1] of the reopening of the school after the

[1] Reported in the *Boston Evening Transcript*, November 9.

evacuation of the town by the British, he read the notes from which I have quoted in the account of his school-boy days. "I dare not attempt to say anything to you [he said in beginning], because in my old age I am forgetting the word I should speak. I cannot remember anybody's name; not even my recollections of the Latin School. I have therefore guarded against absolute silence by bringing you a few reminiscences which I have written."

In 1878, being asked to give a summing-up of the position of the country after the war, and its spiritual needs and prospects for the new generation, he read at the Old South Church in Boston (March 8) the "Fortune of the Republic," a paper of the war-time, with additions from his journals. In September he accompanied his daughter to the Unitarian Convention at Saratoga, visited Niagara Falls, and afterwards went off alone upon a fruitless search of several days, beyond the reach of the railroads, in the western part of the State of New York, for a young mechanic who, some years before, had written him a letter of thankfulness, but also sharp questioning of his complacent optimism. He did not relinquish his efforts until he had found an acquaintance of the young man, and learned that he had left the State. Emerson did not love discussion, but he liked to see the other side, when it was presented by one who showed that he had the right to speak; and a fresh view of his facts, as they were seen by a man of the world or by a struggling young artisan, had a stronger attraction for him than any agreement with himself.

In May, 1879, at the request of the students of the Cambridge Divinity School, he read there the lecture which has been published under the title of " The Preacher," [1] a fitting second part, it seemed to some who heard it, to the address he had delivered in that place forty years before. But his friends saw that it was time his reading in public should come to a close.

It was in the spring of this year that the bust of Emerson, by Mr. French, the sculptor of the Minute-Man, was made ; the best likeness of him, I think, by any artist (except the sun), though unhappily so late in his life. Mr. French writes to me : " I think it is very seldom that a face combines such vigor and strength in the general form and plan with such exceeding delicacy and sensitiveness in the details. Henry James somewhere speaks of ' the over-modelled American face.' No face was ever *more* modelled than was Mr. Emerson's ; there was nothing slurred, nothing accidental ; but it was like the perfection of detail in great sculpture ; it did not interfere with the grand scheme. Neither did it interfere with an almost child-like mobility that admitted of an infinite variety of expression, and made possible that won-

[1] *Collected Writings,* x. 207.

derful 'lighting-up' of the face, so often spoken
of by those who knew him. It was the attempt to
catch that glorifying expression that made me despair of my bust. At the time I made it, as you
know, Mr. Emerson had failed somewhat, and it
was only now and then that I could see, even for
an instant, the expression I sought. As is not un-
common, there was more movement in one side of
Mr. Emerson's face than in the other (the left
side), and there was a great difference in the for-
mation of the two sides; more, probably, at the
time I made the bust than earlier. When the
bust was approaching completion he looked at it
after one of the sittings, and said, 'The trouble is,
the more it resembles me, the worse it looks.'"

In September, he was invited by the Unitarian
Church of Concord, New Hampshire, to attend the
celebration of their fiftieth anniversary; he having
been one of the first preachers. The day appointed
was the 30th; he arrived on the afternoon of the
29th. It was here that he was married to Ellen
Tucker, and he went at once to see the house in
which she and her mother had lived at the time, but
was unable to identify it. The next morning he
remembered that the evening before was the fiftieth
anniversary of his wedding, and that he had unwit-
tingly returned to the place just half a century
afterwards at the same hour. He then learned
from Colonel Kent, the step-brother of Ellen

Tucker, that the house had been moved, and under his guidance went and saw the still familiar-looking rooms. He was asked to take part in the commemorative services of the church, and read the hymn with much feeling, and without being disturbed by the difficulty he found in making out all the words.

His last public readings, if they may be called public, were those of the paper on Carlyle, before the Massachusetts Historical Society, February 10, 1881, and the lecture on "Aristocracy" at the Concord School of Philosophy in July of that year. Constant assistance was now needed to make sure of his recognizing all the words and preserving the order of his pages. There was no very marked change in his appearance; the gracious presence was still there, though it did not retain a very firm hold on the things of the earth.

These last years of Emerson's life were tranquil and happy. His pecuniary circumstances were easy; all solicitudes of that kind had been removed from him by the skilful management of his son-in-law; and there were no others. The port was near, but to all appearance the last waves retained their charm. When I saw him in Concord in 1881, I noticed that he was disinclined to a long walk, and thought the half-mile or so to the post-office a sufficient stint for the afternoon. But at Naushon, at his daughter's house, in the summer, he enjoyed the walk of a mile or two to the bathing-place and back again after a plunge in the sea, and did not object to extending it into the beautiful woods beyond. His chief enjoyment, however, was in sitting on the piazza, watching his grandchildren at their sports, and pleased in the thought how " children nowadays are encouraged to do things, and are taught to do them."

Calmly as he looked forward to the end, the prospect of prolonged illness would have been dreadful to him. This he was spared. Early in the spring of 1882, a cold, rapidly settling into pneumonia, carried him off a few weeks before his seventy-ninth birthday. On Sunday, April 16, he went to church, both morning and evening, as had latterly been his wont, and took a walk in the afternoon. The next day he was hoarse, and the hoarseness and a feeling of heaviness increased during the week, without causing serious alarm to his son, Dr. Emerson, until Saturday, when the fatal symptoms appeared. It was not a severe attack, part only of one lung was affected ; but the power of resistance was gone, and he died on Thursday, April 27th ; without any suffering until the very last. During the first days of his illness, he made light of it, declared that he had no cold, came downstairs and went to walk, only taking more and longer walks than usual, because, he said, he did not feel well in his chair. But, on the fourth day, as he was coming down to breakfast, he stopped, with an exclamation of pain or distress, and said, " I hoped it would not come in this way : I would rather — fall down cellar." Still he persevered two days longer in dressing and coming down to his study, and listened with full enjoyment to the accounts of an address which his son had been delivering before the district medical society. In these last days in his study, his thoughts often lost their connection, and he puzzled over familiar objects. But when his eyes fell on a portrait of Carlyle that was hanging on the wall, he said, with a smile of affection, " *That* is that man, my man." On Saturday, the last day he spent there, he insisted at bedtime on taking apart the brands in the fireplace and making the accustomed arrangements for the night, and declined assistance to go upstairs.

For the day or two before his death he was troubled by the thought that he was away from home, detained by illness at some friend's house, and that he ought to make the effort to get away and relieve him of the inconvenience. But to the last there was no delirium ; in general he recognized every one and understood what was said to him, though he was sometimes unable to make intelligible reply. He took affectionate leave of his family and the friends who came to see him for the last time, and desired to see all who came. To his wife he spoke tenderly of their life together and her loving care of him; they must now part, to meet again and part no more. Then he smiled and said, " Oh, that beautiful boy ! "

A friend who watched by him one of the last nights says : —

" He kept (when awake) repeating in his sonorous voice, not yet weakened, fragments of sentences, almost as if reciting. It seemed strange and solemn in the night, alone with him, to hear these efforts to deliver something evidently with a thread of fine recollection in it; his voice as deep and musical almost as ever."

I was permitted to see him on the day of his death. He knew me at once, greeted me with the familiar smile, and tried to rise and to say something, but I could not catch the words.

He was buried on Sunday, April 30, in Sleepy Hollow, a beautiful grove on the edge of the village, consecrated as a burial-place in 1855, Emerson delivering the address.[1] Here, at the foot of a tall pine-tree upon the top of the ridge in the highest part of the grounds, his body was laid, not far from the graves of Hawthorne and of Thoreau, and surrounded by those of his kindred.

Ten years before, in the illness and depression

[1] Used afterwards in the essay on Immortality. *Collected Writings,* viii. 307.

which followed upon the burning of his house, Emerson wrote in his journal : —

"If I should live another year, I think I shall cite still the last stanza of my own poem, 'The World-Soul.'"

This is the stanza ; and it expresses, I think, the feeling with which the crowd of friends followed him to his rest : —

"Spring still makes spring in the mind
When sixty years are told ;
Love wakes anew this throbbing heart,
And we are never old.
Over the winter glaciers
I see the summer glow,
And through the wild-piled snow-drift
The warm rosebuds below."

APPENDIX.

A.

TO THE SECOND CHURCH AND SOCIETY.

BOSTON, *December* 22, 1832.

CHRISTIAN FRIENDS, — Since the formal resignation
of my official relation to you, in my communication to
the proprietors in September, I had waited anxiously for
an opportunity of addressing you once more from the pulpit, though it were only to say, Let us part in peace and
in the love of God. The state of my health has prevented and continues to prevent me from so doing. I
am now advised to seek the benefit of a sea voyage. I
cannot go away without a brief parting word to friends
who have shown me so much kindness, and to whom I
have felt myself so dearly bound.

Our connection has been very short; I had only begun my work. It is now brought to a sudden close;
and I look back, I own, with a painful sense of weakness, to the little service I have been able to render, after so much expectation on my part; to the checkered
space of time, which domestic affliction and personal infirmities have made yet shorter and more unprofitable.

As long as he remains in the same place, every man flatters himself, however keen may be his sense of his failures and unworthiness, that he shall yet accomplish much ; that the future shall make amends for the past : that his very errors shall prove his instructors, — and what limit is there to hope ?   But a separation from our place, the close of a particular career of duty, shuts the book, bereaves us of this hope, and leaves us only to lament how little has been done.

Yet, my friends, our faith in the great truths of the New Testament makes the change of places and circumstances of less account to us, by fixing our attention upon that which is unalterable.   I find great consolation in the thought that the resignation of my present relations makes so little change to myself.   I am no longer your minister, but am not the less engaged, I hope, to the love and service of the same eternal cause, the advancement, namely, of the kingdom of God in the hearts of men.   The tie that binds each of us to that cause is not created by our connection, and cannot be hurt by our separation.   To me, as one disciple, is the ministry of truth, as far as I can discern and declare it, committed ; and I desire to live nowhere and no longer than that grace of God is imparted to me, — the liberty to seek and the liberty to utter it.

And, more than this, I rejoice to believe that my ceasing to exercise the pastoral office among you does not make any real change in our spiritual relation to each other.   Whatever is most desirable and excellent therein remains to us.   For, truly speaking, whoever provokes me to a good act or thought has given me a pledge of his fidelity to virtue; he has come under bonds to adhere to that cause to which we are jointly attached. And so I say to all you who have been my counsellors and co-operators in our Christian walk, that I am wont to see in your faces the seals and certificates of our mutual obligations. If we have conspired from week to week in the sympathy and expression of devout sentiments; if we have received together the unspeakable gift of God's truth; if we have studied together the sense of any divine word, or striven together in any charity, or conferred together for the relief or instruction of any brother; if together we have laid down the dead in a pious hope, or held up the babe into the baptism of Christianity; above all, if we have shared in any habitual acknowledgment of that benignant God, whose omnipresence raises and glorifies the meanest offices and the lowest ability, and opens heaven in every heart that worships Him, — then indeed are we united; we are mutually debtors to each other of faith and hope, engaged to persist and confirm each other's hearts in obedience to the gospel. We shall not feel that the nominal changes and little separations of this world can release us from the strong cordage of this spiritual bond. And I entreat you to consider how truly blessed will have been our connection, if, in this manner, the memory of it shall serve to bind each one of us more strictly to the practice of our several duties.

It remains to thank you for the goodness you have uniformly extended towards me, for your forgiveness of many defects, and your patient and even partial acceptance of every endeavor to serve you; for the liberal provision you have ever made for my maintenance; and for a thousand acts of kindness which have comforted and assisted me.

To the proprietors I owe a particular acknowledgment, for their recent generous vote for the continuance of my salary, and hereby ask their leave to relinquish this emolument at the end of the present month.

And now, brethren and friends, having returned into your hands the trust you have honored me with, — the charge of public and private instruction in this religious society. — I pray God that whatever seed of truth and virtue we have sown and watered together may bear fruit unto eternal life. I commend you to the Divine Providence. May He grant you, in your ancient sanctuary, the service of able and faithful teachers. May He multiply to your families and to your persons every genuine blessing; and whatever discipline may be appointed to you in this world, may the blessed hope of the resurrection, which He has planted in the constitution of the human soul, and confirmed and manifested by Jesus Christ, be made good to you beyond the grave. In this faith and hope I bid you farewell.

Your affectionate servant,

RALPH WALDO EMERSON.

B.

CORRESPONDENCE WITH REVEREND HENRY WARE, JR.,
CONCERNING THE DIVINITY HALL ADDRESS.

I. WARE TO EMERSON.

CAMBRIDGE, *July* 16, 1838.

MY DEAR SIR, — I do not know how it escaped me
to thank you for the volumes of Carlyle; to make up
for which neglect, I do it now. I am glad to have so
strong a motive as this gives me for reading him carefully and thoroughly. I believe that I am not so far
prejudiced by the affectations and peculiarities of his
later manner as to be unwilling to perceive and enjoy what he has of manly and good ; and I would willingly work myself, if possible, beyond the annoyance of
that poor outside. Indeed, I have always seen enough
of his real merits to wish I could see more, and I heartily thank you for giving me the opportunity.

It has occurred to me that, since I said to you last
night I should probably assent to your unqualified statements if I could take your qualifications with them, I
am bound in fairness to add that this applies only to a
portion, and not to all. With regard to some, I must
confess that they appear to me more than doubtful, and
that their prevalence would tend to overthrow the authority and influence of Christianity. On this account
I look with anxiety and no little sorrow to the course
which your mind has been taking. You will excuse my
saying this, which I probably never should have troubled

you with, if, as I said, a proper frankness did not seem
at this moment to require it.   That I appreciate and rejoice in the lofty ideas and beautiful images of spiritual
life which you throw out, and which stir so many souls,
is what gives me a great deal more pleasure to say.   I
do not believe that any one has had more enjoyment
from them.   If I could have helped it, I would not have
let you know how much I feel the abatement, from the
cause I have referred to.

II. EMERSON TO WARE.

CONCORD, *July* 28, 1838.

What you say about the discourse at Divinity College
is just what I might expect from your truth and charity,
combined with your known opinions.   " I am not a stock
or a stone," as one said in the old time, and could not but
feel pain in saying some things in that place and presence which I supposed might meet dissent, and the dissent, I may say, of dear friends and benefactors of mine.
Yet, as my conviction is perfect in the substantial truth
of the doctrine of the discourse, and is not very new,
you will see at once that it must appear to me very important that it be spoken ; and I thought I would not
pay the nobleness of my friends so mean a compliment
as to suppress my opposition to their supposed views out
of fear of offence.   I would rather say to them : These
things look thus to me ; to you otherwise.   Let us say
out our uttermost word, and be the all-pervading truth,
as it surely will, judge between us.   Either of us would,
I doubt not, be equally glad to be apprised of his error.
Meantime I shall be admonished, by this expression of

your thought, to revise with greater care the address, before it is printed (for the use of the class), and I heartily thank you for this renewed expression of your tried toleration and love.

Respectfully and affectionately yours,

R. W. E.

III. WARE TO EMERSON.

CAMBRIDGE, *October* 3, 1838.

MY DEAR SIR, — By the present mail you will probably receive a copy of a Sermon which I have just printed, and which I am unwilling should fall into your hands without a word from myself accompanying it. It has been regarded as controverting some positions taken by you at various times, and was indeed written partly with a view to them. But I am anxious to have it understood that, as I am not perfectly aware of the precise nature of your opinions on the subject of the discourse, nor upon exactly what speculations they are grounded, I do not therefore pretend especially to enter the lists with them, but rather to give my own views of an important subject, and of the evils which seem to be attendant on a rejection of the established opinions. I hope I have not argued unfairly; and if I assail positions, or reply to arguments, which are none of yours, I am solicitous that nobody should persuade you that I suppose them to be yours; since I do not know by what arguments the doctrine that " the soul knows no persons " is justified to your mind.

To say this is the chief purpose of my writing; and I wish to add that it is a long time since I have been earnestly persuaded that men are suffering from want of sufficiently realizing the fact of the Divine Person. I used to perceive it, as I thought, when I was a minister in Boston, in talking with my people, and to refer to this cause much of the lifelessness of the religious character. I have seen evils from the same cause among young men since I have been where I am; and have been prompted to think much of the question how they should be removed. When, therefore, I was called to discourse at length on the Divine Being, in a series of college sermons, it naturally occurred to me to give prominence to this point, the rather as it was one of those to which attention had been recently drawn, and about which a strong interest was felt.

I confess that I esteem it particularly unhappy to be thus brought into a sort of public opposition to you, for I have a thousand feelings which draw me toward you, but my situation and the circumstances of the times render it unavoidable, and both you and I understand that we are to act on the maxim, "*Amicus Plato, amicus Socrates, sed magis amica Veritas.*" (I believe I quote right.) We would gladly agree with all our friends; but that being impossible, and it being impossible also to *choose* which of them we will differ from, we must submit to the common lot of thinkers, and make up in love of heart what we want in unity of judgment. But I am growing prosy; so I break off.

Yours very truly,　　　　H. WARE, JR.

IV. Emerson to Ware.

Concord, *October* 8, 1838.

My dear Sir, — I ought sooner to have acknowledged your kind letter of last week, and the Sermon it accompanied. The letter was right manly and noble. The Sermon, too, I have read with attention. If it assails any doctrines of mine, perhaps I am not so quick to see it as writers generally, — certainly I did not feel any disposition to depart from my habitual contentment that you should say your thought, whilst I say mine.

I believe I must tell you what I think of my new position. It strikes me very oddly that good and wise men at Cambridge and Boston should think of raising me into an object of criticism. I have always been, from my very incapacity of methodical writing, "a chartered libertine," free to worship and free to rail; lucky when I could make myself understood, but never esteemed near enough to the institutions and mind of society to deserve the notice of the masters of literature and religion. I have appreciated fully the advantage of my position; for I well know that there is no scholar less willing or less able to be a polemic. I could not give account of myself, if challenged. I could not possibly give you one of the "arguments" you cruelly hint at, on which any doctrine of mine stands. For I do not know what arguments mean in reference to any expression of a thought. I delight in telling what I think, but if you ask how I dare say so, or why it is so, I am the most helpless of mortal men. I do not even see that either of these questions admits of an answer. So that, in the present droll posture of my affairs, when I see myself suddenly raised into the importance of a heretic, I am very uneasy when I advert to the supposed duties of such a personage, who is expected to make good his thesis against all comers.

I certainly shall do no such thing. I shall read what you and other good men write, as I have always done, — glad when you speak my thought, and skipping the page that has nothing for me. I shall go on, just as before, seeing whatever I can, and telling what I see; and, I suppose, with the same fortune that has hitherto attended me, — the joy of finding that my abler and better brothers, who work with the sympathy of society, loving and beloved, do now and then unexpectedly confirm my perceptions, and find my nonsense is only their own thought in motley. And so I am

Your affectionate servant,   R. W. EMERSON.

C.

LIST OF MR. EMERSON'S CONTRIBUTIONS TO THE DIAL.

Those marked with an asterisk (*) seem to be his, though I have no very clear evidence. Those marked with a dagger (†) appear to me doubtful. A few more pieces are attributed to him by Mr. Cooke (*Journal of Speculative Philosophy*, July, 1885, page 261), upon grounds which do not seem to me sufficient.

VOL. I. Page 1, The Editors to the Reader; 84, To *** [To Eva, Collected Writings ix. 87]; 122, The Problem; 139, Thoughts on Modern Literature; 158, Silence [Eros, ix. 300]; 220, New Poetry; 242, Wood-Notes; 264, Dana's Two Years before the Mast *; 265, Fourier's Social Destiny of Man †; 339, The Snow-Storm; 347, Suum Cuique; 348, The Sphinx; 367, Thoughts on Art; 401, Michelangelo †; 402, Robbins's Worship of the Soul †; 523, Man the Reformer.

VOL. II. Page 130, Jones Very's Essays and Poems; 205, Painting and Sculpture; Fate; 207, Wood-Notes, II.; 262, W. S. Landor; 373, The Park; Forbearance; Grace; 374, The Senses and the Soul; 382, Transcendentalism *; 408, the Ideal Man †.

VOL. III. Page 1, Lecture on the Times; 72, Tact; 73, Holidays; The Amulet; 77, Prayers; 82, Veeshnoo Sarma; 86, Fourierism and the Socialists; 100, Chardon Street and Bible Conversions; 123, Agriculture of Massachusetts; 127, Borrow's Zincali *; 128, Lockhart's Spanish Ballads *; 129, Colton's Tecumseh *:

132, Exploring Expedition *; 133, Association of Geologists *; Harvard University *; 135, Wordsworth's New Poems; Tennyson and H. Taylor *; 136, Schelling in Berlin *; 181, The Conservative; 227, English Reformers; 265, Saadi; 276, Brownson's Letter to Dr. Channing *; 297, The Transcendentalist; 327, To Eva [Ellen] at the South; 387, Death of Dr. Channing *; 414, Confessions of St. Augustine *; 511, Europe and European Books; 534, Borrow's Bible in Spain *; Browning's Paracelsus †.

Vol. IV. Page 93, Gifts; 96, Past and Present; 104, To Rhea; 134, Pierpont's Anti-Slavery Poems *; Garrison's Poems *; Coffin's America *; Channing's Poems *; 136, To Correspondents *; 247, The Comic; 257, Ode to Beauty; 262, A Letter; 270, Longfellow's Spanish Student †; 271, Percival's Poems †; 357, Tantalus (reprinted in *Nature*, iii. 176–186); 401, Eros; 405, The Times [Blight, ix. 122]; 484, The Young American; 515, The Tragic; 528, The Visit.

D.

LETTER TO MARTIN VAN BUREN, PRESIDENT OF THE
UNITED STATES.

CONCORD, MASS., *April* 23, 1838.

SIR, — The seat you fill places you in a relation of credit and nearness to every citizen. By right and natural position, every citizen is your friend. Before any acts contrary to his own judgment or interest have repelled the affections of any man, each may look with trust and living anticipation to your government. Each has the highest right to call your attention to such subjects as are of a public nature and properly belong to the chief magistrate ; and the good magistrate will feel a joy in meeting such confidence. In this belief and at the instance of a few of my friends and neighbors, I crave of your patience a short hearing for their sentiments and my own : and the circumstance that my name will be utterly unknown to you will only give the fairer chance to your equitable construction of what I have to say.

Sir, my communication respects the sinister rumors that fill this part of the country concerning the Cherokee people. The interest always felt in the aboriginal population — an interest naturally growing as that decays — has been heightened in regard to this tribe. Even in our distant State some good rumor of their worth and civility has arrived. We have learned with joy their improvement in the social arts. We have read their newspapers.

We have seen some of them in our schools and colleges. In common with the great body of the American people, we have witnessed with sympathy the painful labors of these red men to redeem their own race from the doom of eternal inferiority, and to borrow and domesticate in the tribe the arts and customs of the Caucasian race. And notwithstanding the unaccountable apathy with which of late years the Indians have been sometimes abandoned to their enemies, it is not to be doubted that it is the good pleasure and the understanding of all humane persons in the republic, of the men and the matrons sitting in the thriving independent families all over the land, that they shall be duly cared for; that they shall taste justice and love from all to whom we have delegated the office of dealing with them.

The newspapers now inform us that, in December, 1835, a treaty contracting for the exchange of all the Cherokee territory was pretended to be made by an agent on the part of the United States with some persons appearing on the part of the Cherokees; that the fact afterwards transpired that these deputies did by no means represent the will of the nation; and that, out of eighteen thousand souls composing the nation, fifteen thousand six hundred and sixty - eight have protested against the so-called treaty. It now appears that the government of the United States choose to hold the Cherokees to this sham treaty, and are proceeding to execute the same. Almost the entire Cherokee nation stand up and say, " This is not our act. Behold us. Here are we. Do not mistake that handful of deserters for us ; " and the American President and the Cabinet, the Senate and the House of Representatives, neither hear these men nor see them, and are contracting to put this active nation into carts and boats, and to drag them over mountains and rivers to a wilderness at a vast distance beyond the Mississippi. And a paper purporting to be an army-order fixes a month from this day as the hour for this doleful removal.

In the name of God, sir, we ask you if this be so. Do the newspapers rightly inform us? Men and women with pale and perplexed faces meet one another in the streets and churches here, and ask if this be so. We have inquired if this be a gross misrepresentation from the party opposed to the government and anxious to blacken it with the people. We have looked in the newspapers of different parties, and find a horrid confirmation of the tale. We are slow to believe it. We hoped the Indians were misinformed, and that their remonstrance was premature, and will turn out to be a needless act of terror.

The piety, the principle that is left in the United States, — if only in its coarsest form, a regard to the speech of men, — forbid us to entertain it as a fact. Such a dereliction of all faith and virtue, such a denial of justice, and such deafness to screams for mercy were never heard of in times of peace and in the dealing of a nation with its own allies and wards, since the earth was made. Sir, does this government think that the people of the United States are become savage and mad? From their mind are the sentiments of love and a good nature wiped clean out? The soul of man, the justice, the mercy that is the heart's heart in all men, from Maine to Georgia, does abhor this business.

In speaking thus the sentiments of my neighbors and my own, perhaps I overstep the bounds of decorum. But would it not be a higher indecorum coldly to argue a matter like this? We only state the fact that a crime is projected that confounds our understandings by its magnitude, — a crime that really deprives us as well as the Cherokees of a country; for how could we call the conspiracy that should crush these poor Indians our government, or the land that was cursed by their parting and dying imprecations our country, any more? You, sir, will bring down that renowned chair in which you sit into infamy if your seal is set to this instrument of perfidy; and the name of this nation, hitherto the sweet omen of religion and liberty, will stink to the world.

You will not do us the injustice of connecting this remonstrance with any sectional and party feeling. It is in our hearts the simplest commandment of brotherly love. We will not have this great and solemn claim upon national and human justice huddled aside under the flimsy plea of its being a party-act. Sir, to us the questions upon which the government and the people have been agitated during the past year, touching the prostration of the currency and of trade, seem but motes in comparison. These hard times, it is true, have brought the discussion home to every farm-house and poor man's house in this town; but it is the chirping of grasshoppers beside the immortal question whether justice shall be done by the race of civilized to the race of savage man, — whether all the attributes of reason, of civility, of justice, and even of mercy, shall be put off by the American people, and so vast an outrage upon the Cherokee nation and upon human nature shall be consummated.

One circumstance lessens the reluctance with which I intrude at this time on your attention my conviction that the government ought to be admonished of a new historical fact, which the discussion of this question has disclosed, namely, that there exists in a great part of the Northern people a gloomy diffidence in the *moral* character of the government.

On the broaching of this question, a general expression of despondency, of disbelief that any good will accrue from a remonstrance on an act of fraud and robbery, appeared in those men to whom we naturally turn for aid and counsel. Will the American government steal? Will it lie? Will it kill? — we ask triumphantly. Our counsellors and old statesmen here say that ten years ago they would have staked their life on the affirmation that the proposed Indian measures could not be executed; that the unanimous country would put them down. And now the steps of this crime follow each other so fast, at such fatally quick time, that the millions of virtuous citizens, whose agents the government are, have no place to interpose, and must shut their eyes until the last howl and wailing of these tormented villages and tribes shall afflict the ear of the world.

I will not hide from you, as an indication of the alarming distrust, that a letter addressed as mine is, and suggesting to the mind of the executive the plain obligations of man, has a burlesque character in the apprehensions of some of my friends. I, sir, will not beforehand treat you with the contumely of this distrust. I will at least state to you this fact, and show you how plain and humane people, whose love would be honor, regard the policy of the government, and what injurious inferences they draw as to the minds of the governors. A man with your experience in affairs must have seen cause to appreciate the futility of opposition to the moral sentiment. However feeble the sufferer and however great the oppressor, it is in the nature of things that the blow should recoil upon the aggressor. For God is in the sentiment, and it cannot be withstood. The potentate and the people perish before it; but with it, and as its executor, they are omnipotent.

I write thus, sir, to inform you of the state of mind these Indian tidings have awakened here, and to pray with one voice more that you, whose hands are strong with the delegated power of fifteen millions of men, will avert with that might the terrific injury which threatens the Cherokee tribe.

With great respect, sir, I am your fellow citizen,

RALPH WALDO EMERSON.

E.

To the Subscribers to the Fund for the Rebuilding of Mr. Emerson's House after the Fire of July 24, 1872 : —

The death of Mr. Emerson has removed any objection which may have before existed to the printing of the following correspondence. I have now caused this to be done, that each subscriber may have the satisfaction of possessing a copy of the touching and affectionate letters in which he expressed his delight in this, to him, most unexpected demonstration of personal regard and attachment, in the offer to restore for him his ruined home.

No enterprise of the kind was ever more fortunate and successful in its purpose and in its results. The prompt and cordial response to the proposed subscription was most gratifying. No contribution was solicited from any one. The simple suggestion to a few friends of Mr. Emerson that an opportunity was now offered to be of service to him was all that was needed. From the first day on which it was made, the day after the fire, letters began to come in, with checks for large and small amounts, so that in less than three weeks I was enabled to send to Judge Hoar the sum named in his letter as received by him on the 13th of August, and presented by him to Mr. Emerson the next morning, at the Old Manse, with fitting words.

Other subscriptions were afterwards received, increasing the amount on my book to eleven thousand six hundred and twenty dollars. A part of this was handed directly to the builder at Concord. The balance was sent to Mr. Emerson October 7, and acknowledged by him in his letter of October 8, 1872.

All the friends of Mr. Emerson who knew of the plan which was proposed to rebuild his house seemed to feel that it was a privilege to be allowed to express in this way the love and veneration with which he was regarded, and the deep debt of gratitude which they owed to him, and there is no doubt that a much larger amount would have been readily and gladly offered if it had been required for the object in view.

Those who have had the happiness to join in this friendly "conspiracy" may well take pleasure in the thought that what they have done has had the effect to lighten the load of care and anxiety which the calamity of the fire brought with it to Mr. Emerson, and thus perhaps to prolong for some precious years the serene and noble life that was so dear to all of us.

My thanks are due to the friends who have made me the bearer of this message of good-will.

LE BARON RUSSELL.

BOSTON, *May* 8, 1882.

BOSTON, *August* 13, 1872.

DEAR MR. EMERSON, — It seems to have been the spontaneous desire of your friends, on hearing of the burning of your house, to be allowed the pleasure of re-building it.

A few of them have united for this object, and now request your acceptance of the amount which I have to-day deposited to your order at the Concord Bank, through the kindness of our friend, Judge Hoar. They trust that you will receive it as an expression of sincere regard and affection from friends, who will, one and all, esteem it a great privilege to be permitted to assist in the restoration of your home.

And if, in their eagerness to participate in so grateful a work, they may have exceeded the estimate of your architect as to what is required for that pu.pose, they beg that you will devote the remainder to such other objects as may be most convenient to you.

Very sincerely yours,   LE BARON RUSSELL.

CONCORD. *August* 14, 1872.

DR. LE B. RUSSELL : —

Dear Sir, — I received your letters, with the check for ten thousand dollars enclosed, from Mr. Barrett last evening. This morning I deposited it to Mr. Emerson's credit in the Concord National Bank, and took a bank book for him, with his little balance entered at the top, and this following, and carried it to him with your letter. I told him, by way of prelude, that some of his friends had made him treasurer of an association who wished him to go to England and examine Warwick Castle and other noted houses that had been recently injured by fire, in order to get the best ideas possible for restoration, and then apply them to a house which the association was formed to restore in this neighborhood.

When he understood the thing and had read your letter, he seemed very deeply moved. He said that he had been allowed so far in life to stand on his own feet, and that he hardly knew what to say, — that the kindness of his friends was very great. I said what I thought was best in reply, and told him that this was the spontaneous act of friends, who wished the privilege of expressing in this way their respect and affection, and was done only by those who thought it a privilege to do so. I mentioned Hillard, as you desired, and also Mrs. Tappan, who, it seems, had written to him and offered any assistance he might need, to the extent of five thousand dollars, personally.

I think it is all right, but he said he must see the list of contributors, and would then say what he had to say about it. He told me that Mr. F. C. Lowell, who was his classmate and old friend, Mr. Bangs, Mrs. Gurney, and a few other friends had already sent him five thousand dollars, which he seemed to think was as much as he could bear. This makes the whole a very gratifying result, and perhaps explains the absence of some names on your book.

I am glad that Mr. Emerson, who is feeble and ill, can learn what a debt of obligation his friends feel to him, and thank you heartily for what you have done about it. Very truly yours, E. R. HOAR.

CONCORD, *August* 16, 1872.

My DEAR LE BARON, — I have wondered and melted over your letter and its accompaniments till it is high time that I should reply to it if I can. My misfortunes, as I have lived along so far in this world, have been so few that I have never needed to ask direct aid of the host of good men and women who have cheered my life, though many a gift has come to me. And this late calamity, however rude and devastating, soon began to look more wonderful in its salvages than in its ruins, so that I can hardly feel any right to this munificent endowment with which you, and my other friends through you, have astonished me. But I cannot read your letter or think of its message without delight, that my companions and friends bear me so noble a good-will, nor without some new aspirations in the old heart toward a better deserving. Judge Hoar has, up to this time, withheld from me the names of my benefactors, but you may be sure that I shall not rest till I have learned them, every one, to repeat to myself at night and at morning.

Your affectionate friend and debtor,

R. W. EMERSON.

DR. LE BARON RUSSELL.

CONCORD, *October* 8, 1872.

MY DEAR DOCTOR LE BARON, — I received last night your two notes, and the check, enclosed in one of them, for one thousand and twenty dollars.

Are my friends bent on killing me with kindness? No, you will say, but to make me live longer. I thought myself sufficiently loaded with benefits already, and you add more and more. It appears that you all will rebuild my house and rejuvenate me by sending me in my old days abroad on a young man's excursion.

I am a lover of men, but this recent wonderful experience of their tenderness surprises and occupies my thoughts day by day. Now that I have all, or almost all, the names of the men and women who have conspired in this kindness to me (some of whom I have never personally known), I please myself with the thought of meeting each and asking, Why have we not met before? Why have you not told me that we thought alike? Life is not so long, nor sympathy of thought so common, that we can spare the society of those with whom we best agree. Well, 't is probably my own fault by sticking ever to my solitude. Perhaps it is not too late to learn of these friends a better lesson.

Thank them for me whenever you meet them, and say to them that I am not wood or stone, if I have not yet trusted myself so far as to go to each one of them directly.

My wife insists that I shall also send her acknowledgments to them and you. Yours and theirs affectionately,

R. W. EMERSON.

DR. LE BARON RUSSELL.

[I add Mr. Emerson's note of reply to Judge Hoar.]

August 20, 1872.

MY DEAR JUDGE, — I have carried for days a note in my pocket written in Concord to you, but not finished, being myself an imbecile most of the time, and distracted with the multiplicity of nothings I am pretending to do. The note was not finished, and has hid itself, but its main end was answered by your note containing the list, so precious and so surprising, of my benefactors. It cannot be read with dry eyes or pronounced with articulate voice. Names of dear and noble friends; names also of high respect with me, but on which I had no known claims; names, too, that carried me back many years, as they were of friends of friends of mine more than of me, and thus I seemed to be drawing on the virtues of the departed. Indeed, I ought to be in high health to meet such a call on heart and mind, and not the thoughtless invalid I happen to be at present. So you must try to believe that I am not insensible to this extraordinary deed of you and the other angels in behalf of   Yours affectionately,   R. W. EMERSON.

F.

CHRONOLOGICAL LIST OF LECTURES AND ADDRESSES.

In the following list I have endeavored to set down all Mr. Emerson's public discourses (except unpublished sermons) in the order in which they were first delivered, omitting repetitions and rearrangements. If published in his Collected Writings, I have indicated at the end of each note the volume and page where they may be found. Of the unpublished papers I have generally given short abstracts, as far as possible in his own words, with references to passages which have been printed. In courses of lectures the date is that of the first lecture. They were usually continued weekly.

1830.

Feb. 17. Right Hand of Fellowship to Reverend H. B. Goodwin, Concord, Mass. (separately printed 1830).

1832.

Sept. 9. Sermon on the Lord's Supper (xi. 7).

Nov. 4. Introductory Lecture before the Boston Society of Natural History. (At the Masonic Temple, Boston.) Fitness of the study for man. The earth a museum, and the five senses a philosophical apparatus of such perfection that the pleasure they give is trifling in comparison with the natural information they may afford. The Jardin des Plantes, at Paris: the feeling it gives of occult relation between animals and man. Specific advantages of the pursuit: 1. To health. 2. In the discovery of economic uses. 3. The generous enthusiasm it generates. 4. Improvement of mind and character through habits of exact thought. 5. The highest office, to explain man to himself, — or, that correspondence of the outward with the inward world, by which it is fitted to represent what we think.

December. "On the Relation of Man to the Globe." The preparation made for man in the slow and secular changes and melioration of the surface of the planet: his house built, the grounds laid out, the cellar stocked. A most nicely adjusted proportion established betwixt his powers and the forces with which he has to deal. His necessities invite him out to activity, to exploration and commerce. The nimble sailor can change the form of his ship from a butterfly, all wings, to a log, impassive to the storm. Man keeps the world in repair; makes climate and air to suit him. Then, not only a relation of use, but a relation of beauty, subsists between himself and nature, which leads him to science. Other creatures reside in particular places, but the residence of man is the world.

1834.

Jan. 17. "Water." (At the Boston Athenæum before the Mechanic's Institute.) The universal presence of water, and its seen and unseen services to man: plucks down Alps and Andes, and makes habitable land for him; the circulating medium that unites all parts of the earth, equalizes temperature, supports vegetable and animal life. Its external circulation through nature makes the subject of meteorology. Laws of freezing; hydrostatic pressure; capillary attraction; steam.

——. "Italy:" two lectures. Description of the country and its wonders, natural and artificial. Uses of travel: confirmation in unexpected quarters of our simplest sentiments at home. "I was simply a spectator and had no ulterior objects. I collected nothing that could be touched or smelled or tasted, — neither cameo nor painting nor medallion; but we go there to see the utmost that social man can effect, and I valued much, as I went on, the growing picture which the ages had painted and which I reverently surveyed."

May 7. "Naturalist." (At the fourth annual meeting of the Boston Natural History Society.) The place of natural history in a scheme of general education. We cannot all be naturalists, but we may gain from it accuracy of perception, — to be citizens of our own time, which is the era of science. The preëminent claim of natural science is that it seeks directly that which all sciences, arts, and trades seek indirectly, — knowledge of the universe we live in. It shows man in the centre, with a ray of relation passing from him to every created thing. But to gain this advantage we must not lose ourselves in nomenclature. The student must be a poet in his severest analysis; rather, he must make the naturalist subordinate to the man.

1835.

Jan. 29. Six lectures on Biography. (Before the Society for Diffusion of Useful Knowledge, at Masonic Temple, Boston.) I. "Tests of great men." The first question concerning a man: Has he any aim which with all his soul he pursues? 2. Does he work for show?

Luther, Washington, Lafayette, believed in their ends;
Napoleon was no more a believer than the grocer who
displays his shop-window invitingly. 3. The health of
the mind is to work in good-humor. 4. Ability to set
in motion the minds of others. 5. Belief in superhu-
man influence. Attila, esteeming himself the Scourge of
God, opened into himself supernal powers. 6. Unsel-
fish aims. 7. Breadth of vision; to be absolved from
prejudice and to treat trifles as trifles. II. "Michelangelo" (published in *North American Review*, Jan.,
1837). III. "Martin Luther." Great results, with talents and means that are common to all men. His abstract speculations are worthless; he had no appreciation
of scientific truth; his theology is Jewish; if he can
attain the Christianity of the first ages he is content:
the ethical law he states as a Scripture doctrine, not as
a philosophical truth. But he believed deepest what all
believed, and, at the same time, his unsophisticated humanity saved him from fanaticism. He is great because
his head and his heart were sound, and in an extraordinary crisis he obeyed his genius. IV. "Milton" (published in *North American Review*, July, 1838). V.
"George Fox." Religious enthusiasm opens his mind
like liberal discipline; and he was by nature a realist,
even putting a thing for a name. The inward light cannot be confined or transmitted; so the stricken soul
wanders away from churches, and finds himself at first
alone, and afterwards to be in a degree of union with the
good of each name. He and his disciples did magnify
some trifles; their deviations from usage, being sharply
resented, made them exaggerate their importance. The

persecution of the Quakers entitles our town to the name of "that bloody town of Boston." The severities they suffered only gave them an invincible appetite to come hither, and when the master of the ship refused them they sailed for Virginia, for Barbadoes, or some port whence through forests, bogs, and Indian camps they might arrive at the prison, the whipping-post, and the gallows. VI. "Edmund Burke." M. Aurelius and Bacon are examples of philosophers in action, but M. A. is only a moralist, and Bacon left his philosophy when he came to affairs. Burke's intellect was more comprehensive; he was a man of science, and he uses science to harmonize particular aims with the whole constitution of society. He did not take his theory as a basis, but started from facts, and sought to reduce them to the best order which they themselves admitted. His taste, his social disposition, and his affectionate temper prevented his love of liberty from making him a radical reformer. His eloquence was not of the kind of which we have seen eminent examples, in which the heart, not the mind, is addressed, and from which the hearer comes home intoxicated and venting himself in superlatives, but cannot recall a reason, a statement, scarce a sentiment, for the curiosity of inquirers; nor was it that of the man who takes the "practical view," awakens no emotion, but only extorts votes. His was the manly view, such as the reason of nations might consider.

August. Address before the American Institute of Education, "On the Best Mode of Inspiring a Correct Taste in English Literature." Society divides itself into two classes in reference to any influences of learning:

(1) natural scholars ; (2) persons of leisure who read. By being born to the inheritance of the English speech we receive from Nature the key to the noblest treasures of the world. Idle complaint of the number of good books. Books are like the stars in the sky; there are scarce a dozen of the first magnitude. If we should lose all but Shakspeare, Milton, and Bacon, the concentrated attention given to these authors might atone for the loss. Yet if you should read the same number of lines that you read in a day on the newspapers in Hooker or Hume, Clarendon, Harrington, Burke, a short time would suffice to the examination of all the great British authors. And the study of a subject is better than wide *reading.* Chaucer, Spenser, Shakspeare, Bacon, Milton. and Taylor are a class by themselves ; for the second class of the same age, Ben Jonson, Herbert, Herrick, Marvell, Cowley, Cudworth, Dryden ; and, for the third, Pope, Addison, Swift, Hume, Butler, Johnson, Gibbon, Smith. There is no need that all should be scholars, any more than that all should hold the helm, or weave, or sing ; yet I think every man capable of some interest in literature, and that it is the most wholesome and most honorable of recreations. But reading must not be passive ; the pupil must conspire with the teacher. Of inventions and contrivances to aid us, I have no hope from them. The only mechanical means of importance is cheap editions, in good type, of the best authors. Let them go out as magnets to find the atoms of steel that are in the mountains and prairies. (Further passages in Collected Writings, vii. 186; ii. 146.)

Sept. 12. " Historical Discourse at Concord, on the

Second Centennial Anniversary of the Incorporation of the Town." (xi. 33.)

Nov. 5. Ten lectures on "English Literature." (Before the Society for the Diffusion of Useful Knowledge, at the Masonic Temple in Boston.) I. "Introduction." The word literature has in many ears a hollow sound. It is thought to be the harmless entertainment of a few fanciful persons, but it has its deep foundations in the nature and condition of man. The ideas in a man's mind make him what he is. His whole action and endeavor in the world is to utter and give an external shape to his thoughts, to create outside of him a state of things conformed to them. Of the various ways of utterance, the most perfect is language. It is the nature of universal man to think, but human history and our own lives are too close to us: the poet, the philosopher, takes us aside and shows the passage of events as a spectacle. aids us to discern their spiritual meaning, breaks the chains of custom, and lets us see everything as it absolutely exists. The utterance of his thoughts to men proves the poet's faith that all men can receive them, and that all men are poets, though in a less degree. Man stands on the point betwixt spirit and matter, and the native of both elements; the true thinker sees that one represents the other, that the world is the mirror of the soul, and that it is his office to show this beautiful relation. And this is literature. ("Nature," i. 31, 32. 34, 39, 55.) II. "Permanent Traits of English National Genius." Great activity of mind united with a strong will and a vigorous constitution of body characterize the rugged stock from which the splendid flowers of English wit and humanity should bloom. The features that reappear in this race from age to age, in whatever country they are planted, are a certain gravity, humor, love of home, love of utility, accuracy of perception, and a fondness for truth ; a love of fair-play, a respect for birth, a respect for women. The English muse loves the field and the farmyard, the highway and the hearthstone. And the love of gentle behavior, which is at the bottom of the respect for birth and rank, is a stable idea in the English and American mind, now coming to be placed on its true foundation. Welsh and Saxon poetry. III. " The Age of Fable." By the channel of the Norman language, England became acquainted with the metrical romances of the Southern and Western nations in the age when war had reduced the mind of Europe to a state of childishness. Nature and common sense, geography, chronology, and chemistry were set at defiance, and wonder piled on wonder for the delight of credulous nations. Contrast of the beautiful creations of the Greek muse, in which every fable conveys a wise and consistent sense, the stories of Prometheus and of Orpheus with the stories of Merlin and Arthur. Yet, with the progress of refinement, the Romance poet or novelist, seeking to make his picture agreeable, insensibly introduces a fine moral ; uttering, as Plato said, great and wise things which he does not himself understand. Writing only to stimulate and please men, he was led to avail himself of all that familiar imagery which speaks to the common mind. Poetry began to be the vehicle of strong sense, of satire, and of images drawn from the face of nature and com-

mon life. The popular origin of English poetry favored
the unfolding of its peculiar genius, which may be already recognized in the earliest poems whose diction is
completely intelligible to us; the smell of the breath of
cattle, and the household charm of low and ordinary
objects, in Robert of Gloucester and the Vision of Piers
Plowman. ("History," ii. 36–38.) IV. "Chaucer."
The reader of Chaucer is struck everywhere with familiar images and thoughts, for he is in the armory of
English literature. Chaucer is a man of strong and
kindly genius, possessing all his faculties in that balance
and symmetry which constitute an individual a sort of
universal man, and fit him to take up into himself all
the wit and character of his age. But he felt and maintained the dignity of the laurel, and restored it in England to its honor. The ancients quote the poets as we
quote Scripture. But the English poets were forced to
quit the raised platform from which elder bards had
talked down to the people; they had to recur to the
primitive and permanent sources of excitement and delight, and thus laid the foundations of a new literature.
As good sense and increased knowledge resumed their
rights, the poet began to reclaim for himself the ancient
reverence; as Dante, Shakspeare, Spenser, and Milton
have preëminently done. But with the French school
came into English ground a frivolous style, which Scott,
Byron, and Moore have done nothing to dispel. No one
can read Chaucer without being struck with his sense of
the dignity of his art. Equally conspicuous is his humor,
his love of gentle behavior, and his exquisite appreciation of the female character. V. and VI. "Shaks-

peare." Shakspeare stands alone among poets ; to analyze him is to analyze the powers of the human mind.
He possesses above all men the essential gift of imagination, the power of subordinating nature for the purposes
of expression ; and never so purely as in his sonnets, a
little volume whose wonderful merit has been thrown
into the shade by the splendor of his plays. They are
written with so much closeness of thought and such even
drowsy sweetness of rhythm that they are not to be dis-
patched in a hasty paragraph, but deserve to be studied
in the critical manner in which the Italians explain the
verses of Dante and Petrarch. But, however gorgeous
is this power of creation, it leaves us without measure
or standard for comparing thought with thought. Each
passing emotion fills the whole sky of the poet's mind,
and, untempered by other elements, would be a disease.
The healthful mind keeps itself studiously open to all influences ; if its bold speculation carries one thought to
extravagance, presently in its return it carries another
as far. Shakspeare added to a towering imagination
this self-recovering, self-collecting force. His reflective
powers are very active. Questions are ever starting up
in his mind, as in that of the most resolute sceptic, concerning life and death and man and nature. But he is
not merely a poet and a philosopher ; he possesses in at
least as remarkable a degree the clear perception of the
relations of the actual world. He delights in the earth
and earthly things. This drew Shakspeare to the drama.
The action of ordinary life in every sort yielded him the
element he longed for. The secret of his transcendent
superiority lies in the joint activity and constant pres-

ence of all these faculties. He reaches through the three
kingdoms of man's life, the moral, the intellectual, and
the physical being. ("Nature," i. 32, 33, 38, 57.)
VII. "Lord Bacon." Bacon conceived more highly
than perhaps did any other man of the office of the
literary man ; to show, as a thought in the mind, everything that takes place as event. Nothing so great, nothing too small, but he would know its law. He seems to
have taken to heart the taunts against speculative men,
as unfit for business ; he would have the scholar out-
shoot the drudge with his own bow, and even prove his
practical talent by his ability for mischief also. He
surveys every region of human wit, and predicts departments of literature which did not then exist. He is to
be compared with Shakspeare for universality ; but his
work is fragmentary, wants unity. It lies along the
ground like the materials of an unfinished city. Each
of Shakspeare's dramas hath an immortal integrity. To
make Bacon's works complete he must live to the end of
the world. This want of integrity is shown in the importance given to puerile speculations, and in the out-
breaks of a mean spirit ; like the hiss of a snake amid
the discourse of angels. VIII. "Ben Jonson, Herrick,
Herbert, Wotton." Ben Jonson is the president of that
brilliant circle of literary men which illuminated England in Elizabeth's and James's reign. It is the general vigor of his mind, and not the dramatic merit of his
pieces, that has preserved the credit of his name. His
diction is pure, the sentences perfect and strong, but the
plays are dull. Yet it is no vulgar dulness, but the dulness of learning and sense, and presupposes great intel-

lectual activity in the audience ; an Elizabethan age. And, heavy and prosaic as his drama is, he has written some of the most delicate verses in the language. Herrick's merit lies in his power of glorifying common and base objects in his perfect verse. He pushes this privilege of the poet very far, in the wantonness of his power. He delights to show the Muse not nice or squeamish, but treading with firm and elastic step in sordid places, taking no more pollution than the sunbeam, which shines alike on the carrion and the violet. George Herbert is apt to repel the reader, on his first acquaintance, by the quaint epigrammatic style, then in vogue in England. But the reader is struck with the inimitable felicity of the diction. The thought has so much heat as to fuse the words, so that language is wholly flexible in his hands, and his rhyme never stops the progress of the sense. He most excels in exciting that feeling which we call the *moral sublime.* His poems are the breathings of a devout soul reading the riddle of the world with a poet's eye, but with a saint's affections. Sir Henry Wotton deserves attention here more for his fortune than his merit. It would be hard to find another man who stood in personal relations with so great a number of extraordinary men. He has left a few essays and some of his correspondence with his gifted contemporaries ; but he is better known by a few wise maxims and witty sayings.

The most copious department of English literature in the age of Elizabeth and James is the drama. I cannot help thinking that there is a good deal of tradition and custom in the praise that is bestowed upon it. If these plays really exhibit the tone of fashionable society,

we may thank God that he has permitted the English
race in both hemispheres to make a prodigious advancement in purity of conversation and honesty of life. IX.
" Ethical Writers." There is a class of writers who
escape oblivion, not through their learning or their skill,
or from satisfying some demand of the day, but in the
very direction of their thought; because they address
feelings which are alike in all men and all times. The
moral muse is eternal, and speaks a universal language.
Bacon, Spenser, Sidney, Hooker, John Smith, Henry
More, Leighton, Harrington, Milton, Donne, Sir Thomas
Brown, John Bunyan, Clarendon, Addison, Johnson,
Burke, are men from whose writings a selection might
be made of immortal sentences that should vie with that
which any language has to offer, and inspire men with
the feeling of perpetual youth. X. " Byron, Scott.
Stewart. Mackintosh. Coleridge : Modern Aspects of Letters." Byron has a marvellous power of language, but,
from pride and selfishness, which made him an incurious
observer, it lacked food. Our interest dies from famine
of meaning. Cursing will soon be sufficient, in the most
skilful variety of diction. Of Scott it would be ungrateful to speak but with cheerful respect, and we owe
to him some passages of genuine pathos. But, in general, what he contributes is not brought from the deep
places of the mind, and of course cannot reach thither.
The conventions of society are sufficient for him. His
taste and humor happened to be taken with the ringing
of old ballads, with old armor and the turrets of ancient
castles frowning among Scottish hills, and he said, I will
make these tricks of my fancy so great and gay that

they shall take attention like truths and things. By force of talent he accomplished his purpose, but the design was not natural and true, and loses its interest as swarms of new writers appear. Dugald Stewart is an excellent scholar and a lively and elegant essayist rather than an original thinker. Those who remember the brilliant promise of the Introduction to his philosophy, what visions floated before the imagination of the student and how heavily they are disappointed, will be reminded of a description of the entrance of Moscow, which at a distance showed a splendid collection of domes and minarets, but, when the gates were passed, nothing appeared but narrow streets and plain tenements. Sir James Mackintosh is not a writer of that elevation and power of thought to justify a belief that his works shall never be superseded, but his " History of Ethical Philosophy " is valuable for its discrimination, for its suggestions, and for several definitions of much worth. His " English History " is chiefly valuable as it shows how history ought to be written, — not as a narrative of the court, but a treatment of all the topics that interest humanity. Coleridge's true merit is not that of a philosopher or of a poet, but a critic. He possessed extreme subtlety of discrimination, surpassing all men in the fineness of his distinctions, and he has taken the widest survey of the moral, intellectual, and social world. His " Biographia Literaria " is the best book of criticism in the English language; nay, I do not know any to which a modern scholar can be so much indebted. His works are of very unequal interest; in his own judgment half the " Biographia " and part of the third voi-

ume of the " Friend," with a few of his poems, were all
that he would preserve, and if you add the inestimable
little book called " Church and State," I suppose all
good judges would concur.

There remain at least two English authors now alive
[Wordsworth and Carlyle] — and may they live long !
— who deserve particular attention as men of genius
who obey their genius. In general it must be felt that
a torpidity has crept over the greater faculties, a disposition to put forms for things, the plausible for the good,
the appearance for the reality. A degree of humiliation
must be felt by the American scholar when he reviews
the great names of those who in England, from Chaucer
down, have enlarged the limits of wisdom, and then
reckons how little this country, which has enjoyed the
culture of science in the freedom of the wild, has
added to the stock. (" Nature," i. 25, 26.)

1836.

Dec. 8. "The Philosophy of History." (Twelve
lectures at the Masonic Temple, Boston.) I. " Introductory." History dull because badly written. True
history will be commensurate with man's nature : it will
traverse the whole scale of his faculties, and describe
the contrast between his wishes and his position, which
constitutes Tragedy ; his sympathy with the low and his
desire to hide it, which makes Comedy. It will present
other of his social relations besides his conspiracies to
stab and steal ; it will show him in his house, the head
of a little state, served by all and serving all. II.
" Humanity of Science." The first process of the mind

is classification. A tyrannical instinct impels it to reduce all facts to a few laws, to one law. Newton sees
an apple fall, and cries, "The motion of the moon is but
a larger apple-fall." Goethe reduces the plant to a leaf,
the animal to a vertebra. Chladni demonstrates the relation between harmonic sound and proportioned forms.
Lamarck finds a monad of organic life common to every
animal, and becoming a worm, a mastiff, or a man,
according to circumstances. He says to the caterpillar,
How dost thou, brother? Please God, you shall yet be
a philosopher. And the instinct finds no obstacle in the
objects. The blocks fit. All agents, the most diverse,
are pervaded by radical analogies; and in deviations
and degradations we learn that the law is not only firm
and eternal, but also alive; that the creature can turn
itself, not, indeed, into something else, but, within its
own limits, into deformity. Step by step we are apprised of another fact, namely, the humanity of that
spirit in which Nature works; that all proceeds from a
mind congenial with ours. III. and IV. "Art" and
"Literature." Art is man's attempt to rival in new creations that which charms him in external nature. In its
most comprehensive sense, literature is one of its forms,
but in the popular sense they are coördinate and present
a contrast of effects. Art delights in carrying thought
into action; literature is the conversion of action into
thought. The architect executes his dream in stone;
the poet enchants you by idealizing your life and fortunes. In both the highest charm comes from that
which is inevitable in the work; a divine necessity overpowering individual effort, and expressing the thought

of mankind in the time and place. Homer, Shakspeare, Phidias, write or carve as a man ploughs or fights. The poet or the orator speaks that which his countrymen recognize as their own thoughts, but which they were not ready to say. He occupies the whole space between pure mind and the understandings of men. A defect on either side vitiates his success. ("Art," ii. 327–329, 334, 337, 339; "Intellect." ii. 304. 305.) V. "Politics." Another expression of the identical mind of man is the state, the common conscience enveloping the whole population like an invisible net, and bringing the force of the whole against any offender. Government is possible because all men have but one mind, and, in consequence, but one interest. This demands Democracy as the form of government; but it encounters an obstacle in the inequality of property. From the confusion of personal rights and the rights of property have arisen, on the one hand, the sophism of slavery and of despotic government, and, on the other, agrarianism. Sooner or later these forces come into equilibrium. The code at any time is only the high-water mark, showing how high the tide rose the last time. But, with the cultivation of the individuals, forms of government become of less importance; every addition of good sense brings power on the side of justice. ("Politics," iii. 193, 196.)

VI. "Religion." The sense of duty first acquaints us with the great fact of the unity of the mind in all individual men. I seek my own satisfaction at my neighbor's cost, and I find that he has an advocate in my own breast, interfering with my private action and persuading me to act, not for *his* advantage or that of

of all others, for it has no reference to persons, but in
obedience to the dictate of the general mind. Virtue
is this obedience, and religion is the accompanying
emotion, the thrill at the presence of the universal
soul. Right action has a uniform sign in profitable-
ness. All right actions are useful and all wrong actions injurious. But usefulness is only the sign, never
the motive. If the lofty friends of virtue had listened
to prudent counsellors, and not held themselves stiffly to
their own sense, taking counsel of their bosom alone,
the race of mankind would have been impoverished.
Jesus Christ was a minister of the pure reason. The
beatitudes of the Sermon on the Mount are nonsense to
the understanding; the reason affirms their immutable
truth. This is the true Revelation, of which every nation has some more or less perfect transcript. The
effort to embody it in an outward form makes the
church. But all attempts to confine and transmit the
religious feeling by means of formulas and rites have
proved abortive. The truest state of thought rested in
becomes false. Perpetually must we *cast* ourselves, or
we fall into error, starting from the plainest truths and
keeping the straightest road of logic. Every church, the
purest, speedily becomes old and dead. The ages of
belief are succeeded by an age of unbelief and a conversion of the best talents to the active pursuits of life.
A deep sleep creeps over the great functions of man; a
timidity concerning rites and words, diffidence of man's
spiritual nature, whether it can take care of itself, takes
the place of worship. But unbelief never lasts long;
the light rekindles in some obscure heart, who denounces

the deadness of the church, and cries aloud for new and
appropriate forms.   Only a new church is alive ; but all,
while they were new, have taught the same things.
(" Character," x. 95, 96. " Over-Soul," ii. 255, 258, 263,
264, 271. " Spiritual Laws," ii. 150, 151. " Preacher,"
x. 210, 212.) VII. " Society." The man of genius is
he who has received a larger portion of the common
nature. He apprises us not so much of his wealth as of
the common wealth. Are. his thoughts profound ? So
much the less are they his, so much the more the property of all. The attraction of society, of conversation,
friendship, love, is the delight of receiving from another
one's own thoughts and feelings. seeing them out of us
and judging of them as something foreign to us.   (1.)
The first society of nature is that of *marriage*, which has
its own end in an integrity of human nature by the union
of its two great parts, intellect and affection. This is
the rock-foundation of the nuptial bower, which begins
to appear when the air-castle that was built upon it has
faded. (2.) *Friendship*. A man should live among
those with whom he can act naturally, who permit and
provoke the expression of all his thoughts and emotions.
Yet the course of events does steadily thwart any attempt at very dainty and select fellowship, and he who
would live as a man in the world must not wait too
proudly for the presence of the gifted and the good.
The unlike-minded can teach him much. (3.) *The
state*. Seldom a perfect society except at its beginning
or in its crises of peril. A great danger or a strong desire, a war of defence or an enterprise of enthusiasm,
will at any time knit a whole population into one man.

(4.) *Philanthropic association*, which aims to increase the efficiency of individuals by organization. But the gain of power is much less than it seems, since each brings only a mechanical aid; does not apply to the enterprise the infinite force of one man; and in some proportion to the material growth is the spiritual decay. (5.) *Sect or party*, an institution which seems at first sight one of selfishness and voluntary blindness. But the necessity for it is presently seen. There would be no sect if there had been no sect; but each is needed to correct the partiality of some other. The Orthodox Christian builds his system on the fear of sin, the Liberal builds his on the love of goodness. Each, separate from the other, is but a half truth. (6.) The dissolution of society is seen in the *mob*, the action of numbers without individual motives. (7.) A contrast is seen in the effect of eloquence, the power which one man in an age possesses of uniting men by addressing the common soul of them all: if, ignorantly or wilfully, he seeks to uphold a falsehood, his inspiration and erelong his weight with men is lost; instead of leading the whole man he leads only the appetites and passions. A farther advance in civilization would drop our cumbrous modes, and leave the social element to be its own law and to obliterate all formal bonds. ("History," ii. 9. "Friendship," ii. 184, 187. "Compensation," ii. 115.) VIII. "Trades and Professions." A man's trade and tools are a sort of Esop's fable, in which under many forms the same lesson is read. Labor is the act of the individual going out to take possession of the world. In the gratification of his petty wants he is taught, he is armed, he

is exalted. The *farmer* stands on his acres a robust
student of nature, surrounded by his conquests from the
forest, the mountain, and the meadow; prophet of the
seasons, and making, by his skill, rain, wind, and sun
serve him like hired men. The *merchant* is the media-
tor or broker of all the farmers of the earth to exchange
their products; in his head a map of all seaports, a
centre of information concerning the world under the
aspect of production. Look into one of these solitary
fliers that go tilting over the January ocean, and see the
inmate and how he studies his lesson. He is the pensioner
of the wind; his prosperity comes and goes with the fickle
air. He is the man of his hands, all eye, all finger,
muscle, skill, and endurance. He is a great saver of
orts and ends, and a great quiddle. No man well knows
how many fingers he has, nor what are the faculties of a
knife or a needle, or the capabilities of a pine board,
until he has seen the expedients and ambidexter ingenuity of Jack Tar. Less obviously but not less strictly
bound with nature is the *manufacturer*, the artificer in
any kind — nay, every man and woman doing right. Not
only the factory bell or the city clock, but the revolving
sun saith to whomsoever he shines upon, What doest
thou? And every employment is the inlet of power.
All modes of act and thought are good and tolerable;
only not to be dumb and useless, like the larva of the
ant-hill, to be lifted out when it is day, to be lifted in
when it is night, and to be fed.   IX.   " Manners."
The unconscious account that character gives of itself.
The circumstances of the poor and of the middle classes
in civilized countries, being unfavorable to independence

of character, are unfavorable to manners. The habit of
power and authority, the manners of a strong will, are
always imposing. The idea to which they approximate
is that of the hero, or, in modern times, the gentleman or
man of honor; the self-reliant man, exempt from fear
and shame, with a power of beneficence, a power to
execute the conceptions of the soul; the mean between
the life of the savage and the life of the saint. ("History," ii. 28. "Spiritual Laws," ii. 148.)   X. "Ethics,"
or the nature of things, the virtue of the soul of the
world impregnating every atom.   Rise to a certain
height, and you behold and predict what is true for men
in all times. The mind wants nothing but to be roused
from sleep, to be allowed to perceive reality, the mind
common to the universe disclosed to the individual
through his own nature.   XI. "The Present Age."
The age of *trade:* opens all doors; makes peace and
keeps peace; destroys patriotism and substitutes cosmo-
politanism. No man is in a passion, and no man acts
with self-forgetting greatness. You nowhere find a
churl, and nowhere the unkempt Isaiah, the tart tongue
of Milton, the plain integrity of Luther. the sloven
strength of Montaigne.   Diffusion instead of concen-
tration. We have freedom from much nonsense and
superstition, but we pay a great price for it. The old
faith is gone, the new loiters. The world looks bare
and cold. We have lost reverence, yet are timid and
flattering. See the despondency of those who are putting
on the manly robe ; when they are to direct themselves,
all hope. wisdom, and power sink flat down. Tendency
to reflection, introversion, morbid views. It is the age

of second-thought. But there is always a presumption against the truth of a gloomy view. This nakedness and want of object are only the hesitation, while the man sees the hollowness of the old, and does not yet know the resources of the soul. In another age its good fruits will appear. XII. "Individualism." The habit of reflection which characterizes the age, when carried to its height, emancipates the spirit from fear. The ruin which the Copernican astronomy brought to our carnal notions of man's importance is made good by the perception which places reason at the centre. The individual learns that his place is as good as any place; his fortunes as good as any. When he looks at the rainbow he is the centre of its arch; everything out of him corresponds to his states of mind, and becomes intelligible as he arrives at the thought to which it belongs. He stands on the top of the world, and with him, if he will, is the Divinity. ("Self-Reliance," ii. 82, 84. "History," ii. 13, 30, 32.)

1837.

June 10. "Address on Education," at Green Street School, Providence, R. I. The disease of which the world lies sick is the inaction of the higher faculties of man. Men are subject to things. A man is an appendage to a fortune, to an institution. The object of education is to emancipate us from this subjection, to inspire the youthful man with an interest and a trust in himself, and thus to conspire with the Divine Providence. If it fall short of this, it only arms the senses to pursue their low ends; it makes only more skilful servants of Mammon. ("Education," x. 128, 129, 130–132, 134.)

"The American Scholar." Phi Beta Kappa oration at Cambridge, August 31. (i. 81.)

November. "Slavery: an address delivered in the Second Church in Concord, Tuesday, November, 1837, at the request of several gentlemen."

Dec. 6. Ten lectures on "Human Culture," at the Masonic Temple, Boston. I. "Introduction." The aim of former periods was a shining social prosperity: they compromised the individuals to the nation. The modern mind teaches (in extremes) that the nation exists for the individual. The church of Calvin and of the Friends have ever preached this doctrine; our democracy is a stammering effort to declare it. The individual has ceased to be regarded as a part, and has come to be regarded as a whole. He is the world. The new view has for its basis the ideal, the comparison of every action and object with the perfect. The office of culture is to domesticate man in his true place in nature, to demonstrate that no part of a man was made in vain, and to give everything a just measure of importance. II. "Doctrine of the Hands." In the mechanical works which occupy the majority of men, any falseness immediately appears. Wheat will not grow nor iron bend unless the lesson they teach is learned and obeyed, though we should talk a year. This prospective working of nature makes the din and smoke of the city, the incessant drudgery, agreeable to the imagination. Nature is immensely rich, and man is welcome to her store; but she speaks no word, will not beckon or laugh; if he blunders and starves she says nothing. She forces each to his proper work, and makes him happy in it. I confess I hear with more satisfaction the honest avowal of here and there a man to his shuddering neighbors, that he is quite content with this world and does not wish any other, than the hope or the suggestion that heaven will emancipate us from labor. The true rule for the choice of pursuit is that you may do nothing to get money that is not worth your doing on its own account. III. "The Head." The animal has only a joint possession of his nature; nothing in severalty. He does after his kind. The intellect emancipates the individual, for infinite good and also for infinite ill. Man drinks of that nature whose property it is to be *Cause*. With the first surge of that ocean he affirms, *I am*. Only Cause can say I. But as soon as he has uttered this word he transfers this *me* from that which it really is to the frontier region of effects, to his body and its appurtenances, to place and time. Yet is he continually wooed to abstract himself from effects and dwell with causes; to ascend into the region of law. Few men enter it, but all men belong there. A man's progress is measured by what he includes in his *me:* if only the *dining* part, he has not got far. The main thing we can do for the culture of the intellect is to stand out of the way; to trust to its divine power. Two expedients may be of service : (1.) Sit alone : in your arrangements for residence see you have a chamber to yourself, though you sell your coat and wear a blanket. (2.) Keep a journal : pay so much honor to the visits of truth to your mind as to record them. IV. "Eye and Ear." They furnish the external elements of beauty. All body is the effect of spirit, and all beauty the effect of truth. The work of art represents all nature within its little circuit. The perception of beauty belongs to the nature of every man, yet, from defective organization, it is very unequal in different persons. Nothing marks the distance of actual from ideal man more than the want of it. To a true life beauty would be an hourly neighbor. A man should be all eye, all ear, to the intimations of the soul reflected to him from the forms of things; he should purge his organs by purity and self-denial. Then shall the name of the world be beauty, at last as it was at first. (Mostly in " Poet," iii. 9, 19. " History," ii. 17. " Art," ii. 334. " Beauty," vi. 281, etc.) V. " The Heart." In strictness the soul has nothing to do with persons : they are embodied thoughts and affections on which, as upon diagrams, the student reads his own nature and law. Meantime let not this absolute condition be any moment confounded with the relative and actual. This solitude of essence is not to be mistaken for a view of our position in nature. Our position in nature is the reverse of this. Let none wrong the truth by too stiffly standing on the cold and proud doctrine of self-sufficiency. We are partial and social creatures. Our being is shared by thousands who live in us and we in them. This impulse of affection is not to be analyzed, but obeyed. Welcome each to his part, and let relations to them form as they will. If we believed in the existence of strict *individuals*, in an infinity of hostility in the enemy, we should never dare to fight. The rule of conduct in respect to this part of our nature seems to be implicit obedience. The heart in a cultivated nature knows its own, knows that such and

such persons are constitutionally its friends, because they
are lovers of the same things. ("Love," ii. 177.
" Friendship," ii. 183, 185, 187, 197, 199, 202. 203; vi.
258.) VI. "Being and Seeming." We yield to the
promptings of natural affection, the divine leading which
relieves us of individual responsibility; but the excess of
social tendency, of *otherism* in us, leads to affectation.
On the entrance of the second person hypocrisy begins :
the man breaks his being into shows. Yet it is shallow
to think the world full of vice because the conventions
of society, measured by an ideal standard, are little
worth. Adam and John, Edith and Mary, are generous
and tender-hearted and of scrupulous conduct, while yet
they are immersed in these poor forms. They may attain much growth before they shall become impatient of
all but what is real. ("Spiritual Laws," ii. 148, 149.
" Experience," iii. 51.) VII. " Prudence." Needful
that the soul come out to the external world and take
hands and feet. The man of genius may scorn worldly
matters in his devotion to his thought, but the scorned
world will have its revenge. *Health :* use the great
medicines of sleep, fasting, exercise, and diversion.
Sleep, though only for five minutes, is the indispensable
cordial, — this abdication of will and accepting supernatural aid, introduction of the supernatural into the familiar day. *Diversion :* Sir H. Wotton says that souls
grow wiser by lounging. As dangerous a specific as
wine for the whole, but better than wine for the sick.
Good manners have high value for their convenience :
the cool equilibrium, the mild, exact decorum of the
English, saves from many annoyances. (" Prudence,"

ii. 210–225. "Manners." iii. 124.) VIII. "Heroism." (The manuscript wanting. Probably printed, ii. 231.) IX. "Holiness." Heroism is the exaltation of the individual, he regarding external evils and dangers as the measure of his greatness. It is the life of souls of great activity, who have never discriminated between their individual and their universal nature ; really resting on the last, esteem it their private property. The saint, on the other hand, discriminates too sharply : cuts it off and puts it far from him ; calls it God and worships it, and calls the other himself and flouts it. We miss in the devotee the heroic, sprightly, intrepid motions of the soul, and feel no beauty in his life. Two extremes, superstition and atheism, between which our being oscillates : the right religion must be found somewhere between. ("Preacher," x. 213. "Over-Soul," ii. 252, 276–278.) X. "General Views." (MS. wanting.)

1838.

March 12. "War." Seventh lecture in a course before the Am. Peace Soc. at the Odeon, Boston. (xi. 177.)

July 15. "Address delivered before the Senior Class in Divinity College, Cambridge." (i. 117.)

July 24. "Literary Ethics : an oration delivered before the literary societies of Dartmouth College." (i. 149.)

Dec. 5. Ten lectures on "Human Life," at Masonic Temple, Boston, beginning Dec. 5 and continued weekly. I. "The Doctrine of the Soul." Man is related by his form to the world about him ; by his soul to the universe, — passing through what a scale, from reptile sympathies to enthusiasm and ecstasy. Modern history has an ethical character. Even in its outbursts of ferocious passion it is the assertion of justice and freedom. The universal relation manifests itself in the tendency to inquire into the ulterior connection of all parts. Geology opens the crust of the earth that, like a material conscience, it may tell its own tale. In politics the democratic spirit : men are possessed with the belief that man has not had justice done him by himself. Much of the stir and activity exhibits but a half-consciousness of the new thought, but in literature a higher melody has made itself heard. The fame of Mr. Wordsworth is one of the most instructive facts, when it is considered how hostile his genius seemed to the reigning taste, and with what feeble poetic talents it has been established. (" Intellect," ii. 306. " Over-Soul," ii. 251, 254, 255, 260, 263, 267, 268, 270. " History," ii. 12.) II. " Home." The instinct of the mind, its sense of stability, demands some outward type, a *home*, and as fast as one and another are seen to be impermanent transfers its regard. To the infant, the mother, the bed, the house, and furniture supply the object. Presently these pass away ; the boy finds that he and they can part and he remain whole. The old ties fade and are succeeded by new, which prove equally fleeting. He is not yet a man if he have not learned the household laws, the precepts of economy, and how to reconcile them with the promptings of love, of humanity. A wise man can better afford to spare all the marts and temples and galleries and state-houses and libraries than this key that deciphers them all. But the progress of culture is to a deeper home in law, the perceived order and perfection beneath the surface of accident and change. Whilst he is an individual he has in him no assurance of permanence. What security in the affections of a few mortals groping like him for an immovable foundation? But by happy inspiration or slow experience he learns that wherever he goes he is attended by that which he seeks. He no longer dies daily in the perishing of local and temporary relations, but finds in the Divine soul the rest which in so many types he had sought, and learns to look on them as the movables and furniture of the City of God. ("Education," x. 127, 128. Passage in "Domestic Life.") III. "School." Man's teachers are Instinct, Condition, Persons, Books, Facts. *Instinct*, in the high sense, is so much our teacher as almost to exclude all other teaching, but its means and weapons are the secondary instincts, the wants and faculties that belong to our organization. Magnitude and duration make a guide for beginners, as the Linnæan botany leads the way to the natural classification. Next the incarnation of the spirit in *persons*. Every man carries in him a piece of me, which I cannot forego. And we learn as much from the sick as from the well. To be sure, he 's a poor creature, as bad as you or I. What of that? What have you to do with his nonsense ? He is not to have any ray of light, any pulse of goodness, that I do not make my own. Yet if a man suffer himself to depend on persons, he will become deaf and blind. Persons are for sympathy, not for guidance. *Books :* they are not only the history, they are the uttermost achieve-

ments of the human intellect. My great brothers have
seen that which I have not seen. Whilst we read, the
drawbridge is down; nothing hinders that we should pass
with the author. And somewhere, somehow, the passage
must be made; books must make us creative, else they
are hurtful. Another tuition which follows us from the
dawn of consciousness is that of *facts*. Nature, one in
law, falls upon us in subdivision, in showers of facts,
blinding and overwhelming us unless we can dissolve
them by spiritual perception. ("The Times," i. 250.
"History," ii. 35. "Spiritual Laws," ii. 127, 136.
"Over-Soul," ii. 256, 259. "Education," x. 127, 130,
132. "Self-Reliance," ii. 64, 65.) IV. "Love." (Printed
almost entire, ii. 159.) V. "Genius." The enchantment of the intellect, as love is the enchantment of
the affections. The man of genius is the typical man,
the measure of all the possibilities of the soul. See the
effect of eloquence; go into Faneuil Hall. and see how
the pinched, wedged, elbowed, sweltering assembly, when
the chosen man rises, hangs suspended on his lips. Each,
while he hears, thinks he too can speak; life is communicated to our torpid powers, and an infinite hope. Such
is this essence as it is a sentiment. Within we feel
its inspirations; out there in history we see its fatal
strength. It is in the world, and by it the world was
made. ("History," ii. 19. "Self-Reliance," ii. 47.
"Intellect," ii. 314. "Poet," iii. 27.) VI. "The
Protest." The man of genius is the representative man,
because he is the entirely sane man, through whom the
great intellect speaks unobstructed. The tragedy of life
is the presence of the same energy, but obstructed by

unfavorable circumstances. The painful dissonance of the actual. Each new-comer finds himself an unlooked-for guest; there is no place for him congenial to his aspirations. Few men feel that they are doing what is commensurate with their powers. But the obstruction comes in truth from himself, because he shares the inertia of which he complains. If his warlike attitude is made good by new impulse from within, his path is made clear to him. The opposition has only the strength that we give to it. Formidable in appearance, it is tractable to valor and self-trust. VII. "Tragedy." (Printed in the *Dial*, iv. 515.) VIII. "Comedy." (Collected Writings, viii. 149.) IX. "Duty." When we look at life, and see the snatches of thought, the gleams of goodness, amid the wide and wild madness, does it not seem to be a god dreaming? The actual life and the intellectual intervals seem to lie in parallel lines, and never meet. Virtue is the spontaneity of the will bursting up into the world as a sunbeam out of the aboriginal cause. The measure of its force is in the temptations of sense, and character is the cumulative force of the will acquired by the uniform resistance of temptation. (" Self-Reliance," ii. 67, 78, 87. " Compensation," ii. 96, 97, 102, 108, 117. " Spiritual Laws." ii. 132.) X. " Demonology." (x. 7 ; ii. 141.)

1839.

Dec. 4. Ten lectures on the " Present Age," at the Masonic Temple in Boston. I. " Introduction." II. and III. " Literature." There is no luck in literature; it proceeds by fate; yet it is in some sort a creature of

time; the occasion is administered by the low antago-
nisms of circumstances which break the perfect circulation of thought and allow the spark to pass. The char-
acteristics of the age: (1.) That it has all books. (2.)
The multitude and variety of the writers: soldiers, sailors,
nobles, women, write books. There is determined realism; all facts are gathered and sifted by being subjected
to the criticism of common sense. Another trait is the
feeling of the Infinite. The child in the nursery doubts
and philosophizes. He who has most united in himself
the tendencies of the times is Goethe. He can use all
the material. Yet the subjectiveness, the egotism, that is
the vice of the time, infested him also. I am provoked
with his Olympian self-complacency and his total want of
frankness. He works to astonish. (ii. 39, 40, 61. x.
307, 308. Much in the *Dial.*) IV. "Politics." The
State and the Church guard their purlieus with a jealous
decorum. I sometimes wonder where their books find
readers among mere mortals, who must sometimes laugh
and are liable to the infirmity of sleep. Yet politics
rest on real foundations, and cannot be treated with
levity. But the foundation is not numbers or force, but
character. Men do not see that all force comes from
this, and that the disuse of force is the education of
men to do without it. Character is the true theocracy.
It will one day suffice for the government of the world.
Absolutely speaking, I can only work for myself. The
fight of Leonidas, the hemlock of Socrates, the cross
of Christ, is not a personal sacrifice for others, but
fulfils a high necessity of his proper character: the
benefit to others is merely contingent. (ii. 61: iii. 94.

191, 192, 206. 254.) V. " Private Life." A fact full
of meaning, the infinite self-trust of men. No man
likes anybody's intemperance or scepticism but his own.
Yet nothing but God is self-dependent. Man is powerful only by the multitude of his affinities. Our being
is a reproduction of all the past ; a congress of nations.
Men doubt a Divine Power because to our best medi-
tation the Divine Nature refuses to impersonate itself.
They think God is not; when behold all around them
the great Cause is alive, is life itself, and matter seems
but the soft wax in his hand. We are the planters of
various grains in the acre of time ; it is so pretty to
scatter this poisoned dust. and we don't believe we shall
hear of it again. But when it has rooted and grown
and ripened, we eat sickness and infamy and curses, like
bread. With a fidelity not less admirable, Time re-
ceives into its faithful bosom the brave and just deed.
the humble prayer, and it turns out that the universe
was all ear, that the solitude saw, and choirs of witnesses shall testify the eternal approbation. A man's
conviction of the perfectness of Divine justice is the
best measure of his culture. VI. " Reforms." Every
reform shows me that there is somewhat I can spare ;
and thus how rich I am ! Let us catch a golden boon
of purity and temperance and mercy from these faithful
men of one idea. Other creatures eat without shame,
but our eating and drinking are not agreeable to the
imagination. All the objects of nature accuse our
manner of life ; we are touched with inferiority in the
presence of the pine and the hemlock. Meantime, the
reforms of diet are made odious to us by the foolish

detachment of temperance from the rest of life. It should be the sign of virtue and health, but, sought of itself, it is phlegm or conceit. Our institution for property also involves many abuses. A man cannot get his own bread, much less scatter bread to others, without stooping himself to the petty system of monopoly, force, and distrust. You will not take my word that I have labored honestly and added to the amount of value in the world, but demand a certificate in the shape of a piece of silver. Then, the certificates of labor pass without labor, to the undeserving. If it represented character, money would be given and taken without shame : but now, in acknowledgment of the highest services, of a priest or a friend, it seems unfit. Non-resistance : doctrine of manual labor, etc. With regard to all these criticisms of our social ways the individual must resist the degradation of a man to a measure. But, when his time comes, let him cheerfully insist on playing his game out, without being scared by the resistance he may find. People hold to you so long as you treat the ideal life as a petty dream; but if you propose a mode of domestic life in which trifles shall descend to their place and character shall rule, this is an incredible proposition. And yet nature is in earnest. Prayer and aspiration predict their answer in facts. Let us not heed the awkwardness and half-apprehension of its first attempts. What is separate in them do thou blend ; what is finite, exalt to an infinite aim. VII. " Religion." The annals of the world are found first in the mind. An impulse of sentiment in the heart of some Oriental shepherd explodes all considerations of prudence, all ties of custom, and installs him as the interpreter of nature to half mankind. There seems no proportion between cause and effect. But who can tell from what profound crater that spark shot up? The most wonderful fact in history is Christianity. A knot of young, ardent men, probably of ingenuous and bashful complexion, their simple devotion has resounded farther than they dreamed. At the present day the sacred tradition is fast losing its force. It is felt by all the young that the entire catechism and creed on which they were bred may be forgotten with impunity. It stands now on the poor footing of respect. Religion lurks in the philanthropic assemblies and private efforts for reform. The mind of the age begins to see the infinity shed abroad in the present moment, and cannot quit this to go star-gazing after parish circumstances or Jewish prodigies. Open my eyes by new virtue, and I shall see miracles enough in the current moment. Religion does not seem to tend now to a *cultus*, but to a heroic life. He who would undertake it is to front a corrupt society and speak rude truth; and he must be ready to meet collision and suffering. VIII. " Prospects. Duties." There is something low and impertinent in the tone of sorrow and anxiety that characterizes much of the speculation of the present time. We are saturated with good; our blunders lead to success, and "the more falls we get, move faster on." Our attitude should be reception and transmission of the same. The men who evince the force of the moral sentiment are not normal, canonical people, but enormous, indefinite, hastening out of all limitation. The

age is rich and indefinable, far-retreating as the depths
of the horizon. Let us not be too early old. Our ignorance is as handsome as knowledge, whilst we are advancing. If we are not plumed like birds of paradise,
but like sparrows and plebeian birds, let that fact be
humbly and happily borne with. Perhaps all that is
not performance is preparation. The times, the men, —
what are we all but the instant manifestation of the Divine energy? The church, which should represent this
idea, is poor. What I hear there I never meet elsewhere. It speaks in a dialect. It refers to a narrow
circle of experiences and of persons. IX. " Education." What is called education fails because of its
low aim. It would make amends for the Fall of Man
by teaching him feats and games. It aims not to re-
trieve, but to conceal. Yet to be taught is the main
design hung out in the sky and earth. He that has no
ambition to be taught, let him creep into his grave : the
play is not worth the candle. The sun grudges his
light, the air his breath, to him who stands with his
hands folded in the great school of God. A man is not
a man who does not yet draw on the universal and eternal soul. (x. 133, 135–137, 141, 142, 149, 151–155 ; iii.
254, 255; ii. 50, 129, 131.) X. " Tendencies." Society
is divided between two opinions : the assiduous endeavor
to govern, to manage, to repair, to supply buckles and
supports by which the world may be made to last our
day, and the resistance of the young, who throw away
first one, then another habitude, until the world fears
the loss of all regulated energy in the dreams of idealism. All progress tends to a quiet yet sublime re-

ligion, the hem of whose vesture we dare not touch, whilst from afar we predict its coming; whose temple shall be the household hearth, and under whose light each man shall do that work in which his genius delights, — shall have property in entire nature through renouncement of all selfish and sensual aim. (ii. 40, 52, 55–59, 128, 135, 258 ; x. 88.)

1840.

Jan. 15. " Address to the People of East Lexington on the Dedication of their Church." The building of a church may be as profane a business as the building of a hotel. It may proceed from a love of liturgies, the pleasure of partaking in a quiet social ceremony, a tasteful and intellectual entertainment; but there yet remains a whole paradise beyond, unattained, — the enthusiasm, the great ardor that catches men up from time to time for a moment into its height. They may well build churches to refresh their own memory and affection, to certify to their sons that such a thing can be. Know, then, that your church is not builded when the last clapboard is laid, but then first when the consciousness of union with the Supreme Soul dawns on the lowly heart of the worshipper.

1841.

Jan. 25. " Man the Reformer," before the Mercantile Library Association. (i. 215.)

Aug. 11. " The Method of Nature." Address at Waterville College, Me. (i. 181.)

Dec. 2. Eight lectures on " The Times," at Masonic

Temple, in Boston. The MSS. mostly wanting. Largely printed in the *Dial* and in Collected Writings. I. " Introduction." (i. 245.) II. "The Conservative." (i. 277.) III. "The Poet." (Seems not to have been the " Poet " of second " Essays," but mostly "Poetry and Imagination." viii. 7.) IV. "The Transcendentalist." (i. 309.) V. " Manners." (iii. 117.) VI. " Character." (In part, iii. 87.) VII. " Relation to Nature." VIII. " Prospects."

1843.

February. Five lectures on " New England," in the city of New York, beginning Feb. 7. (Reported in *New York Weekly Tribune*, Feb. 11.) I. "Genius of the Anglo-Saxon Race." II. "Trade." III. "Manners and Customs of New England." IV. " Recent Literature and Spiritual Influences." V. " Results." (The MSS. only partially preserved.) The English race from the oldest accounts were marked by a love of liberty, yielding to settled authority more than direct command, and by a respect for women. When the Puritans came to America, the distinguishing traits were, conscience and common sense ; or, in view of their objects, *religion* and *trade*. (1.) The depth of the religious sentiment as it may still be remembered was itself an education : it raised every trivial incident to a colossal dignity. Another result was the culture of the intellect. The universality of elementary education in New England is her praise and her power in the world. To the school succeeds the lyceum, a college for the young farmers throughout the country towns. New England furnishes preachers and school-masters for the whole country, and, besides these, book-peddlers, who thus at small cost see the world and supply the defects of their training. (2.) The other element conspicuous in the Anglo-Saxon mind is the determination of blood to the hand. The favorite employment is trade, and agriculture as the basis of trade. Farming in New England a cold, surly business. Hard work ill-rewarded makes the farmer a narrow and selfish drudge. The best part of the class drained off to the city. Behold the result in the cities that line the Atlantic coast, and the intellectual circulation they nourish. Trade flagellates that melancholy temperament into health and contentment. The good merchant is a very considerable person. He puts more than labor, he puts character and ambition into his business. This runs to excess and overpowers sentiment. That repose which is the ornament and ripeness of man is not in America. In our culture we are too easily pleased. A hint like phrenology is exalted into a science, to outwit the laws of nature and pierce to the courts of power and light by this dull trick. In the scholars an impatience to rush into the lists without enduring the training. Our books are turning into newspapers : our reformers are wearisome talkers ; we put all on the first die we cast. Our genius is tame : our poems are chaste, faultless, but uncharacterized. So of art and eloquence. We are receptive, not creative. We go to school to Europe. The influence of Wordsworth, Coleridge. and Carlyle found readier reception here than at home. It is remarkable that we have our intellectual culture from one country and our duties from another. A wide gulf yawns for the young American between his education and his work. We are sent to a feudal school to learn democracy. But there is an ethical element in the mind of our people that will never let them long rest without finding exercise for the deeper thoughts. It very soon found both Wordsworth and Carlyle insufficient. The criticism which began to be felt upon our church generally was that it was poor, that it did not represent the deepest idea in man. Meantime, this unbelief proceeds out of a deeper belief. We are in transition from that Jewish idea before which the ages were driven like sifted snows, which all the literatures of Europe have tingled with, to a more human and universal thought.

1843.

July 4. "Address to the Temperance Society at Harvard, Mass." A fitting celebration of the national anniversary. The drum is good only for boys and holidays ; the militia is very innocent, and getting a little ridiculous. War is over, but the elements of war remain ; the antagonism has shifted to higher ground. A man's foes are of his own household, within his own skin, a war between the body and the soul. The topic not to be disconnected from the whole subject of that beautiful self-command by which alone a man's life is worth keeping and transmitting. Whatever we may think of particular rules we must rejoice in the general design that every man be master of his organs. Cannot this blood, which in all men rolls with such a burden of disease, roll pure ? To be temperate is to be men ; and for what shall we sell that birthright? It seems to me that the conscience in the coming age is to extend its jurisdiction over the intellectual as over the moral sensibility, that men shall feel the crime of being stupid as they now feel the crime of being fraudulent. Yet it is not in bands nor by pledges to each other that the victory will be achieved, but in the isolated will and devotion of each; in the resolution to give himself no holidays, no indulgences, no hesitations in his clear election of the right and rejection of the wrong.

1844.

Feb. 7. "The Young American:" a lecture read before the Mercantile Library Association, at Amory Hall, in Boston. (i. 341.)

March 10. "Address at Second Church."

Aug. 1. "Address on Emancipation in the British West Indies." (xi. 129.)

Notes for speech on the expulsion of Mr. Samuel Hoar. (I know not if delivered, nor the precise date of writing.) Inevitable effect of the education of any people to disunite and detach the individuals from that mere animal association which is strongest in the most barbarous societies. There is but one man in South Carolina as far as I can see; the rest are repeaters of his mind: here there are so many that it is impossible to combine them by any calculation. I hope when the transgressor comes here, clothed with the earnings of the slave, he shall find a new accuser and judge in every man, and will feel that he is not helped by dealing with the last man to deal with him who comes next. I am far from wishing that we should retaliate. We cannot. We cannot bring down the New England culture and intellect to the South Carolina standard. Let the Carolinian who comes hither receive the grave rebuke of your sanity, your freedom. Let him see that Massachusetts is not a bloody prison, but open as the air, with no guards, no secrets, no fears. We can do nothing, only let us not do wrong. Let us call things by right names. Let us not pretend a union where there is none. Let us not treat with false politeness men who have avowed themselves man-stealers. Let us now put all persons on their guard. Then if a nation exclude every gentleman, every free man from its territory, whose loss is it? Who is the worse?

1845.

July 22. " Discourse at Middlebury College," Vt. (Mostly in x. 249, and iv. 249.)

Aug. 1. Remarks at a meeting in Waltham on the anniversary of the W. I. Emancipation. (Reported in *New York Tribune,* Aug. 7.)

Sept. 22. " Politics." (Apparently remarks at a meeting in Concord, concerning the annexation of Texas.)

Dec. 11. Seven lectures on "Representative Men." Before the Boston Lyceum, at the Odeon. (iv.)

1847.

Feb. 10. " Eloquence." Before the Mercantile Library Association, Tremont Temple, Boston. Reported in *Boston Journal,* Feb. 12. (vii. 61.)

May 8. Discourse at Nantucket. (See Memoir, p. 498.)

November. " Books or a Course of Reading ; " " Superlative." At Manchester, England.

1848.

Feb. —. " Natural Aristocracy." At Edinburgh (x. 33.)

June 7. " Mind and Manners of the XIX. Century." (So reported in Douglas Jerrold's newspaper. The title on the covers of the first three lectures is " The Natural History of the Intellect.") At the Portman Square Literary and Scientific Institution, London. I. " Powers and Laws of Thought." II. " Relation of Intellect to Natural Science." III. " Tendencies and Duties of Men of Thought." (These three were new : their general import has been given in the Memoir ; they were repeated in the course in 1849 and 1850 in Boston and New York, and were substantially the same with some of the lectures on the " Natural Method of Mental Philosophy," in 1858, and " Philosophy for the People," in 1866.) IV. " Politics and Socialism " (apparently the fourth lecture of the course on the " Present Age," 1839 - 40). V. " Poetry and Eloquence " (a Boston lecture of 1847). VI. " Natural Aristocracy " (the Edinburgh lecture).

June —. (At Exeter Hall.) " Napoleon," " Shakspeare," " Domestic Life." (The first two form " Representative Men," 1845 ; the third perhaps " Home," 1838.)

Dec. 27. " England." (Before the Mercantile Library

Association at the Tremont Temple, Boston. Mostly in " English Traits.")

1851.

March 21. Six lectures on the "Conduct of Life," at Pittsburgh, Pa. (Repeated in Boston and elsewhere, and printed in vol. vi. of Collected Writings.)

May 3. "Address to the Citizens of Concord," Sunday evening. (On the Fugitive Slave Law.)

1852.

May 11. Address to Kossuth. (xi. 357.)

1853.

Jan. 10. "Anglo-Saxon." at Springfield. Ill. (Substantially in " English Traits.")

Feb. 27 ? "Anglo - American," at Philadelphia. "American " (in Europe) means *speedy*, everything new and slight. An irresistibility like Nature's, and, like Nature, without conscience. The American's motto is, " The country, right or wrong." He builds shingle palaces, shingle cities, picnic universities, extemporizes a state. An admirable fruit, but you shall not find one good, sound, well-developed apple on the tree. Nature was in a hurry with the race, and never finished one. His leather is not tanned ; his white-lead, whiting ; his sulphuric acid. half strength ; his stone, well-sanded pumpkin pine. The engine is built in the boat, — which does not commend it to the Englishman. The knees, instead of grand old oak, are sawed out of refuse sapling. At the Mississippi your Western romance fades into a reality of some grimness. The men " follow the river ; "

the people as well as the country are the work of the river, and are tinged with its mud. The American is a wilderness of capabilities, of a many-turning Ulyssean culture. More chambers opened in his mind than in the Englishman's. It is the country of opportunity, inviting out all faculties. Every one tasked beyond his strength, and grows early old. Careless in his voting, because he never feels seriously threatened. Yet it is to be remembered that the flowering time is the end : we ought to be thankful that no hero or poet hastens to be born. (Much in " Fortune of the Republic," xi. 393.)

1854.

Jan. 3. A course of six lectures in Philadelphia, of which the following were new : —

I. "Norseman, and English Influence in Modern Civilization." In all that is done or begun towards right thinking and practice, we Americans are met by a civilization already settled and overpowering, the influence of England. The culture of the day, the thoughts of men, their aims, are English thoughts and aims. The practical common sense of modern society is the natural genius of the British mind. The American is only its continuation into new conditions. (The MSS. fragmentary; probably in great part in " English Traits.")
III. " Poetry and English Poetry." (Substantially in " Poetry and Imagination," viii. 7.) V. " France, or Urbanity." France is aggressively cosmopolitan ; has built Paris for the world ; the traveller eats lotus and forgets his home. From every corner of the earth, men who have made their fortunes come to spend their old

age in Paris. The endless facilities, the boundless good-
humor and politeness of the people, full of entertainment, lively as lizards, make it easy to live with them.
It was said of Balzac that he did not need the freedom
of cities to be given to him, but was cheered and welcomed by bands of admirers wherever he presented himself. In their proverb, *Le bon Dieu est Français,* —
God belongs to their tribe. In what I have to say of
France I shall not begin by canting. I am born, I suppose, to my full share of Saxon nationality, and I confess
I have observed that all people of Teutonic stock believe there are certain limits to the Frenchman, not so
quickly found in the neighboring race. They have good
heads, system, clearness, and correct taste. Heine said
the test of any philosophy was to translate it into French.
They are excellent in exact science. Everything is
geometrical. The French muse is Arithmetic. In literature, lucid and agreeable. If life were long enough.
we could spend agreeable years in libraries of French
Mémoires. But they have few examples of a profounder
class, no single example of imagination, and never a
poet; no jet of fire. The office of France is to popu-
larize ideas. Their purpose is to be amused, and they
turn everything to amusement : " wise in pleasures, foolish in affairs." Everything bubbles up at the surface of
that enormous whirlpool, and gives place as fast to a
newer spectacle. They attitudinize ; they dramatize
their own deaths. They write and they act, for effect.
They have no homes, but live in public. I suppose
there was never anything more excellent in its way than
the play of talent, wit, science. and epicureanism in the

French *salons* at the best period. A nation of talkers. Late and early it will be found that they have reasoned best and best discussed what other nations have best done. Then I think that the sense which they give to the word *amour* is the serious bar to their civilization. The French ideas are subversive of what Saxon men understand by society. Yet perhaps these things which disparage the French are the salient points which must strike the spectator, but not really the essential traits. Here was born Fénelon the saint; Montesquieu, who "found the lost titles of the human race;" Pascal : Mme. Guion ; Mme. de Staël. And, to all good readers in French books, there is conclusive proof of moderation, culture, practical judgment, love of the best, or wisdom.

March 7. "The Seventh of March." Lecture read in the Tabernacle, New York city. (xi. 203.)

Aug. 15. "Address to the Adelphi Union of Williamstown College." The scholars an organic caste or class in the State. Men toil and sweat, earn money, save, consent to servile compliance, all to raise themselves out of the necessity of being menial and overborne. For this they educate their children, to expiate their own shortcomings. Art, libraries, colleges, churches, attest the respect to what is ulterior, — to theism, to thought, which superexist by the same elemental necessity as flame above fire. Our Anglo-Saxon society is a great industrial corporation. It sees very well the rules indispensable to success. You must make trade everything. Trade is not to know friends, or wife, or child, or country. But this walking ledger knows

that though he, poor fellow, has put off his royal robes,
somewhere the noble humanity survives, and this con-
soles him for the brevity and meanness of his street-life.
He has not been able to hide from himself that this devotion to means is an absurdity ; is, for a livelihood, to
defeat the ends of living. And it is out of the wish to
preserve sanity, to establish the minor propositions without throwing overboard the major proposition, how not
to lose the troop in the care for the baggage, that he has
said, Let there be schools, a clergy, art, music, poetry,
the college. But if the youth, looking over the college-
wall at the houses and the lives of the founders, make
the mistake of imitating them, they may well say, " We
paid you that you might not be a merchant. We bought
and sold that you might not buy and sell, but reveal the
reason of trade. We did not want apes of us, but guides
and commanders." This atheism of the priest, this prose
in the poet, this cowardice and succumbing before material greatness, is a treason one knows not how to excuse. Let the scholar stand by his order. I wish the
college not to make you rich or great, but to show you
that the material pomps and possessions, that all the
feats of our civility, were the thoughts of good heads.
The shopkeeper's yardstick is measured from a degree
of the meridian. All powers by which a man lays his
hand on those advantages are intellectual ; it is thoughts
that make men great and strong ; the material results are
bubbles, filled only and colored by this divine air. But
this great ocean which in itself is always equal and full,
in regard to men, ebbs and flows. Now, for us, it is in
ebb. It is the vulgarity of this country — it came to us,

with commerce, out of England — to believe that naked wealth, unrelieved by any use or design, is merit. Who is accountable for this materialism? Who but the scholars? When the poets do not believe in their own poetry, how should the bats and the swine? The world is always as bad as it dares to be, and if the majority are evil it is because the minority are not good. If the heathen rage, it is because the Christians doubt. People wish to be amused, and they summon a lecturer or a poet to read to them for an hour; and so they do with a priest. They want leaders : intellect is the thread on which all their worldly prosperity is strung. Yet I speak badly for the scholar if I seem to limit myself to secular and outward benefit. All that is urged by the saint for the superiority of faith over works is as truly urged for the highest state of intellectual perception over any performance. I too am an American and value practical ability. I delight in people who can do things. I prize talent, — perhaps no man more. But I think of the wind, and not of the weathercocks.

1855.

Jan. 25. Lecture on Slavery, in the course, by various persons, at the Tremont Temple, Boston. (Reported in *Boston Traveller*, Jan. 26.)

March. " Beauty and Manners." at Concord (Mass.) Lyceum. Life should not be prosaic. Life tends ever to be picturesque, and the reason why life is prosaic is that it is false, and violates the laws of the mind. The life of man is environed by beauty. Strange that the door to it should be through the prudent, the punctual,

the frugal, the careful; and that the adorers of beauty,
musicians, painters, Byrons, Shelleys, Keatses, should
turn themselves out of doors, out of sympathies, and out
of themselves!

Sept. 20. "Address at the Woman's Rights Convention," Boston. (xi. 335.)

Sept. 29. "Address to the Inhabitants of Concord at
the Consecration of Sleepy Hollow." We see the futility of the old arts of preserving the body; we see the
defects of the old theology; we learn that the race never
dies, the individual is never spared. We give our earth
to earth. We will not jealously guard a few atoms,
selfishly and impossibly sequestering them from the vast
circulations of nature; but at the same time we fully
admit the divine hope and love which belong to our nature, and wish to make one spot tender to our children
who shall come hither in the next century to read the
dates of these lives. Our people, accepting the lesson of
science, yet touched by the tenderness which Christianity
breathes, have found a mean in the consecration of gardens, of pleasant woods and waters, in the midst of which
to lay the corpse. Shadows haunt these groves. All
that ever lived about them clings to them. You can almost see the Indian with bow and arrow lurking yet,
exploring the traces of the old trail. Our use will not
displace the old tenants. To this modest spot of God's
earth shall repair every sweet and friendly influence;
the beautiful night and the beautiful day will come in
turn to sit upon the grass. The well-beloved birds will
not sing one song the less; they will find out the hospitality of this asylum. Sleepy Hollow, — in this quiet

valley, as in the palm of Nature's hand, we shall sleep well, when we have finished our day. And when these acorns that are falling at our feet are oaks overshadowing our children in a remote century, this mute green bank will be full of history: the good, the wise, and great will have left their names and virtues on the trees, will have made the air tunable and articulate. I have heard that death takes us away from ill things, not from good. The being that can share thoughts and feelings so sublime is no mushroom. Our dissatisfaction with any other solution is the blazing evidence of immortality. (Used in the essay on "Immortality," viii. 305.)

1856.

May 26. "The Assault upon Mr. Sumner." (xi. 231.)

Sept. 10. Speech at the Kansas Relief Meeting in Cambridge. (xi. 239.)

1857.

Jan. —. "Works and Days," at Cincinnati. (vii. 149.)

April —. "Memory," at Concord Lyceum.

July 4. "Ode," in the Town Hall, Concord. (ix. 173.)

December. "Country Life," at Concord Lyceum. When I go into a good garden, I think, if it were mine, I should never go out of it. It requires some geometry in the head to lay it out rightly, and there are many who can enjoy, to one that can create it. But the place where a thoughtful man in the country feels the joy of eminent domain is his wood-lot. If he suffer from

accident or low spirits, his spirits rise when he enters it.
I could not find it in my heart to chide the citizen who
should ruin himself to buy a patch of heavy oak-timber.
I approve the taste which makes the avenue to the
house — were the house never so small — through a
wood; as it disposes the mind of the inhabitant and of
his guest to the deference due to each. I admire in
trees the creation of property so clean of tears, of
crime, even of care. They grow at nobody's cost and
for everybody's comfort. When Nero advertised for a
new luxury, a walk in the woods should have been
offered. 'T is the consolation of mortal men. I think
no pursuit has more breath of immortality in it. 'T is
one of the secrets for dodging old age; for Nature
makes a like impression on age as on youth. It is the
best of humanity, I think, that goes out to walk. In
happy hours all affairs may be wisely postponed for this.
Dr. Johnson said, "Few men know how to take a
walk," and it is pretty certain that Dr. Johnson was not
one of those few. 'T is a fine art; there are degrees of
proficiency, and we distinguish the professors from the
apprentices. The qualifications are endurance, plain
clothes, old shoes, an eye for nature, good-humor, vast
curiosity, good speech, good silence, and nothing too
much. Good observers have the manners of trees and
animals, and if they add words, 't is only when words
are better than silence. But a vain talker profanes the
river and the forest, and is nothing like so good company as a dog. We have the finest climate in the world
for this purpose. If we have coarse days and dogdays
and white days, we have also yellow days and crystal

days, — days neither hot nor cold, but the perfection of temperature. The world has nothing to offer more rich than the days that October always brings us, when, after the first frosts, a steady shower of gold falls in the strong south wind from the maples and hickories. All the trees are wind-harps, filling the air with music, and all men are poets. And in summer we have scores of days when the heat is so rich, yet so tempered, that it is delicious to live. For walking you must have a broken country, neither flat like the prairie nor precipitous like New Hampshire. The more reason we have to be content with the felicity of our slopes in Massachusetts, rocky, broken, and surprising, but without this Alpine inconveniency.

1858.

March 3. Six lectures on the "Natural Method of Mental Philosophy," at Freeman Place Chapel, Boston. I. "Country Life." (Abstract included in that of the Concord lecture, 1857.) II. "Works and Days." (Probably the Cincinnati lecture, January, 1857.) III. "Powers of the Mind." Metaphysics owes little to metaphysicians, but much to the incidental remarks of deep men everywhere : Montaigne, Pascal, Montesquieu, even Molière; not D'Alembert, Condillac, or Jouffroy. Taking to pieces is the trade of those who cannot construct. For it is incidental experiences that belong to us; not serial or systematic. We are confined in this vertebrate body, convenient but ridiculously provincial. There is affectation in assuming to give our chart or orrery of the universe; Nature flouts those who do so,

trips up their heels, and throws them on their back.
But so long as each sticks to his private experience, each
may be interesting and irrefutable. Every man knows all
that Plato or Kant can teach him. He was already
that which they say, and more profoundly than they
can say it. We are conscious of an Intellect that arches
over us like a sky, and externizes itself in our perceptions. IV. " Natural Method of Mental Philosophy."
The game of intellect is the perception that whatever
befalls us is a universal proposition ; and contrariwise.
that every general statement is poetical again by being
particularized or impersonated. The mental faculties
are the transcendency of the physical, and thereby we
acquire a key to the sublimities which skulk and hide in
the caverns of human consciousness. Being fashioned
out of one and the same lump, all things have the same
taste and quality. It makes little difference what I
learn, I have the key to all existences. The laws of
each department of nature are duly found repeated
on a higher plane in the mind, — gravity, polarity, the
phenomena of chemistry, of vegetable and animal life.
The progress of science is the carrying out in the mind
of the perpetual metamorphosis in nature. Transition.
becoming somewhat else, is the whole game of nature.
and death is the penalty of standing still. 'T is not less
so in thought. Inspiration to carry on and complete
the metamorphosis which, in the imperfect kinds, is
arrested for ages. Every generalization shows the way
to a larger. The number of saltations the nimble
thought can make measures the difference between the
highest and lowest of mankind. The commonest re-

mark, if the man could extend it a little, would make
him a genius. V. "Memory." The cement, the ma-
trix in which the other faculties lie embedded; the
thread that holds experience together. The difference
in men is in the swiftness with which memory flies after
and re-collects the flying leaves ; or in power to grasp
so firmly at first that the fact does not escape. Memory
is as the affection : we remember the things which we
love and those which we hate. It depends on the cardinal fact of identity, and on a right adjustment to the
poles of nature. The reason of short memory is shallow thought. A deeper thought would hold in solution
more facts. We lose something for everything we gain.
Yet defect of memory is not always want of genius,
but sometimes excellence of genius; presence of mind,
that does not need to rely on its stores. Newton could
remember the reasons involved in his discoveries, but
not the discoveries. VI. "Self-Possession." An individual soul is a momentary eddy, in which certain sciences and powers are taken up and work and minister in
petty circles. Excellence is an inflamed personality.
Every man is right, or, to make him right, only needs a
larger dose. He is excellent in his own way by virtue
of not apprehending the gift of another. Men row
with one hand and back water with the other; not giving to any manner of life the strength of their constitution. In excess, if not subordinated to the supreme
reason, it makes monotones, men of one idea, who must
be humored. The opposite temperament is the disper-
sive, people who are impatient of continued attention,
and must relieve themselves by new objects ; heaps of

beginnings, always beginners. The first rule is to obey your genius; the second, choose what is positive, what is advancing, affirmative. But the affirmative of affirmatives is love. Good-will makes insight. All that we aim at is reception; self-possession and self-surrender. Yet so inextricably is the thread of free-will interwoven into this necessity that the will to receive avails much. Will is always miraculous; when it appears, metaphysics is at fault, it being the presence of God to men. We are embosomed in the spiritual world, yet none ever saw angel or spirit. Whence does all our knowledge come? Where is the source of power? The soul of God is poured into the world through the thoughts of men. Thought resists the brute whirl of fate by higher laws, and gives to nature a master.

Sept. 29. "The Man with the Hoe," at the exhibition of the Middlesex Agricultural Society. ("Farming," vii. 131.)

Dec. 14. "Success," at Hartford, Conn. (vii. 265.)

1859.

Jan. 25. Speech at the celebration of the Burns Centenary. (xi. 363.)

March 23. Six lectures at the Freeman Place Chapel, Boston. I. "The Law of Success." (Probably a repetition of lecture at Hartford, Dec. 14, 1858.) II. "Originality." (viii. 167.) III. "Clubs." (vii. 211.) IV. "Art and Criticism." The advance of the Third Estate, the transformation of laborer into reader and writer, has compelled the learned to import the petulance of the street into correct discourse. The language of the street is always strong. I envy the boys the force of the double negative, and I confess to some titillation of my ears from a rattling oath. What traveller has not listened to the vigor of the French postilion's *sacré*, the *sia ammazato* of the Italian, the deep stomach of the English drayman's execration? Montaigne must have the credit of giving to literature that which we listen for in bar-rooms; words and phrases that no scholar coined, that have neatness and necessity through use in the vocabulary of work and appetite. Herrick is a remarkable example of the low style. Like Montaigne, he took his level, where he did not write up to his subject, but wrote down, with the easiness of strength, and from whence he can soar to a fine lyric delicacy. Luther said, " I preach coarsely ; that giveth content to all." Shakspeare might be studied for his dexterity in the use of these weapons. His fun is as wise as his earnest ; its foundations are below the frost. Dante is the master that shall teach both the noble low style, the power of working up all his experience into heaven and hell, and also the sculpture of compression, the science of omitting, which exalts every syllable he writes. A good writer must convey the feeling of a flamboyant richness, and at the same time of chemic selection ; in his densest period no cramp, but room to turn a chariot and horses between his valid words. I sometimes wish that the Board of Education might carry out the project of a college for graduates, to which editors and members of Congress and writers of books might repair and learn to sink what we could best spare of our words, and to gazette those Americanisms which offend us in all journals: the use of *balance* for remainder ; *some* as an adverb ; *graphic, considerable,* and the like, and the showy words that catch young writers. The best service Carlyle has rendered is to rhetoric. In his books the vicious conventions are dropped; he has gone nigher to the wind than any other craft. As soon as you read aloud you will find what sentences drag. Blot them out and read again, and you will find what words drag. If you use a word for a fraction of its meaning, it must drag. 'T is like a pebble inserted in a mosaic. Blot out the superlatives, the negatives, the dismals, the adjectives, and *very.* And, finally, see that you have not omitted the word which the piece was written to state. Have a good style, of course, but occupy the reader's attention incessantly with new matter, so that he shall not have an instant's leisure to think of the style. Classic and romantic. Classic art is the art of necessity; organic. The romantic bears the stamp of caprice. When I read Plutarch or look at a Greek vase, I incline to the common opinion of scholars that the Greeks had clearer wits than any other people. But there is anything but time in my idea of the antique. A clear and natural expression is what we mean when we love and praise the antique. Dumas or Eugène Sue, when he begins a story, does not know how it is to end. But Scott, in "Bride of Lammermoor," knew, and Shakspeare in "Macbeth" had no choice. V. "Manners." Not to be directly cultivated, but recognized as the dial-hand that divulges our real rank. We must look at the mark, not at the arrow. Common sense is so far true that it demands in manners what belongs to a high state of nature. Manners are named well the minor morals, and they call out the energy of love and dislike which the major morals do. (Largely in " Behavior," vi. 171.) VI. " Morals." (" Character " and " Sovereignty of Ethics," x. 91 and 175.)

May 22. " The Superlative or Mental Temperance," at Music Hall, Boston. (x. 157.)

Oct. 2. " Beauty in Art," at Music Hall.

Nov. 8. " Courage." (vii. 237.)

Nov. 13. " Domestic Life," at Music Hall. (vii. 99.)

Nov. 18. Remarks at a meeting for the relief of the family of John Brown, at Tremont Temple, Boston. (xi. 249.)

Dec. 25. " Conversation," Music Hall, Boston.

1860.

Jan. 6. " John Brown." Speech at Salem. (xi. 237.)

March —. " Poetry and Criticism, at Montreal." Modern criticism is coming to look on literature and arts as history; that is, as growths. Those who were in the fray could not guess the result; those who come after see it as an incident in the history of the race. The Christian religion looked to us as a finality, as universal truth, and we looked down on the rest of mankind as heathens. Now. spiritism shows us that we were sceptics, who can believe only by a grip or a whisper. The amount of revelation from these new doctrines has not been large, but as criticism they have been useful.

March 18. " Moral Sense," at the Music Hall. Boston. Everything in nature is so nicely graduated and linked together that the eye is led round the circle with-

out finding a beginning or end, or ever coming to the
chasm where the Cause acted.   The understanding
would run forever in the round of second causes, did
not somewhat higher startle us now and then with impatient questions: Why do we exist? and what are we?
There is somewhat droll in seeing such a creature as is
a man going in and out for seventy years amid the
shows of nature and humanity, making up his mouth
every day to express surprise at every impertinent trifle,
and never suspecting all the time that it is even singular
that he should exist.   I take it to be a main end of education to touch the springs of wonder in us.   Look at
the house of nature, in which man is so magnificently
bestowed!   But the inventory of his wealth reminds us
of the unworthiness of the owner.   These splendors and
pomps and the control of all that exists, all this he has
inherited.   But does he dwell in this palace of power?
No, he skulks like a gypsy or a robber in the gates and
archways of his house.   What a country muster, what
a Vanity Fair, is the life of man; full of noise and
squibs and whiskey!   Yet see where the final emphasis,
the consent of mankind, lies.   Go into the theatre and
see what the audience applauds when it loves itself for
applauding.   Go into the mass meeting and see the reception which a noble sentiment awakens.   Don't be
deceived by the mean and devilish complaisances.   We
are the dwarfs of ourselves, but the good spirit is never
totally withdrawn from us, cheaply as we hold ourselves.

   June 17.   "Theodore Parker."   Address at the Memorial Meeting at the Music Hall, Boston.   (xi. 265.)

Nov. 3. "Reform," before Mr. Parker's congregation at the Music Hall, Boston. It is not an old impulse by which we move, like a stone thrown into the air, but an incessant impulse, like that of gravitation. We are not potted and buried in our bodies, but every body newly created from day to day and every moment. Reformers are our benefactors and practical poets, hindering us of absurdity and self-stultification. Yet the emphasis that is laid on the popular reforms shows how drowsy and atheistic men are. It is of small importance your activity in them, more or less. What is imperative is that you be on the right side; on the side of man and the Divine justice. The forward class, the innovators, interest us because they stand for thoughts. The part of man is to advance, to stand always for the Better, and not for his grandmother's spoons and his shop-till. The rowdy eyes that glare on you from the mob say plainly that they feel that you are doing them to death; your six per cent. is as deadly a weapon as gun or tomahawk: there is a wrong somewhere, though they know not where.

Nov. 20. "Classes of Men," at Music Hall, on Sunday. Man is a classifier. Love of method appears in the child ; every man has his theory, his objects of interest which appear to him the only interesting, and his classification classifies him. Some people are born public souls, with all their doors open; others are so much annoyed by publicity that they had rather go to prison. The *contrary* temperament, stung to contradict and assault and batter; stiff-necked, with the nose of the rhinoceros, as if remainders of the snapping-turtle

that bites fiercely before yet the eyes are open. *National*
men, who carry the idea or genius of their races, and
so naturally lead them. Men of the world, properly
so called. Archimedes, Columbus, Copernicus, Humboldt, astronomic or mundane brains, adapted to the
world which they study. The two abiding and supreme classes, the executive and the intellectual men :
the head which is good for combining means to ends;
and the demonstrative, who can illuminate the thing to
the eyes of the million. The class who begin by expecting everything, and the other class, who expect nothing,
and thankfully receive every good fortune as pure gain.
The only men of any account in nature are the three
or five whom we have beheld who have a will. The
strength of a man is to be born with a strong polarity,
which, in excess, makes the monotones. But to have no
polarity, no serious interest, inspires the deepest pity.
I do not see any benefit derived to the universe from
this negative class.

1861.

Jan. 6. "Cause and Effect," at Music Hall, before
Theodore Parker's congregation. I think the South
quite right in the danger they ascribe to free speaking.
And if a gag-law could reach to whispers and winks and
discontented looks, why you might plant a very pretty des-
potism, and convert your boisterous cities into deaf-and-
dumb asylums. But no machine has yet been devised
to shut out gravitation, or space, or time, or thought.
War universal in nature, from the highest to the lowest
race. What does it signify? It covers a great and
beneficent principle, — self-help, struggle to be, to resist

oppression, to attain the security of a permanent self-defended being. War is a beastly game, but, when our duty calls us, it is no impediment. Life a perpetual instructor in cause and effect. Every good man does in all his nature point at the existence and well-being of the state. Throughout his being he is loyal. See how fast Trade changes its politics. Yesterday it was all for concession : it said, Oh yes, slavery, if you like it; so long as you will buy goods of me, and pay your debts, slavery shall be good and beneficent. Yes, but Reality does not say the same thing : Reality finds it a pestilent mischief ; and at last Trade says, It must stop ; we shall never have sound business until we settle it finally. In short, to-day Trade goes for free speech, and is an abolitionist. (Much in x. 207.)

Jan. 24. Attempted speech at the annual meeting of the Mass. Anti-Slavery Society, Tremont Temple, Boston. (See report in *Liberator*, Feb. 1.)

Feb. 3. "Natural Religion:" Sunday discourse to Mr. Parker's congregation at the Music Hall. There is nothing arbitrary in creeds : the most barbarous we can translate into our own. They all taught the same lesson : realism, to judge not after appearances, and self-command, the gaining of power by serving that life for which each was created. All indicate the presence of sensible and worthy men who had a law and were a law to themselves. We should not contradict or censure these well-meant, best-meant approximations, but point out the identity of their summits. The distinctions of sects are fast fading away. The old flags still wave on our towers, but 't is a little ostentatiously, with a pride in

being the last to leave them. We measure religions by
their civilizing power. That which is contrary to equity
is doomed. We are not afraid that justice will not be
done, but that we shall not live to see it. So with the
institution of slavery; it must come to an end, for all
things oppose it. We should be so pre-occupied with this
perpetual revelation from within that we cannot listen
to any creed, but only nod assent when they utter somewhat that agrees with our own.

April 9. Six lectures on "Life and Literature," at
the Meionaon, Boston. I. "Genius and Temperament."
Satisfaction at meeting again his accustomed audience.
who do not demand a formal method, but detect fast
enough what is important, without need to have it set in
perspective. Our topic is not excluded by the critical
times which shake and threaten our character-destroying
civilization. Genius is a consoler of our mortal condition, because not the skill of a man, but more than man,
worketh. Genius is the inside of things. Science keeps
us on the surface : talent is a knack to be applied according to the demand ; but genius is sensibility to the
laws of the universe. II. "Art." The activity of nations
is periodic, ebbs and flows. Man is happy and creative ;
then he loses his temper, his arts disappear in the one
art of war. The cumulative onward movement of civilization, the potency of experience, disappears, and the
uncouth, forked, nasty savage stands on the charred desert, to begin anew his first fight with wolf and snake.
and build his dismal shanty on the sand. Perhaps our
America offers that calamitous spectacle to the universe
at this moment. The first aspect of the crisis is like

that of the fool's paradise which Paris wore in 1789 ; the insane vanity of little men, who, finding themselves of no consequence, can make themselves of consequence by mischief. But the facility with which a great political fabric can be broken is instructive, and perhaps indicates that these frivolous persons are wiser than they know, and that the hour is struck, so long predicted by philosophy, when the civil machinery that has been the religion of the world decomposes before the now adult individualism. Yet the height of man is to create. He is the artist. Justice can be administered on a heath, and God can be worshipped in a barn, — yet it is fit that there should be halls and temples, and not merely booths and warehouses ; that man should animate all his surroundings, and impress upon them his character and culture. In America the effect of beauty has been superficial. Our art is nothing more than the national taste for whittling ; the choice of subject is fantastic. Art does not lie in making the subject prominent, but in choosing one that is prominent. The genius of man is a continuation of the power that made him. The hints of Nature tell on us, and when we see an intention of hers we set at work to carry it out ; we feel the eloquence of form and the sting of color. But original and independent representation requires an artist charged in his single head with a nation's force. This determination does not exist in our nation, or but with feeble force : it reaches to taste, not to creation. III. " Civilization at a Pinch." IV. " Some Good Books." It is absurd to rail at books : it is as certain there will always be books as that there will be clothes. 'T is a delicate matter,

this offering to stand deputy for the human race, and
writing all one's secret history colossally out as philosophy or universal experience. We must not inquire too
curiously into the absolute value of literature, yet books
are to us angels of entertainment, sympathy, and provocation. These silent wise, these tractable prophets and
singers, who now and then cast their moonlight illumination over solitude, weariness, and fallen fortunes. The
power of a book. Every letter of our venerable Bible
has been a seed of revolution. What vitality has the
Platonic philosophy! I remember I expected a revival
in the churches to be caused by the reading of Iambli-
chus. And Plutarch: if the world's library were burning, I should fly to save that, with our Bible and Shakspeare and Plato. Our debt to Thomas Taylor, the trans-
lator of the Platonists. A Greek born out of time, and
dropped on the ridicule of a blind and frivolous age.
V. "Poetry and Criticism in England and America."
Something, in every action, of doubt and fear. In the
picture or story this element is taken out; you have the
purity or soul of the thing without any disturbance of
affection. Poetry is the only verity; the speech of man
after the real, not after the apparent. Chaucer, Milton,
Shakspeare, have seen mountains; the young writers
seem to have seen pictures of mountains. How sufficing
is mere melody! What a youth we find in Collins' "Ode
to Evening." and in some lines of Gray's to Eton College! It is a pretty good test of poetry, the facility of
reading it aloud. We have enjoyed the full flowering
of the genius of Tennyson. His dirge on Wellington
combines his name inextricably not only to his hero, but

to the annals of England. "In Memoriam" is the commonplace of condolence among good Unitarians in the first week of mourning: all the merit is on the surface. Recall the verses with which we prompt and prick ourselves in dangerous moments, and you will see how few such he supplies. Like Burke or Mirabeau he says better than all what all think. Music is proper to poetry, but within the high organic music are inferior harmonies and melodies, which it avails itself of at pleasure. Scott is the best example of the mastery of metrical commonplaces. But "Dinas Emlinn" and "Helvellyn" show how near a poet he was. Byron had declamation, he had delicious music, but he knew not the mania which gives creative power. — Criticism has its right place as well as poetry. The virtue of criticism is to correct mere talent by good sense. An ingenious man is the victim of his rhetoric, when really there is no such matter as he is depicting. When Anaximander sang, the boys derided him, whereupon he said, "We must learn to sing better for the boys." And I think the journals, whose shallow criticism we affect to scorn, are right. They miss the firm tone which commands every good reader. The virtue of books is to be readable, and if the book is dull 't is likely the writer is in fault. VI. "Boston." The old physiologists watched the effect of climate. They believed the air was a good republican ; that the air of mountains and the seashore predispose to rebellion. What Vasari said three hundred years ago of Florence might be said of Boston, " that the desire for glory and honor is powerfully generated by the air of that place, in the man of every pro-

fession : whereby all who possess talent are impelled to
struggle, that they may not remain in the same grade with
those whom they perceive to be only men like themselves,
but all labor by every means to be foremost."
We find no less stimulus in our native air. This town
has a history. It is not an accident, a railroad station,
cross-roads, tavern, or army-barracks, grown up by time
and luck to a place of wealth, but a seat of men of
principle, obeying a sentiment. I do not speak with any
fondness, but the language of coldest history, when I say
that Boston commands attention as the town which was
appointed in the destiny of nations to lead the civilization of North America. The leaders were well-edu-
cated, polite persons, of good estate and still more ele-
vated by devout lives. They were precisely the idealists
of England, the most religious in a religious era. And
they brought their government with them. They could
say to themselves, "Well, at least this yoke of man, of
bishops and courtiers, is off my neck. We are a little
too close to the wolf and famine than that anybody
should give himself airs here in the swamp." The religious sentiment gave the iron purpose and arm. When
one thinks of the Zoars, New Harmonies and Brook
Farms, Oakdales and phalansteries, which end in a pro-
tracted picnic, we see with increased respect the solid,
well-calculated scheme of these emigrants, sitting down
hard and fast, and building their empire by due degrees.
Moral values became money values when men saw that
these people would stand by each other at all hazards.
A house in Boston was worth as much again as a house
just as good in a town of timorous people, or in a torpid

place, where nothing is doing. In Boston they were sure to see something going forward; for here was the moving principle itself always agitating the mass. From Roger Williams and Ann Hutchinson down to Abner Kneeland and William Garrison there never was wanting some thorn of innovation and heresy. There is no strong performance without a little fanaticism in the performer. It is the men who are never contented who carry their point. The American idea, emancipation, has its sinister side, which appears in our bad politics; but, if followed, it leads to heavenly places. These people did not gather where they had not sown. They did not try to unlock the treasure of the world except by honest keys of labor and skill. They accepted the divine ordination that man is for use, and that it is ruin to live for pleasure and for show. And when some flippant senator wished to taunt them by calling them " the mud-sills of society," he paid them ignorantly a true praise. Nature is a frugal mother, and never gives without measure. When she has work to do she qualifies men for that. In America she did not want epic poems and dramas yet, but, first, planters of towns and farmers to till and harvest corn for the world. Yet the literary ability our fathers brought with them was never lost. Benjamin Franklin knew how to write, and Jonathan Edwards to think. There was a long period, from 1790 to 1820, when, with rare exceptions, no finished writer appeared. But from the day when Buckminster read a discourse before the Phi Beta Kappa Society at Cambridge an impulse was given to polite literature which seems to date the *renaissance* in Boston.

It is almost a proverb that a great man has not a great son. But, in Boston, nature is more indulgent and has given good sons to good sires. I confess I do not find in our educated people a fair share of originality, any broad generalization, any equal power of imagination. And I know that the history of this town contains many black lines of cruel injustice. No doubt all manner of vices can be found in this as in every city; infinite meanness, scarlet crime. But there is yet in every city a certain permanent tone, a tendency to audacity or slowness, labor or luxury, giving or parsimony; and I hold that a community, as a man, is entitled to be judged by his best. Here stands to-day as of yore our little city of the rocks. and here let it stand forever on the man-bearing granite of the North. Let her stand fast by herself. She has grown great, but she can only prosper by adding to her faith. Let every child that is born of her and every child of her adoption see to it to keep the name of Boston as clean as the sun! And in distant ages her motto shall be the prayer of millions on all the hills that gird the town: *Sicut patribus sit Deus nobis!*

July 10. "Address at Tufts College" (Somerville, Mass.). The brute noise of cannon has a most poetic echo in these days, as instrument of the primal sentiments of humanity. But here in the college we are in the presence of the principle itself. It is the ark in which the law is deposited. If there be national failure, it is because the college was not in its duty. Then power oozes out of it; it is a hospital for decayed tutors, a musty shop of old books. Sanity consists in not being subdued by your means. If the intellectual interest be, as I hold, no hypocrisy, but the only reality, it behooves us to enthrone it and give it possession of us and ours. You, gentlemen, are selected out of the great multitude of your mates, and set apart, through some strong persuasion of your own or of your friends that you are capable of the high privilege of thought. And need enough there is of such. All superiority is this or related to this; for I conceive morals and mind to be in eternal bond. Men are as they think, as they believe. A certain quantity of power belongs to a certain quantity of truth. The exertions of this force are the eminent experiences; out of a long life all that is worth remembering. And yet, with this divine oracle, the world is not saved. Nay, in the class called intellectual, in the institutions of education, there is a want of faith in their own cause. We have many revivals of religion. I wish to see a revival of the human mind; to see men's sense of duty extend to the cherishing and use of their intellectual powers. I wish the revival of thought in the literary class. For greatness, we have ambition; for poetry, ingenuity; for art, sensuality; and the young, coming up with innocent hope and looking around them at education, at the professions and employments, at religious and literary teachers and teaching, are confused, and become sceptical and forlorn. Talents and facilities are excellent as long as subordinated, all wasted and mischievous when they assume to lead and not obey. Now the idea of a college is an assembly of men obedient each to this pure light, and drawing from it illumination. A college should have no mean ambition, but should aim at a reverent discipline and invitation of the soul. Here if nowhere else genius should find its home; imagination should be greeted; the noblest tasks proposed, and the most cordial and honoring rewards. Enthusiasm for liberty and wisdom should breed enthusiasm, and form heroes for the state.

Sept. 27. Address at Yarmouth, Mass., on Education. The world is a system of mutual instruction. Every man is, for his hour or minute, my tutor. Can I teach him something? As surely can he me. Deal kindly and truly with every man, and you convert him into an invaluable teacher of his science; and every man has a science. To set up my stove I want a piece of iron thirty inches square, and that want entitles me to call on all the professors of tin and iron in the village, and to see all the beautiful contrivances for working with them; I only paying for the iron and labor. If I want the underpinning or the frame of a barn, I call on the professors of stone or of wood; and for labor on my garden, I pass by the college chairs, and go to the working botanists and the sweating geometers. The whole art of education consists in habitual respect to wholes, by an eye capable of all the particulars. When I saw Mr. Rarey's treatment of the horse, I could not help suspecting that he must know what sarcastic lessons he was reading to schools and universities. He has turned a new leaf in civilization. What an extension and nobility in his maxim that "he who would deal with a horse must know neither fear nor anger." And the horses see that he is a solid good fellow, up to all their ways, and a little better than they are in their own way.

The school-master must stand in as real a relation to his subjects. The boy must feel that he is not an old pedant, but has been a boy once. (Mostly in "Education," x. 123.)

Nov. 12. "American Nationality." In the Fraternity course, at the Music Hall, Boston. (Reported in *Boston Evening Transcript*, Nov. 13.) It is a mortification that because a nation had no enemy it should become its own, and because it has an immense future should commit suicide. But this mania has been met by a resistance proportioned to the danger. We have often fancied that our country was too large to permit any strong nationality. But we reckoned without the instincts. The waters held in solution substances the most remote, but when the flagstaff of Sumter was shot down and fell into the sea, fibres shot to it from every part. All the evils that have yet ensued are inconsiderable, compared with the relief it has operated to public and private health. Do you suppose that we shall crawl into that collar again? I hope the war is to heal a deeper wound than any it makes; that it is to heal that scepticism, that frivolous mind, which is the spoiled child of a great material prosperity. The war for the Union is broader than any state policy or sectional interest; but, at last, the Union is not broad enough, because of slavery; and we must come to emancipation, with compensation to loyal States. This is a principle. Everything else is an intrigue. Who would build a house on a solfatara, or a quicksand? The wise builder lets down his stone foundations to rest on the strata of the planet. The result at which the government aims, and rightly, is repos-

session of all its territory. But, in the present aspect of
the war, separation is a contingency to be contemplated;
and I say, in view of that, it is vastly better than what
we called the integrity of the republic, with slavery. Now
that we have learned that two railroads are as good as a
river, we begin to think we could spare the Mississippi,
until it has better people on its banks. The war searches
character, acquits those whom I acquit, whom life acquits; those whose reality and spontaneous honesty and
singleness appears. Force it requires. 'T is not so
much that you are moral as that you are genuine, sincere, frank, and bold. I do not approve those who give
their money or their voices for liberty from long habit,
but the rough democrat, who hates abolition but detests
these Southern traitors. There is a word which I like
to hear, " the logic of events." We are in better keeping than of our vacillating authorities, military or civil.
We are like Captain Parry's party of sledges on the
drifting ice, who travelled for weeks north, and then
found themselves further south than when they started;
the ice had moved.

———. " Truth." (Before Mr. Parker's congregation at Music Hall?) In the noise of war we come up
to the house of social worship to school our affections,
drenched in personal and patriotic hopes and fears, by
lifting them out of the blinding tumult into a region where
the air is pure and serene ; the region of eternal laws,
which hold on their beneficent way through all temporary
and partial suffering, and so assure, not only the general good but the welfare of all the suffering individuals.
For evil times have their root in falsehood. At a mo-

ment in our history the mind's eye opens, and we become aware of spiritual facts, of rights, duties, thoughts, — a thousand faces of one essence, Truth. Having seen them, we are no longer brute lumps whirled by Fate, but come into the council-chamber and government of nature. It is rare to find a truth-speaker, in the common sense. Few people have accurate perceptions, or see the importance of exactness. A house-parrot, though not reckoned by political economists a producer, has many uses. She is a socialist, and knits a neighborhood together with her democratic discourse. And she is a delicate test of truth. Hear what stories respectable witnesses will tell of Poll! This want of veracity does not remain in speech; it proceeds instantly to manners and behavior. How any want of frankness on one part destroys all sweetness of discourse! But veracity is an external virtue, compared with that inner and higher truth we call honesty; which is to act entirely, not partially. You may attract by your talents and character and the need others have of you; but the attempt to attract directly is the beginning of falsehood. You were sent into the world to decorate and honor that poverty, that singularity, that destitution, by your tranquil acceptance of it. If a man is capable of such steadfastness, though he see no fruit to his labor, the seed will not die; his son or his son's son may yet thank his sublime faith, and find, in the third generation, the slow, sure maturation. Let us sit here contented with our poverty and deaf - and - dumb estate from youth to age, rather than adorn ourselves with any red rag of false church or false association. It is our homage to truth, which

is honored by our abstaining, not by our superservice-
ableness.

Dec. 29. "Immortality." In the Parker Fraternity
course, at the Music Hall. (viii. 305.)

1862.

Jan. 31. "American Civilization." At the Smithsonian Institution, Washington. (vii. 21, and xi.
275.)

March 16. "Essential Principles of Religion." On
Sunday, before Mr. Parker's congregation at the Music
Hall. (Mostly in "Character" and "Sovereignty of
Ethics," x. 91 and 175.) The great physicists have
signified their belief that our analysis will reach at last
a sublime simplicity, and find two elements, or one element with two polarities, at the base of things; and in
morals we are struck with the steady return of a few
principles: we are always finding new applications of
the maxims and proverbs of the nursery.

April 13. "Moral Forces." At the Music Hall, before the Twenty-Eighth Congregational Society, on a
Fast Day appointed by the President of the United
States. In recommending to the country to take thankful remembrance of the better aspect of our affairs, the
President echoes the general sentiment that we should
carry our relief thankfully to the Heart of hearts, to
Him whom none can name, who hideth himself, and is
only known to us by immense and eternal benefit. Let
us use these words, thanks and praise, cautiously, tenderly, discriminating in our mind as reason of gratitude
that which all men that breathe might join to be glad

for. Let us rejoice in every success and in every overthrow, which a wise and good soul, whether among our
enemies or in other nations, would see to be for the right,
for ideas, for the good of humanity. We are rightly
glad only in as far as we believe that the victories of
our cause are real grounds of joy for all mankind. Yet,
leaving this thin and difficult air of pure reason, and accepting our common and popular sympathies as right
and safe, there is certainly much which the patriot and
the philanthropist will regard with satisfaction. Things
point the right way. A position is taken by the American Executive, — that is much ; and it has been supported by the legislature. What an amount of power
released from doing harm and now ready to do good !
The world is nothing but a bundle of forces, and all the
rest is a clod which it uses. In all works of man there
is a constant resistance to be overcome, and constant
loss by friction. But the tree rises into the air without
any violence, by its own unfolding, which is as easy as
shining is to the sun, or warming to fire. It is the same
with the moral forces. People, in proportion to their intelligence and virtue, are friends to a good measure ;
whilst any wrong measure will find a hitch somewhere.
Inspiration and sympathy, — these are the cords that
draw power to the front, and not the harness of the
cannon. The power of victory is in the imagination.
The moral powers are thirsts for action. We are listless and apologizing and imitating ; we are straws and
nobodies, and then the mighty thought comes sailing on
a silent wind and fills us with its virtue.

June 29. " Thoreau," at the Music Hall, on Sunday.

(MSS. fragmentary; probably used in the Biographical Sketch prefixed to Thoreau's "Excursions," 1863.)

Oct. 12. "The Emancipation Proclamation." (xi. 291.)

Nov. 18. "Perpetual Forces." Fraternity lecture at Tremont Temple. (x. 69.)

Dec. 14. "Health." Health is the obedience of all the members to the genius or character. As soon as any part makes itself felt, there is disease. Perfectness of influx and efflux. There is a certain medicinal value to every intellectual action. Thoughts refresh and dignify us. The most powerful means are the cheapest: pure water, fresh air, the stroke of the hand, a kind eye, a gentle voice, a serene face.

1863.

Jan. 1. "Boston Hymn," at the Music Hall. (ix. 174.)

July 22. "Discourse before the Literary Societies of Dartmouth College." Repeated Aug. 11, at Waterville College. (x. 229.)

Dec. 1. "The Fortune of the Republic." In the Parker Fraternity course, Boston. (xi. 393, with some additions.)

1864.

Aug. 9. "Discourse before the Literary Societies of Middlebury College, Vt."

Nov. 27. Course of six weekly lectures before the Parker Fraternity at the Melodeon, in Boston. I. "Education." II. "Social Aims." (viii. 77.) III. "Resources." (viii. 131.) IV. "Table-Talk." The books that record conversation are incomparably better than the formal biographies, — indeed, the real source of these. The pain of loneliness is to be heeded, just as the toothache is. It was not given for torment, but for useful warning. It says to us, Seek society; keep your friendships in repair; answer your letters; meet good-will half-way. Strict discourse with a friend is the magazine out of which all good writing is drawn. Fine conversation is a game of expansions; like boys trying who will take the longest leap. Many parties in discourse give you liberty, hint, and scope; but a master more purely. Americans have not cultivated conversation as an art, as other nations have done. Indeed, there are some drawbacks in our institutions. A town in Europe is a place where you can go into a café at a certain hour of every day, buy a cup of coffee, and at that price have the company of wits, artists, and philosophers. Our clubbing is more costly and cumbersome. The capital advantage of our republic is that by the organic hospitality of its institutions it is drawing the health and strength of all nations into its territory, and promises by perpetual intermixture to yield the most vigorous qualities and accomplishments of all. What is Europe but a larger chance of meeting a cultivated man? (Mostly in "Social Aims" and in "Clubs.") V. "Books." We expect a great man to be a good reader. In proportion to the spontaneous power should be the assimilating power. 'T is easy to disparage literature, to call it eavesdropping, a naming of things that does not add anything; to say that books draw the mind from things to words; but I find an asylum and a com-

forter in the library. There is no hour and no vexation,
in ordinary health, in which, on a little reflection, I cannot think of the book that will operate an instant diversion and relief. How we turn them to account! It is
not the grammar and dictionary, it is French novels
that teach us French, and German novels that teach us
German. The passions rush through all resistance of
grammar and vocabulary. Provide always a good book
for a journey, as Horace, or Pascal, — some book which
lifts quite out of prosaic surroundings. The important
difference is whether they are written from life or from
a literary point of view. I read lately with delight a
casual notice of Wordsworth, in a London journal, in
which with perfect *aplomb* his highest merits were affirmed, and his unquestionable superiority to all English
poets since Milton. I thought how long I travelled and
talked in England, and found no person, or only one
(Clough), in sympathy with him and admiring him
aright, in face of Tennyson's culminating talent and genius in melodious verse. This rugged countryman walks
and sits alone for years, assured of his sanity and his inspiration, sneered at and disparaged, yet no more doubt-
ing the fine oracles that visited him than if Apollo had
visibly descended to him on Helvellyn. Now, so few
years after, it is lawful in that obese England to affirm,
unresisted, the superiority of his genius. Only the great
generalizations survive. The sharp words of the Decla-
ration of Independence, lampooned then and since as
" glittering generalities," have turned out blazing ubi-
quities, that will burn forever and ever. Our American
culture is a hasty fruit; our scholars are hurried from

the pupil's desk to the master's chair, and do not get ripened; they are like my Catawbas, that need a fortnight more of sun. But it admits what expansion! For good reading, there must be some yielding to the book. Some minds are incapable of any surrender. They " carve at the meal in gloves of steel, and drink the red wine through the helmet barred." Of course their dining is unsatisfactory. VI. " Character." (x. 91.)

1865.

April 19. " Abraham Lincoln." Remarks at the funeral services in Concord. (xi. 305.)

July 21. " Harvard Commemoration Speech." (xi. 317.)

July 31. " Address before the Adelphi Union, Williams College, Williamstown : compiled from my lectures on Art and Criticism; Books; Some Good Books; Success."

1866.

April 14. Six lectures on the " Philosophy of the People," at Chickering's Hall, Boston. I. " Seven Metres of Intellect." (1.) Perception of identity. (2.) Power of generalizing. (3.) Advancing steps, or the number of shocks the battery can communicate. (4.) Pace. (5.) Organic unfolding, classic and romantic. (6.) Nearness. (7.) Imaginative power. The highest measure is such insight and faculty as can convert the daily and hourly circumstance into universal symbols. Nature is always working, in wholes and in details, after the laws of the human mind. Science adopts the method of the universe, as fast as it appears, as its own.

The reality of things is thought. The first measure of a mind is its centrality. We require a certain absoluteness in the orator, the leader, the statesman; and if they have it not, they simulate it. Right perception sees nothing alone, but sees each particular object in the All. The English think that if you add a hundred facts, you will have made a right step towards a theory; if a thousand, so much the nearer. But a good mind infers from two or three facts, or from one, as readily as from a legion. Kepler and Newton are born with a taste for the manners of Nature, and catch the whole tune from a few bars, usually from one; for they know that the single fact indicates the universal law. Power of generalizing differences in men; and the number of successive saltations this nimble thought can make. Habitual speed of combination. Time is an inverse measure of the amount of spirit. II. "Instinct, Perception, Talent." None of the metaphysicians have prospered in describing the power which constitutes sanity, the corrector of private excesses and mistakes. This is *instinct;* and inspiration is only this power excited and breaking its silence. Instinct is a shapeless giant in the cave, without hands or articulating lips, not educated or educable; Behemoth, disdaining speech, disdaining particulars, never condescending to explanation, but pointing in the direction you should go; makes no progress, but was wise in youth as in age. *Perception* is generalization; and every perception is a power. Differs from instinct by adding the will. Insight assimilates the thing seen, **sees nothing alone,** but sees each particular in just connection, sees all in God. In all

good souls an inborn necessity of presupposing for each
particular fact a prior Being which compels it to a
harmony with all other natures. *Talent* is habitual
facility of execution. It formulates thought, and sets it
to work for something practical, which will pay. You
must formulate your thought, or it is all sky and no
stars. All men know the truth, but it is rare to find one
that knows how to speak it. The same thing happens
in power to do the right. Without talent his rectitude
is ridiculous, his organs do not play him true. The various talents are organic, each related to that part of
nature it is to explore and utilize. III. "Genius, Imagination, Taste." Talent grows out of the severalty of
the man, but *genius* out of his universality. It is the
levity of this country to forgive everything to talents.
We have a juvenile love of smartness. But it is higher
to prize the power, above the idea individualized or domesticated. Power, new power, is the good which the
soul seeks. It cares not if it do not yet appear in a
talent ; likes it better if it have no talent. Genius is a
sensibility to all the impressions of the outer world. It
is the organic motion of the soul. It does not rest in
contemplation, but passes over into act. Thus it is always new and creative. *Imagination* uses an organic
classification, joins what God has joined. It is vision,
and knows the symbol and explores it for the sense.
IV. "Laws of mind." (1.) *Individualism.* An individual mind is a momentary eddy, a fixation of certain
sciences and powers. The universe is traversed with
paths or bridges : to every soul is its path, invisible to
all but itself. Every man is a new method, and distrib-

utes things anew. Every persecution shows how dear
and sacred their thoughts are to men. The leaders were
perhaps rogues, but they could not have done their work
but for the sincere indignation of good people behind
them. (2.) *Identity.* What we see once we see again.
What is here, that is there, and it makes little difference
what we learn. In the mind, all the laws of each department of nature are repeated, and each faculty.
Memory, imagination, reason, are only modes of the
same power; as lampblack and diamond are different
arrangements of the same chemical matter. (3.) *Subjectiveness.* The sun borrows his beams from you. Joy
and sorrow are radiations from us. The material world
in strict science is illusory. Perception makes. All
our desires are procreant. What we are, that we see,
love, and hate. A man externizes himself in his friends,
his enemies, and his gods. Good-will makes insight.
All is beautiful that beauty sees. (4.) *Transition. flux:*
the blunder of the *savants* is to fancy science to be a
finality. But the mind cares for a fact, not as a finality, but only as a convertibility into every other fact and
system, and so indicative of the First Cause. Wisdom
consists in keeping the soul liquid; in resisting the tendency to rapid petrifaction. (5.) *Detachment.* A man
is intellectual in proportion as he can detach his thought
from himself, and has no engagement in it which can
hinder him from looking at it as somewhat foreign, seeing it not under a personal but a universal light. What
is vulgar but the laying the emphasis on persons and
facts, instead of on the quality of the fact? Yet this
privilege is guarded with costly penalty. This detach-

ment paralyzes the will. There is this vice about men of thought, that you cannot quite trust them. They have a hankering to play providence, and excuse themselves from the rules which they apply to the human race. This interval even comes between the thinker and his conversation, which he cannot inform with his genius. V. "Conduct of the Intellect." The condition of sanity is to respect the order in the intellectual world ; to keep down talent in its place ; to enthrone instinct. The primary rule for the conduct of intellect is to have control of the thoughts without losing their natural attitudes and action. They are the oracles ; we are not to poke and force, but to follow them. Yet the spirits of the prophets are subject to the prophets. A master can formulate his thought. There are men of great apprehension, who can easily entertain ideas, but are not exact, severe with themselves. One wishes to lock them up and compel them to perfect their work. Will is the measure of power. He alone is strong and happy who has a will. Genius certifies its possession of a thought by translating it into a fact which perfectly represents it. But the consolation of being the victim of noble agents is at times all that appears. The ground position is that the intellect grows by moral obedience. VI. " Relation of the Intellect to Morals." The spiritual power of man is twofold ; intellect and will. mind and heart. Each is easily exalted in our thought until it seems to fill the universe and become the synonym of God. Each has its vices, obvious enough when the opposite element is deficient. Intellect is sceptical. and runs down into talent. On the other side, the affections are blind guides. But all great minds and all great hearts have mutually allowed the absolute necessity of the twain. Action and idea are man and woman, both indispensable : why should they rail at and exclude each other ?

Dec. 11. "Man of the World," before the Parker Fraternity. The earth shows age, and the benefits of age. It is a very refined air that we breathe ; a refined world. It attests the presence of man and how long he has been here. He is a born collector, not of coins or pictures, but of arts, manners. thoughts, achievements. My man of the world is no monotone or man of one idea, but has the whole scale of speech to use as occasion requires ; the scholastic with clerks. the polite in the parlor. and the speech of the street. He has a certain toleration, a letting-be and letting-do ; a consideration for the faults of others, but a severity to his own. But, with all his secular merits, he belongs to the other world. too. He knows the joys of the imagination ; he prefers a middle condition : he is capable of humility, he is capable of sacrifices. He is the man of the world who can lift the sense of other men, since he knows the real value of money, culture, languages, art, science, and religion. The one evil of the world is blockheads. and its salvation is the sensible men, of catholicity and of individual bias.

1867.

March 4. "Eloquence," at Chicago. (viii. 107.)

April 14. Remarks at the funeral of George L. Stearns, at Medford, Mass. (Reported in *Commonwealth*, April 27.)

April 19.   Address at the dedication of the Soldiers' Monument. Concord, Mass.   (xi. 99.)

May 12.   "Rule of Life."   At Horticultural Hall, before the Radical Association.   (Mostly in "Sovereignty of Ethics," x. 175, and " Preacher," x. 207.)

May 30.   "Remarks at the Organization of the Free Religious Association."   At Horticultural Hall, Boston.   (xi. 379.)

Aug. 21.   Speech at the dinner, in Boston, to the Chinese Embassy.   (Reported in *Boston Daily Advertiser.* Aug. 27.)

Sept. 16.   "The Preacher."   At a meeting at Reverend J. T. Sargent's.   (x. 207.)

1868.

Oct 12.   Six lectures at the Meionaon, Boston.   IV. "Leasts and Mosts."   (The lecture for which "Civilization at a Pinch" was substituted, April, 1861.) Aristotle said the nature of everything is best seen in its smallest portions.   Size is of no account; the snow-flake is a small glacier, the glacier a large snow-flake.   See everywhere the simplicity of the means by which great things are done.   Earth-worms preserve the ground in a state fit for vegetation.   Corallines build continents.   And in daily life it is certain that what is memorable to us is short passages of happy experience.   The essence of our lives is contained sometimes in a few days or hours.   So in literature : a few anecdotes. a few poems, perhaps a few lines of a poem, refuse to be forgotten ; the rest lies undisturbed in the library.   'T is a narrow line that divides an awkward act from the finish of gracefulness.   England, France,

America, are proud nations, as Romans and Greeks were before them. *Volvox globator*, the initial microscopic mite from which man draws his pedigree, has got on so far. He has rolled and rotated to some purpose. Power resides in small things, and wisdom is always marked by simplicity, temperance, and humility. Worship, indeed, is the perception of the Power which constructs the greatness of the centuries out of the paltriness of the hours. V. "Hospitality, Homes." In Scott's poem, the stranger, arriving at the mountaineer's camp and asked what he requires, replies: "Rest, and a guide, and food, and fire." That seems little, but each of these four wants admits of large interpretation. "Rest" means peace of mind; "guide," a guardian angel; "food" means bread of life; and "fire," love. The household are put to their extremity of means even to attempt such heavenly hospitality. I do not know that any city is big enough to meet these demands. And as God made the country and man made the town, I think we must supplement the weakness of the entertainer by leading the traveller thither where Nature bears the expense. A thoughtful man, if he has liberty to choose, will easily prefer the country for his home, because here no man is poor; nature takes charge of furnishing the beauty and magnificence, gratis. Hospitality is in degrees. Give the elements, be sure, and as good as you can; but there are higher hospitalities, — of thoroughly simple and good manners; hospitality to the thought of the guest. See what he can do, and aid him to do that. Let him feel that his aspirations are felt and honored by you. In every family there is some one inmate or visitor who has taught the young people how to distinguish truth from falsehood, and not to regard follies as merits ; perhaps some grave senior, or some maiden aunt, lover of solitude, has deserted her remote village and its church, to refresh herself awhile with young faces, and defend them from parental routine. She knows well the way to the heart of children by speaking to their imagination, by rejoicing in theirs ; by feeding them with high anecdotes, unforgettable, lifting them from book to book, inspiring curiosity and even ambition prematurely in young bosoms; teasing, flattering, chiding, spoiling them for the simple delight of her sympathy and pride. Perhaps they will not find in all the colleges so real a benefactor. VI. "Greatness." (viii. 283, in part.)

1869.

Jan. 2. " Readings of English Poetry and Prose." At Chickering's Hall, Boston, on ten Saturday afternoons. I. " Chivalry." Extracts from Robert Gloucester's Chronicle, etc. II. "Chaucer." III. (Wanting.) IV. "Shakspeare." V. " Ben Jonson and Lord Bacon." VI. "Herrick, Donne, Herbert, Vaughan, Marvell." VII. " Milton." VIII. (Wanting.) IX. " Johnson, Gibbon, Burke, Cowper, Wordsworth." X. (Wanting.)

March 1. "Mary Moody Emerson." Before the Woman's Club, in Boston. (x. 371.)

April 4. " Natural Religion." At Horticultural Hall, Boston. (Mostly in " Sovereignty of Ethics," x. 175.)

May 17. A reading on "Religion," at Rev. J. T. Sargent's.

May 28.   Speech at the second annual meeting of the
Free Religious Association; Tremont Temple, Boston.
(xi. 385.)

Sept. 14.   Speech at the evening reception on the
centennial anniversary of Alexander von Humboldt's
birth.   (In the publication of the proceedings by the Boston Society of Natural History, 1870, p. 71.)

1870.

April 26.   Sixteen university lectures at Harvard
College, on " The Natural History of the Intellect."   1.
Introduction ; Praise of Knowledge.   2. Transcendency
of Physics.   3, 4. Perception.   5, 6. Memory.   7. Im-
agination.   8. Inspiration.   9. Genius.   10. Common
Sense.   11. Identity.   12, 13. Metres of Mind.   14.
Platonists.   15. Conduct of Intellect.   16. Relation of
Intellect to Morals.   (Repeated in 1871, in a slightly
different order, omitting 11, 14, and adding Wit and
Humor, Demonology, and another lecture on the Conduct of Intellect.   In substance, these lectures are mostly
the same with the first three in the course on " Mind and
Manners in the XIX. Century " (1848), and with some of
those on the " Natural Method of Mental Philosophy "
(1858), and " Philosophy for the People " (1866.)   Most
of what was new is given in " Poetry and Imagination,"
Collected Writings, viii. 7.)

Dec. 22.   Speech before the New England Society,
at Delmonico's, New York.   (Printed in the Proceedings of the Society.)

Dec. 23.   " Discourse on the Anniversary of the Land-
ing of the Pilgrims at Plymouth."   Before the New

England Society, at Steinway Hall, New York. (Reported in *New York Tribune*, Dec. 24, and *Boston Daily Advertiser*, Dec. 26.)

1871.

Feb. 3. Speech at the meeting for organizing the Museum of Fine Arts in Boston. (Reported in *Boston Daily Advertiser*, Feb. 4.)

Aug. 15. "Walter Scott." At Massachusetts Historical Society, on the centennial anniversary of Scott's birth. (xi. 370.)

1872.

Jan. 4. " Inspiration : " one of a course of four lectures at Peabody Institute, Baltimore. (viii. 255.)

Jan. 7. " Books and Reading." At Howard University, Washington. (Reported in *Boston Evening Transcript*, Jan. 22.)

April 15. Six readings at Mechanics Hall, Boston. I. " Books. Read Thoreau's ' Inspiration,' H. Hunt's ' Thought.' II. Poetry and Imagination [as printed in viii. 7], as far as through *Creation*, and read Wordsworth's ' Schill,' Byron's ' Soul,' lines from ' Island,' and ' Licoo,' ' Ballad of Thomas the Rhymer,' Lewis' ' Lines to Pope,' Scott's ' Look not thou on Beauty,' B. Jonson, ' Ode to Himself.' III. Poetry and Imagination, concluded, and read Taliessin, ' Dinas Emlinn ' Saadi, from ' Westöstliche Divan,' Arab ballad from W. O. D. IV. Criticism : Klephtic ballads, ' Lochinvar,' Timrod's poem, ' Boy of Egremont.' V. Culture. Goethe, Pascal, Pope, Bolingbroke, Lionardo da Vinci, Varnhagen v. Ense. VI. Morals, Religion."

Aug. 2.   Speech at the dinner in Boston to the Japanese envoys.   (Reported in *Commonwealth*, Aug. 10.)

Oct. 15.   Speech at dinner for Mr. J. A. Froude, at New York.   (Reported in *New York Tribune*, Oct. 16.)

1873.

Oct. 1.   Address at the opening of the Monroe Public Library, Concord, Mass.

Dec. 16.   Read in Faneuil Hall the poem "Boston." (ix. 182.)

1875.

April 19.   Address at the unveiling of the statue of the Minute-Man at Concord Bridge.   (Reported in *Commonwealth*, April 24.)

1876.

June 28.   Oration to the Senior Class of the University of Virginia.   (x. 247.)

Nov. 8.   Speech at the meeting of the Latin School Association in Boston, on the centennial anniversary of the reopening of the school after the evacuation of the town by the British troops.   (Reported in *Boston Evening Transcript*, Nov. 9.)

1877.

April 20.   "Boston."   At Old South Church, Boston.   (From the course on "Life and Literature," in 1861, with some additions.)

1878.

March 30.   "The Fortune of the Republic."   At Old South Church, Boston.   (A lecture of 1863, with additions.   Published, xi. 393.)

1879.

May 5. "The Preacher." At Divinity School Chapel. Cambridge. (The lecture of Sept. 16, 1867. Published, x. 207.)

1881.

Feb. 10. "Carlyle." At Massachusetts Historical Society. (Published, x. 453.)

INDEX.

THE END.

Printed by R. & R. CLARK, *Edinburgh.*